image comics presents

THE WALKING DEAD™

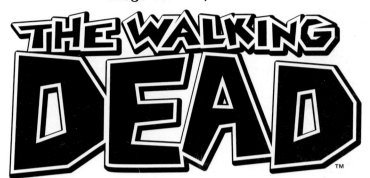

ROBERT KIRKMAN
CREATOR, WRITER

CHARLIE ADLARD
PENCILER

STEFANO GAUDIANO
INKER

CLIFF RATHBURN
GRAY TONES

RUS WOOTON
LETTERER

CHARLIE ADLARD
&
DAVE STEWART
COVER

SEAN MACKIEWICZ
EDITOR

For SKYBOUND ENTERTAINMENT
Robert Kirkman - CEO
Sean Mackiewicz - Editorial Director
Shawn Kirkham - Director of Business Development
Brian Huntington - Online Editorial Director
June Alian - Publicity Director
Rachel Skidmore - Director of Media Development
Michael Williamson - Assistant Editor
Dan Petersen - Operations Manager
Sarah Effinger - Office Manager
Nick Palmer - Operations Coordinator
Lizzy Iverson - Administrative Assistant
Stephan Murillo - Administrative Assistant

International inquiries: foreign@skybound.com
Licensing inquiries: contact@skybound.com
WWW.SKYBOUND.COM

IMAGE COMICS, INC.
Robert Kirkman – Chief Operating Officer
Erik Larsen – Chief Financial Officer
Todd McFarlane – President
Marc Silvestri – Chief Executive Officer
Jim Valentino – Vice-President

Eric Stephenson – Publisher
Ron Richards – Director of Business Development
Jennifer de Guzman – Director of Trade Book Sales
Kat Salazar – Director of PR & Marketing
Corey Murphy – Director of Retail Sales
Jeremy Sullivan – Director of Digital Sales
Emilio Bautista – Sales Assistant
Branwyn Bigglestone – Senior Accounts Manager
Emily Miller – Accounts Manager
Jessica Ambriz – Administrative Assistant
Tyler Shainline – Events Coordinator
David Brothers – Content Manager
Jonathan Chan – Production Manager
Drew Gill – Art Director
Meredith Wallace – Print Manager
Addison Duke – Production Artist
Vincent Kukua – Production Artist
Tricia Ramos – Production Assistant
IMAGECOMICS.COM

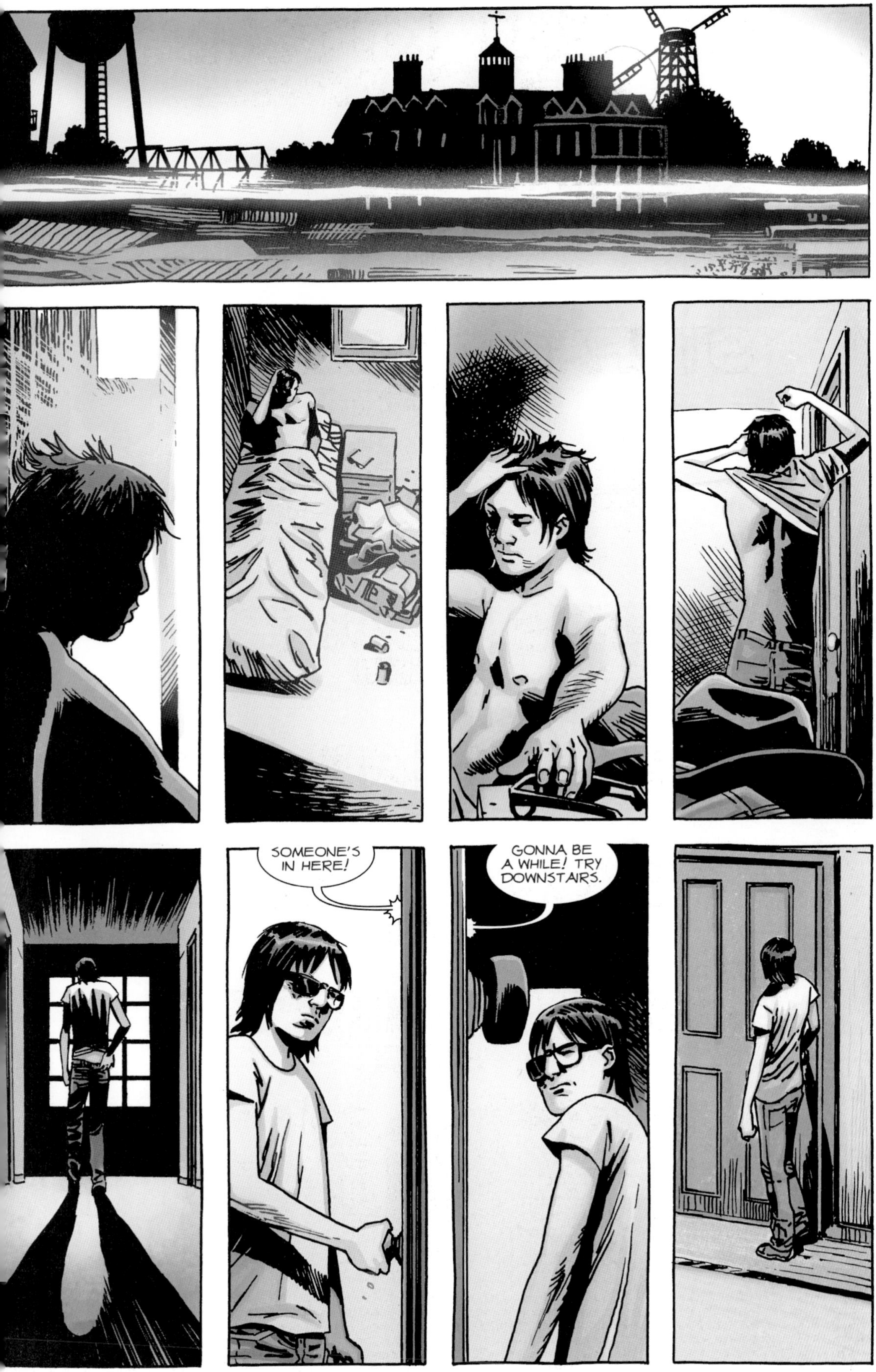
SOMEONE'S IN HERE!
GONNA BE A WHILE! TRY DOWNSTAIRS.

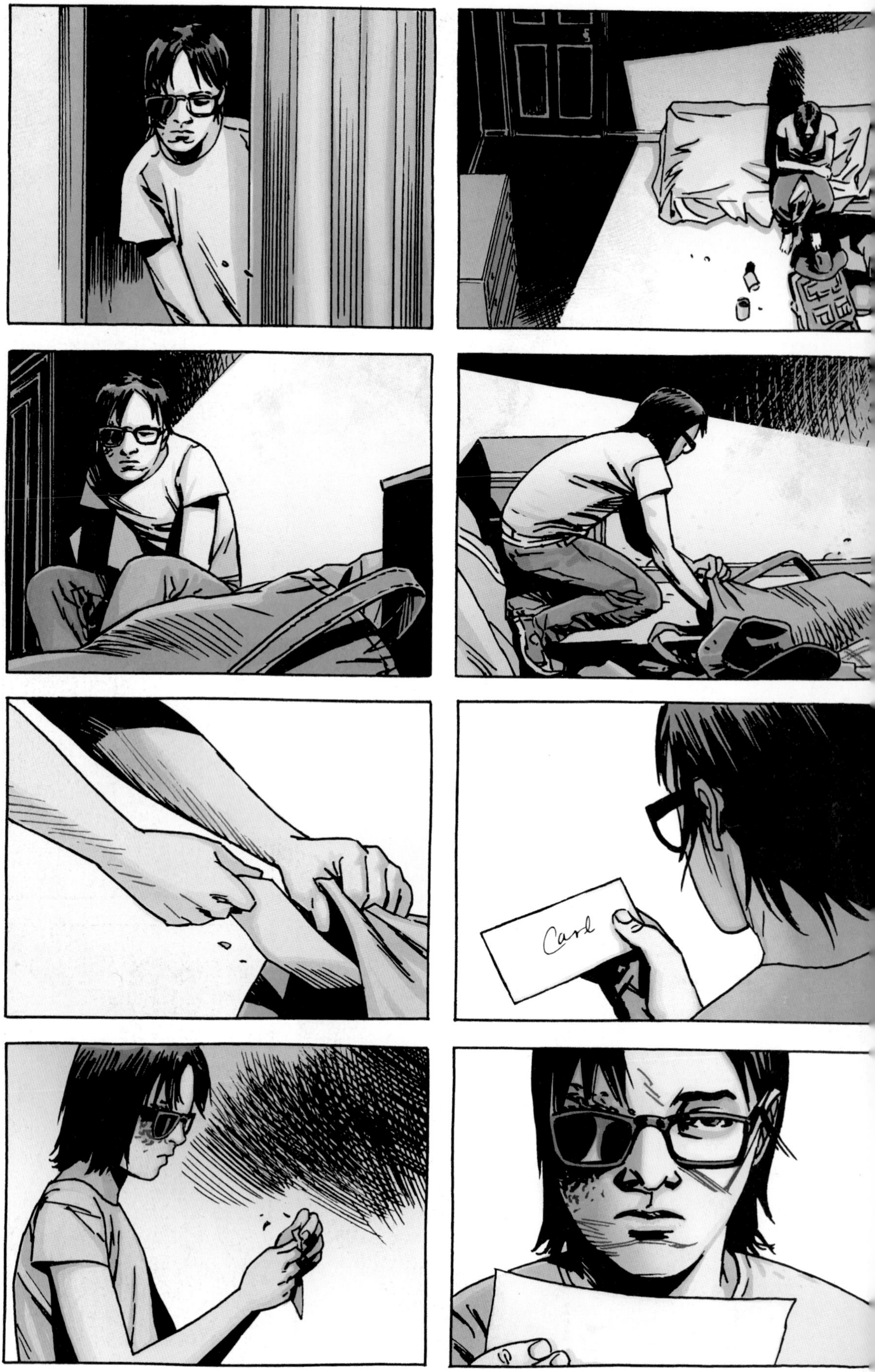
Carl

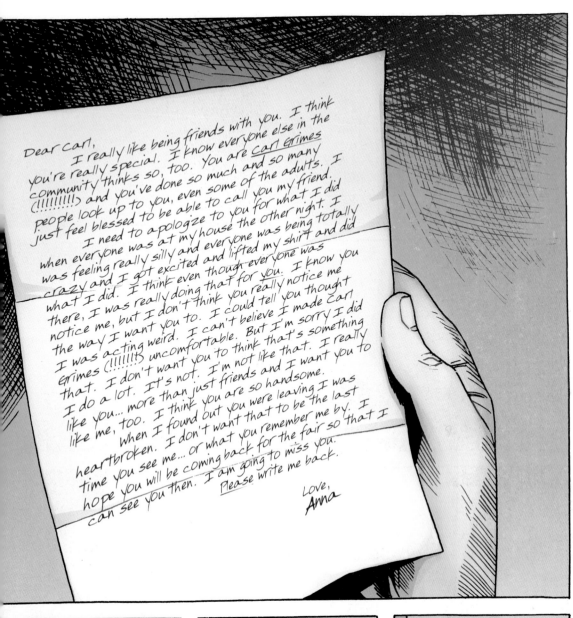

Dear Carl,

    I really like being friends with you. I think you're really special. I know everyone else in the community thinks so, too. You are Carl Grimes (!!!!!!!!) and you've done so much and so many people look up to you, even some of the adults. I just feel blessed to be able to call you my friend.

    I need to apologize to you for what I did when everyone was at my house the other night. I was feeling really silly and everyone was being totally crazy and I got excited and lifted my shirt and did what I did. I think even though everyone was there, I was really doing that for you. I know you notice me, but I don't think you really notice me the way I want you to. I could tell you thought I was acting weird. I can't believe I made Carl Grimes (!!!!!!!!) uncomfortable. But I'm sorry I did that. I don't want you to think that's something I do a lot. It's not. I'm not like that. I really like you... more than just friends and I want you to like me, too. I think you are so handsome.

    When I found out you were leaving I was heartbroken. I don't want that to be the last time you see me... or what you remember me by. I hope you will be coming back for the fair so that I can see you then. I am going to miss you. Please write me back.

                   Love,
                   Anna

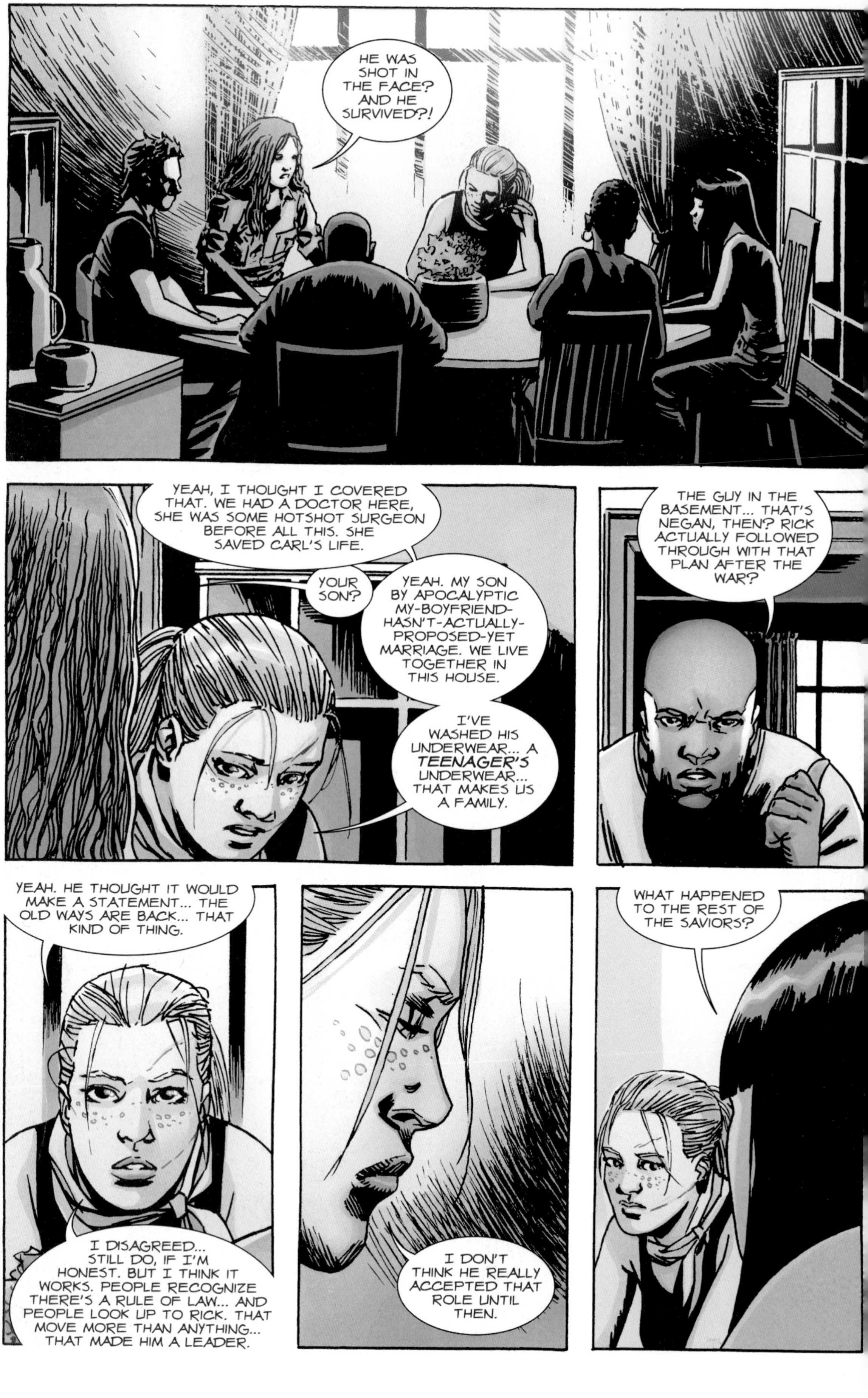
HE WAS SHOT IN THE FACE? AND HE SURVIVED?!
YEAH, I THOUGHT I COVERED THAT. WE HAD A DOCTOR HERE, SHE WAS SOME HOTSHOT SURGEON BEFORE ALL THIS. SHE SAVED CARL'S LIFE.
YOUR SON?
YEAH. MY SON BY APOCALYPTIC MY-BOYFRIEND-HASN'T-ACTUALLY-PROPOSED-YET MARRIAGE. WE LIVE TOGETHER IN THIS HOUSE.
I'VE WASHED HIS UNDERWEAR... A *TEENAGER'S* UNDERWEAR... THAT MAKES US A FAMILY.
THE GUY IN THE BASEMENT... THAT'S NEGAN, THEN? RICK ACTUALLY FOLLOWED THROUGH WITH THAT PLAN AFTER THE WAR?
YEAH. HE THOUGHT IT WOULD MAKE A STATEMENT... THE OLD WAYS ARE BACK... THAT KIND OF THING.
I DISAGREED... STILL DO, IF I'M HONEST. BUT I THINK IT WORKS. PEOPLE RECOGNIZE THERE'S A RULE OF LAW... AND PEOPLE LOOK UP TO RICK. THAT MOVE MORE THAN ANYTHING... THAT MADE HIM A LEADER.
I DON'T THINK HE REALLY ACCEPTED THAT ROLE UNTIL THEN.
WHAT HAPPENED TO THE REST OF THE SAVIORS?

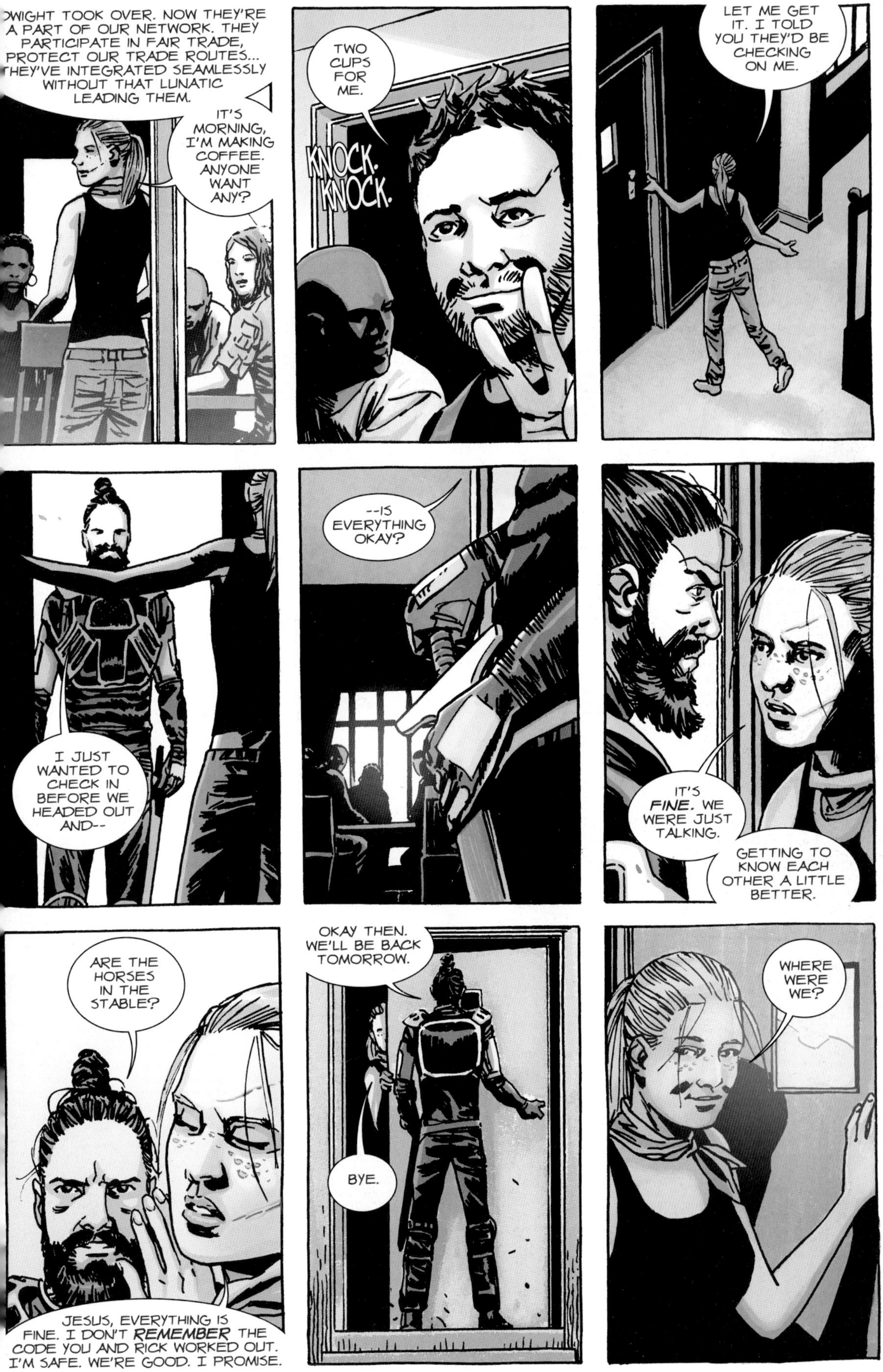
DWIGHT TOOK OVER. NOW THEY'RE A PART OF OUR NETWORK. THEY PARTICIPATE IN FAIR TRADE, PROTECT OUR TRADE ROUTES... THEY'VE INTEGRATED SEAMLESSLY WITHOUT THAT LUNATIC LEADING THEM.
IT'S MORNING, I'M MAKING COFFEE. ANYONE WANT ANY?
TWO CUPS FOR ME.
KNOCK. KNOCK.
LET ME GET IT. I TOLD YOU THEY'D BE CHECKING ON ME.
I JUST WANTED TO CHECK IN BEFORE WE HEADED OUT AND--
--IS EVERYTHING OKAY?
IT'S FINE. WE WERE JUST TALKING.
GETTING TO KNOW EACH OTHER A LITTLE BETTER.
ARE THE HORSES IN THE STABLE?
JESUS, EVERYTHING IS FINE. I DON'T REMEMBER THE CODE YOU AND RICK WORKED OUT. I'M SAFE. WE'RE GOOD. I PROMISE.
OKAY THEN. WE'LL BE BACK TOMORROW.
BYE.
WHERE WERE WE?

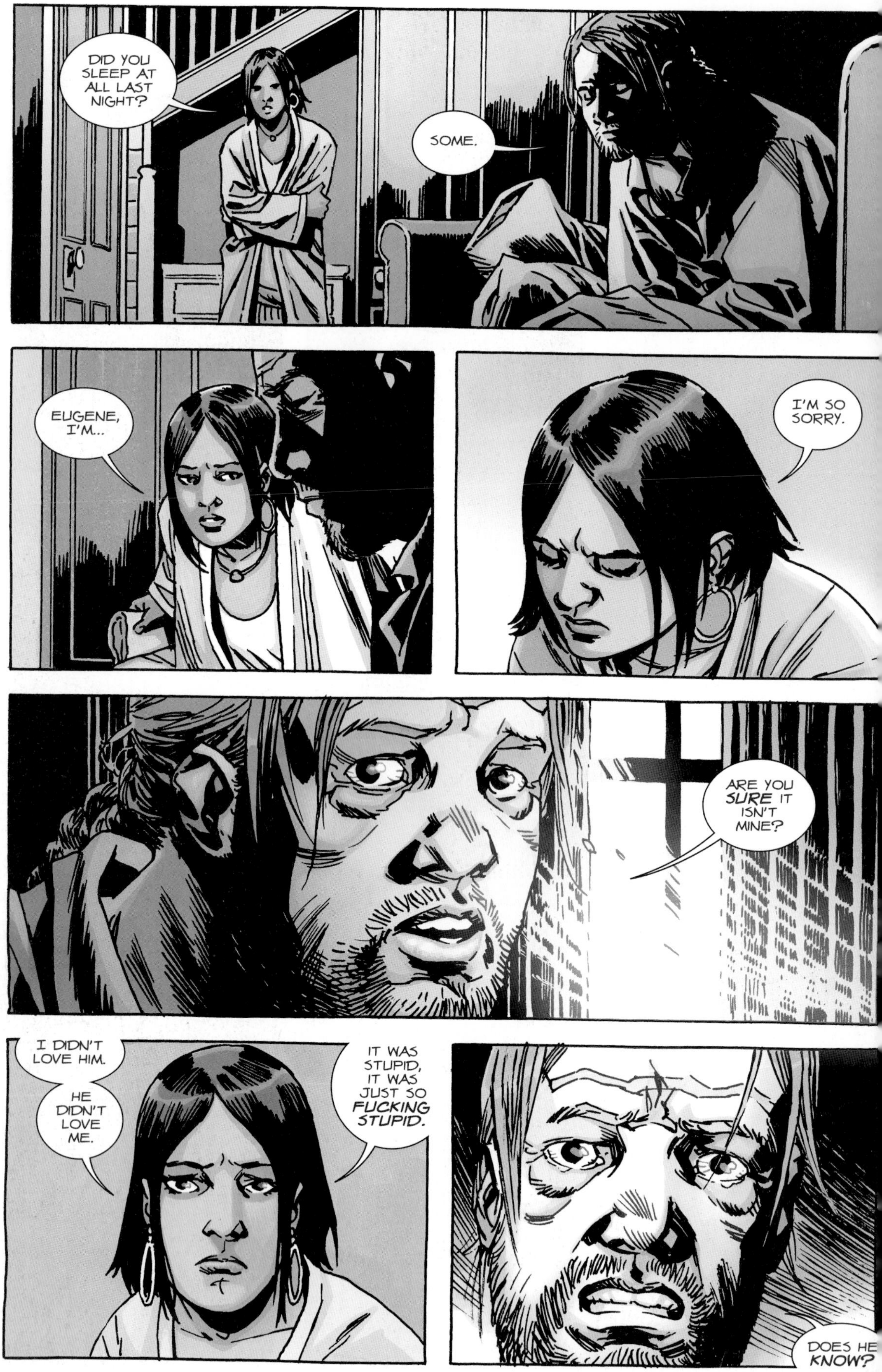
DID YOU SLEEP AT ALL LAST NIGHT?
SOME.
EUGENE, I'M...
I'M SO SORRY.
ARE YOU *SURE* IT ISN'T MINE?
I DIDN'T LOVE HIM.
HE DIDN'T LOVE ME.
IT WAS STUPID, IT WAS JUST SO *FUCKING STUPID.*
DOES HE *KNOW?*

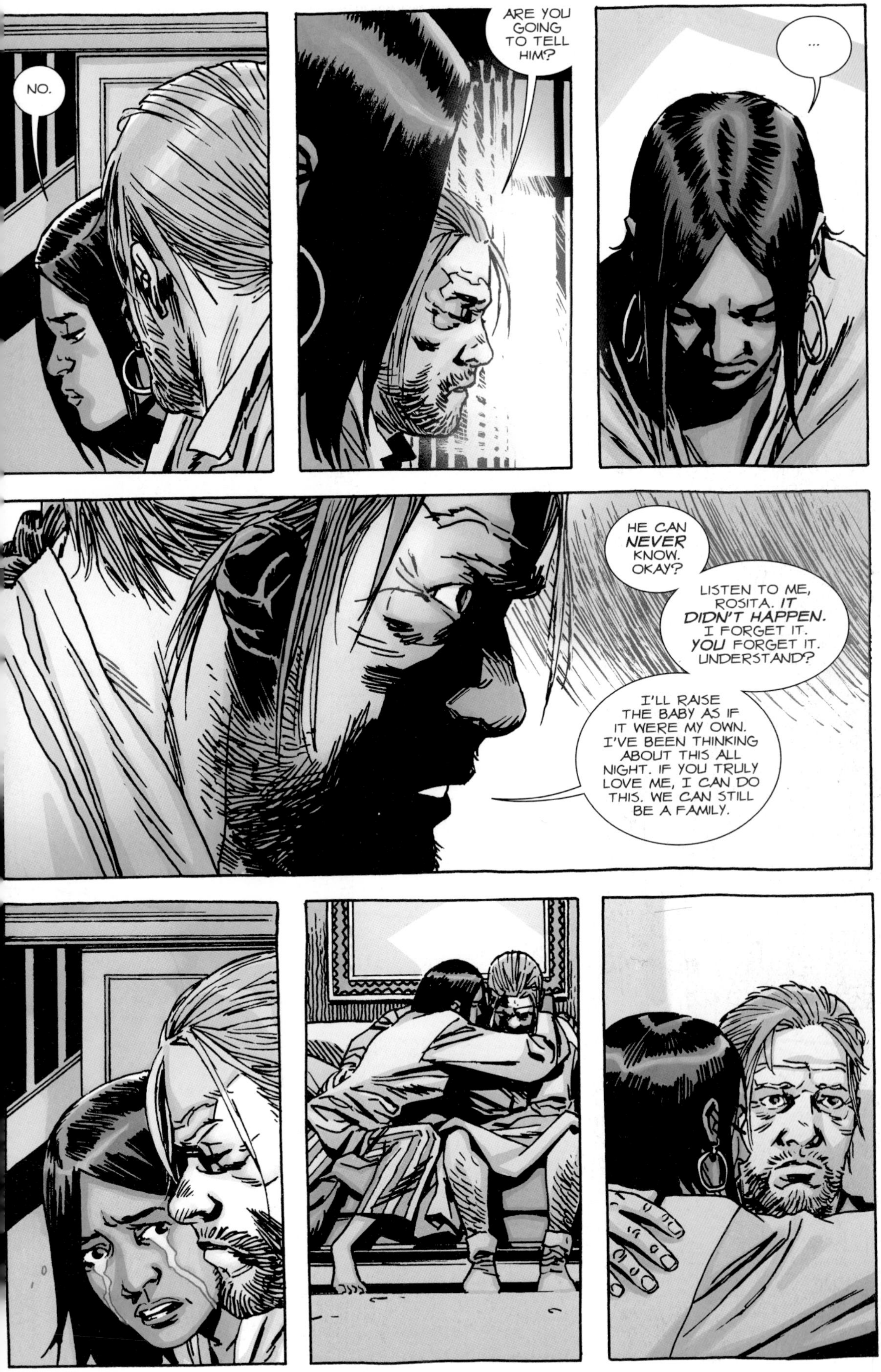

NO.
ARE YOU GOING TO TELL HIM?
...
HE CAN NEVER KNOW. OKAY?
LISTEN TO ME, ROSITA. IT DIDN'T HAPPEN. I FORGET IT. YOU FORGET IT. UNDERSTAND?
I'LL RAISE THE BABY AS IF IT WERE MY OWN. I'VE BEEN THINKING ABOUT THIS ALL NIGHT. IF YOU TRULY LOVE ME, I CAN DO THIS. WE CAN STILL BE A FAMILY.

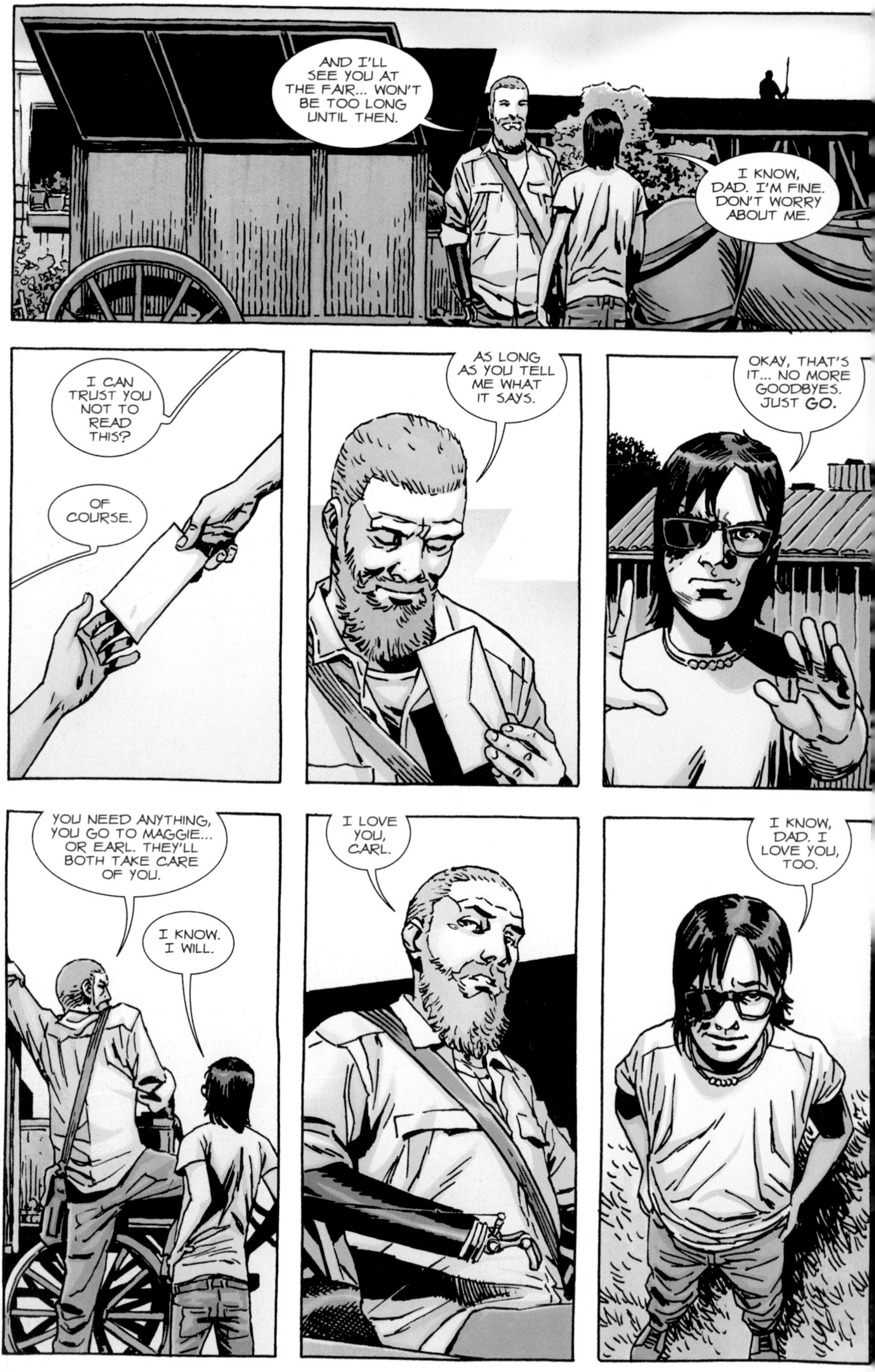
AND I'LL SEE YOU AT THE FAIR... WON'T BE TOO LONG UNTIL THEN.
I KNOW, DAD. I'M FINE. DON'T WORRY ABOUT ME.
I CAN TRUST YOU NOT TO READ THIS?
OF COURSE.
AS LONG AS YOU TELL ME WHAT IT SAYS.
OKAY, THAT'S IT... NO MORE GOODBYES. JUST GO.
YOU NEED ANYTHING, YOU GO TO MAGGIE... OR EARL. THEY'LL BOTH TAKE CARE OF YOU.
I KNOW. I WILL.
I LOVE YOU, CARL.
I KNOW, DAD. I LOVE YOU, TOO.

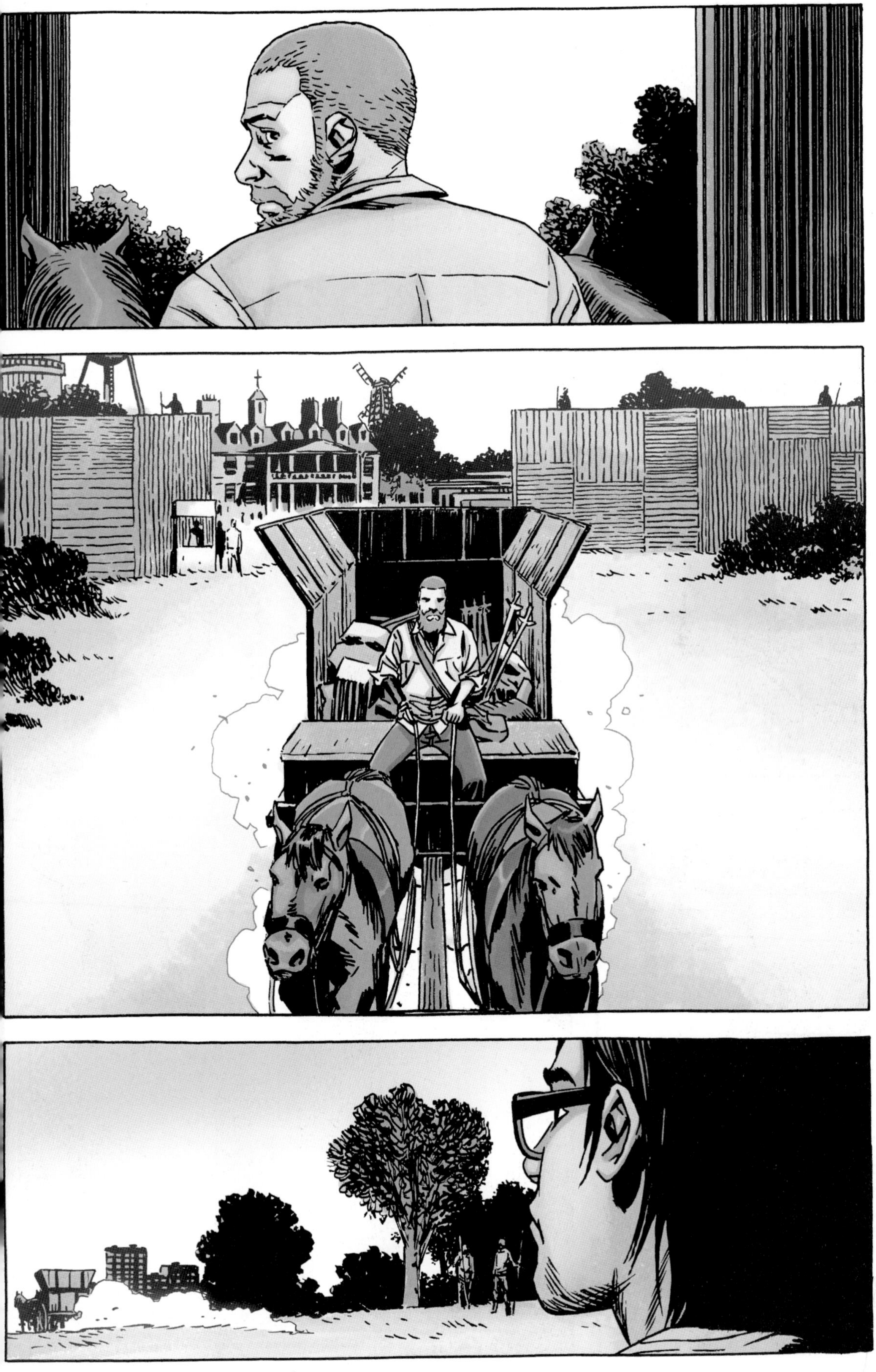

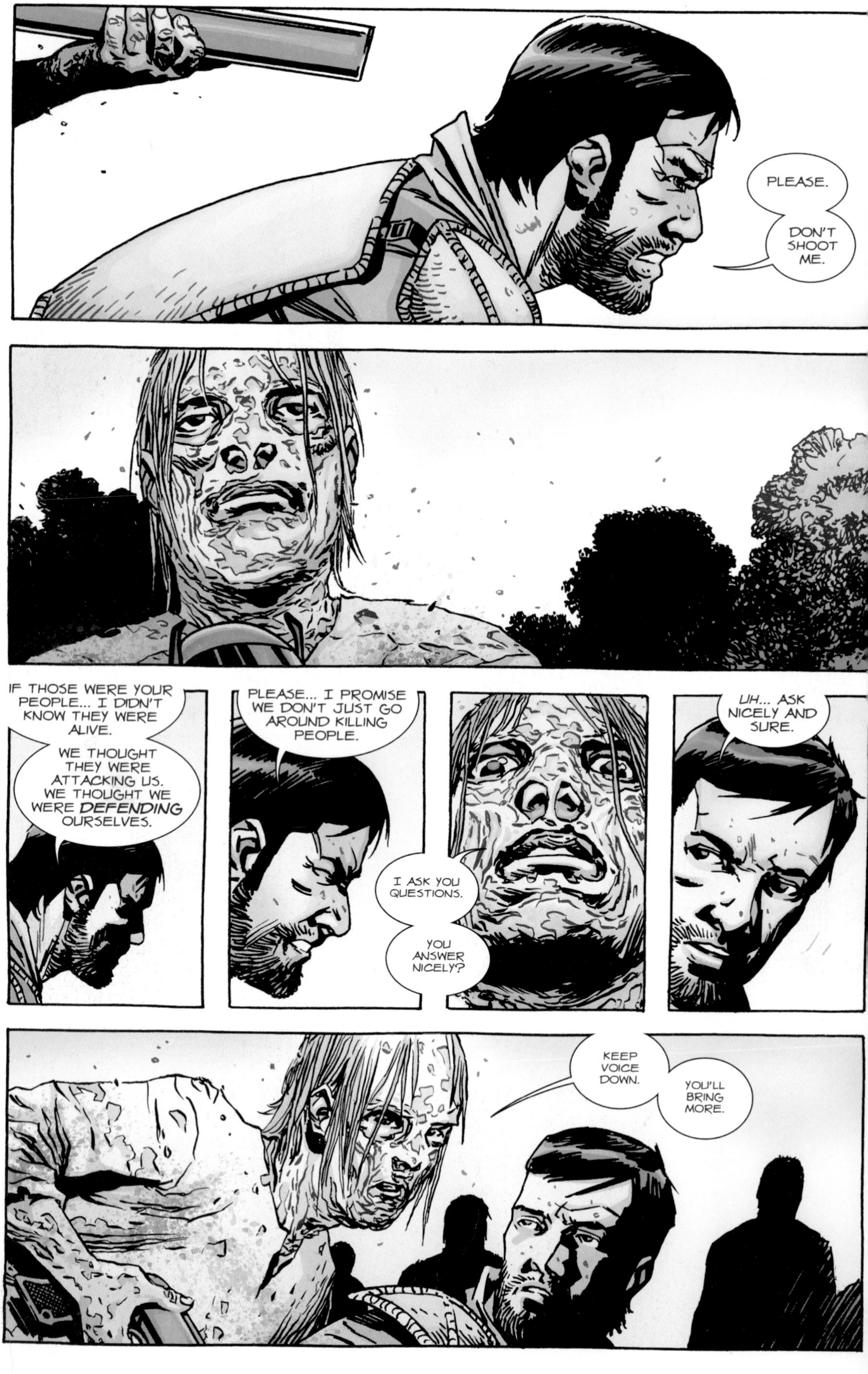
PLEASE.
DON'T SHOOT ME.
IF THOSE WERE YOUR PEOPLE... I DIDN'T KNOW THEY WERE ALIVE.
WE THOUGHT THEY WERE ATTACKING US. WE THOUGHT WE WERE *DEFENDING* OURSELVES.
PLEASE... I PROMISE WE DON'T JUST GO AROUND KILLING PEOPLE.
I ASK YOU QUESTIONS.
YOU ANSWER NICELY?
UH... ASK NICELY AND SURE.
KEEP VOICE DOWN.
YOU'LL BRING MORE.

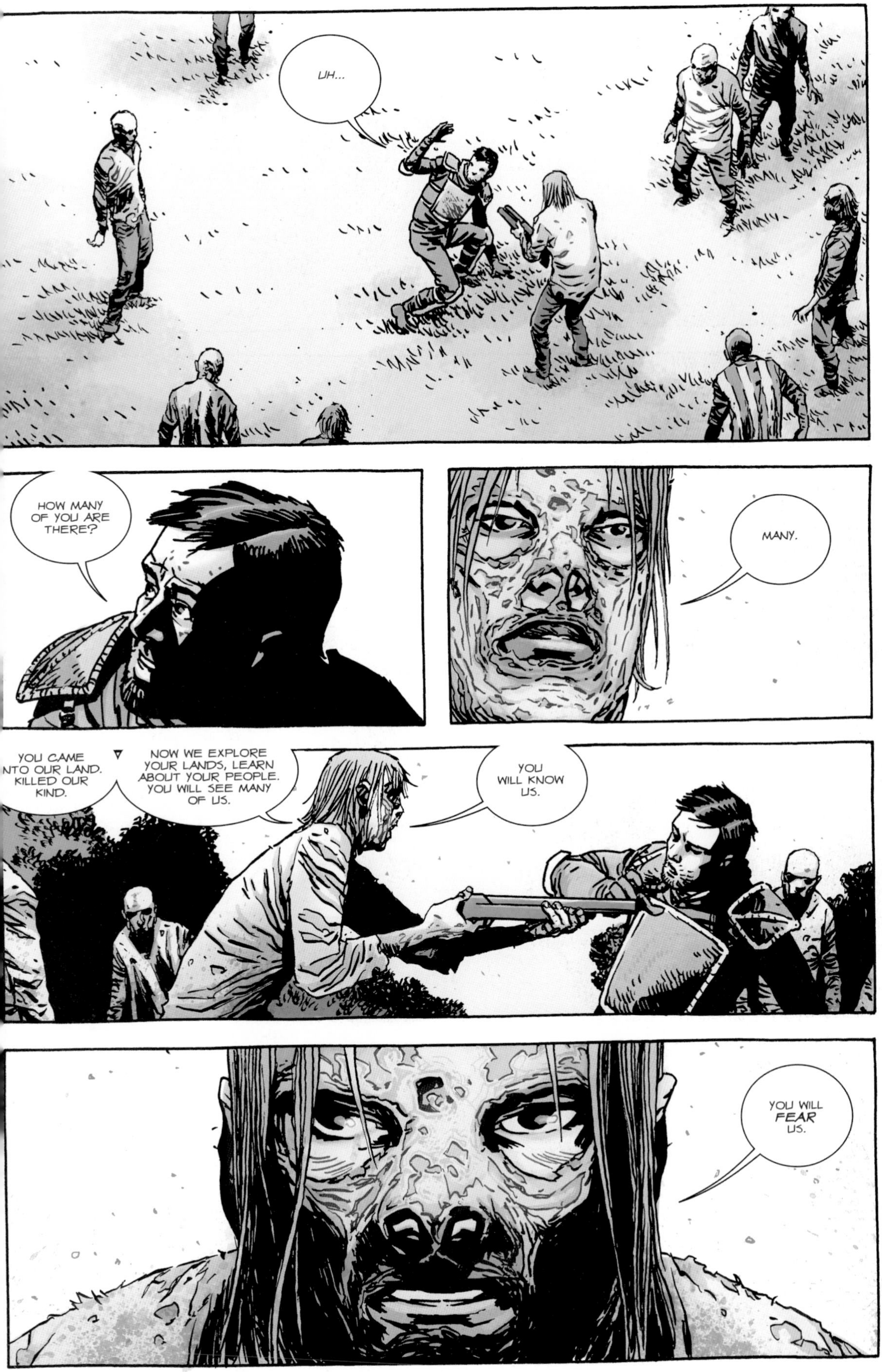
UH...
HOW MANY OF YOU ARE THERE?
MANY.
YOU CAME NTO OUR LAND. KILLED OUR KIND.
NOW WE EXPLORE YOUR LANDS, LEARN ABOUT YOUR PEOPLE. YOU WILL SEE MANY OF US.
YOU WILL KNOW US.
YOU WILL *FEAR* US.

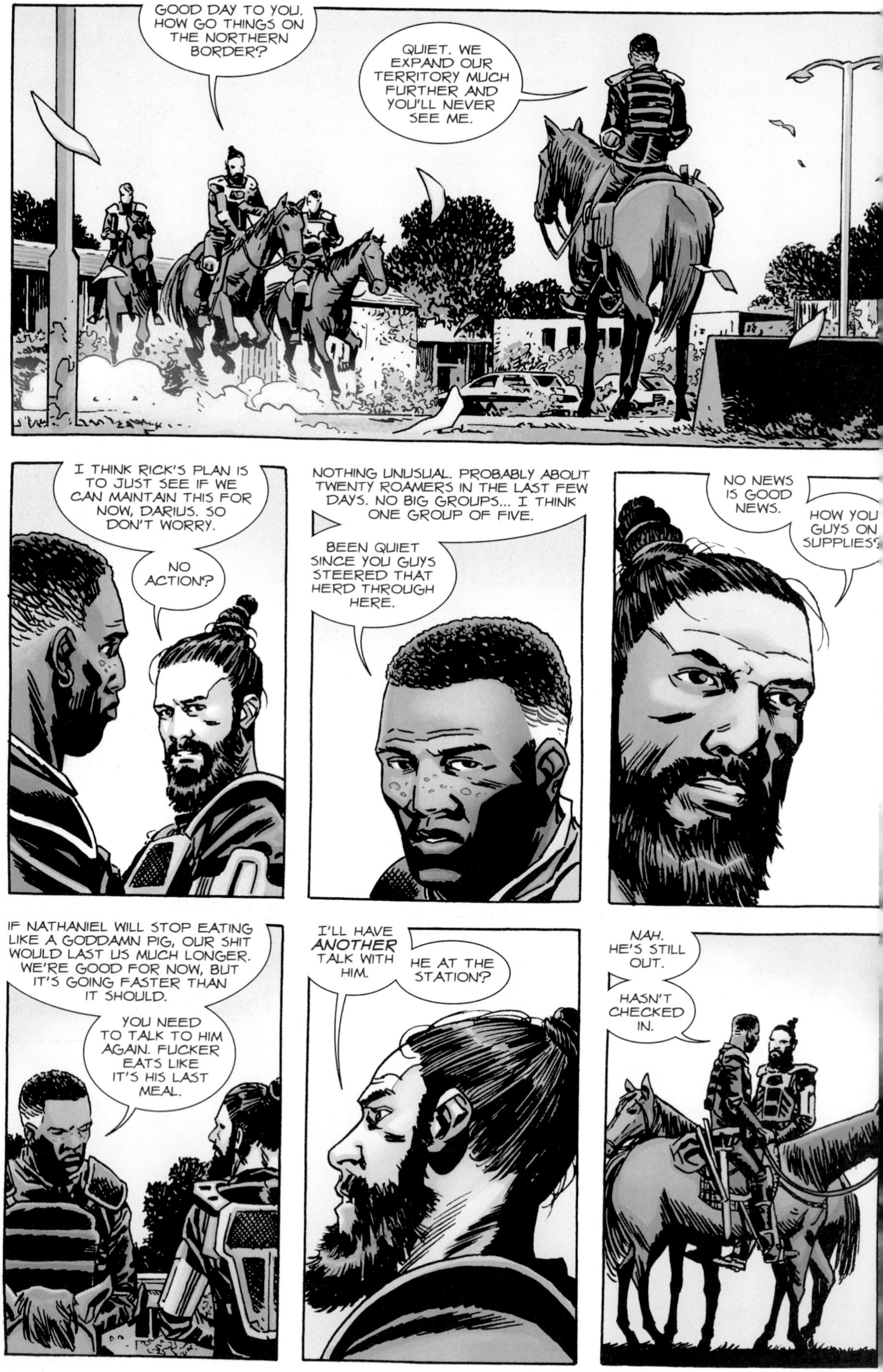

GOOD DAY TO YOU. HOW GO THINGS ON THE NORTHERN BORDER?
QUIET. WE EXPAND OUR TERRITORY MUCH FURTHER AND YOU'LL NEVER SEE ME.
I THINK RICK'S PLAN IS TO JUST SEE IF WE CAN MAINTAIN THIS FOR NOW, DARIUS. SO DON'T WORRY.
NO ACTION?
NOTHING UNUSUAL. PROBABLY ABOUT TWENTY ROAMERS IN THE LAST FEW DAYS. NO BIG GROUPS... I THINK ONE GROUP OF FIVE.
BEEN QUIET SINCE YOU GUYS STEERED THAT HERD THROUGH HERE.
NO NEWS IS GOOD NEWS.
HOW YOU GUYS ON SUPPLIES?
IF NATHANIEL WILL STOP EATING LIKE A GODDAMN PIG, OUR SHIT WOULD LAST US MUCH LONGER. WE'RE GOOD FOR NOW, BUT IT'S GOING FASTER THAN IT SHOULD.
YOU NEED TO TALK TO HIM AGAIN. FUCKER EATS LIKE IT'S HIS LAST MEAL.
I'LL HAVE **ANOTHER** TALK WITH HIM.
HE AT THE STATION?
NAH. HE'S STILL OUT.
HASN'T CHECKED IN.

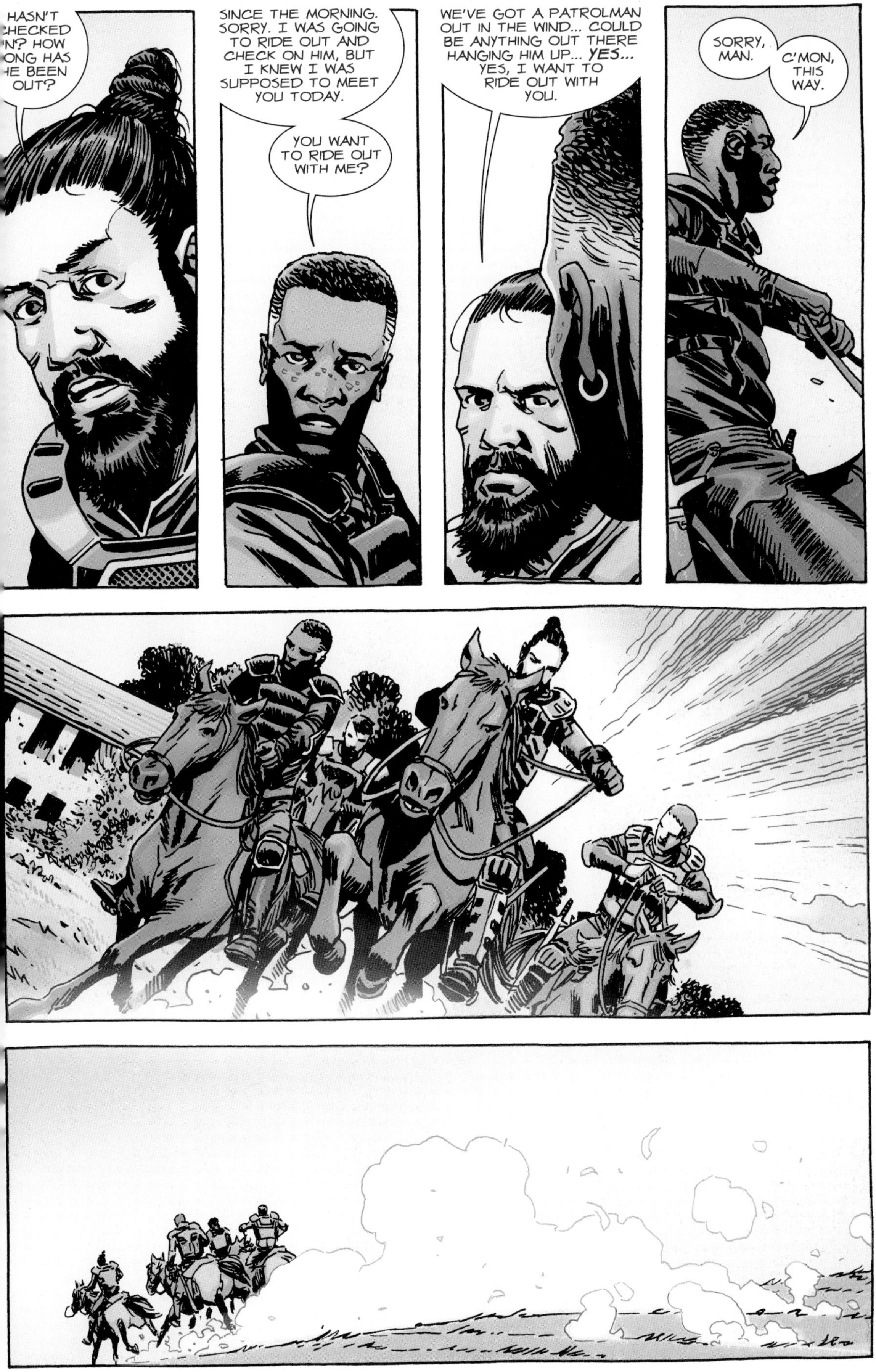
HASN'T CHECKED N? HOW ONG HAS HE BEEN OUT?
SINCE THE MORNING. SORRY. I WAS GOING TO RIDE OUT AND CHECK ON HIM, BUT I KNEW I WAS SUPPOSED TO MEET YOU TODAY.
YOU WANT TO RIDE OUT WITH ME?
WE'VE GOT A PATROLMAN OUT IN THE WIND... COULD BE ANYTHING OUT THERE HANGING HIM UP... YES... YES, I WANT TO RIDE OUT WITH YOU.
SORRY, MAN.
C'MON, THIS WAY.

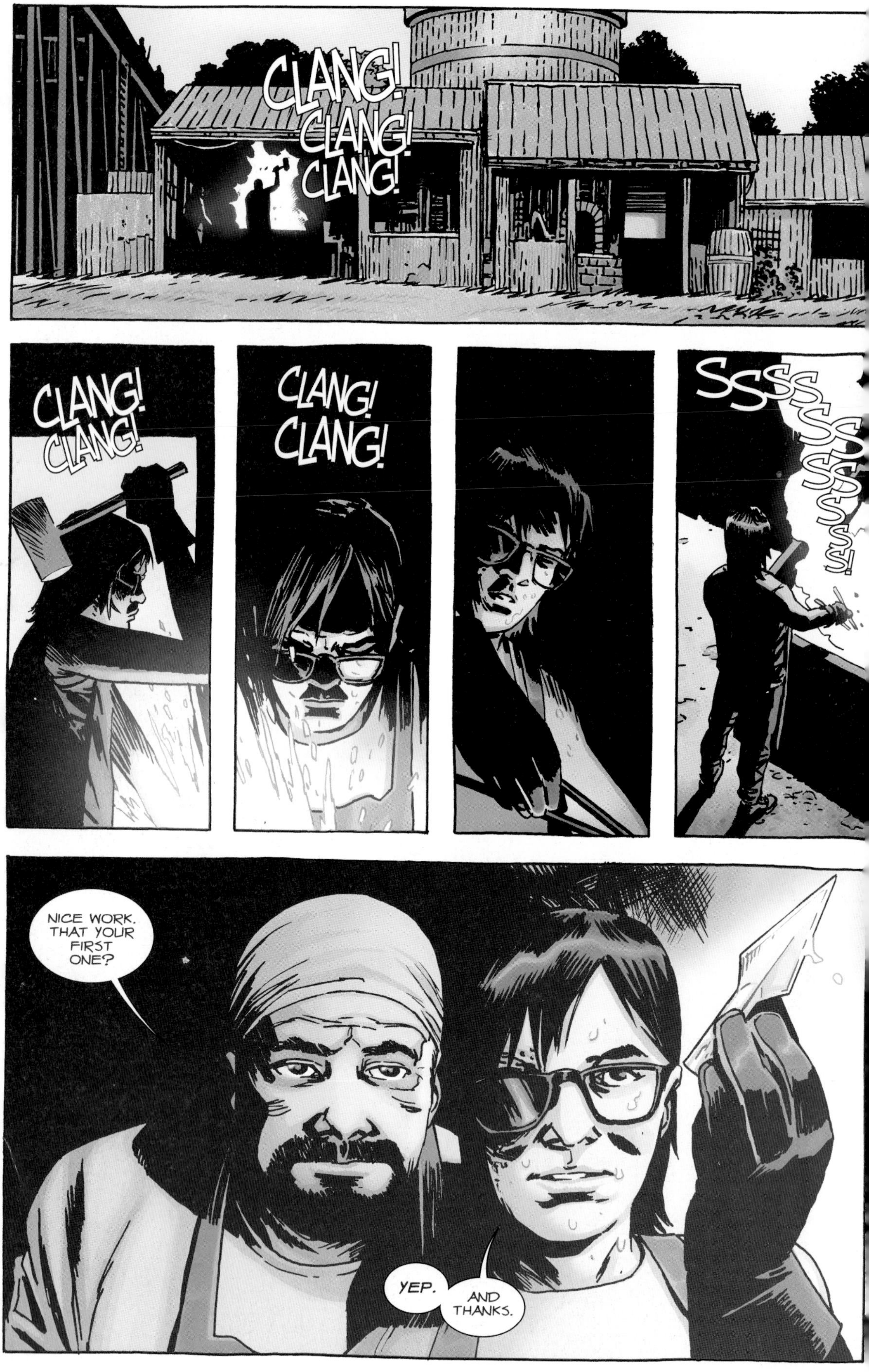

CLANG! CLANG! CLANG!
CLANG! CLANG!
CLANG! CLANG!
SSSSSSSSSSSSSS!
NICE WORK. THAT YOUR FIRST ONE?
YEP.
AND THANKS.

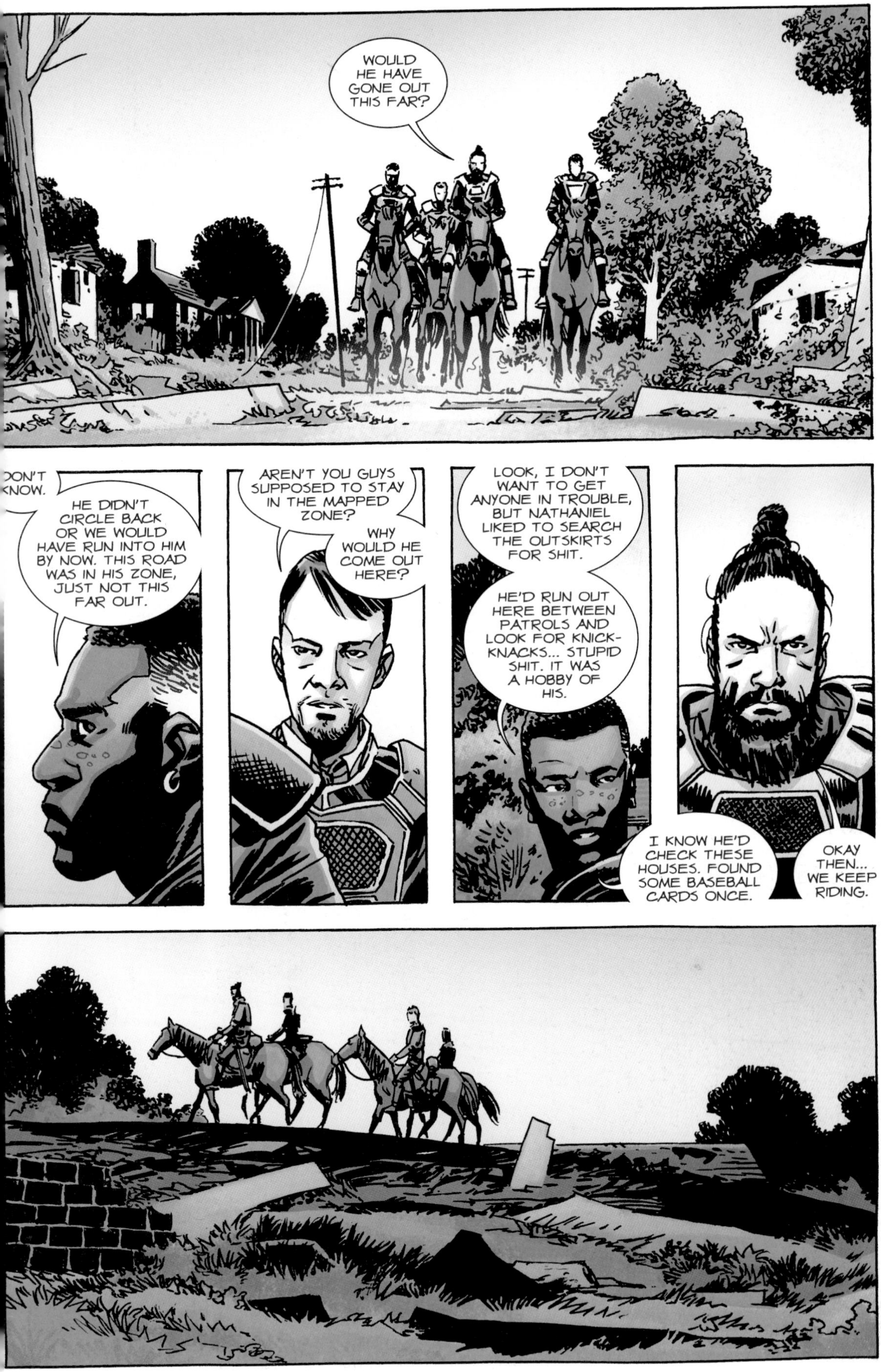
WOULD HE HAVE GONE OUT THIS FAR?
DON'T KNOW.
HE DIDN'T CIRCLE BACK OR WE WOULD HAVE RUN INTO HIM BY NOW. THIS ROAD WAS IN HIS ZONE, JUST NOT THIS FAR OUT.
AREN'T YOU GUYS SUPPOSED TO STAY IN THE MAPPED ZONE?
WHY WOULD HE COME OUT HERE?
LOOK, I DON'T WANT TO GET ANYONE IN TROUBLE, BUT NATHANIEL LIKED TO SEARCH THE OUTSKIRTS FOR SHIT.
HE'D RUN OUT HERE BETWEEN PATROLS AND LOOK FOR KNICK-KNACKS... STUPID SHIT. IT WAS A HOBBY OF HIS.
I KNOW HE'D CHECK THESE HOUSES. FOUND SOME BASEBALL CARDS ONCE.
OKAY THEN... WE KEEP RIDING.

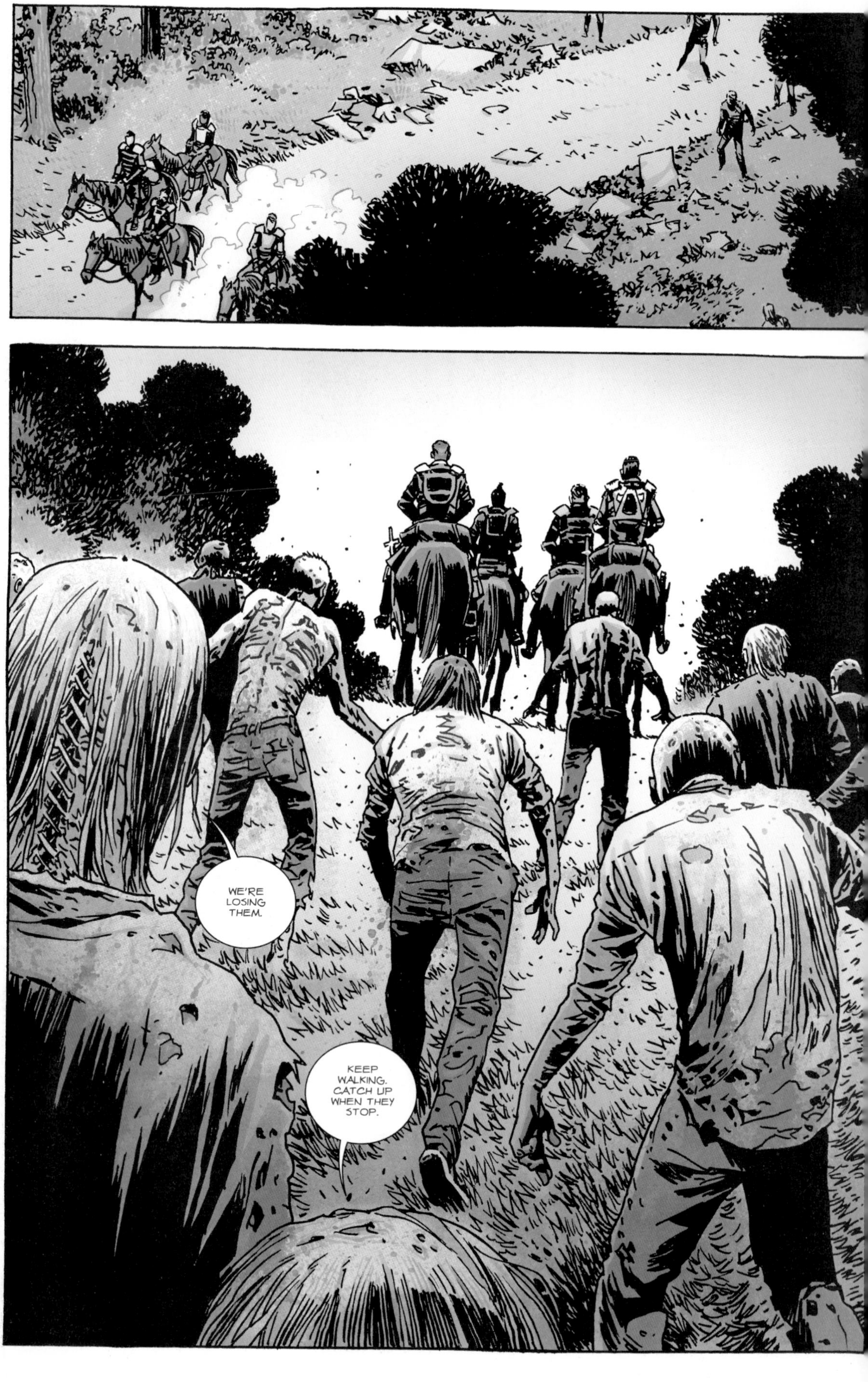
WE'RE LOSING THEM.
KEEP WALKING. CATCH UP WHEN THEY STOP.

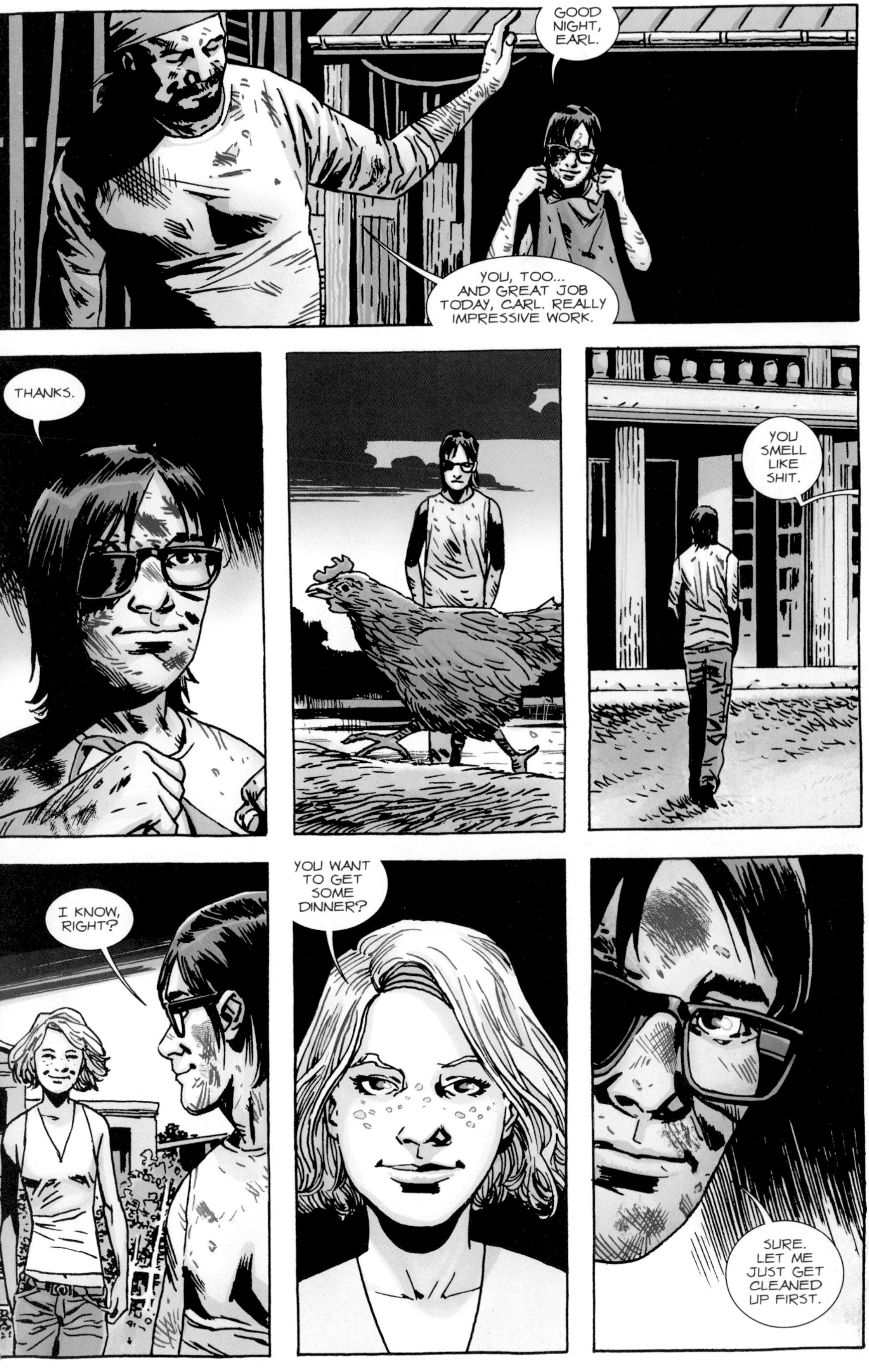
GOOD NIGHT, EARL.
YOU, TOO... AND GREAT JOB TODAY, CARL. REALLY IMPRESSIVE WORK.
THANKS.
YOU SMELL LIKE SHIT.
I KNOW, RIGHT?
YOU WANT TO GET SOME DINNER?
SURE. LET ME JUST GET CLEANED UP FIRST.

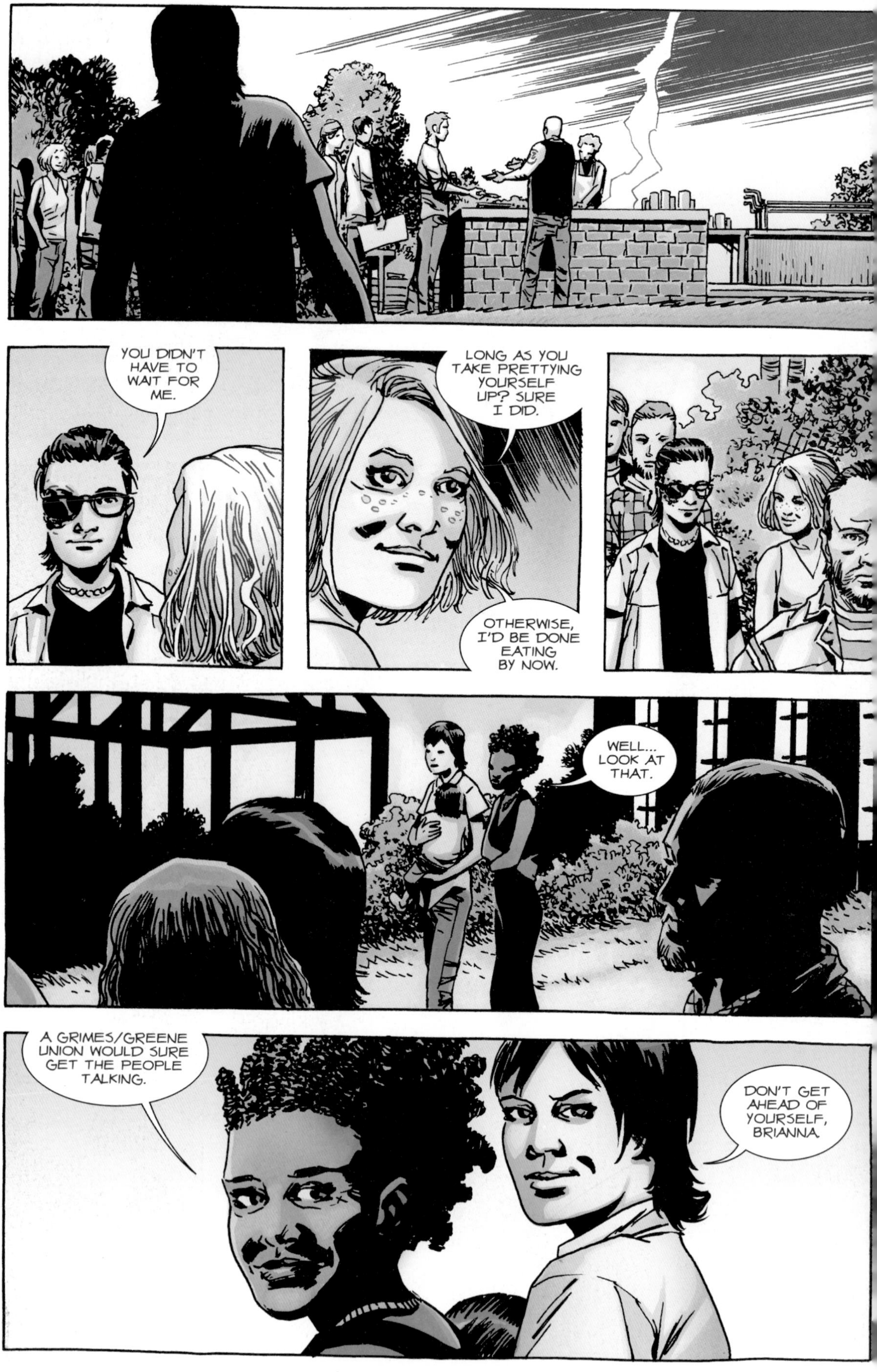

YOU DIDN'T HAVE TO WAIT FOR ME.
LONG AS YOU TAKE PRETTYING YOURSELF UP? SURE I DID.
OTHERWISE, I'D BE DONE EATING BY NOW.
WELL... LOOK AT THAT.
A GRIMES/GREENE UNION WOULD SURE GET THE PEOPLE TALKING.
DON'T GET AHEAD OF YOURSELF, BRIANNA.

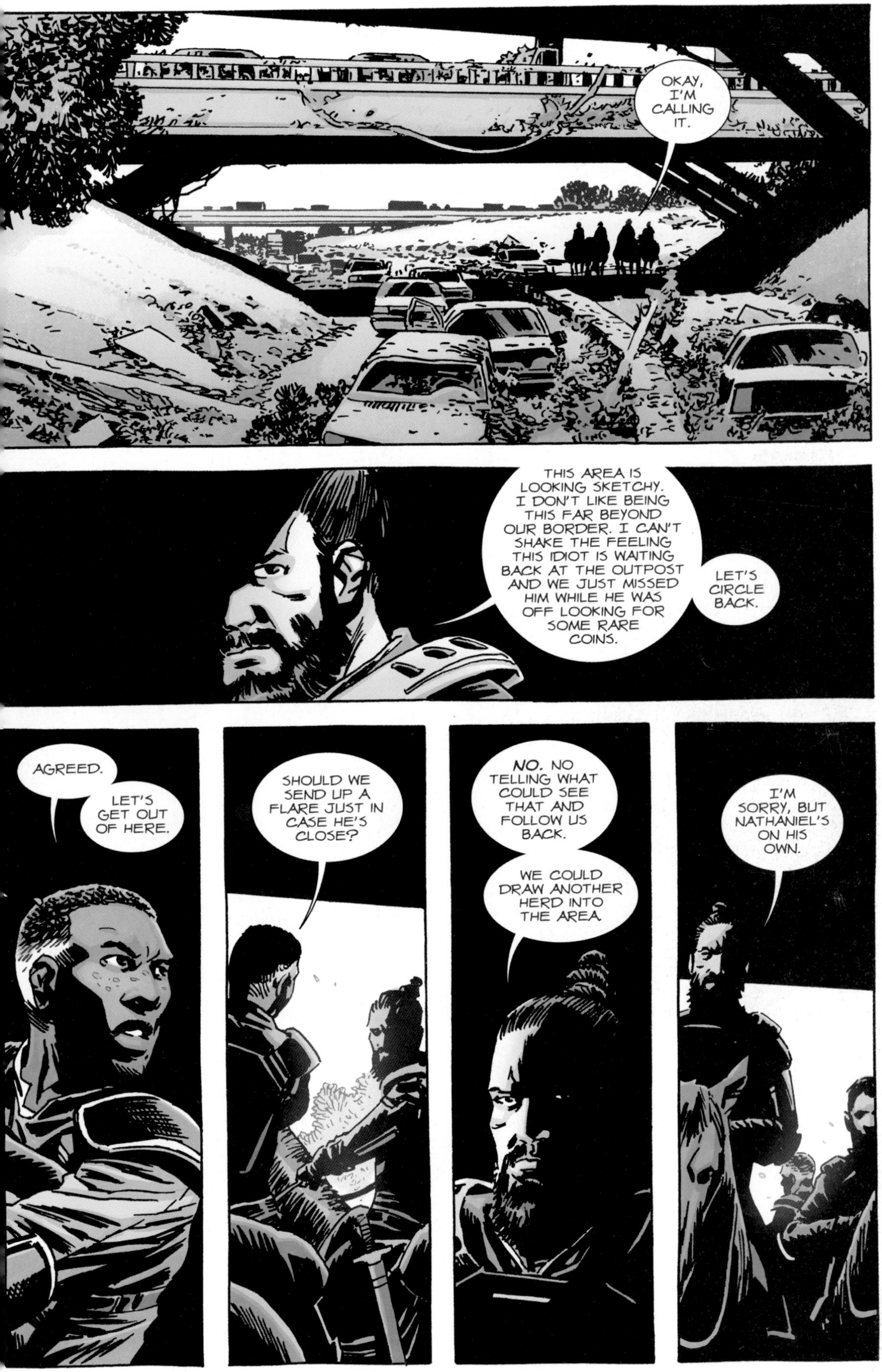
OKAY, I'M CALLING IT.
THIS AREA IS LOOKING SKETCHY. I DON'T LIKE BEING THIS FAR BEYOND OUR BORDER. I CAN'T SHAKE THE FEELING THIS IDIOT IS WAITING BACK AT THE OUTPOST AND WE JUST MISSED HIM WHILE HE WAS OFF LOOKING FOR SOME RARE COINS.
LET'S CIRCLE BACK.
AGREED.
LET'S GET OUT OF HERE.
SHOULD WE SEND UP A FLARE JUST IN CASE HE'S CLOSE?
NO. NO TELLING WHAT COULD SEE THAT AND FOLLOW US BACK.
WE COULD DRAW ANOTHER HERD INTO THE AREA.
I'M SORRY, BUT NATHANIEL'S ON HIS OWN.

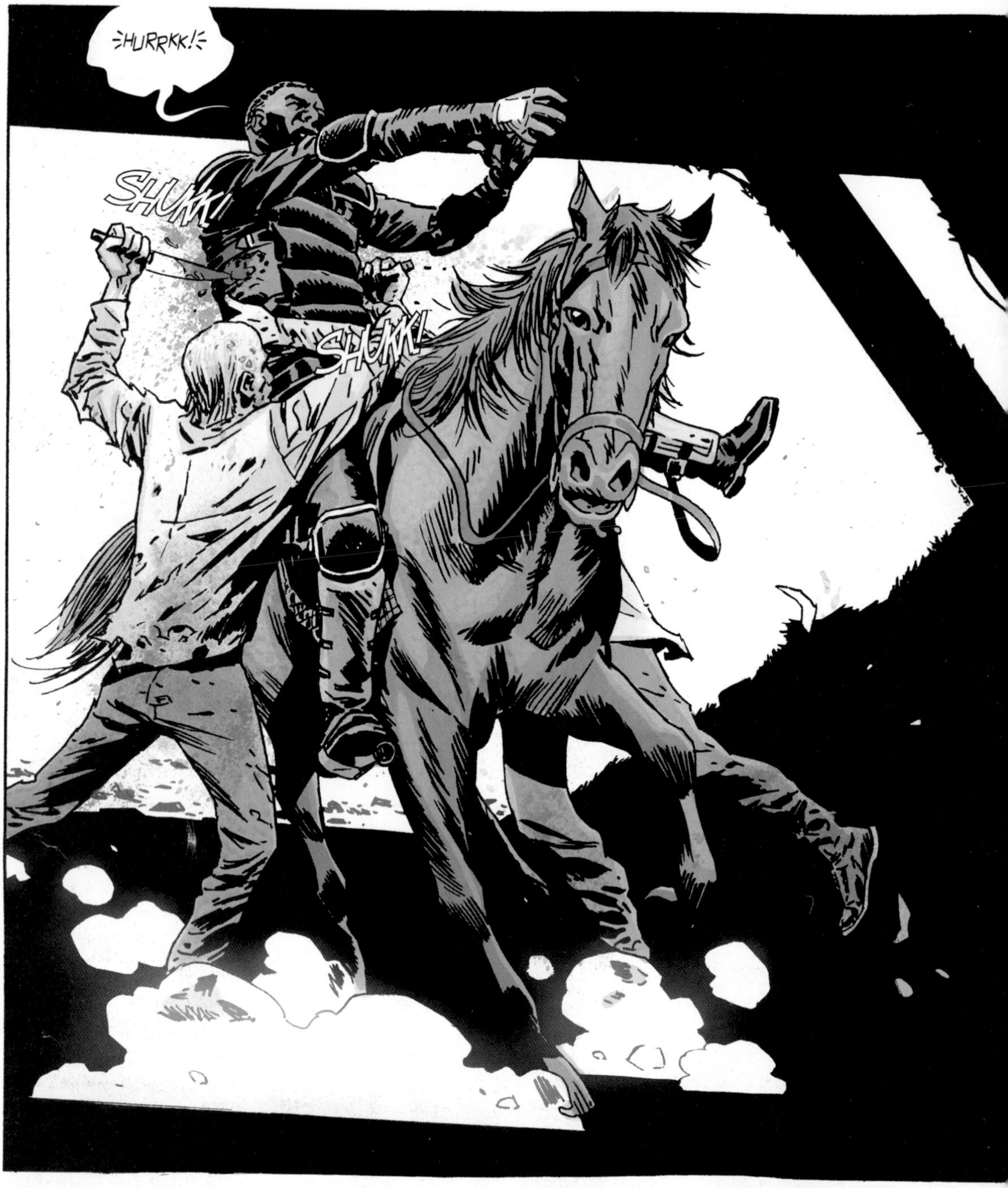
HURRKK!
SHUKK!
SHUKK!

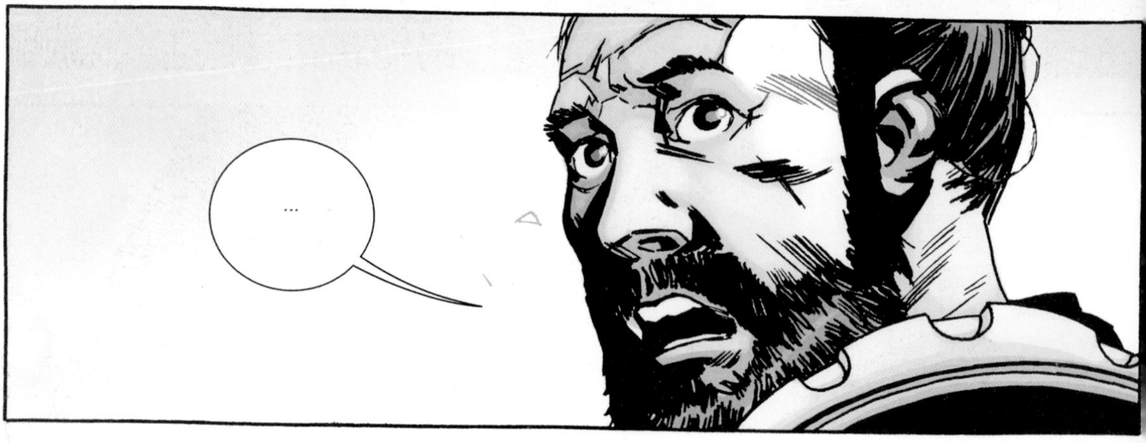
...

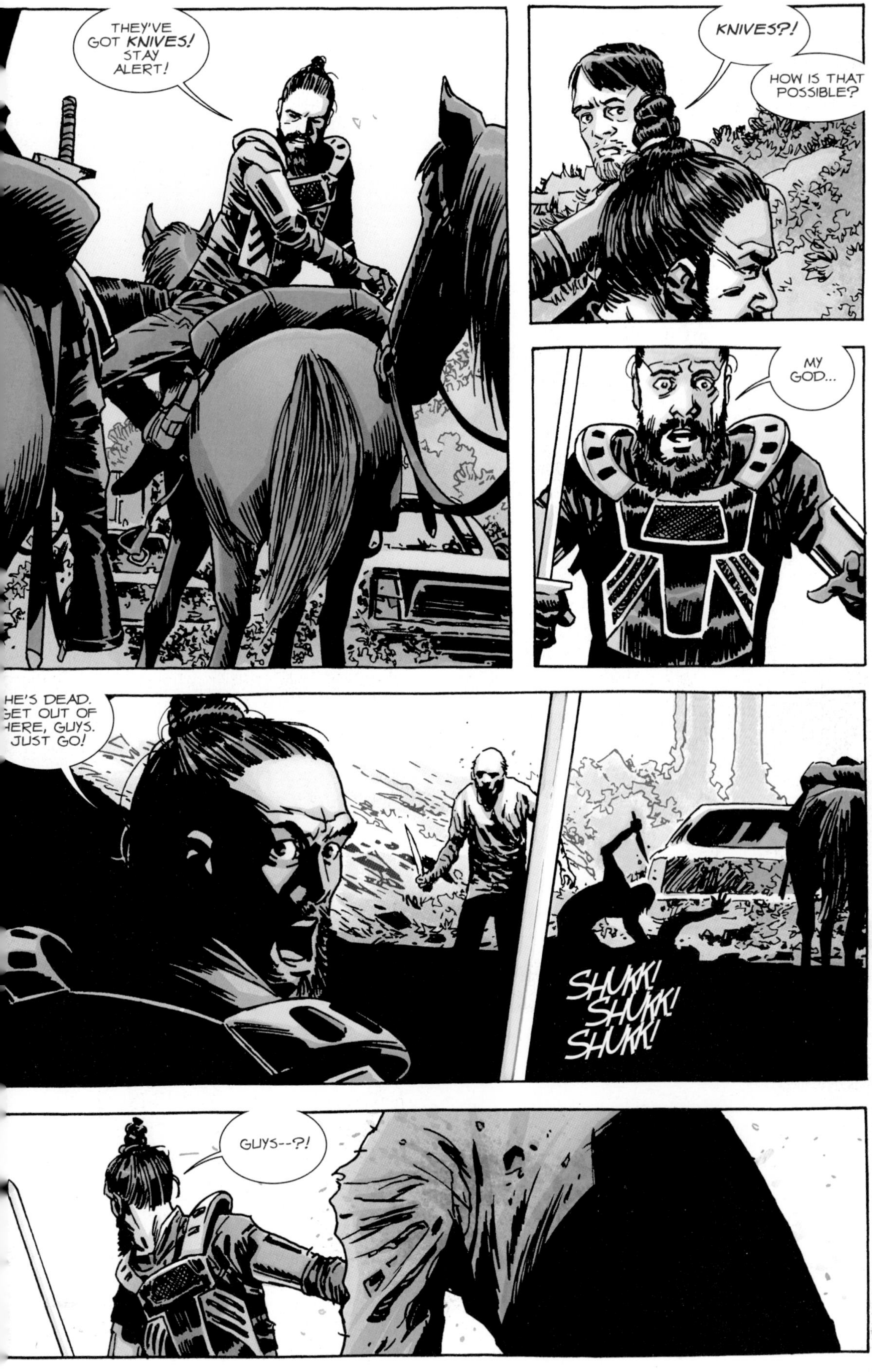
THEY'VE GOT KNIVES! STAY ALERT!
KNIVES?!
HOW IS THAT POSSIBLE?
MY GOD...
HE'S DEAD. GET OUT OF HERE, GUYS. JUST GO!
SHUKK! SHUKK! SHUKK!
GUYS--?!

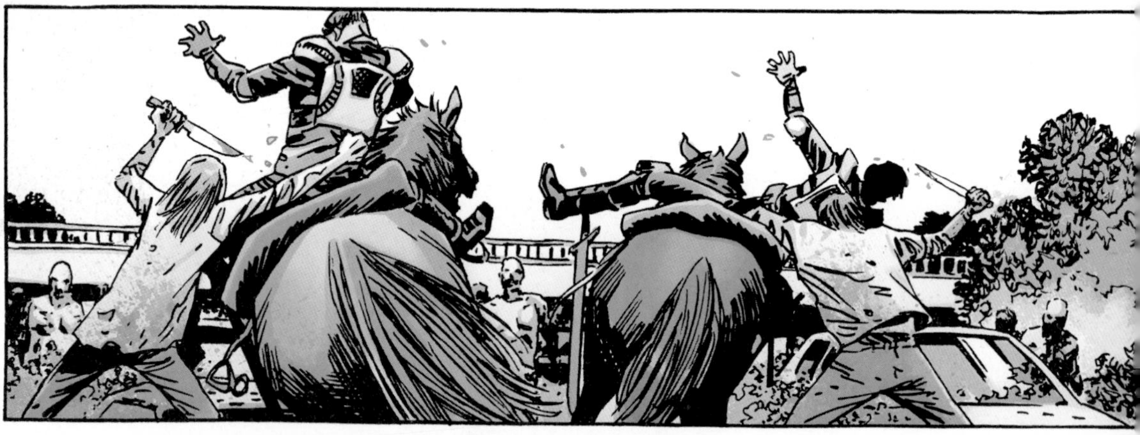

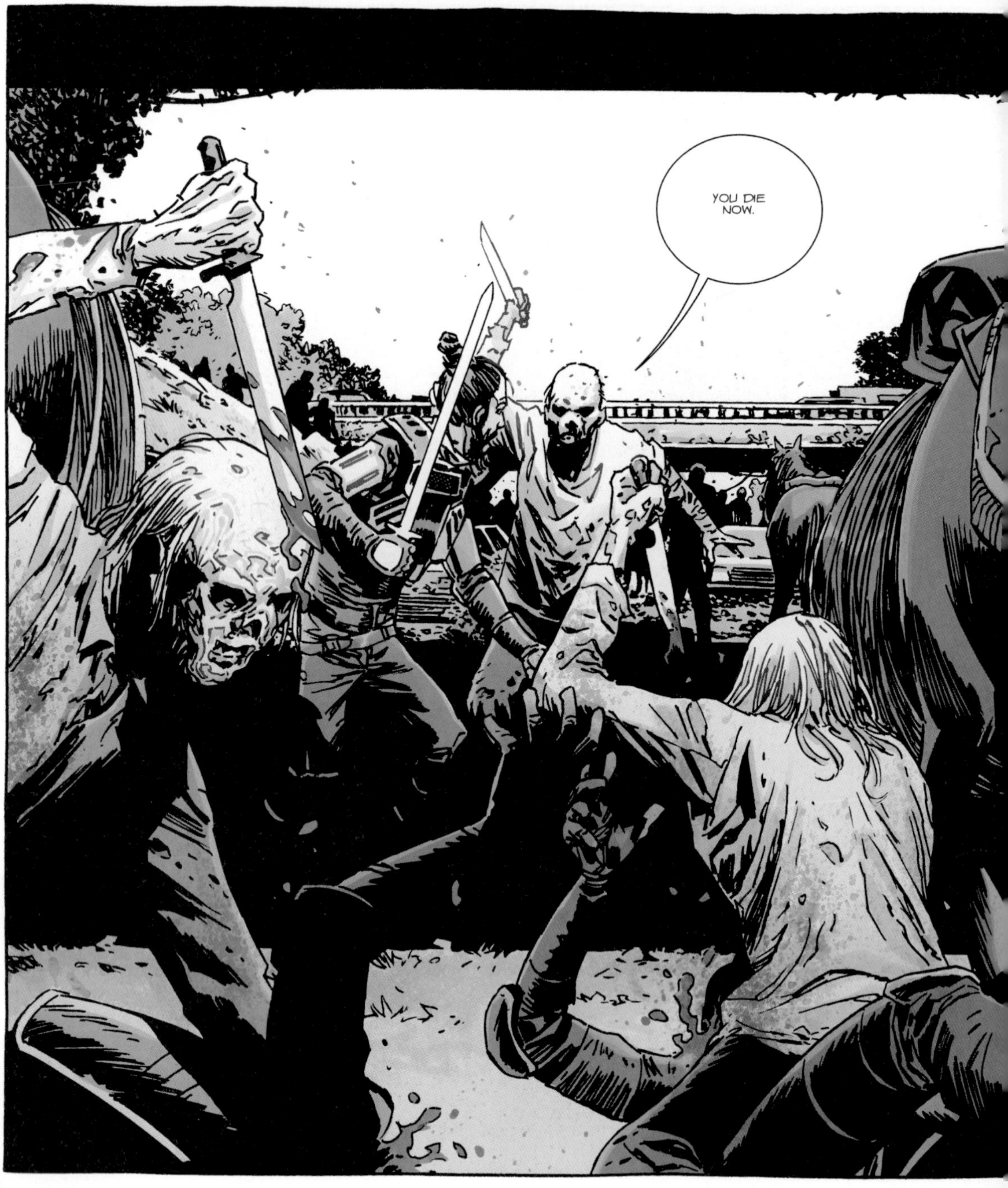
YOU DIE NOW.

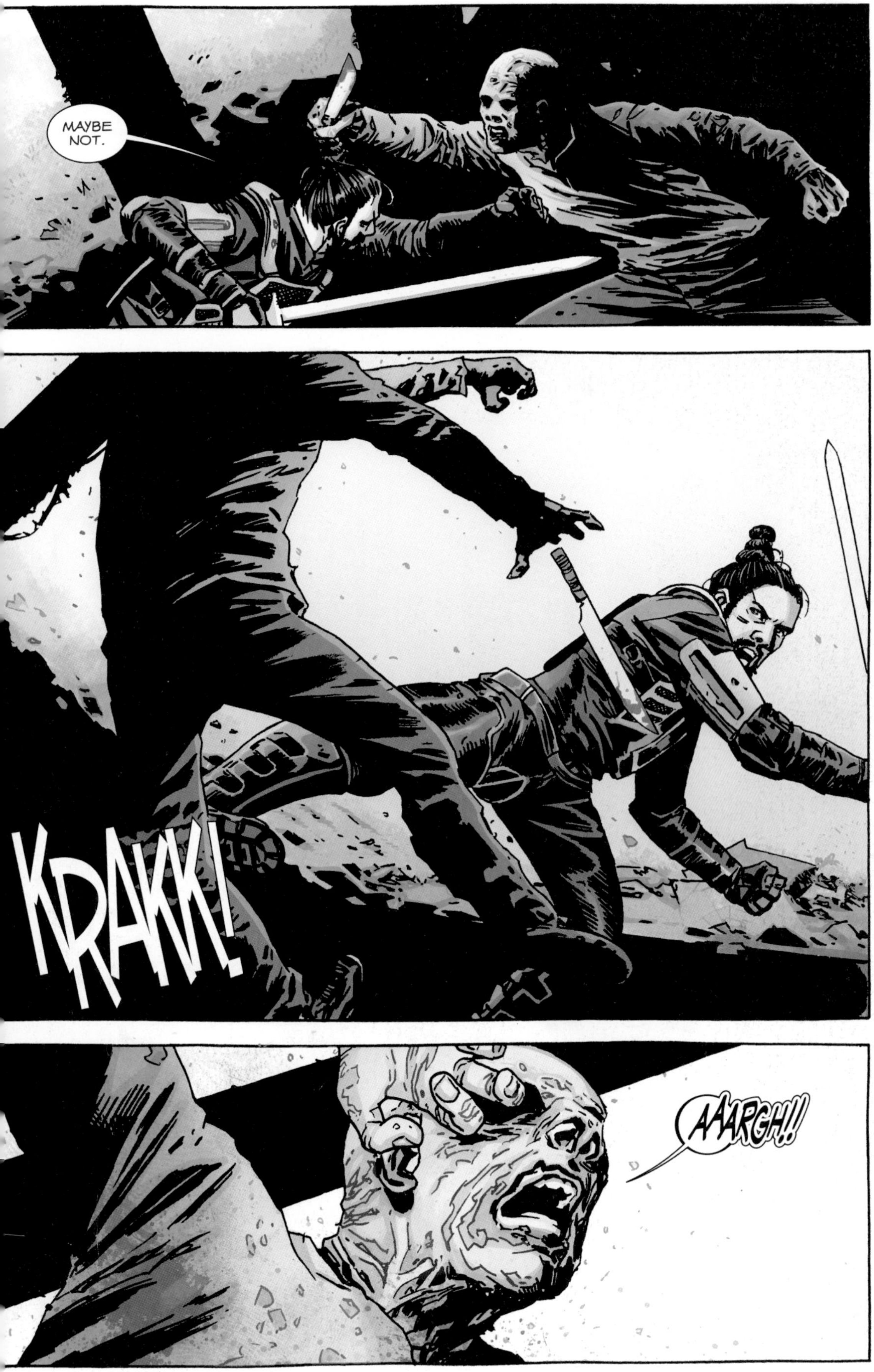

MAYBE NOT.
KRAKK!
AAARGH!!

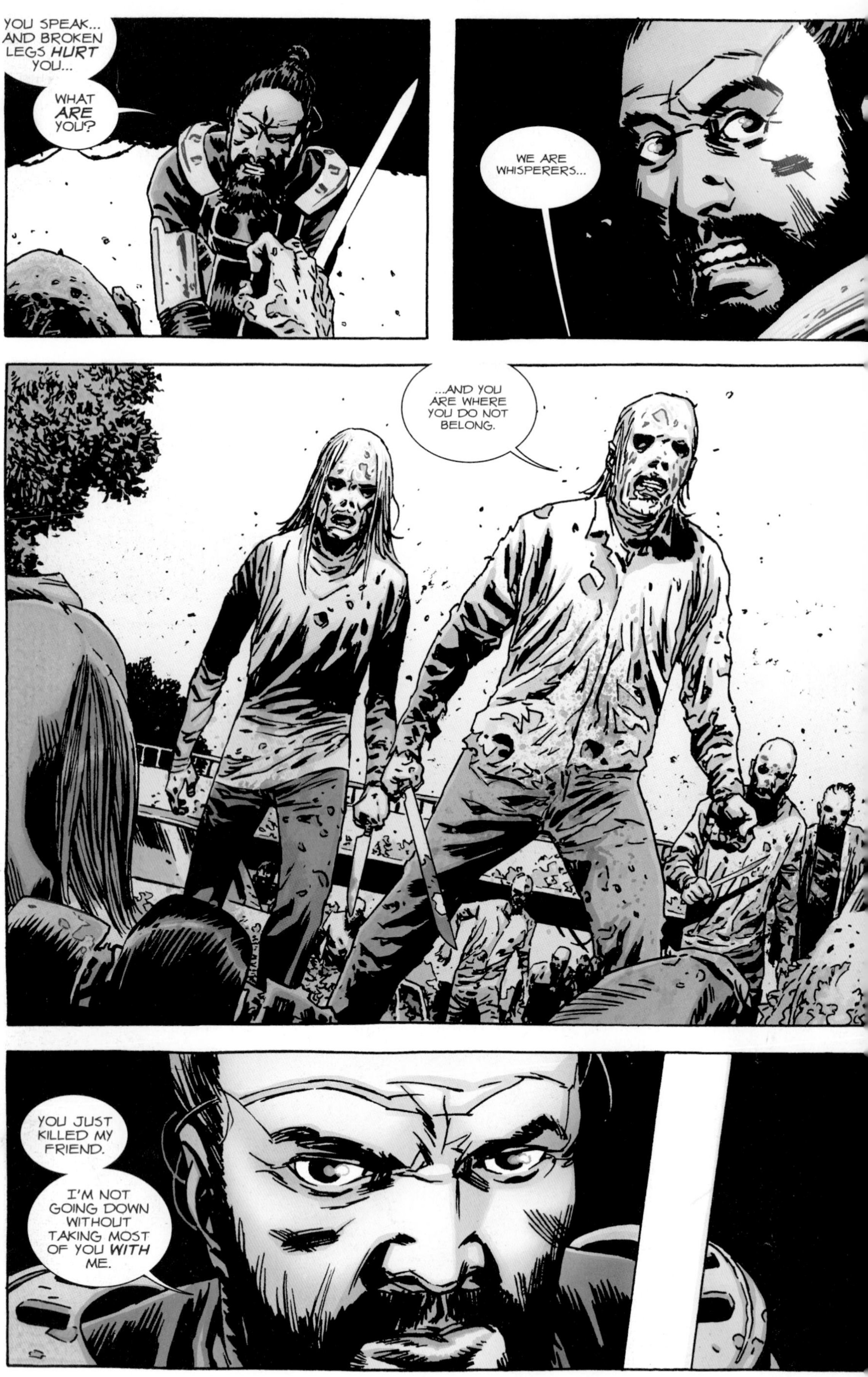
YOU SPEAK... AND BROKEN LEGS HURT YOU...
WHAT ARE YOU?
WE ARE WHISPERERS...
...AND YOU ARE WHERE YOU DO NOT BELONG.
YOU JUST KILLED MY FRIEND.
I'M NOT GOING DOWN WITHOUT TAKING MOST OF YOU WITH ME.

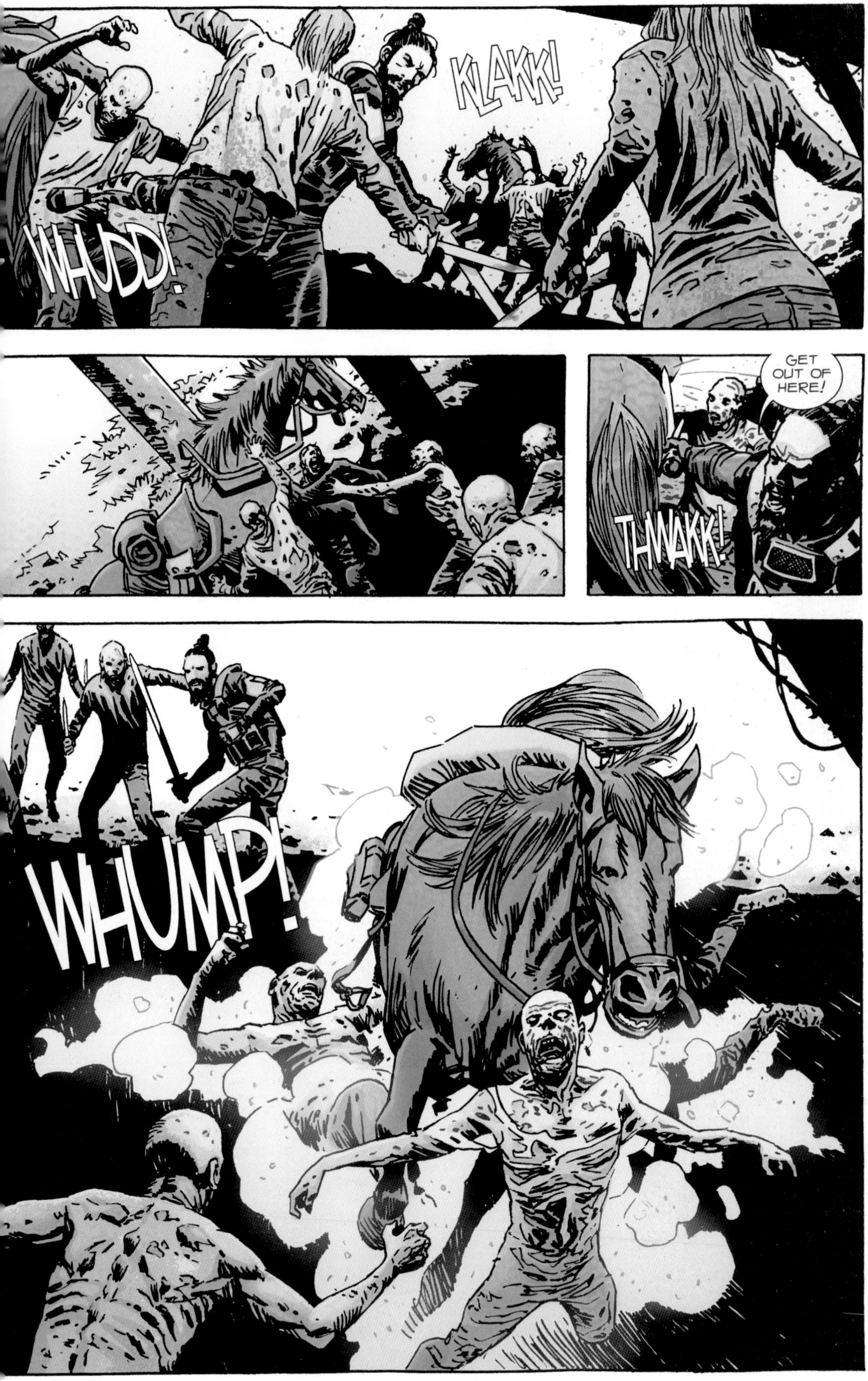
KLAKK!
WHUDD!
GET OUT OF HERE!
THWAKK!
WHUMP!

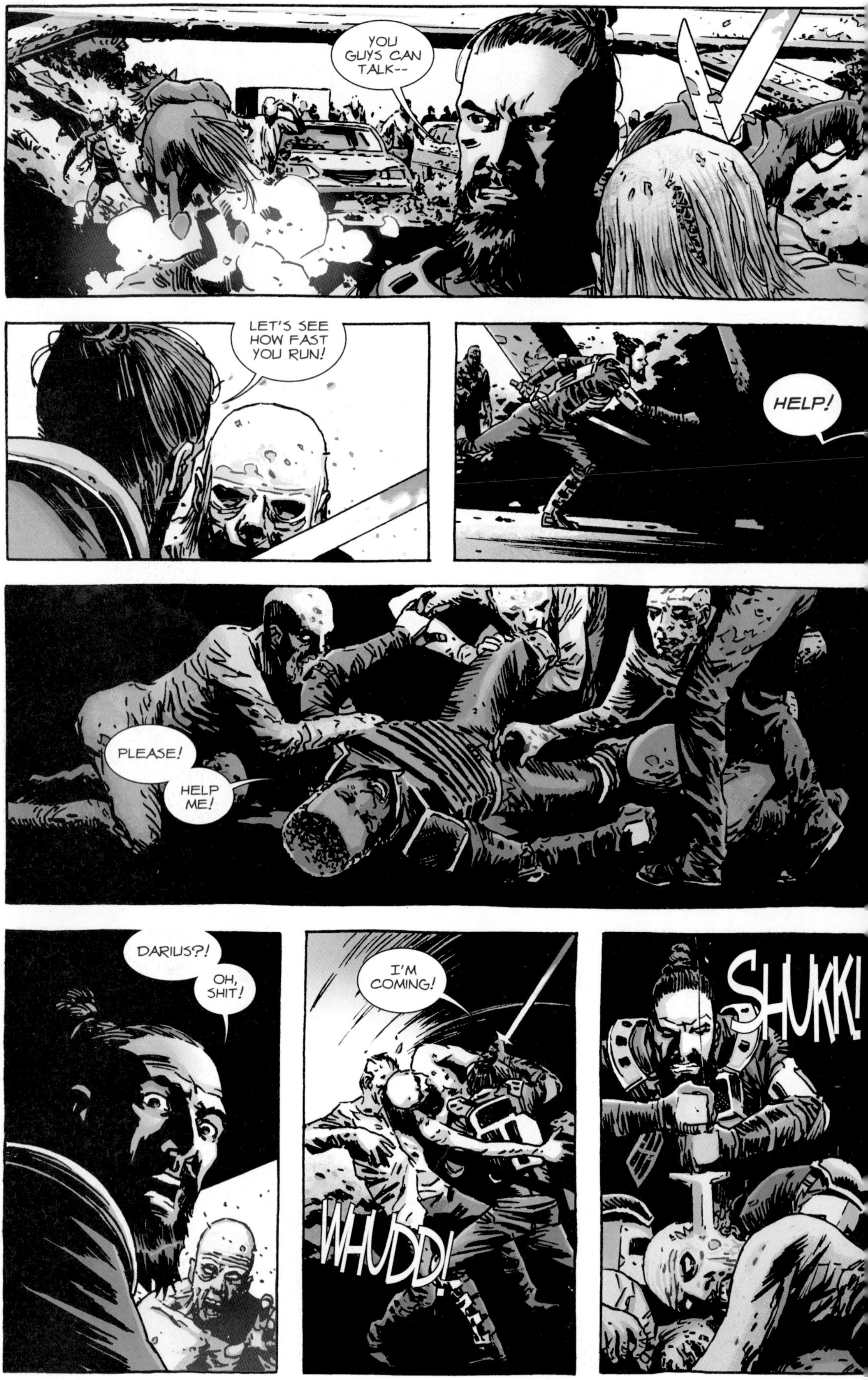
YOU GUYS CAN TALK--
LET'S SEE HOW FAST YOU RUN!
HELP!
PLEASE!
HELP ME!
DARIUS?!
OH, SHIT!
I'M COMING!
WHUDD!
SHUKK!

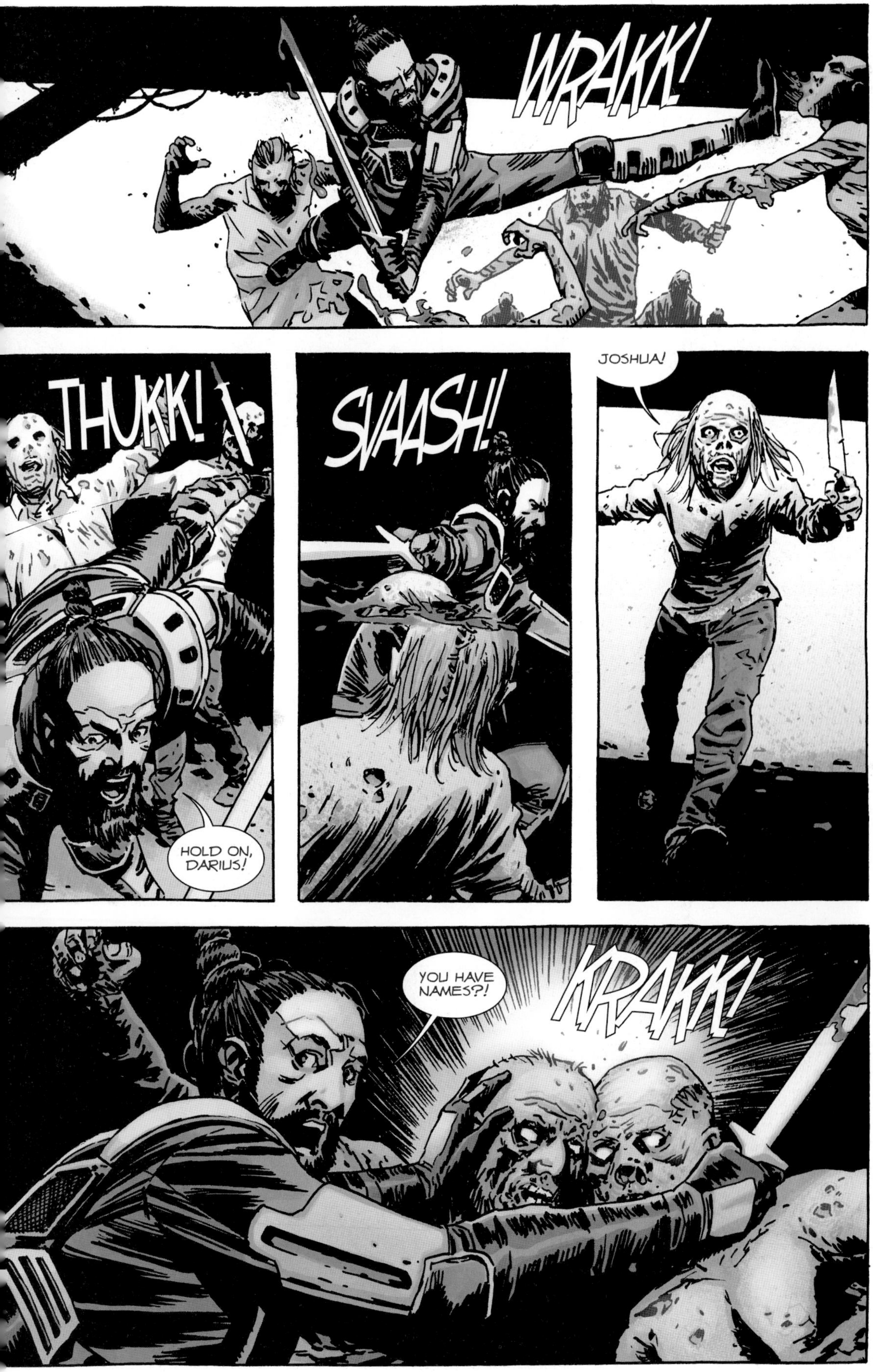
WRAKK!
THUKK!
HOLD ON, DARIUS!
SVAASH!
JOSHUA!
YOU HAVE NAMES?!
KRAKK!

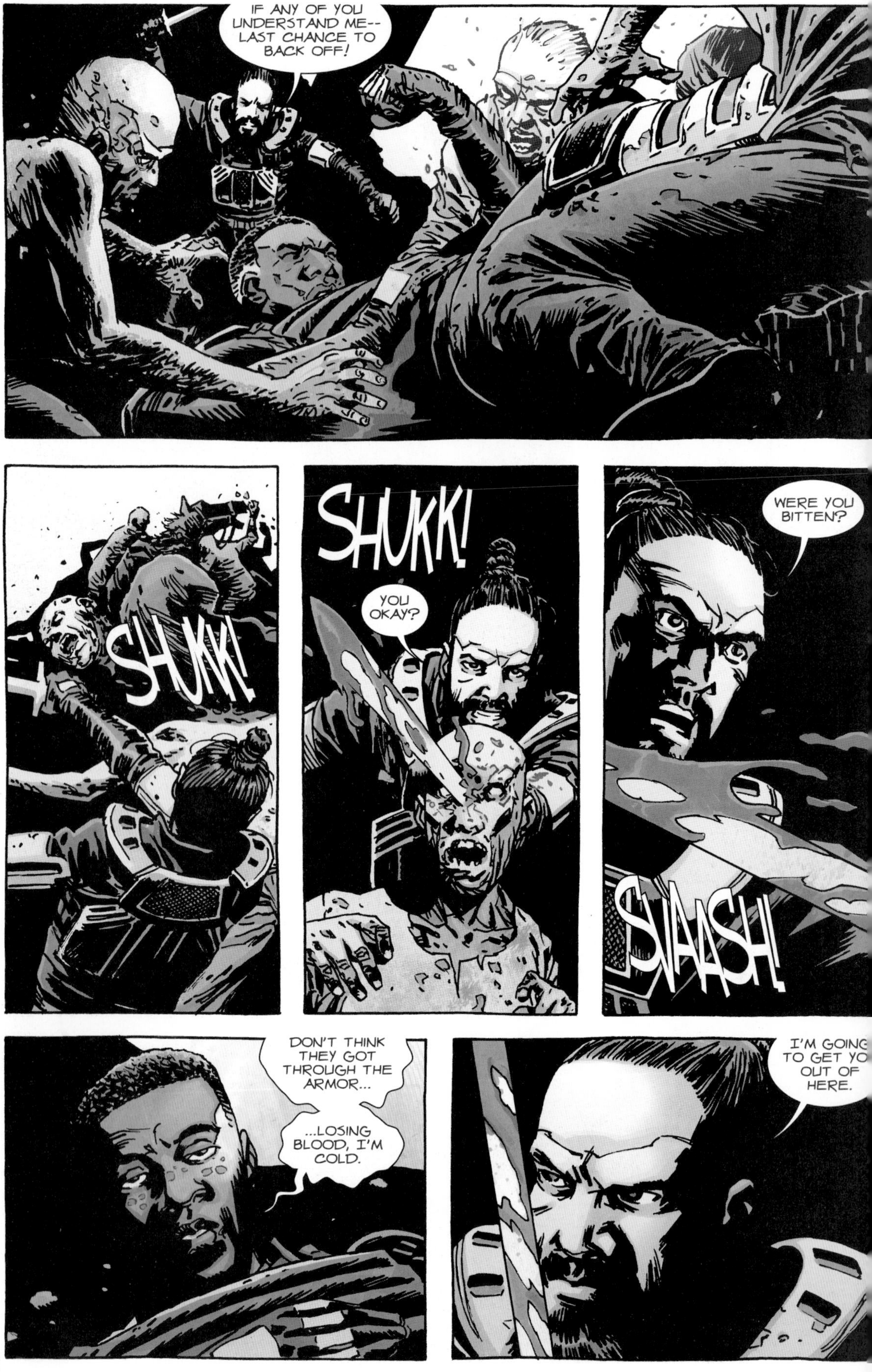
IF ANY OF YOU UNDERSTAND ME-- LAST CHANCE TO BACK OFF!
SHUKK!
SHUKK!
YOU OKAY?
WERE YOU BITTEN?
SWAASH!
DON'T THINK THEY GOT THROUGH THE ARMOR...
...LOSING BLOOD, I'M COLD.
I'M GOING TO GET YO OUT OF HERE.

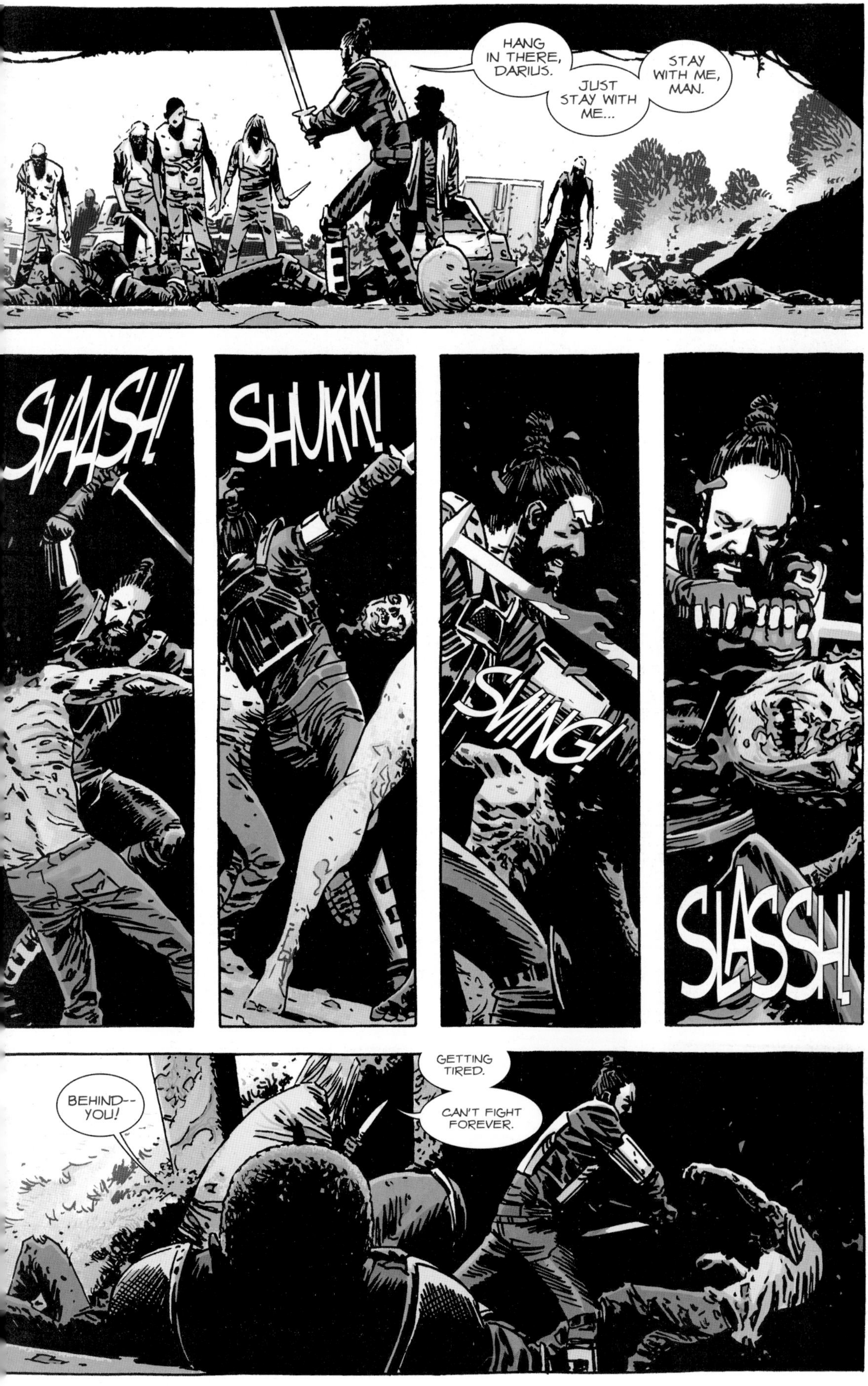
HANG IN THERE, DARIUS.
JUST STAY WITH ME...
STAY WITH ME, MAN.
SWAASH!
SHUKK!
SWING!
SLASSH!
BEHIND-- YOU!
GETTING TIRED.
CAN'T FIGHT FOREVER.

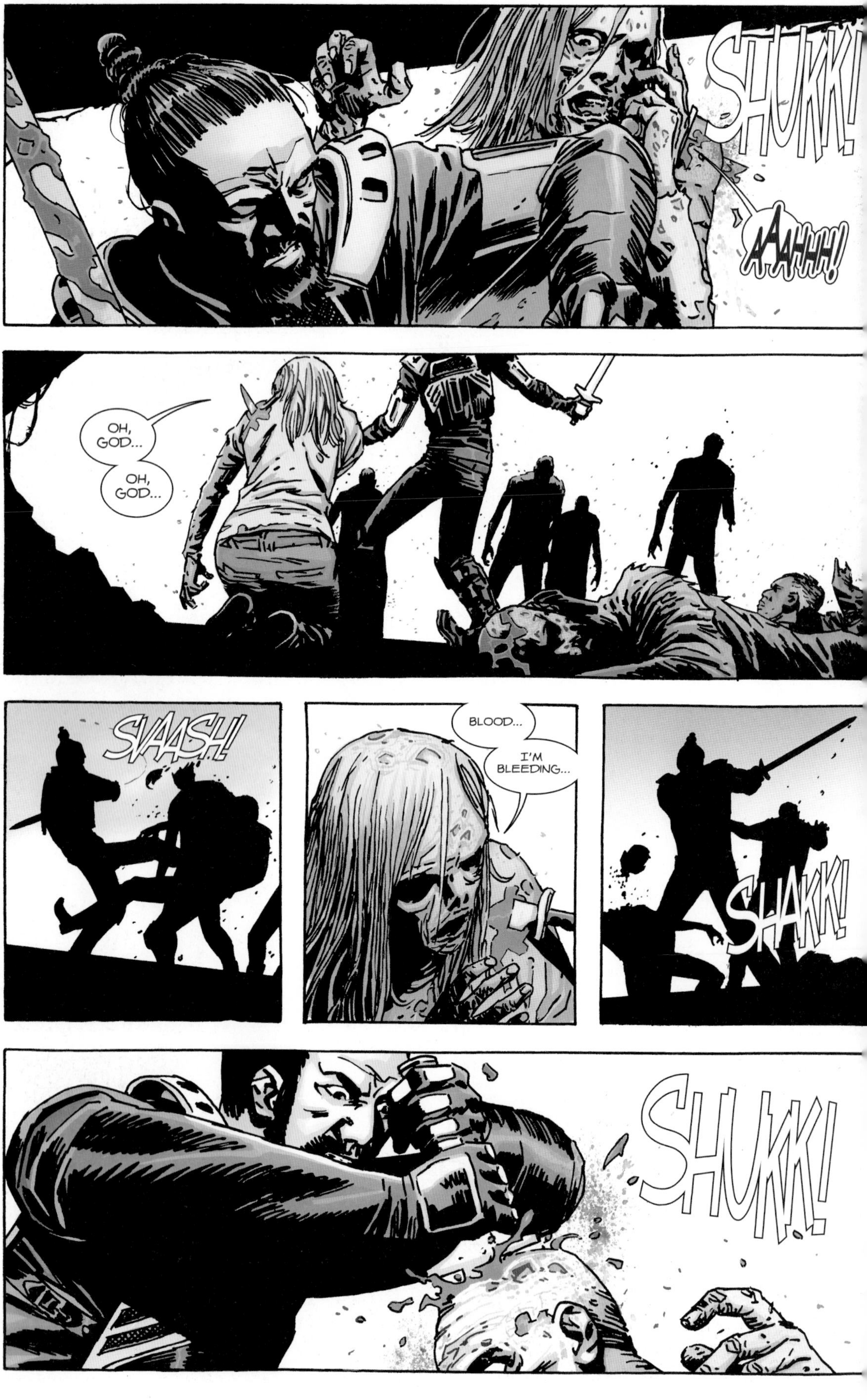
SHUKK!
AAAHHH!
OH, GOD...
OH, GOD...
SVAASH!
BLOOD...
I'M BLEEDING...
SHAKK!
SHUKK!

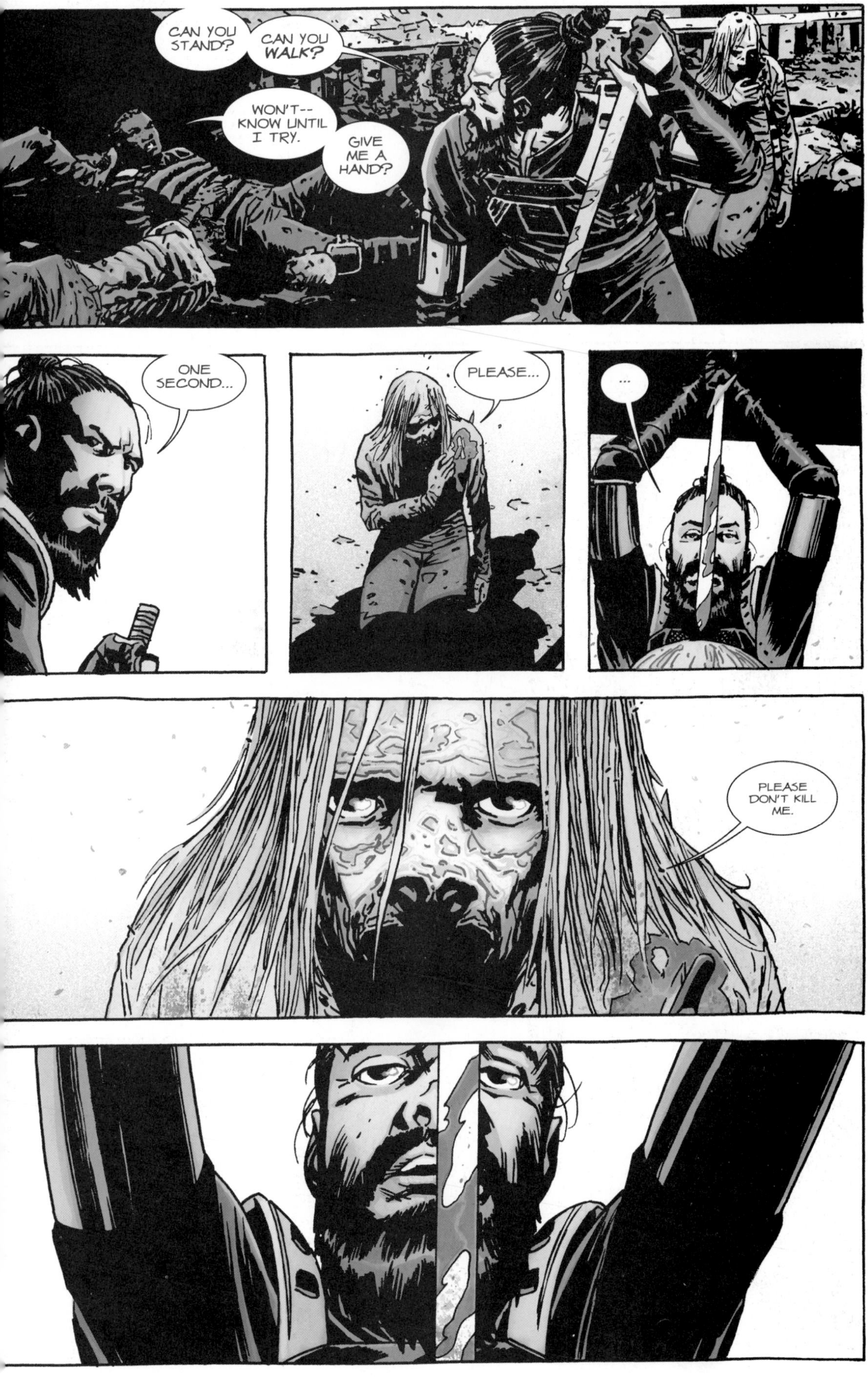
CAN YOU STAND?
CAN YOU WALK?
WON'T-- KNOW UNTIL I TRY.
GIVE ME A HAND?
ONE SECOND...
PLEASE...
...
PLEASE DON'T KILL ME.

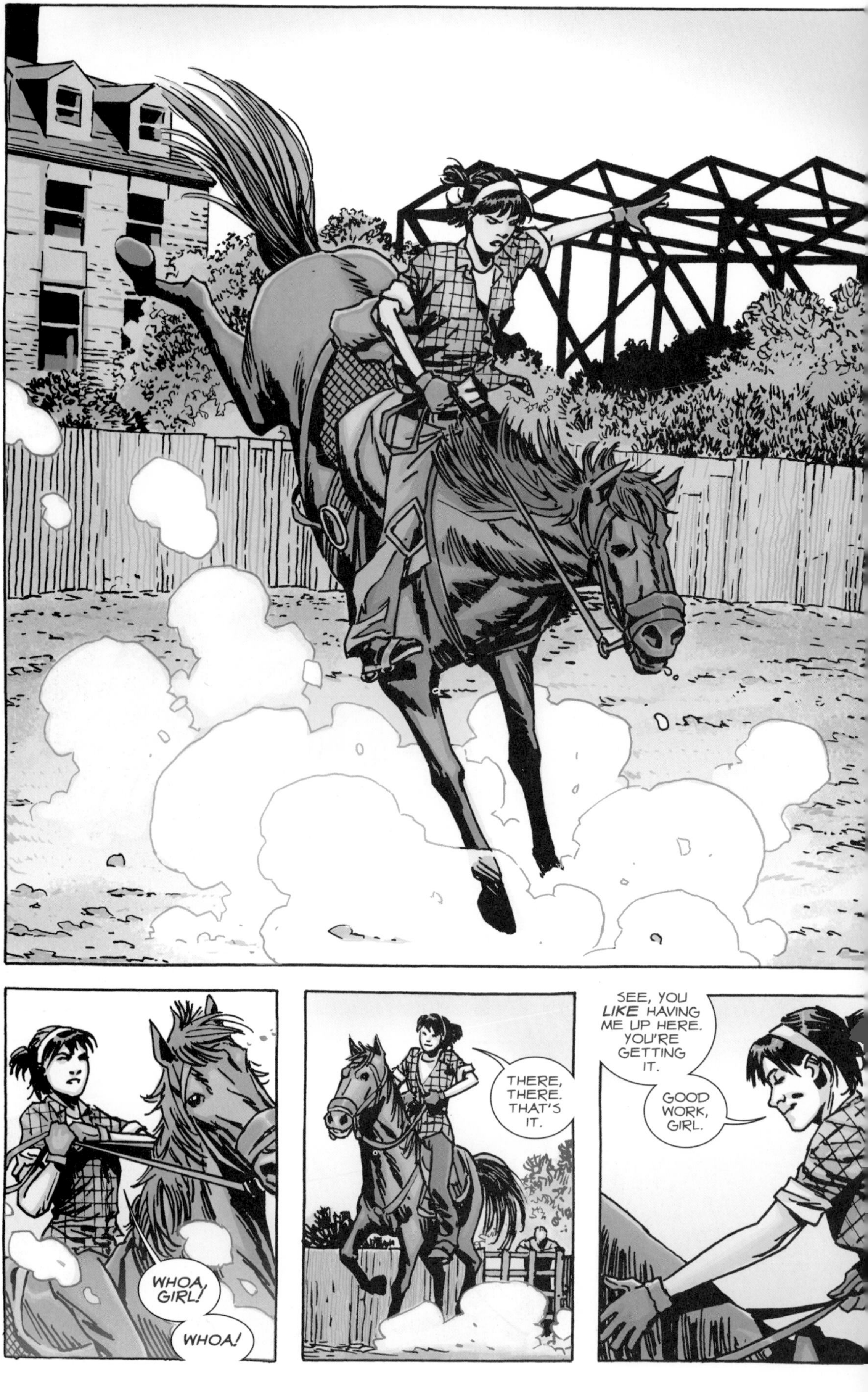
WHOA, GIRL!
WHOA!
THERE, THERE. THAT'S IT.
SEE, YOU LIKE HAVING ME UP HERE. YOU'RE GETTING IT.
GOOD WORK, GIRL.

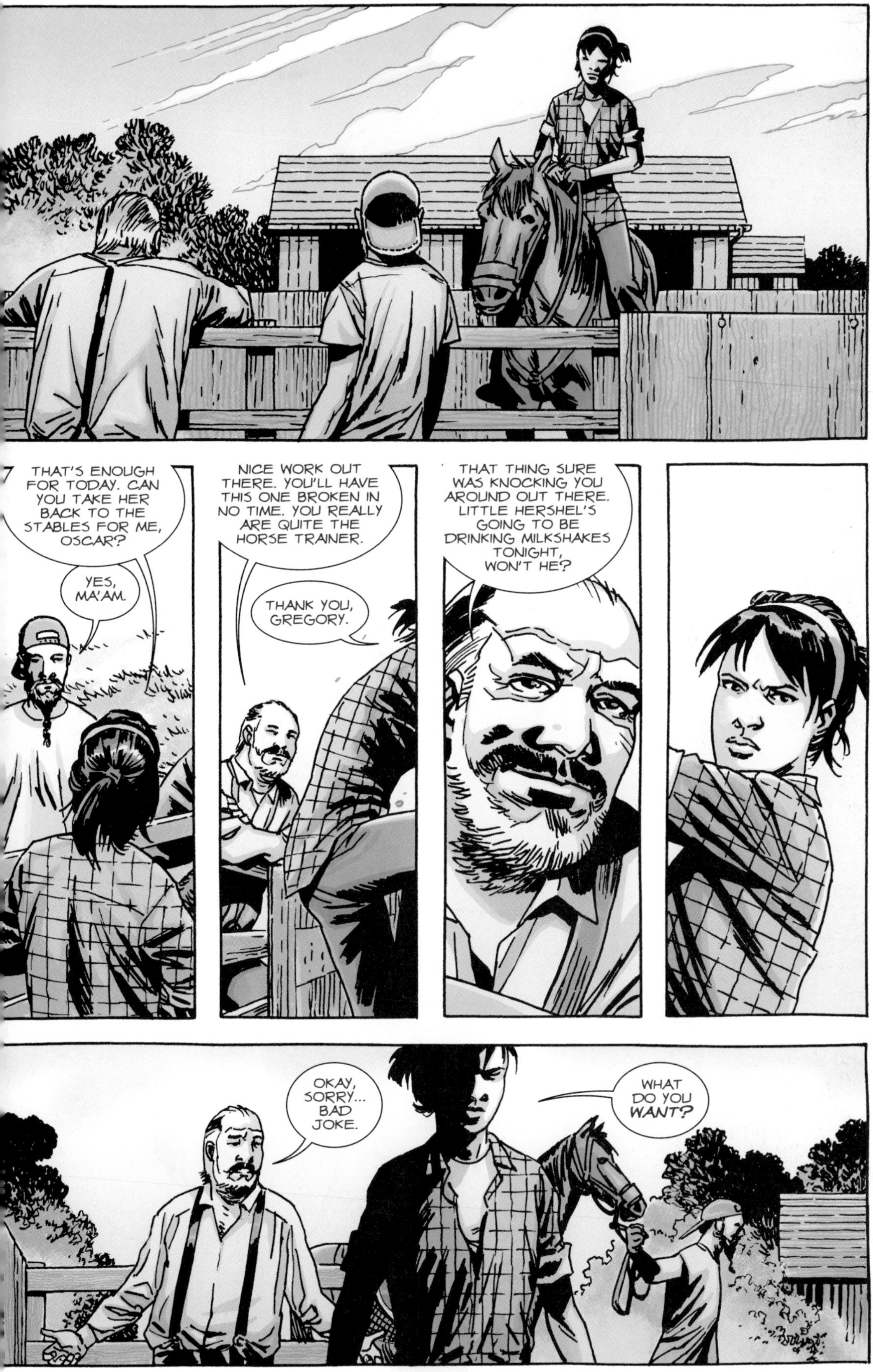
THAT'S ENOUGH FOR TODAY. CAN YOU TAKE HER BACK TO THE STABLES FOR ME, OSCAR?
YES, MA'AM.
NICE WORK OUT THERE. YOU'LL HAVE THIS ONE BROKEN IN NO TIME. YOU REALLY ARE QUITE THE HORSE TRAINER.
THANK YOU, GREGORY.
THAT THING SURE WAS KNOCKING YOU AROUND OUT THERE. LITTLE HERSHEL'S GOING TO BE DRINKING MILKSHAKES TONIGHT, WON'T HE?
OKAY, SORRY... BAD JOKE.
WHAT DO YOU *WANT?*

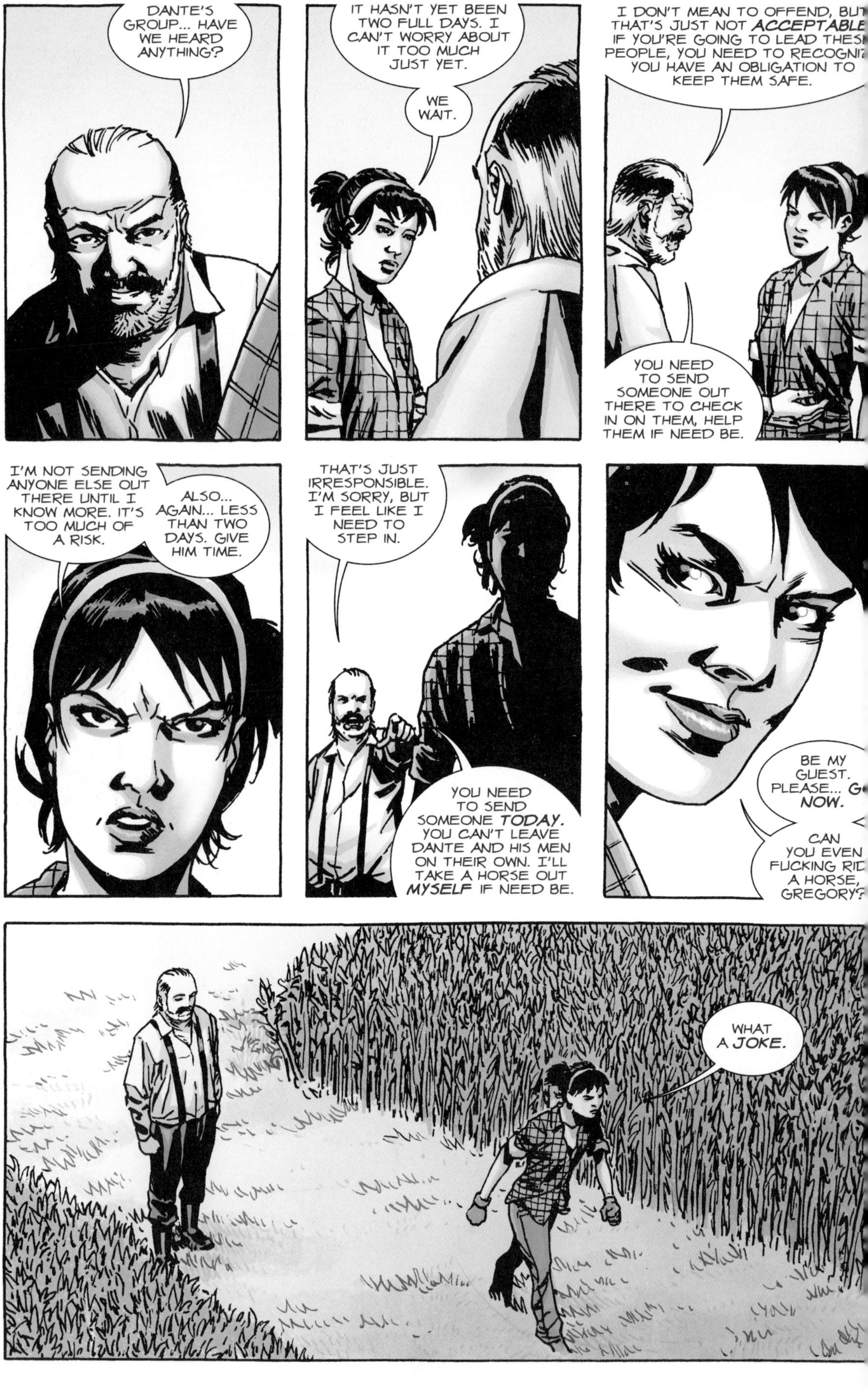
DANTE'S GROUP... HAVE WE HEARD ANYTHING?
IT HASN'T YET BEEN TWO FULL DAYS. I CAN'T WORRY ABOUT IT TOO MUCH JUST YET.
WE WAIT.
I DON'T MEAN TO OFFEND, BUT THAT'S JUST NOT ACCEPTABLE IF YOU'RE GOING TO LEAD THES PEOPLE, YOU NEED TO RECOGNI YOU HAVE AN OBLIGATION TO KEEP THEM SAFE.
YOU NEED TO SEND SOMEONE OUT THERE TO CHECK IN ON THEM, HELP THEM IF NEED BE.
I'M NOT SENDING ANYONE ELSE OUT THERE UNTIL I KNOW MORE. IT'S TOO MUCH OF A RISK.
ALSO... AGAIN... LESS THAN TWO DAYS. GIVE HIM TIME.
THAT'S JUST IRRESPONSIBLE. I'M SORRY, BUT I FEEL LIKE I NEED TO STEP IN.
YOU NEED TO SEND SOMEONE TODAY. YOU CAN'T LEAVE DANTE AND HIS MEN ON THEIR OWN. I'LL TAKE A HORSE OUT MYSELF IF NEED BE.
BE MY GUEST. PLEASE... G NOW.
CAN YOU EVEN FUCKING RID A HORSE, GREGORY?
WHAT A JOKE.

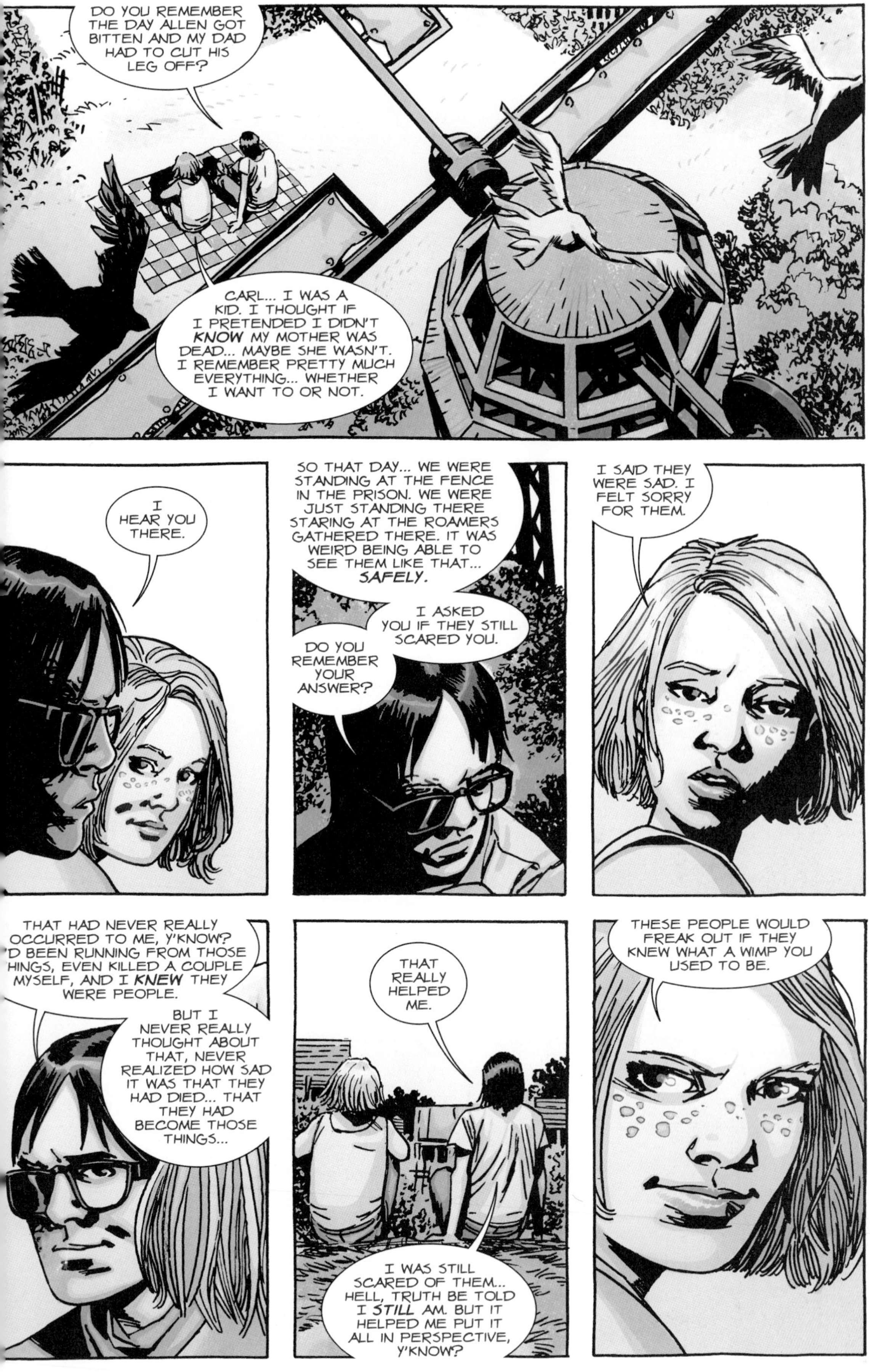
DO YOU REMEMBER THE DAY ALLEN GOT BITTEN AND MY DAD HAD TO CUT HIS LEG OFF?
CARL... I WAS A KID. I THOUGHT IF I PRETENDED I DIDN'T **KNOW** MY MOTHER WAS DEAD... MAYBE SHE WASN'T. I REMEMBER PRETTY MUCH EVERYTHING... WHETHER I WANT TO OR NOT.
I HEAR YOU THERE.
SO THAT DAY... WE WERE STANDING AT THE FENCE IN THE PRISON. WE WERE JUST STANDING THERE STARING AT THE ROAMERS GATHERED THERE. IT WAS WEIRD BEING ABLE TO SEE THEM LIKE THAT... ***SAFELY.***
I ASKED YOU IF THEY STILL SCARED YOU.
DO YOU REMEMBER YOUR ANSWER?
I SAID THEY WERE SAD. I FELT SORRY FOR THEM.
THAT HAD NEVER REALLY OCCURRED TO ME, Y'KNOW? 'D BEEN RUNNING FROM THOSE HINGS, EVEN KILLED A COUPLE MYSELF, AND I ***KNEW*** THEY WERE PEOPLE.
BUT I NEVER REALLY THOUGHT ABOUT THAT, NEVER REALIZED HOW SAD IT WAS THAT THEY HAD DIED... THAT THEY HAD BECOME THOSE THINGS...
THAT REALLY HELPED ME.
I WAS STILL SCARED OF THEM... HELL, TRUTH BE TOLD I ***STILL*** AM. BUT IT HELPED ME PUT IT ALL IN PERSPECTIVE, Y'KNOW?
THESE PEOPLE WOULD FREAK OUT IF THEY KNEW WHAT A WIMP YOU USED TO BE.

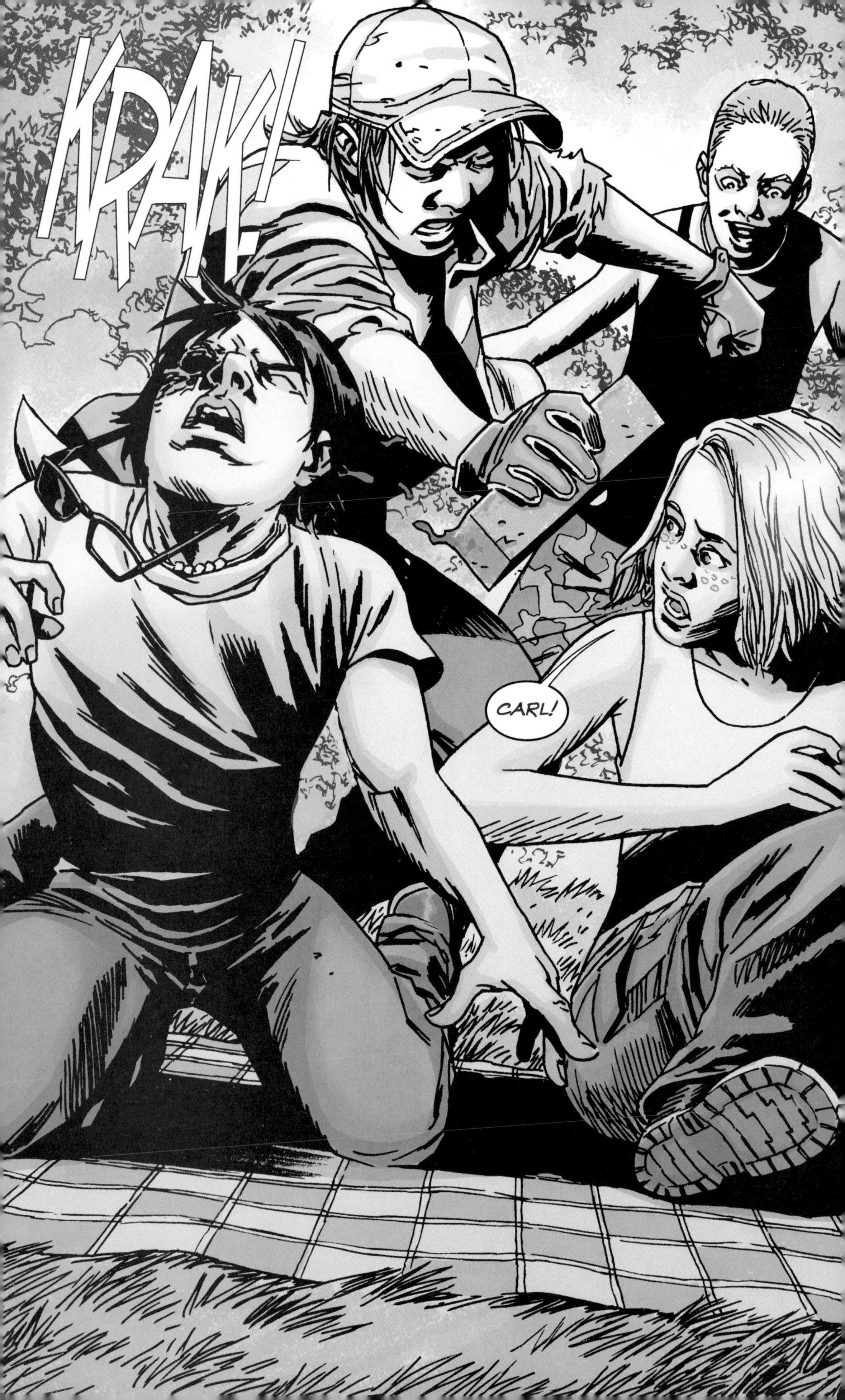
KRAK!
CARL!

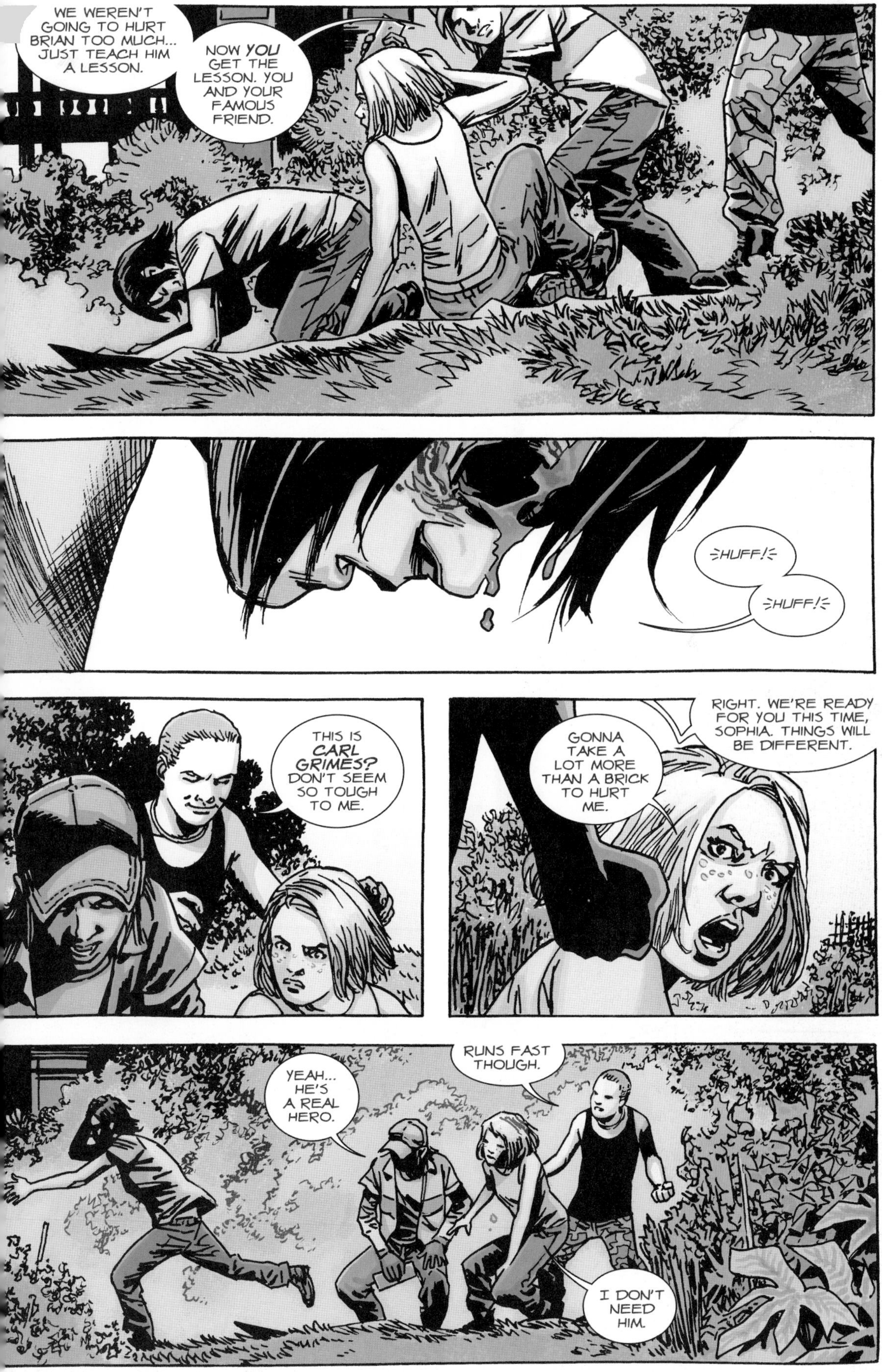
WE WEREN'T GOING TO HURT BRIAN TOO MUCH... JUST TEACH HIM A LESSON.
NOW *YOU* GET THE LESSON. YOU AND YOUR FAMOUS FRIEND.
HUFF!
HUFF!
THIS IS **CARL GRIMES?** DON'T SEEM SO TOUGH TO ME.
GONNA TAKE A LOT MORE THAN A BRICK TO HURT ME.
RIGHT. WE'RE READY FOR YOU THIS TIME, SOPHIA. THINGS WILL BE DIFFERENT.
YEAH... HE'S A REAL HERO.
RUNS FAST THOUGH.
I DON'T NEED HIM.

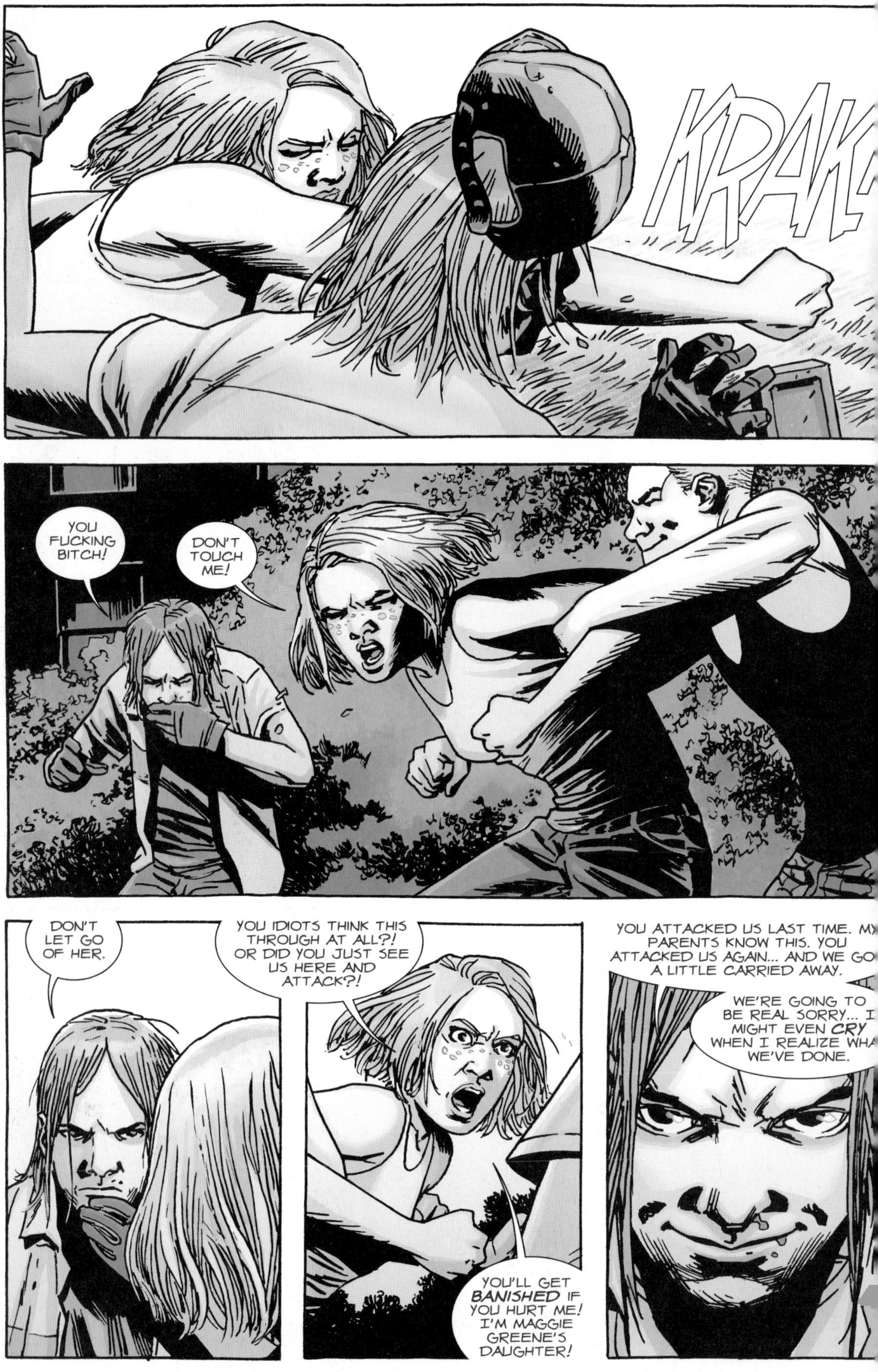
KRAK
YOU FUCKING BITCH!
DON'T TOUCH ME!
DON'T LET GO OF HER.
YOU IDIOTS THINK THIS THROUGH AT ALL?! OR DID YOU JUST SEE US HERE AND ATTACK?!
YOU'LL GET BANISHED IF YOU HURT ME! I'M MAGGIE GREENE'S DAUGHTER!
YOU ATTACKED US LAST TIME. MY PARENTS KNOW THIS. YOU ATTACKED US AGAIN... AND WE GO A LITTLE CARRIED AWAY.
WE'RE GOING TO BE REAL SORRY... I MIGHT EVEN CRY WHEN I REALIZE WHA WE'VE DONE.

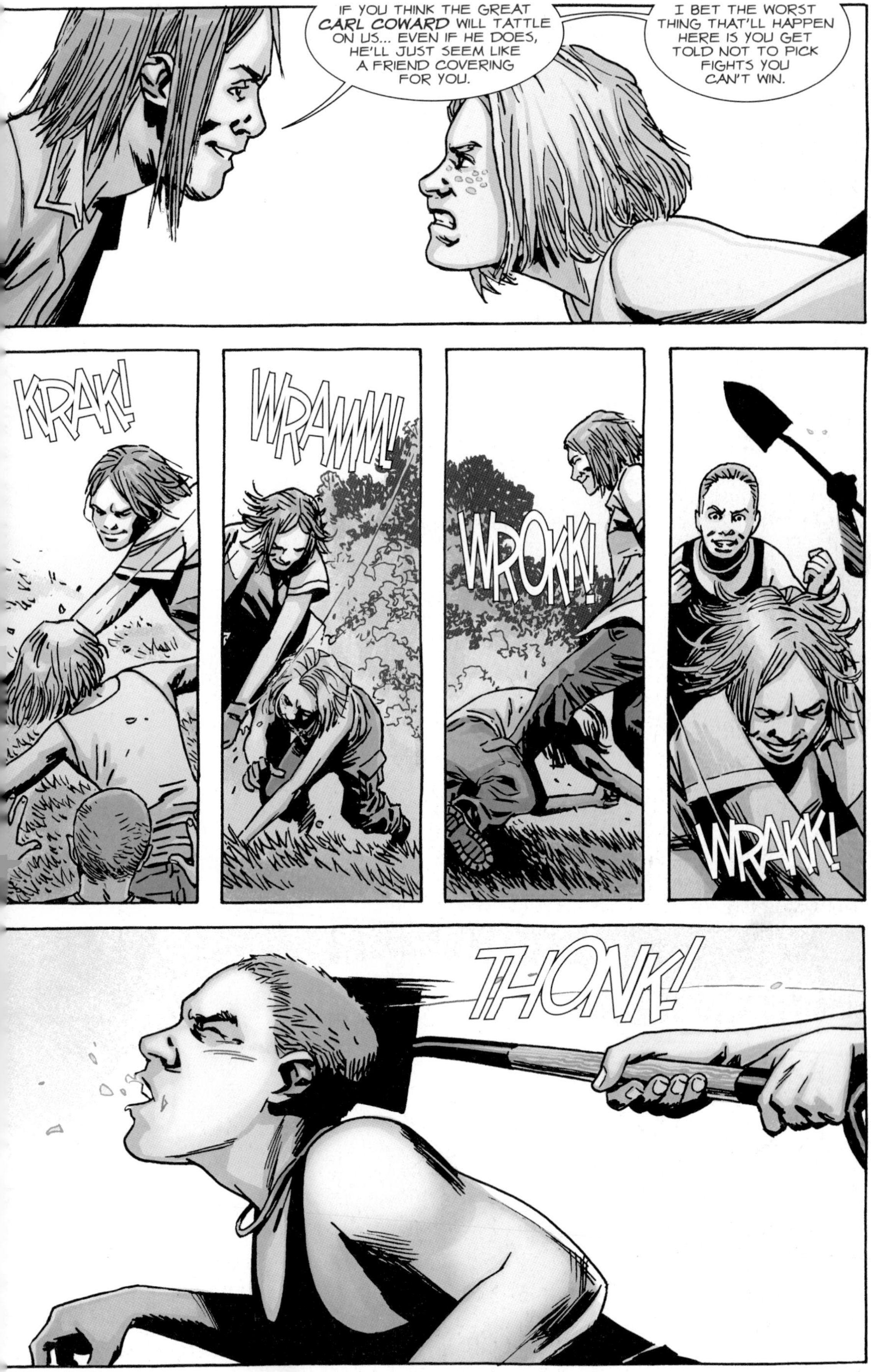
IF YOU THINK THE GREAT CARL COWARD WILL TATTLE ON US... EVEN IF HE DOES, HE'LL JUST SEEM LIKE A FRIEND COVERING FOR YOU.
I BET THE WORST THING THAT'LL HAPPEN HERE IS YOU GET TOLD NOT TO PICK FIGHTS YOU CAN'T WIN.
KRAK!
WRAMM!
WROKK!
WRAKK!
THONK!

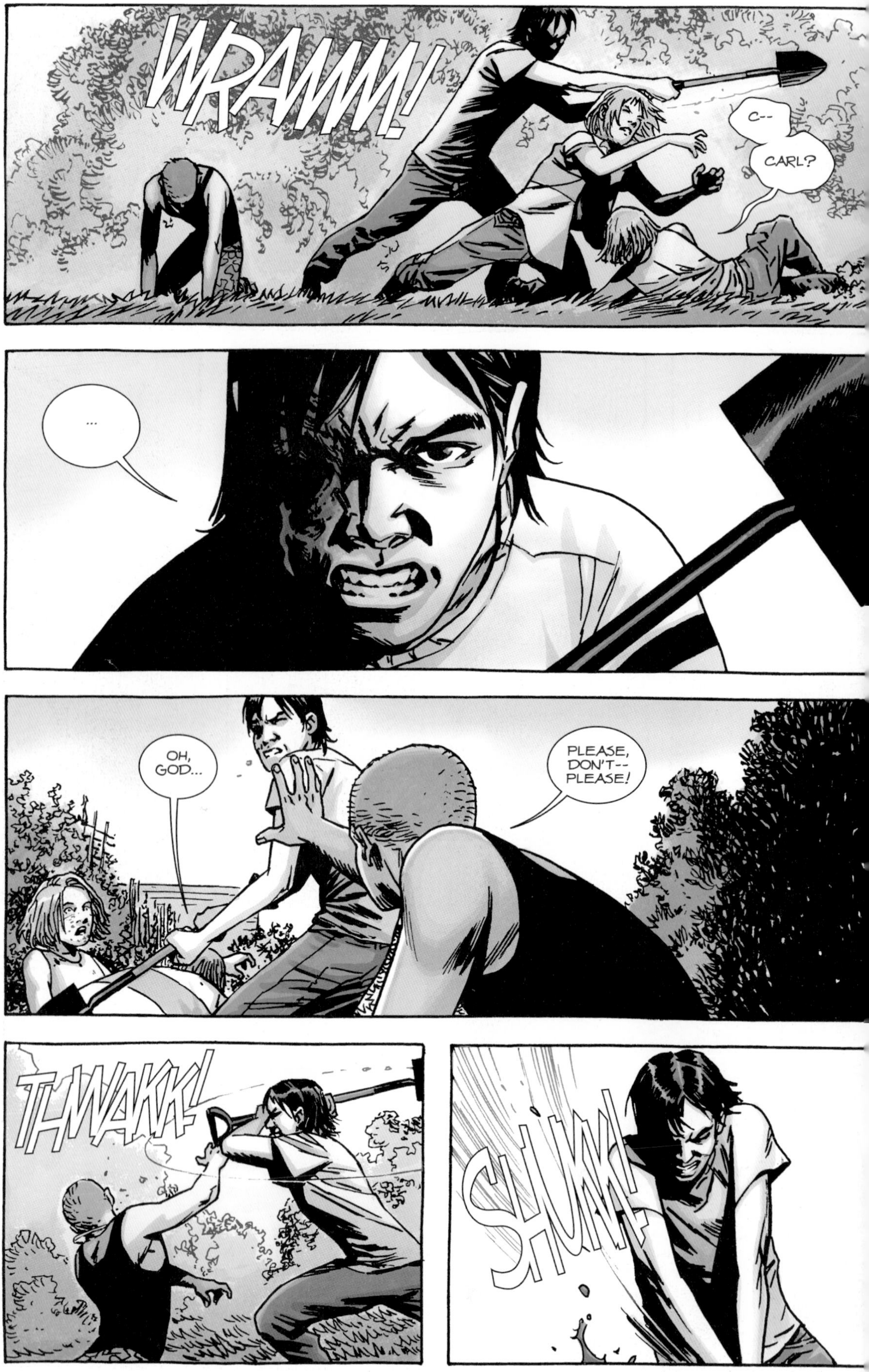
WRAMM!
C--
CARL?
...
OH, GOD...
PLEASE, DON'T-- PLEASE!
THWAKK!
SHUNK!

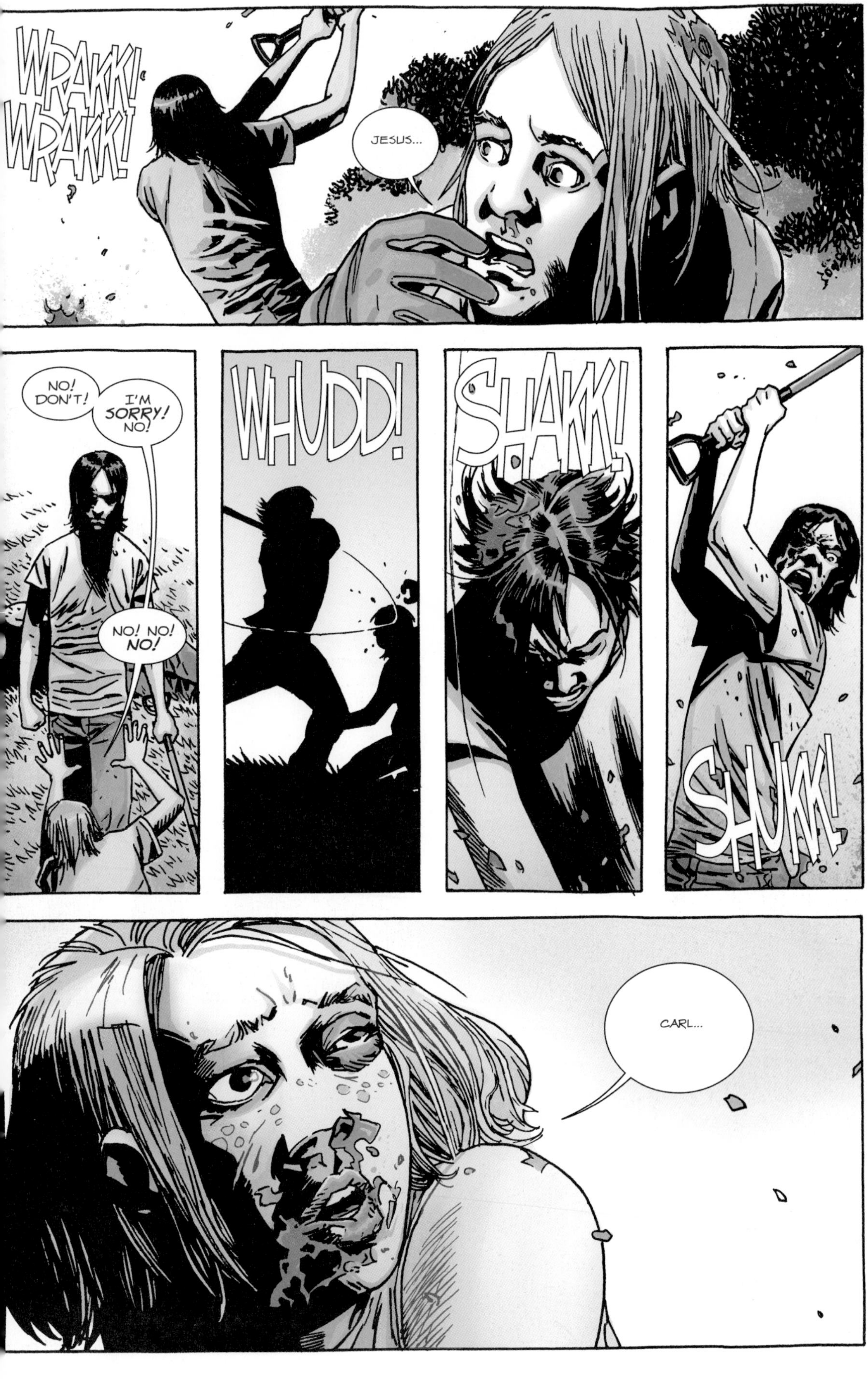

WRAKK! WRAKK!
JESUS...
NO! DON'T!
I'M SORRY! NO!
NO! NO! NO!
WHUDD!
SHAKK!
SHUKK!
CARL...

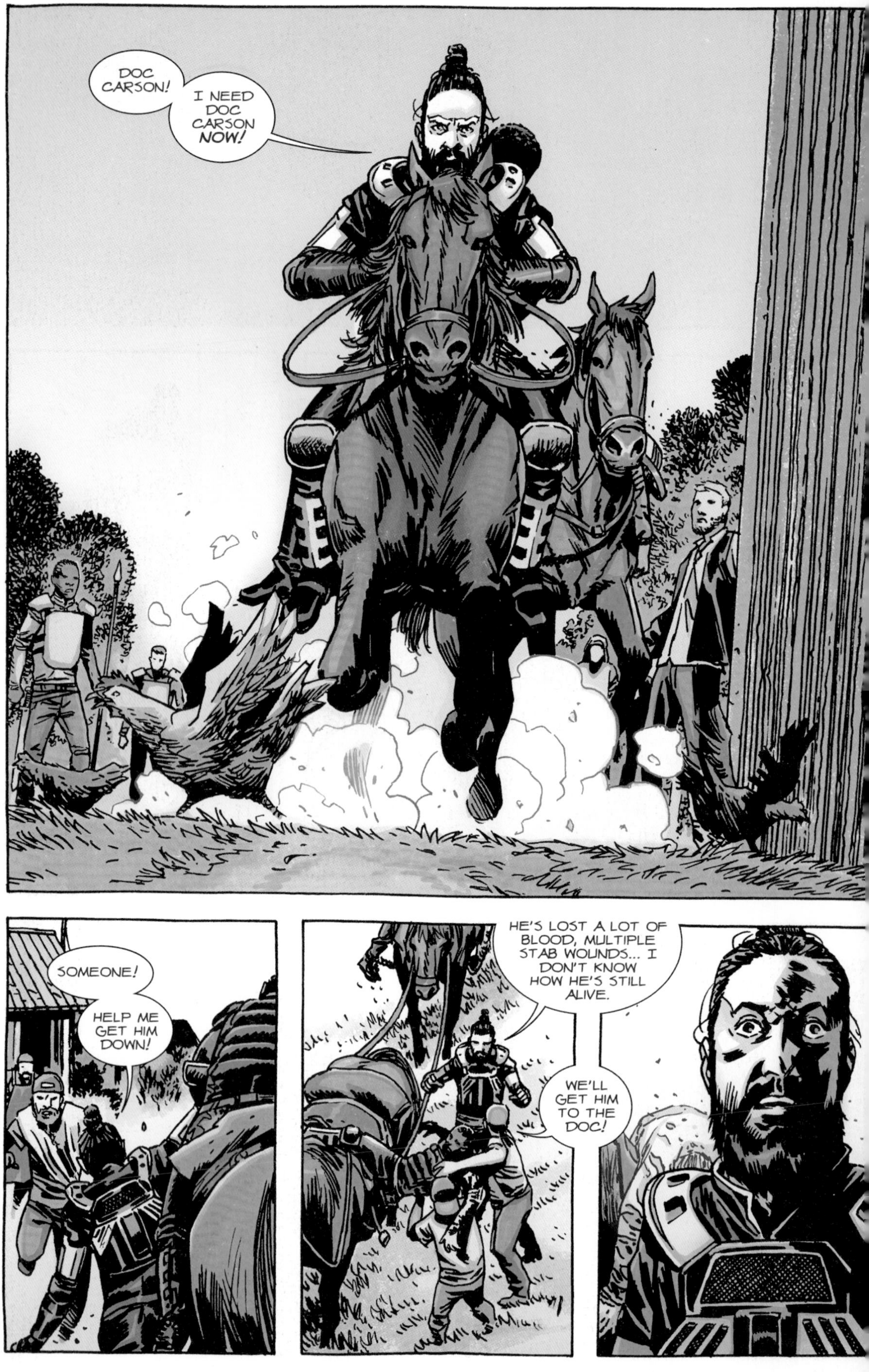
DOC CARSON!
I NEED DOC CARSON NOW!
SOMEONE!
HELP ME GET HIM DOWN!
HE'S LOST A LOT OF BLOOD, MULTIPLE STAB WOUNDS... I DON'T KNOW HOW HE'S STILL ALIVE.
WE'LL GET HIM TO THE DOC!

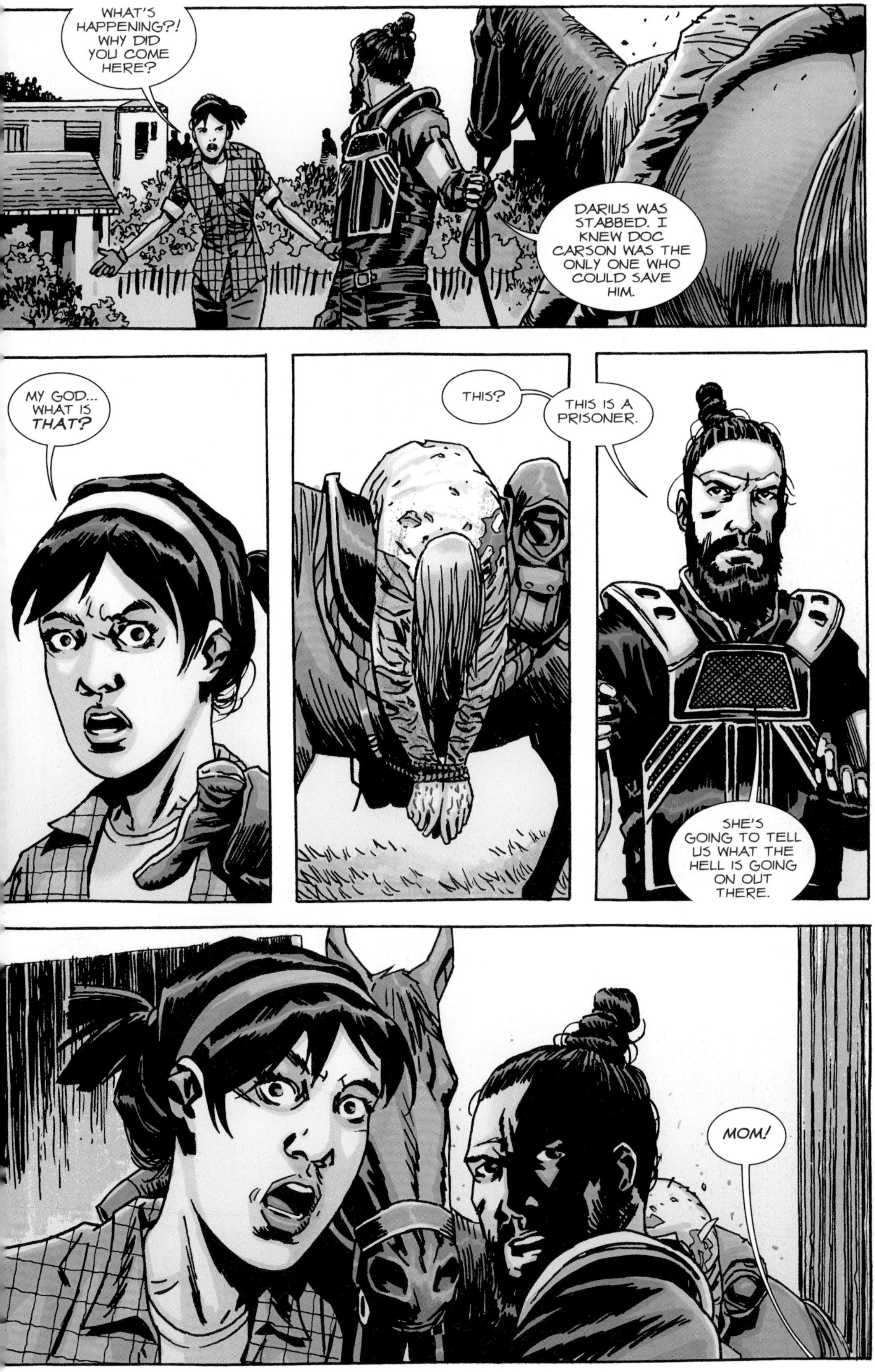
WHAT'S HAPPENING?! WHY DID YOU COME HERE?
DARIUS WAS STABBED. I KNEW DOC CARSON WAS THE ONLY ONE WHO COULD SAVE HIM.
MY GOD... WHAT IS *THAT?*
THIS?
THIS IS A PRISONER.
SHE'S GOING TO TELL US WHAT THE HELL IS GOING ON OUT THERE.
MOM!

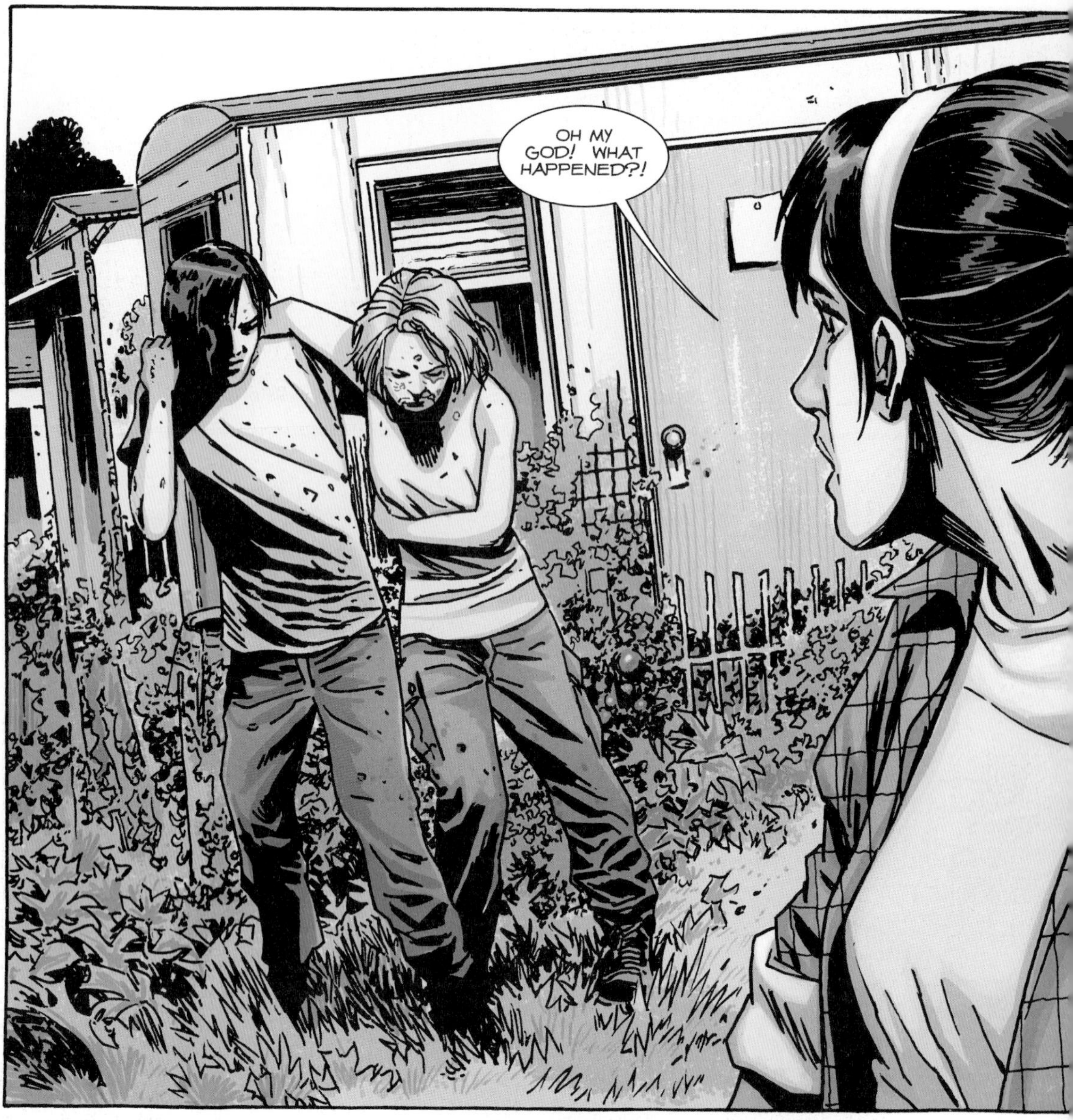
OH MY GOD! WHAT HAPPENED?!

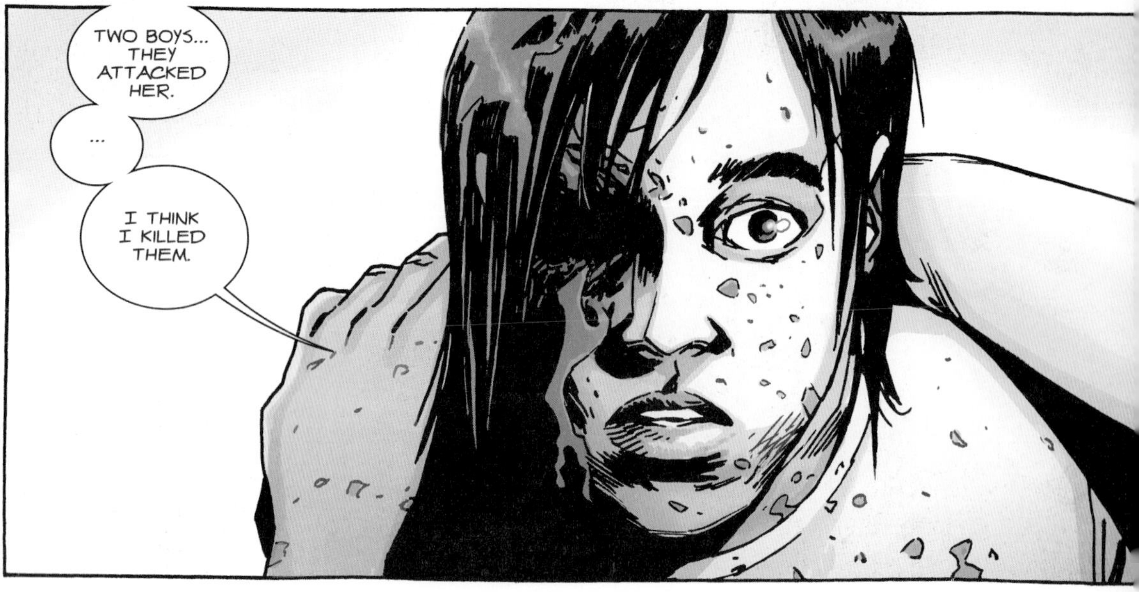
TWO BOYS... THEY ATTACKED HER.
...
I THINK I KILLED THEM.

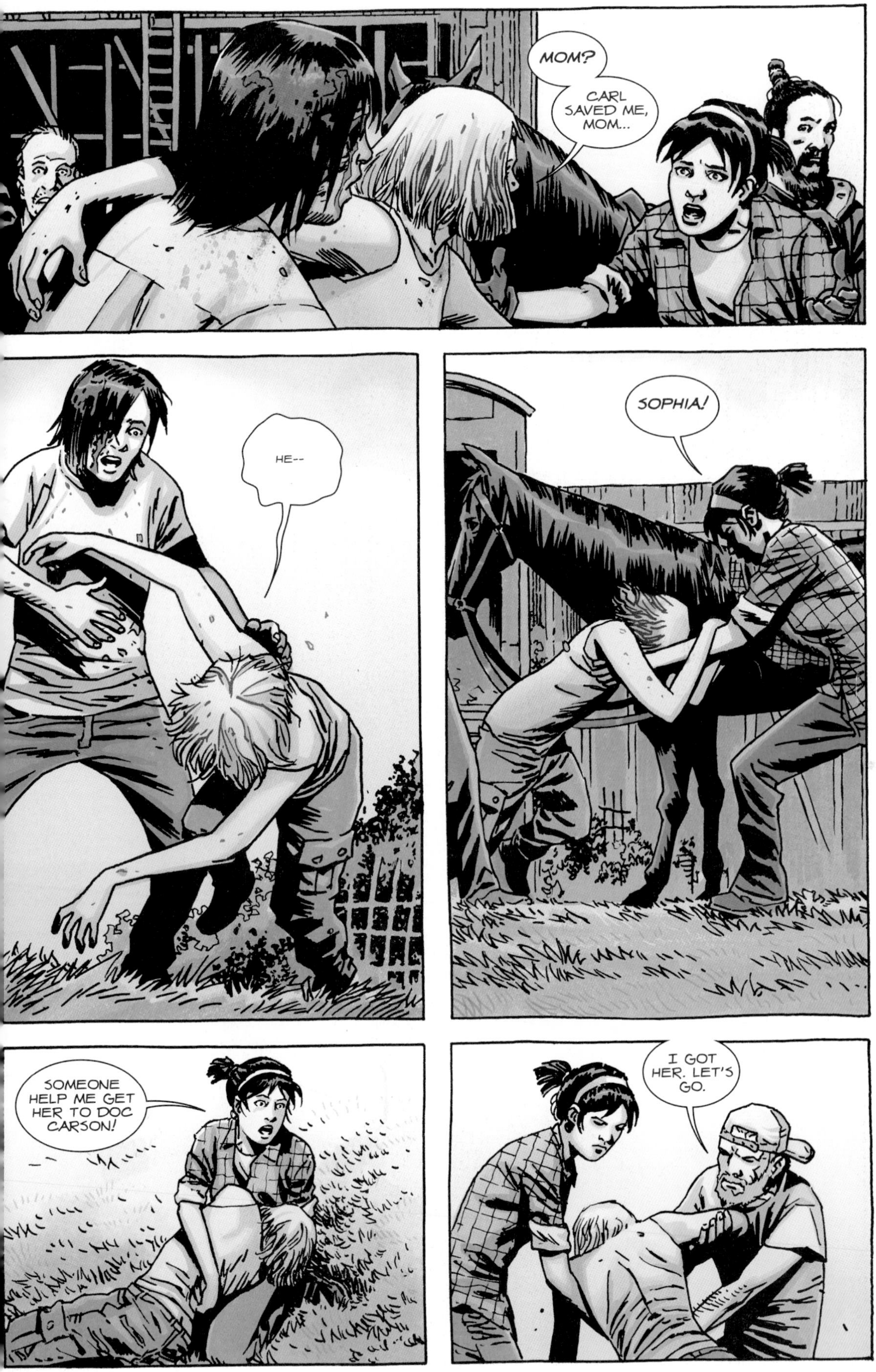
MOM?
CARL SAVED ME, MOM...
HE--
SOPHIA!
SOMEONE HELP ME GET HER TO DOC CARSON!
I GOT HER. LET'S GO.

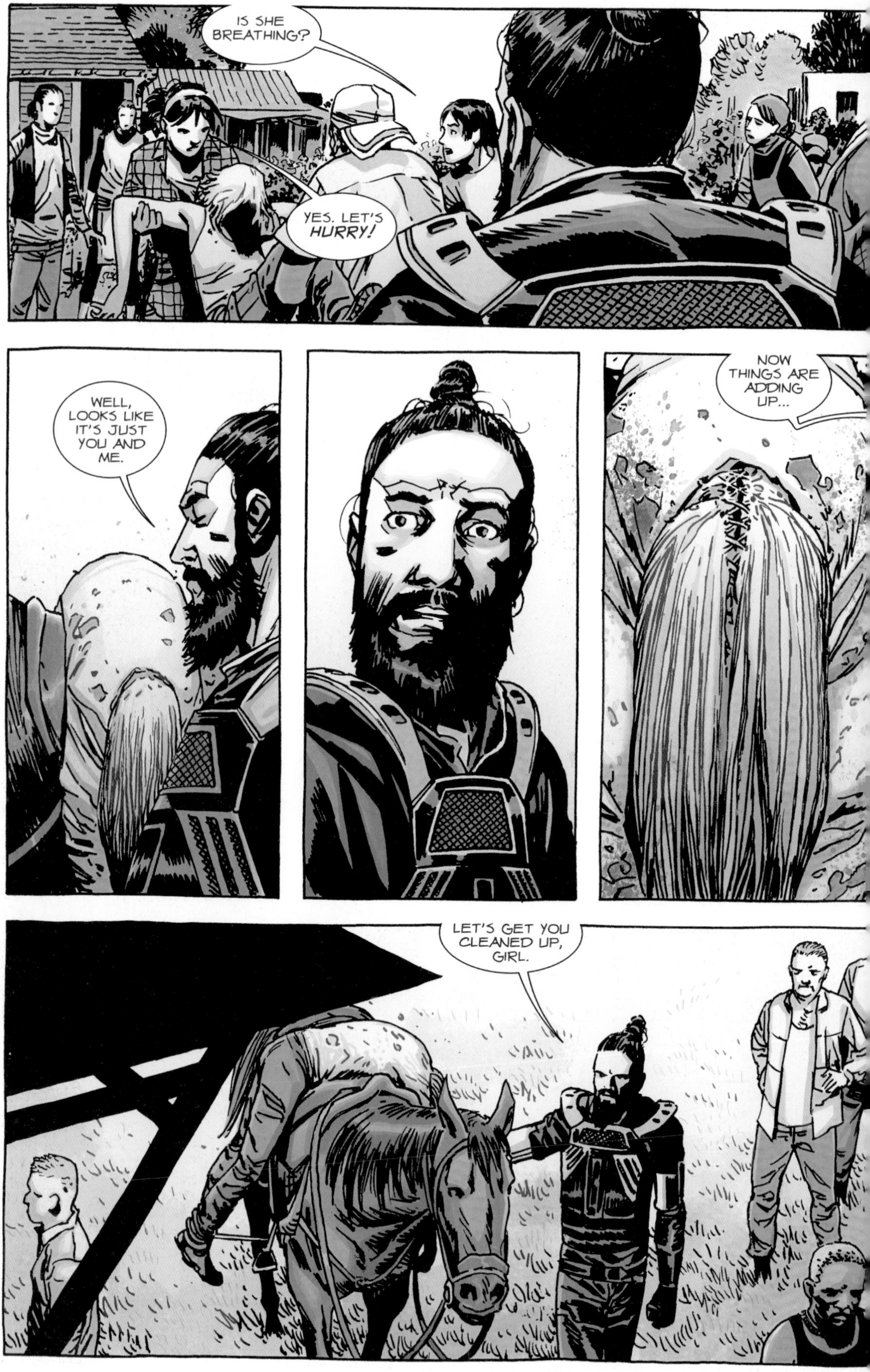
IS SHE BREATHING?
YES. LET'S HURRY!
WELL, LOOKS LIKE IT'S JUST YOU AND ME.
NOW THINGS ARE ADDING UP...
LET'S GET YOU CLEANED UP, GIRL.

WHAT DO YOU THINK, ALEX? IS SHE GOING TO BE OKAY?

SHE'S PRETTY BANGED UP... AND SHE'S PROBABLY GOT A CONCUSSION... BUT I THINK SHE'S GOING TO BE *FINE.*

DOC CARSON NEEDS TO FINISH UP WITH DARIUS... THEN HE'LL PATCH HER UP.

IT'S JUST A MATTER OF TIME.

TRY NOT TO WORRY, CARL. YOU HEARD ALEX. SHE'S GOING TO BE FINE.

I'M GLAD YOU WERE THERE FOR HER.

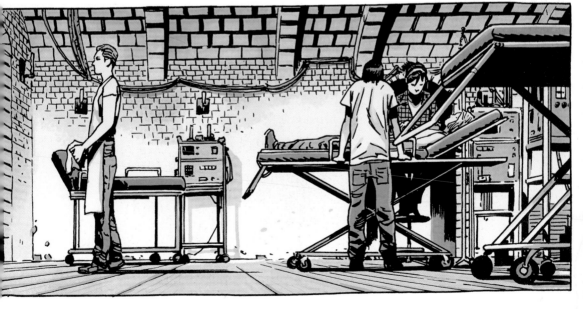

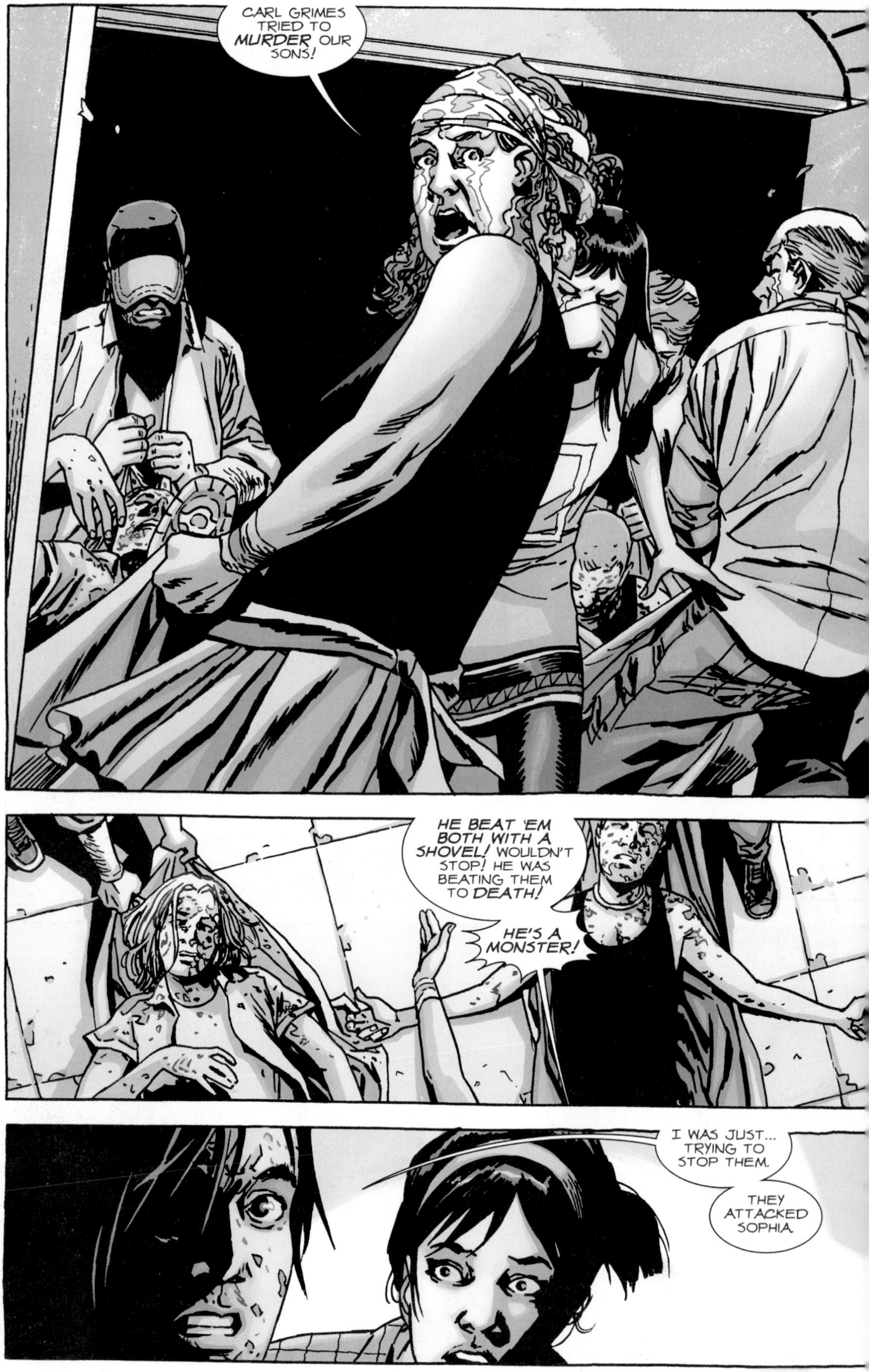

CARL GRIMES TRIED TO MURDER OUR SONS!
HE BEAT 'EM BOTH WITH A SHOVEL! WOULDN'T STOP! HE WAS BEATING THEM TO DEATH!
HE'S A MONSTER!
I WAS JUST... TRYING TO STOP THEM.
THEY ATTACKED SOPHIA.

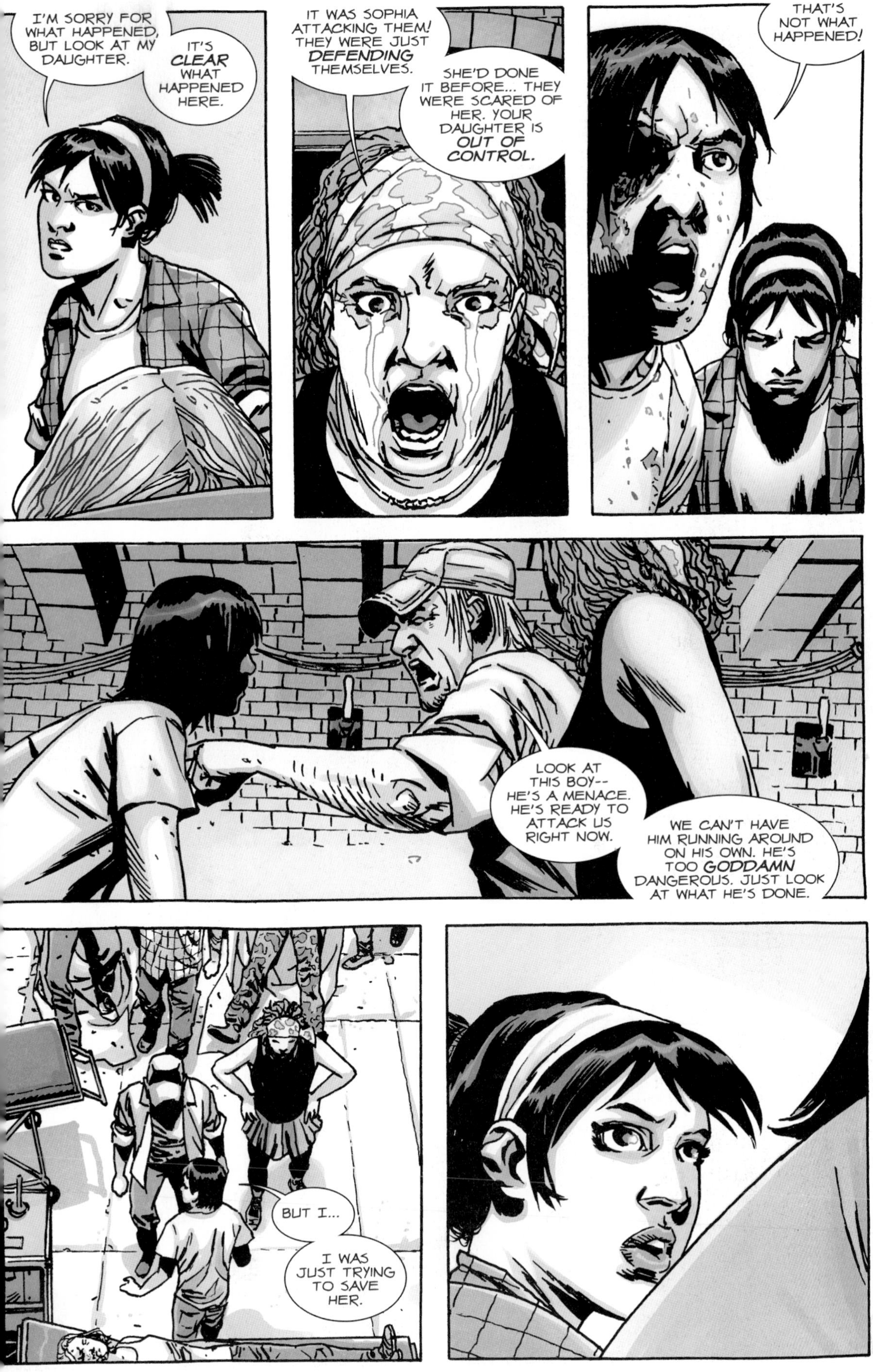
I'M SORRY FOR WHAT HAPPENED, BUT LOOK AT MY DAUGHTER.
IT'S *CLEAR* WHAT HAPPENED HERE.
IT WAS SOPHIA ATTACKING THEM! THEY WERE JUST *DEFENDING* THEMSELVES.
SHE'D DONE IT BEFORE... THEY WERE SCARED OF HER. YOUR DAUGHTER IS ***OUT OF CONTROL.***
THAT'S NOT WHAT HAPPENED!
LOOK AT THIS BOY-- HE'S A MENACE. HE'S READY TO ATTACK US RIGHT NOW.
WE CAN'T HAVE HIM RUNNING AROUND ON HIS OWN. HE'S TOO **GODDAMN** DANGEROUS. JUST LOOK AT WHAT HE'S DONE.
BUT I...
I WAS JUST TRYING TO SAVE HER.

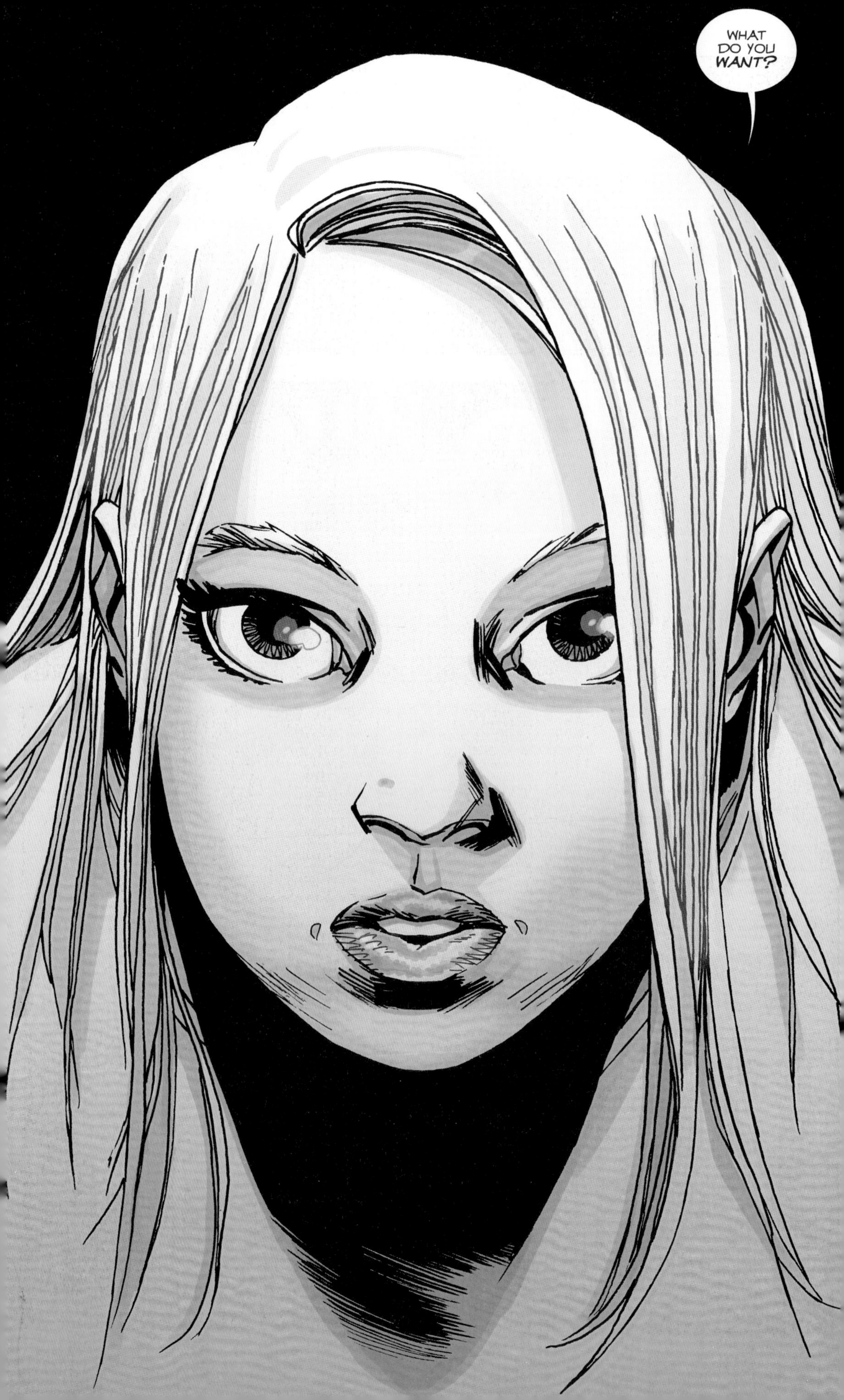
WHAT DO YOU WANT?

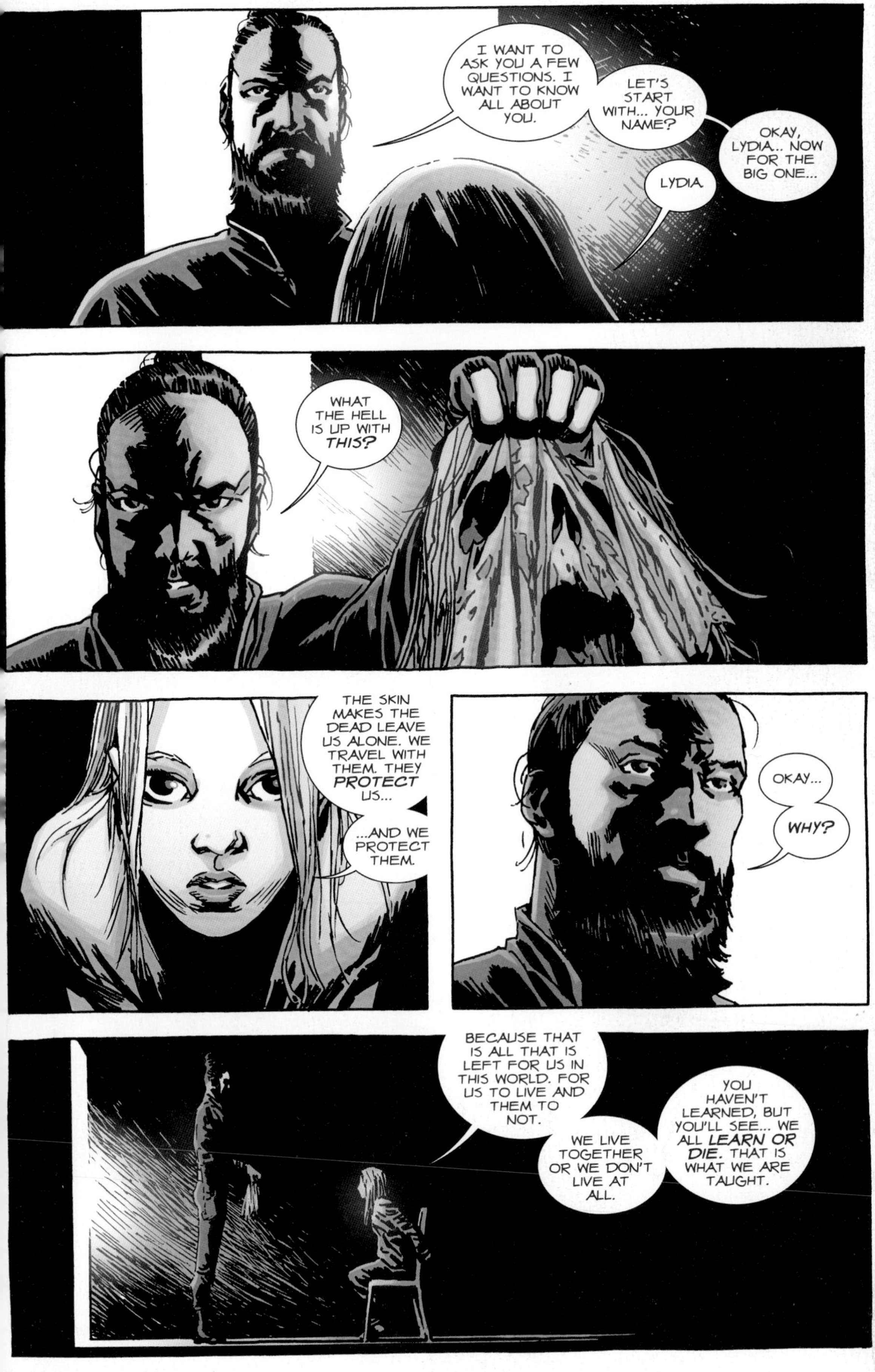
I WANT TO ASK YOU A FEW QUESTIONS. I WANT TO KNOW ALL ABOUT YOU.
LET'S START WITH... YOUR NAME?
LYDIA.
OKAY, LYDIA... NOW FOR THE BIG ONE...
WHAT THE HELL IS UP WITH *THIS?*
THE SKIN MAKES THE DEAD LEAVE US ALONE. WE TRAVEL WITH THEM. THEY *PROTECT* US...
...AND WE PROTECT THEM.
OKAY...
WHY?
BECAUSE THAT IS ALL THAT IS LEFT FOR US IN THIS WORLD. FOR US TO LIVE AND THEM TO NOT.
WE LIVE TOGETHER OR WE DON'T LIVE AT ALL.
YOU HAVEN'T LEARNED, BUT YOU'LL SEE... WE ALL *LEARN OR DIE.* THAT IS WHAT WE ARE TAUGHT.

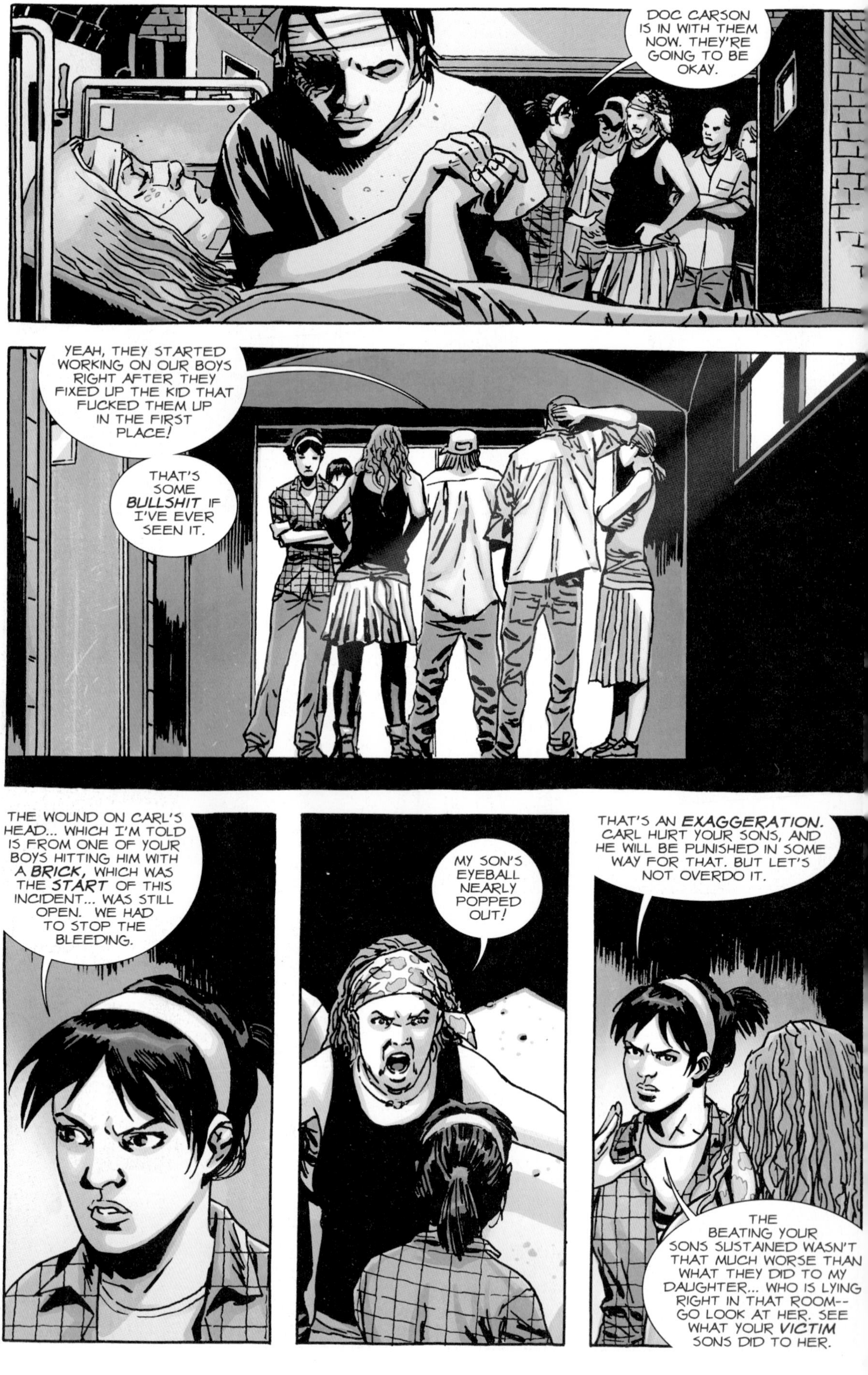
DOC CARSON IS IN WITH THEM NOW. THEY'RE GOING TO BE OKAY.
YEAH, THEY STARTED WORKING ON OUR BOYS RIGHT AFTER THEY FIXED UP THE KID THAT FUCKED THEM UP IN THE FIRST PLACE!
THAT'S SOME BULLSHIT IF I'VE EVER SEEN IT.
THE WOUND ON CARL'S HEAD... WHICH I'M TOLD IS FROM ONE OF YOUR BOYS HITTING HIM WITH A BRICK, WHICH WAS THE START OF THIS INCIDENT... WAS STILL OPEN. WE HAD TO STOP THE BLEEDING.
MY SON'S EYEBALL NEARLY POPPED OUT!
THAT'S AN EXAGGERATION. CARL HURT YOUR SONS, AND HE WILL BE PUNISHED IN SOME WAY FOR THAT. BUT LET'S NOT OVERDO IT.
THE BEATING YOUR SONS SUSTAINED WASN'T THAT MUCH WORSE THAN WHAT THEY DID TO MY DAUGHTER... WHO IS LYING RIGHT IN THAT ROOM-- GO LOOK AT HER. SEE WHAT YOUR VICTIM SONS DID TO HER.

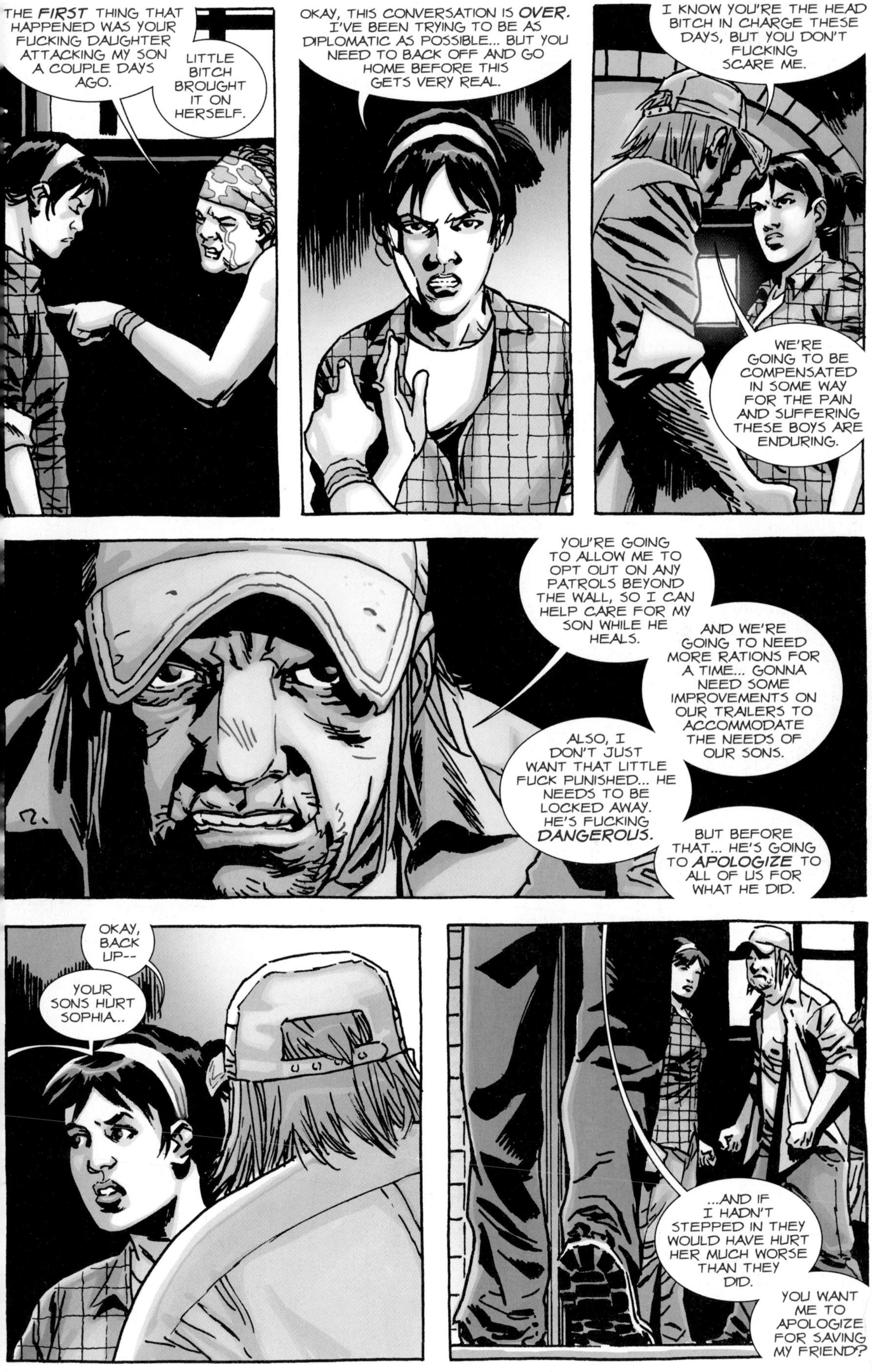
THE FIRST THING THAT HAPPENED WAS YOUR FUCKING DAUGHTER ATTACKING MY SON A COUPLE DAYS AGO.
LITTLE BITCH BROUGHT IT ON HERSELF.
OKAY, THIS CONVERSATION IS OVER. I'VE BEEN TRYING TO BE AS DIPLOMATIC AS POSSIBLE... BUT YOU NEED TO BACK OFF AND GO HOME BEFORE THIS GETS VERY REAL.
I KNOW YOU'RE THE HEAD BITCH IN CHARGE THESE DAYS, BUT YOU DON'T FUCKING SCARE ME.
WE'RE GOING TO BE COMPENSATED IN SOME WAY FOR THE PAIN AND SUFFERING THESE BOYS ARE ENDURING.
YOU'RE GOING TO ALLOW ME TO OPT OUT ON ANY PATROLS BEYOND THE WALL, SO I CAN HELP CARE FOR MY SON WHILE HE HEALS.
AND WE'RE GOING TO NEED MORE RATIONS FOR A TIME... GONNA NEED SOME IMPROVEMENTS ON OUR TRAILERS TO ACCOMMODATE THE NEEDS OF OUR SONS.
ALSO, I DON'T JUST WANT THAT LITTLE FUCK PUNISHED... HE NEEDS TO BE LOCKED AWAY. HE'S FUCKING DANGEROUS.
BUT BEFORE THAT... HE'S GOING TO APOLOGIZE TO ALL OF US FOR WHAT HE DID.
OKAY, BACK UP--
YOUR SONS HURT SOPHIA...
...AND IF I HADN'T STEPPED IN THEY WOULD HAVE HURT HER MUCH WORSE THAN THEY DID.
YOU WANT ME TO APOLOGIZE FOR SAVING MY FRIEND?

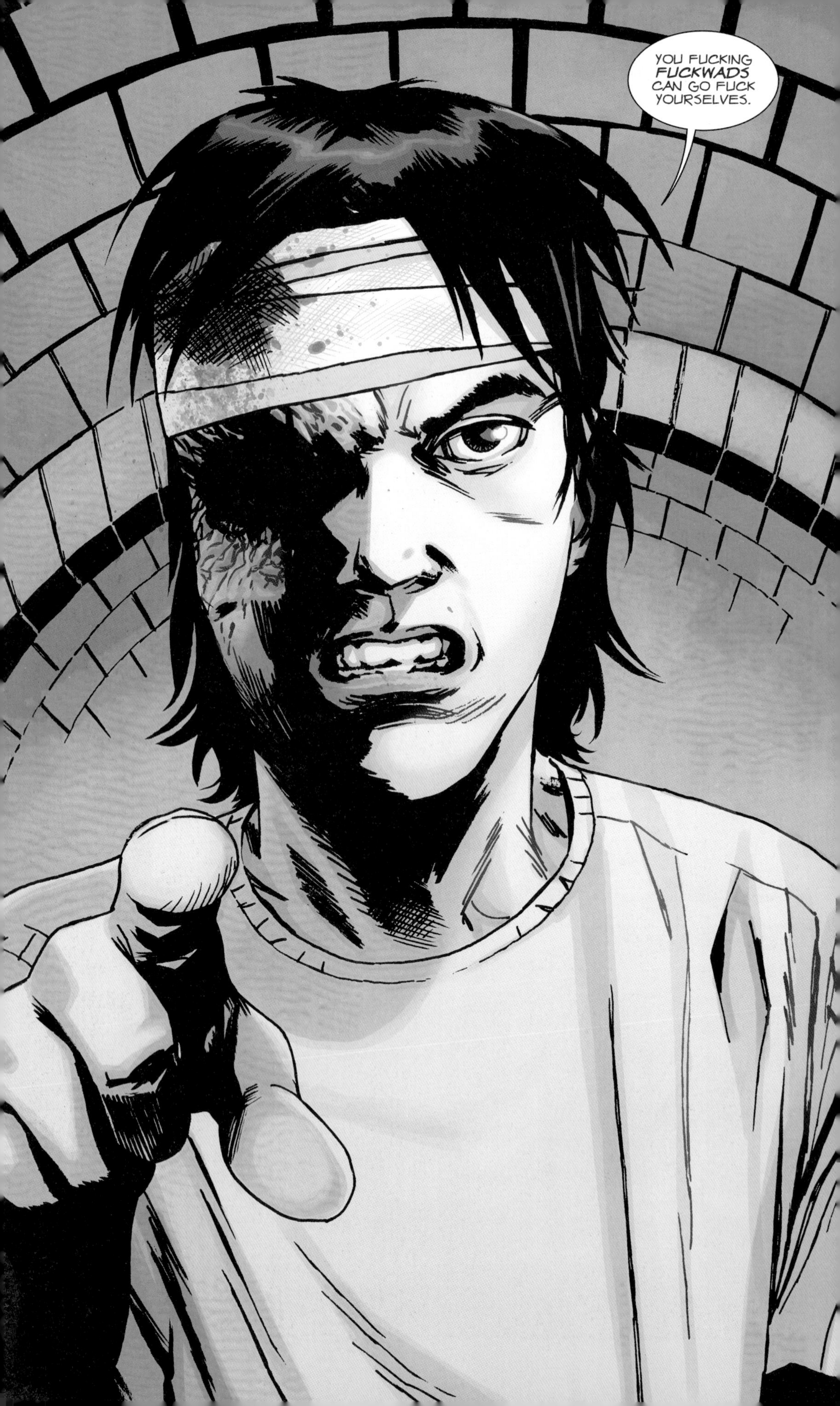
YOU FUCKING FUCKWADS CAN GO FUCK YOURSELVES.

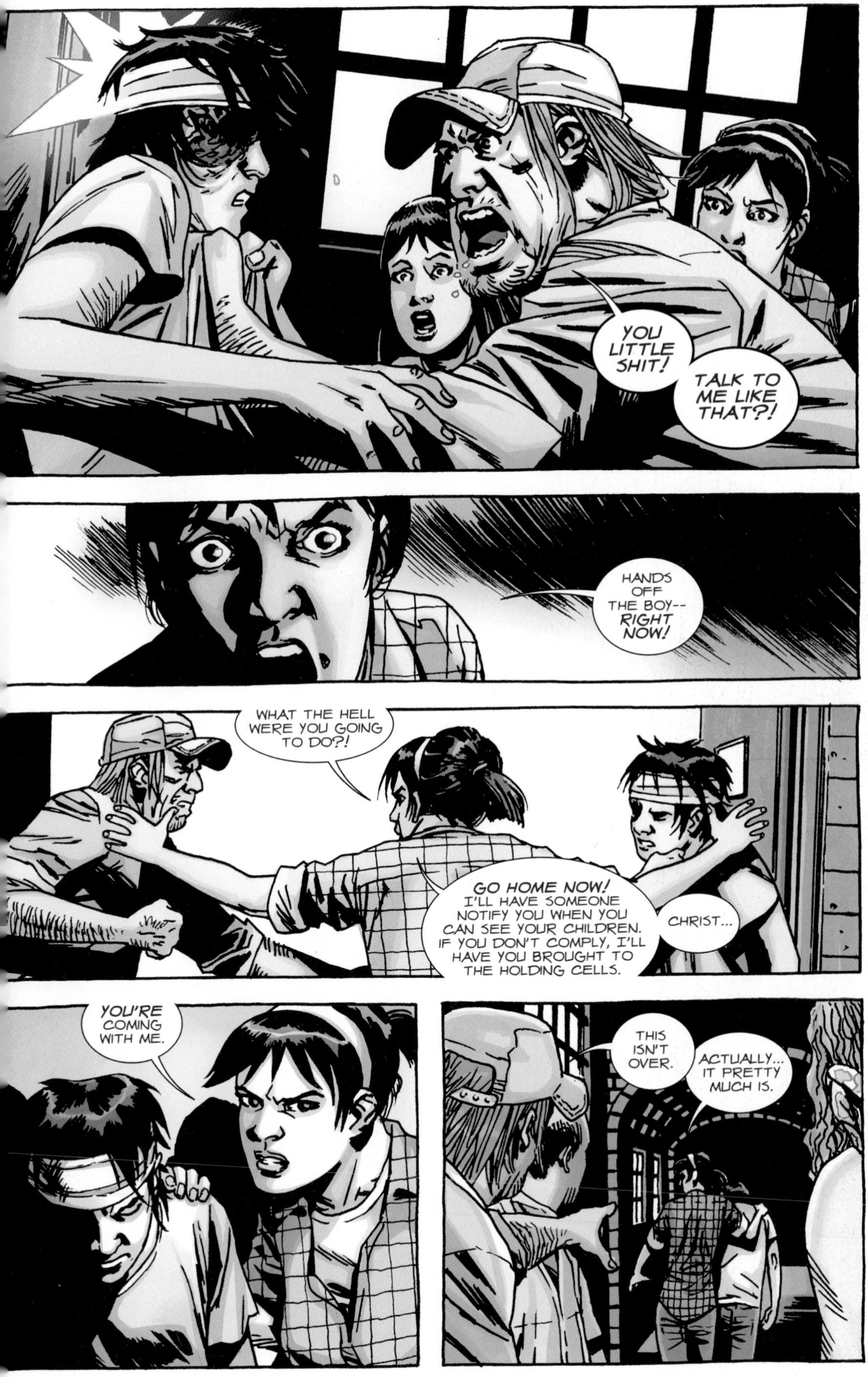
YOU LITTLE SHIT!
TALK TO ME LIKE THAT?!
HANDS OFF THE BOY-- RIGHT NOW!
WHAT THE HELL WERE YOU GOING TO DO?!
GO HOME NOW! I'LL HAVE SOMEONE NOTIFY YOU WHEN YOU CAN SEE YOUR CHILDREN. IF YOU DON'T COMPLY, I'LL HAVE YOU BROUGHT TO THE HOLDING CELLS.
CHRIST...
YOU'RE COMING WITH ME.
THIS ISN'T OVER.
ACTUALLY... IT PRETTY MUCH IS.

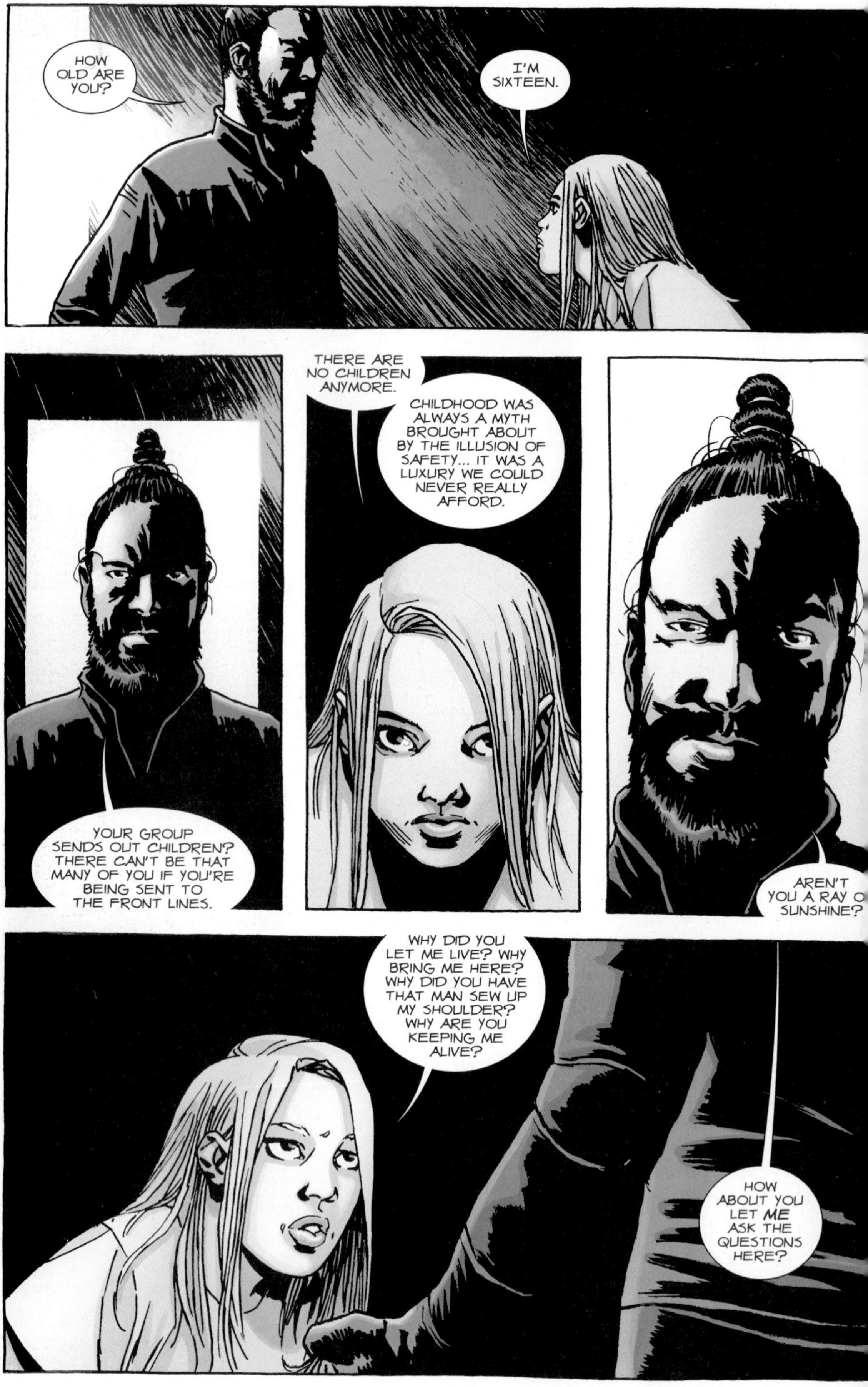
HOW OLD ARE YOU?
I'M SIXTEEN.
YOUR GROUP SENDS OUT CHILDREN? THERE CAN'T BE THAT MANY OF YOU IF YOU'RE BEING SENT TO THE FRONT LINES.
THERE ARE NO CHILDREN ANYMORE.
CHILDHOOD WAS ALWAYS A MYTH BROUGHT ABOUT BY THE ILLUSION OF SAFETY... IT WAS A LUXURY WE COULD NEVER REALLY AFFORD.
AREN'T YOU A RAY O SUNSHINE?
WHY DID YOU LET ME LIVE? WHY BRING ME HERE? WHY DID YOU HAVE THAT MAN SEW UP MY SHOULDER? WHY ARE YOU KEEPING ME ALIVE?
HOW ABOUT YOU LET *ME* ASK THE QUESTIONS HERE?

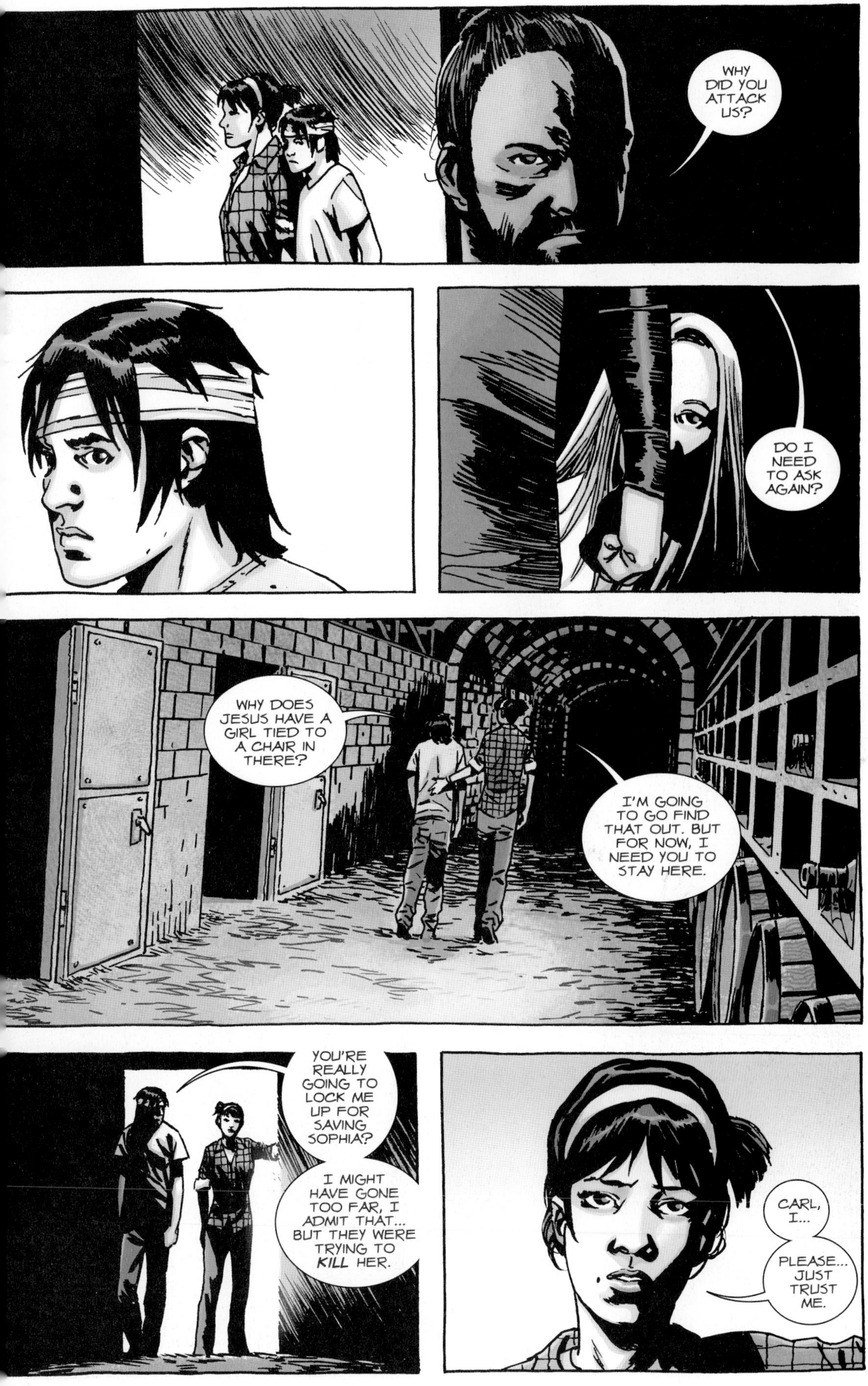
WHY DID YOU ATTACK US?
DO I NEED TO ASK AGAIN?
WHY DOES JESUS HAVE A GIRL TIED TO A CHAIR IN THERE?
I'M GOING TO GO FIND THAT OUT. BUT FOR NOW, I NEED YOU TO STAY HERE.
YOU'RE REALLY GOING TO LOCK ME UP FOR SAVING SOPHIA?
I MIGHT HAVE GONE TOO FAR, I ADMIT THAT... BUT THEY WERE TRYING TO **KILL** HER.
CARL, I...
PLEASE... JUST TRUST ME.

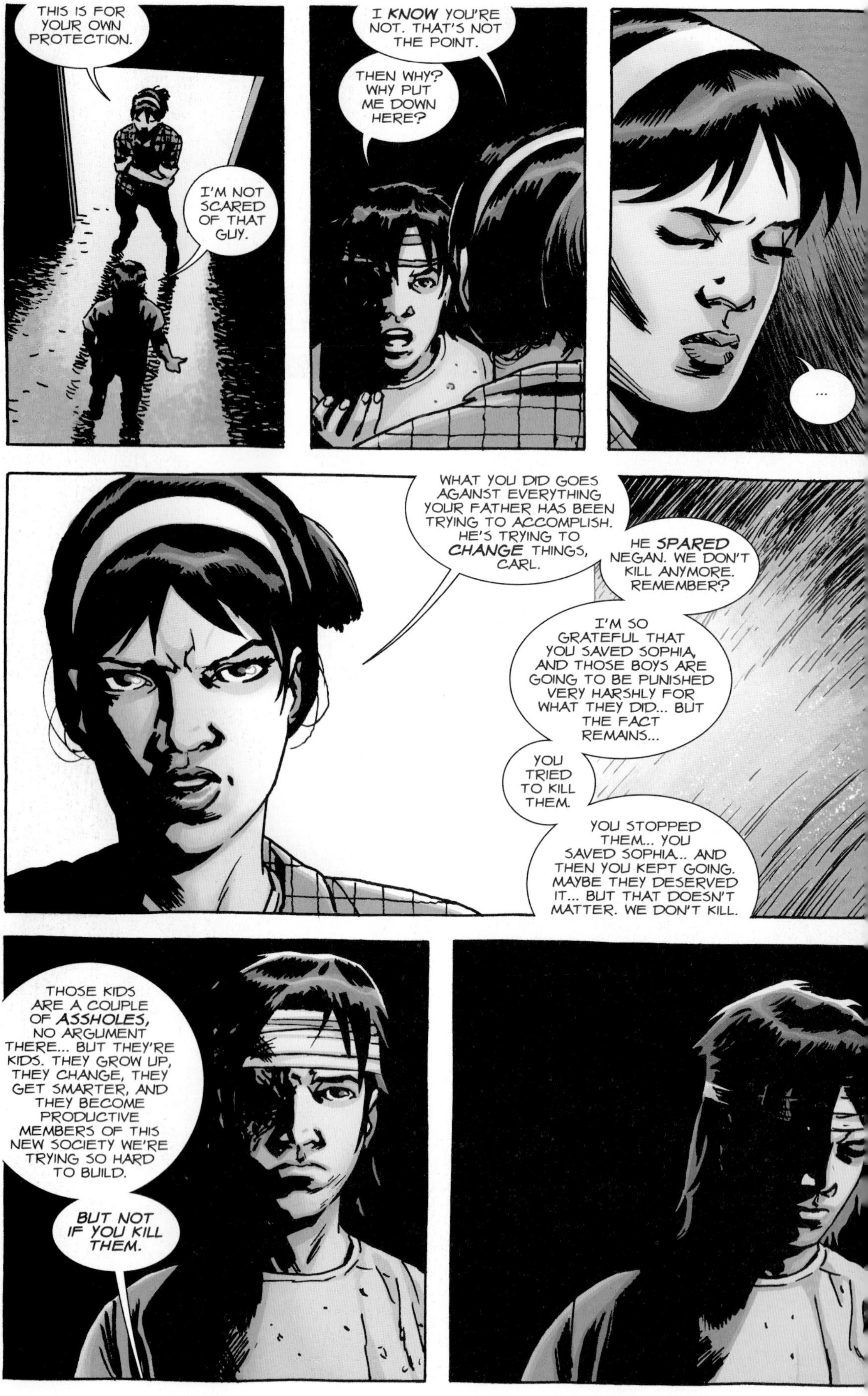
THIS IS FOR YOUR OWN PROTECTION.
I'M NOT SCARED OF THAT GUY.
I KNOW YOU'RE NOT. THAT'S NOT THE POINT.
THEN WHY? WHY PUT ME DOWN HERE?
...
WHAT YOU DID GOES AGAINST EVERYTHING YOUR FATHER HAS BEEN TRYING TO ACCOMPLISH. HE'S TRYING TO CHANGE THINGS, CARL.
HE SPARED NEGAN. WE DON'T KILL ANYMORE. REMEMBER?
I'M SO GRATEFUL THAT YOU SAVED SOPHIA, AND THOSE BOYS ARE GOING TO BE PUNISHED VERY HARSHLY FOR WHAT THEY DID... BUT THE FACT REMAINS...
YOU TRIED TO KILL THEM.
YOU STOPPED THEM... YOU SAVED SOPHIA... AND THEN YOU KEPT GOING. MAYBE THEY DESERVED IT... BUT THAT DOESN'T MATTER. WE DON'T KILL.
THOSE KIDS ARE A COUPLE OF ASSHOLES, NO ARGUMENT THERE... BUT THEY'RE KIDS. THEY GROW UP, THEY CHANGE, THEY GET SMARTER, AND THEY BECOME PRODUCTIVE MEMBERS OF THIS NEW SOCIETY WE'RE TRYING SO HARD TO BUILD.
BUT NOT IF YOU KILL THEM.

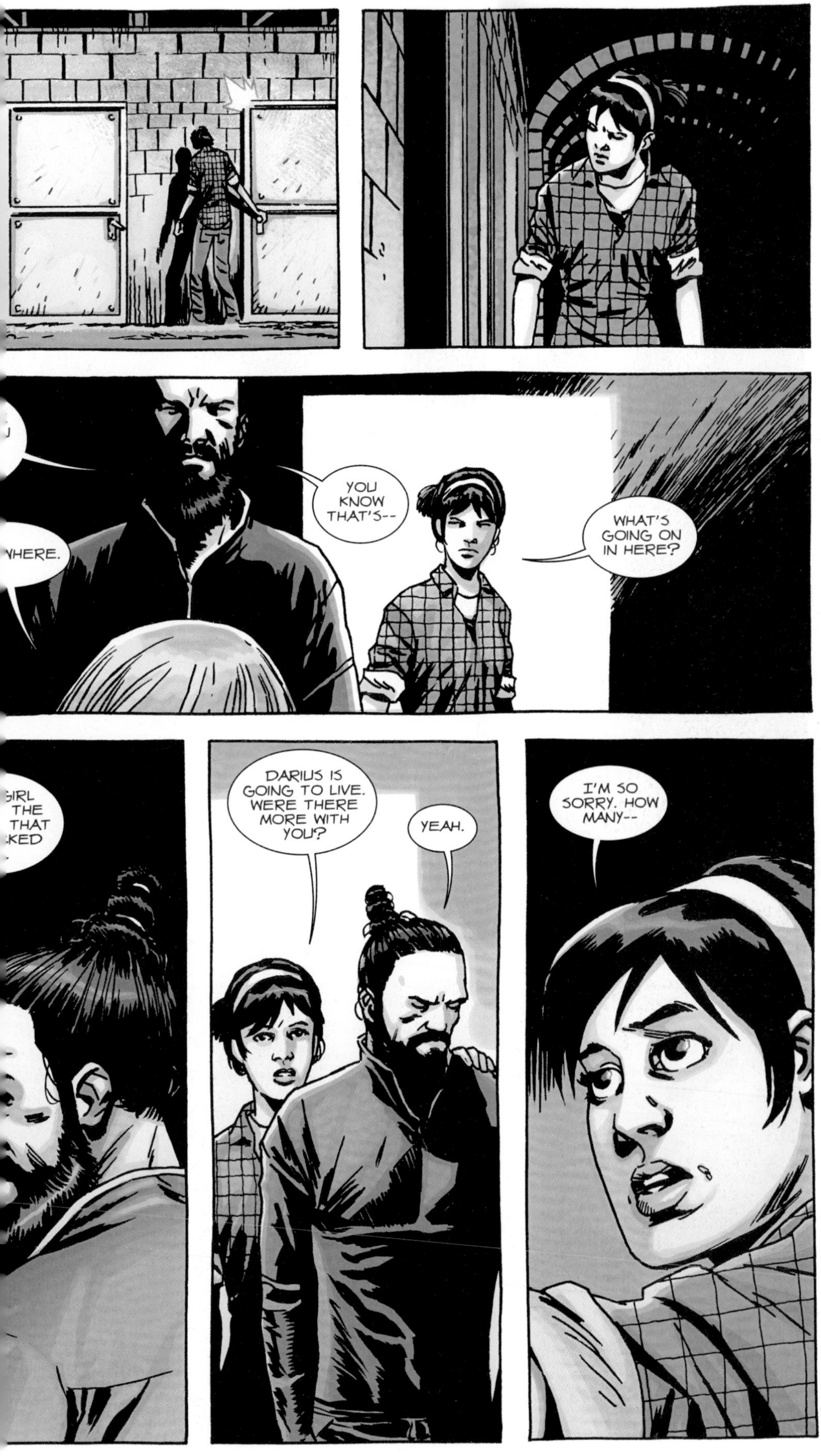
YOU KNOW THAT'S--
WHAT'S GOING ON IN HERE?
DARIUS IS GOING TO LIVE. WERE THERE MORE WITH YOU?
YEAH.
I'M SO SORRY. HOW MANY--

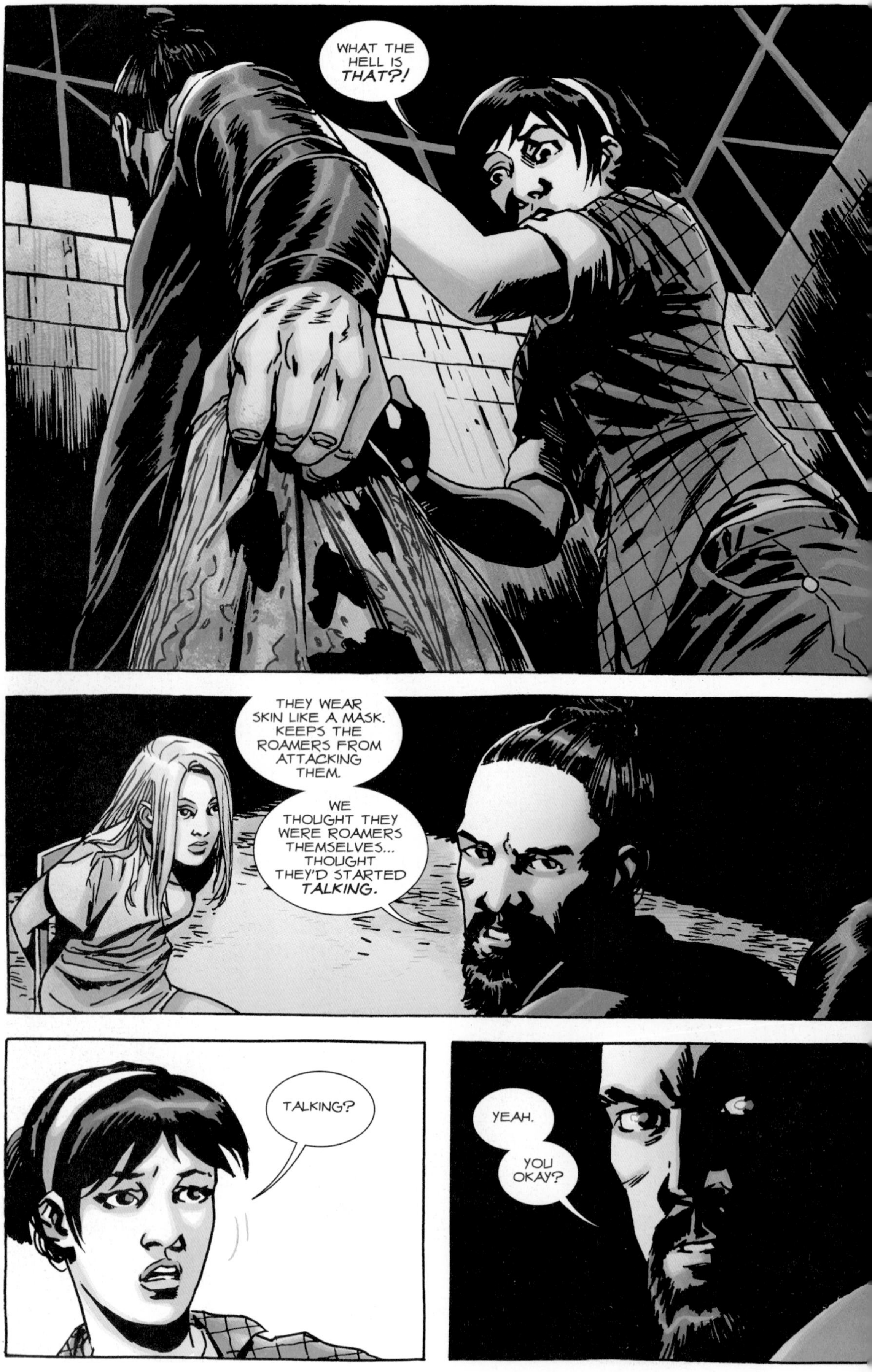
WHAT THE HELL IS THAT?!
THEY WEAR SKIN LIKE A MASK. KEEPS THE ROAMERS FROM ATTACKING THEM.
WE THOUGHT THEY WERE ROAMERS THEMSELVES... THOUGHT THEY'D STARTED TALKING.
TALKING?
YEAH.
YOU OKAY?

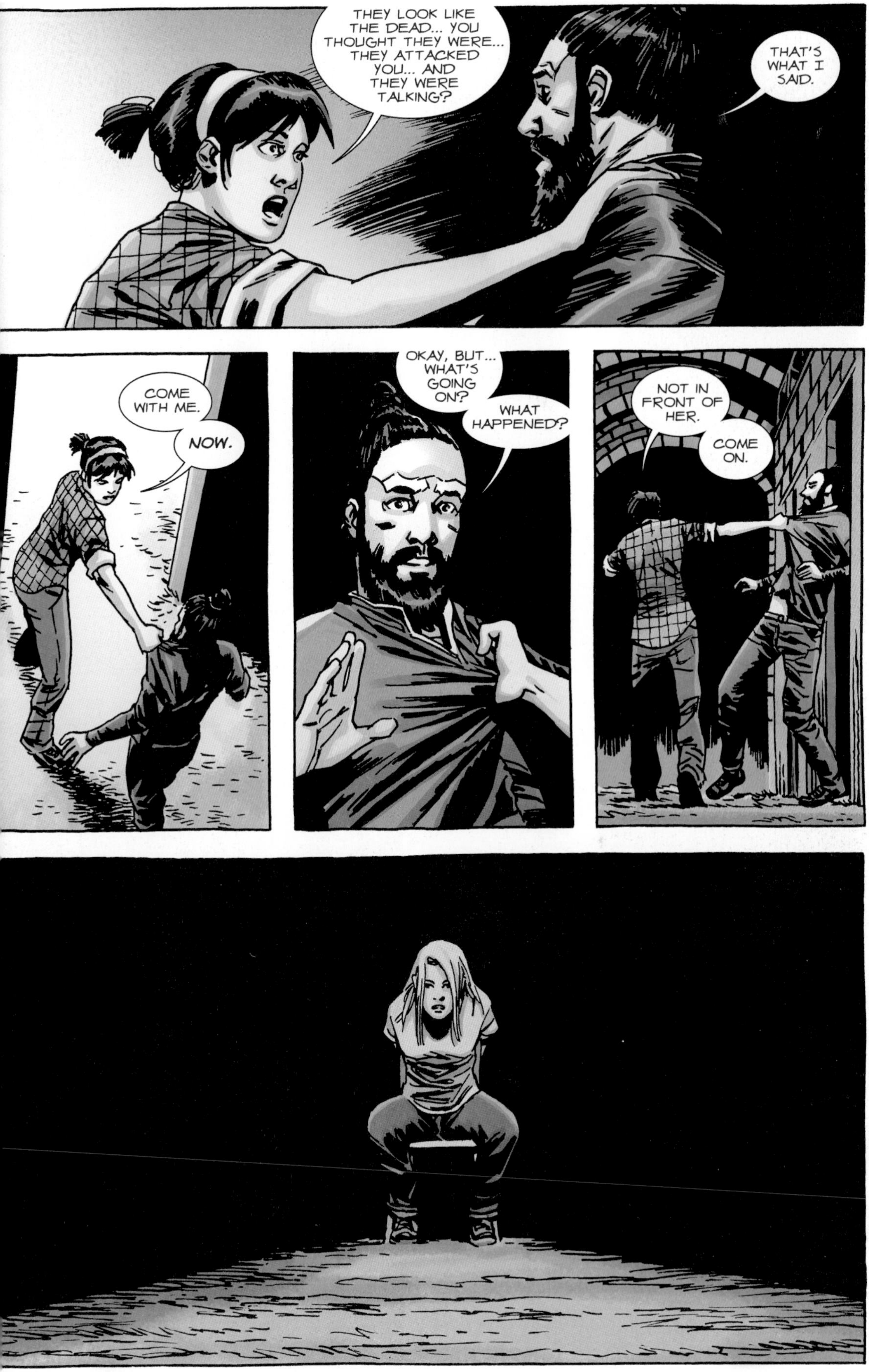
THEY LOOK LIKE THE DEAD... YOU THOUGHT THEY WERE... THEY ATTACKED YOU... AND THEY WERE TALKING?
THAT'S WHAT I SAID.
COME WITH ME.
NOW.
OKAY, BUT... WHAT'S GOING ON?
WHAT HAPPENED?
NOT IN FRONT OF HER.
COME ON.

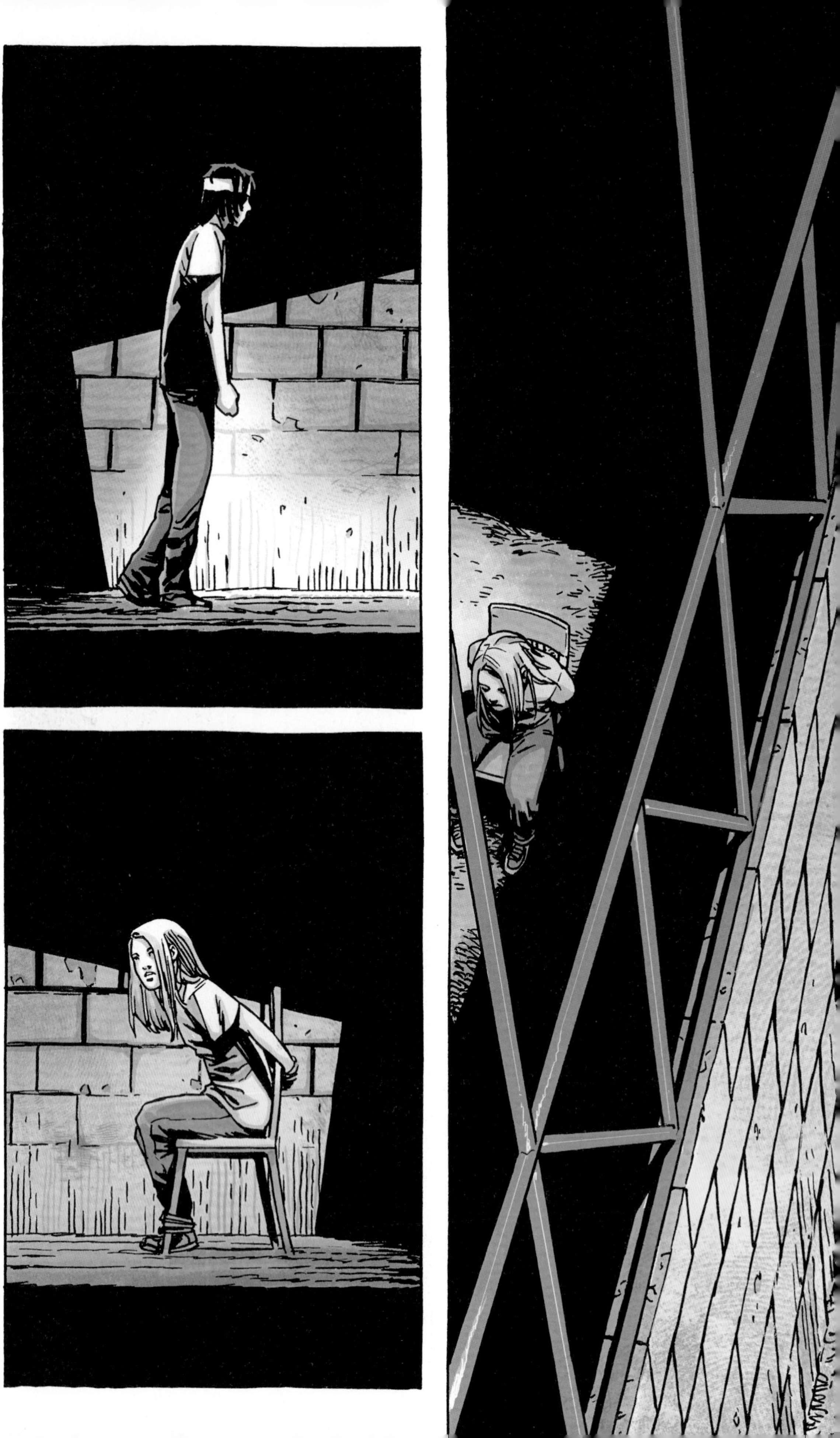

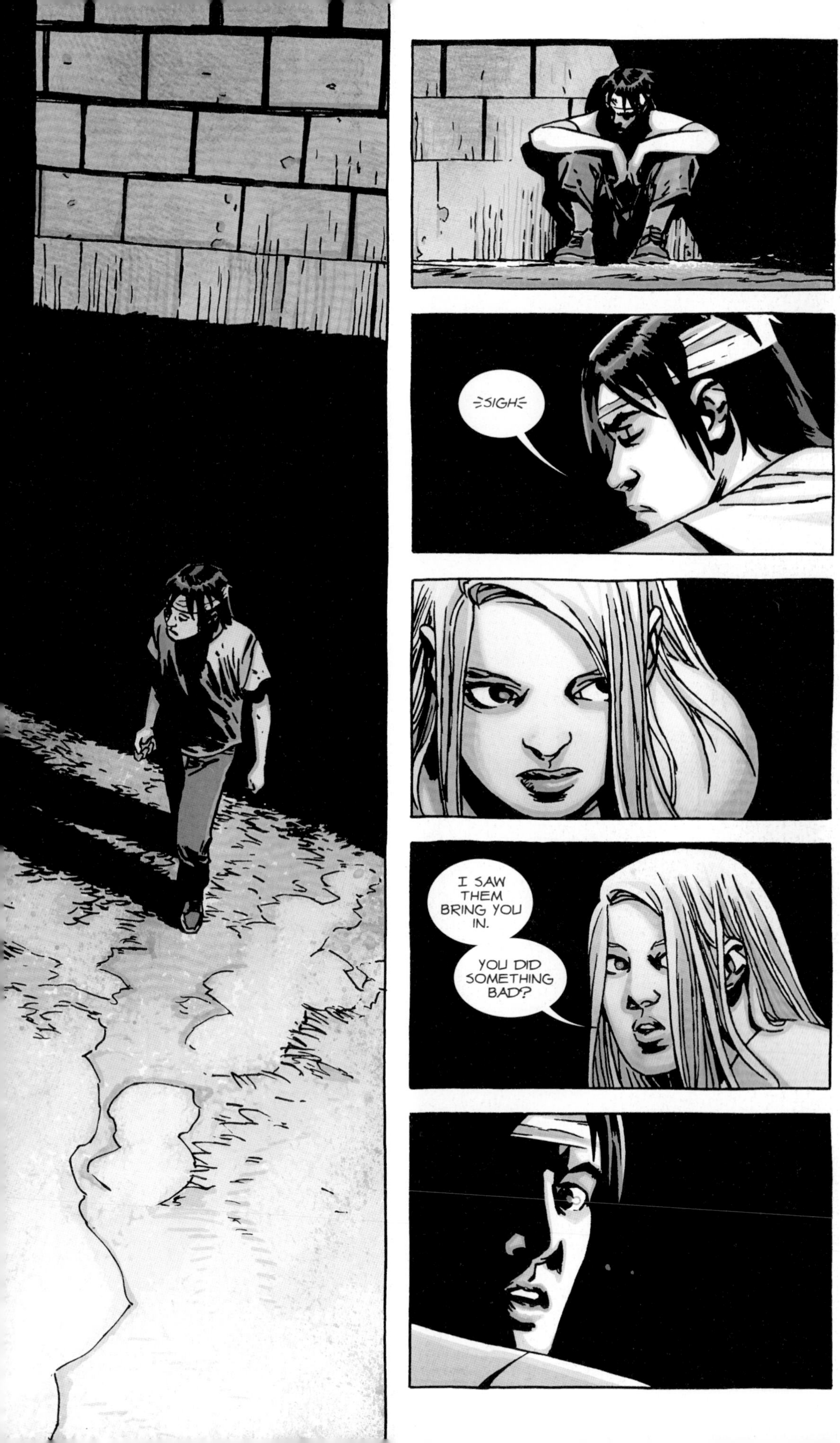
SIGH
I SAW THEM BRING YOU IN.
YOU DID SOMETHING BAD?

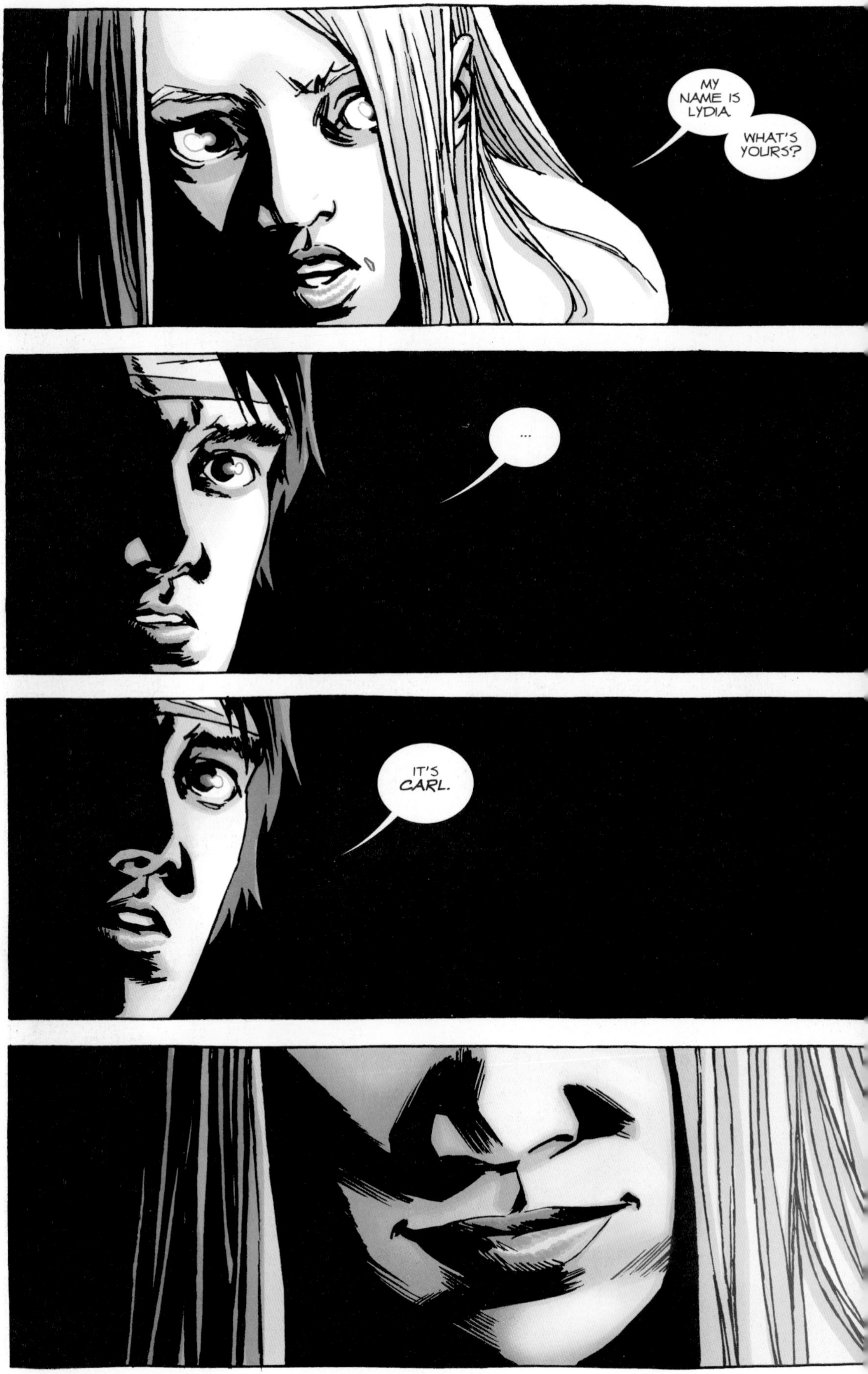
MY NAME IS LYDIA.
WHAT'S YOURS?
...
IT'S CARL.

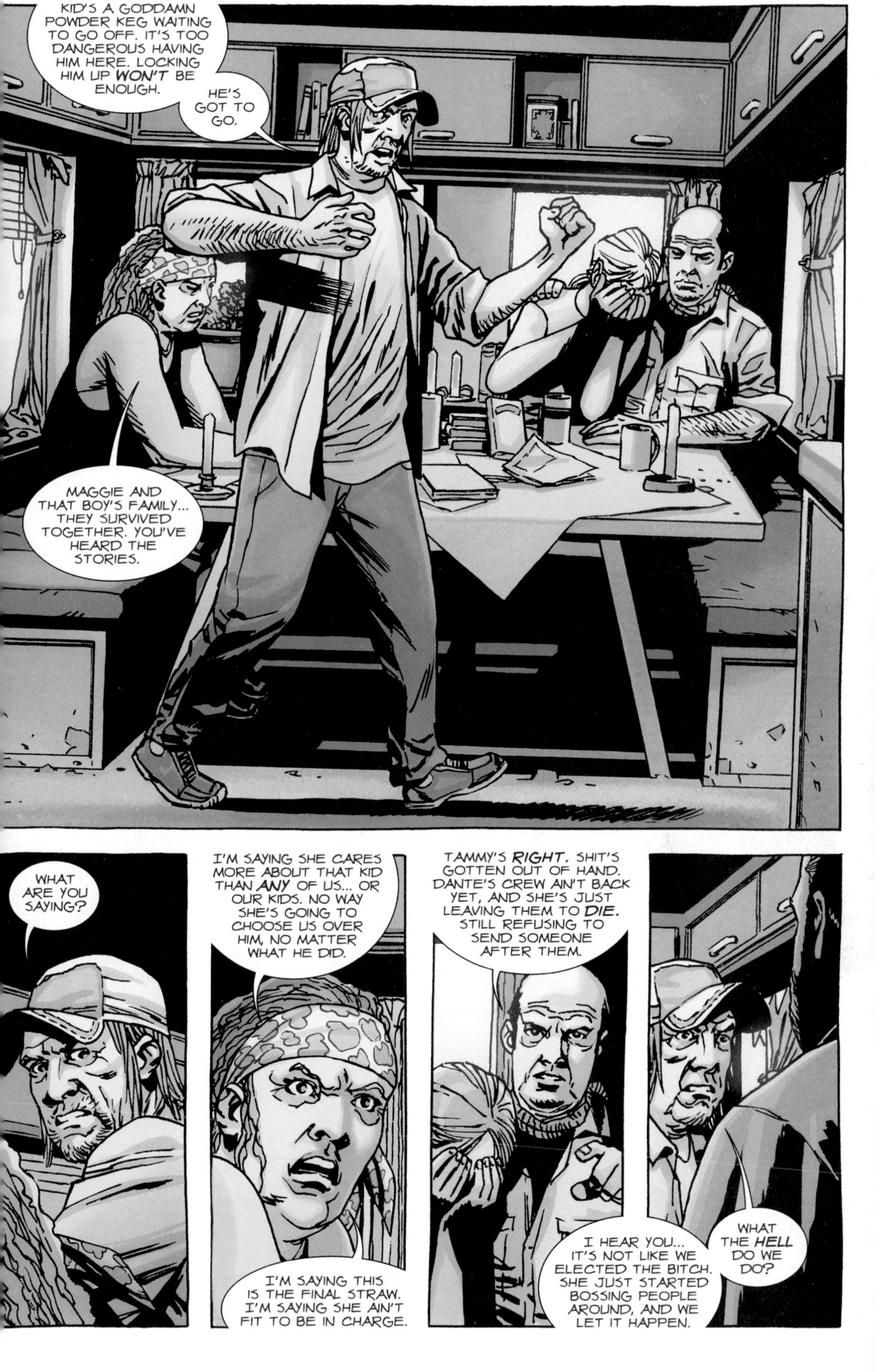
KID'S A GODDAMN POWDER KEG WAITING TO GO OFF. IT'S TOO DANGEROUS HAVING HIM HERE. LOCKING HIM UP *WON'T* BE ENOUGH.
HE'S GOT TO GO.
MAGGIE AND THAT BOY'S FAMILY... THEY SURVIVED TOGETHER. YOU'VE HEARD THE STORIES.
WHAT ARE YOU SAYING?
I'M SAYING SHE CARES MORE ABOUT THAT KID THAN *ANY* OF US... OR OUR KIDS. NO WAY SHE'S GOING TO CHOOSE US OVER HIM, NO MATTER WHAT HE DID.
I'M SAYING THIS IS THE FINAL STRAW. I'M SAYING SHE AIN'T FIT TO BE IN CHARGE.
TAMMY'S *RIGHT.* SHIT'S GOTTEN OUT OF HAND. DANTE'S CREW AIN'T BACK YET, AND SHE'S JUST LEAVING THEM TO *DIE.* STILL REFUSING TO SEND SOMEONE AFTER THEM.
I HEAR YOU... IT'S NOT LIKE WE ELECTED THE BITCH. SHE JUST STARTED BOSSING PEOPLE AROUND, AND WE LET IT HAPPEN.
WHAT THE *HELL* DO WE DO?

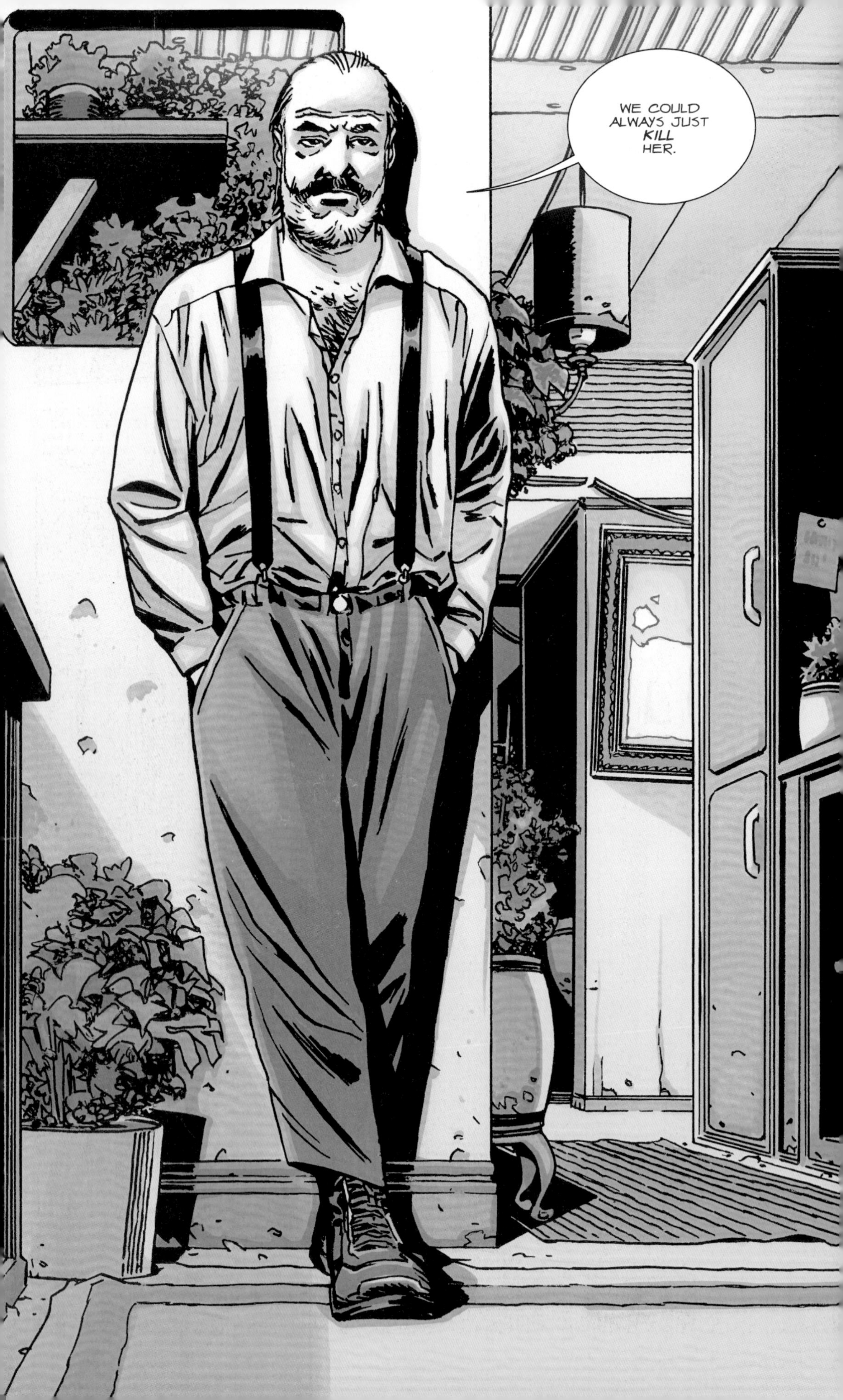
WE COULD ALWAYS JUST **KILL** HER.

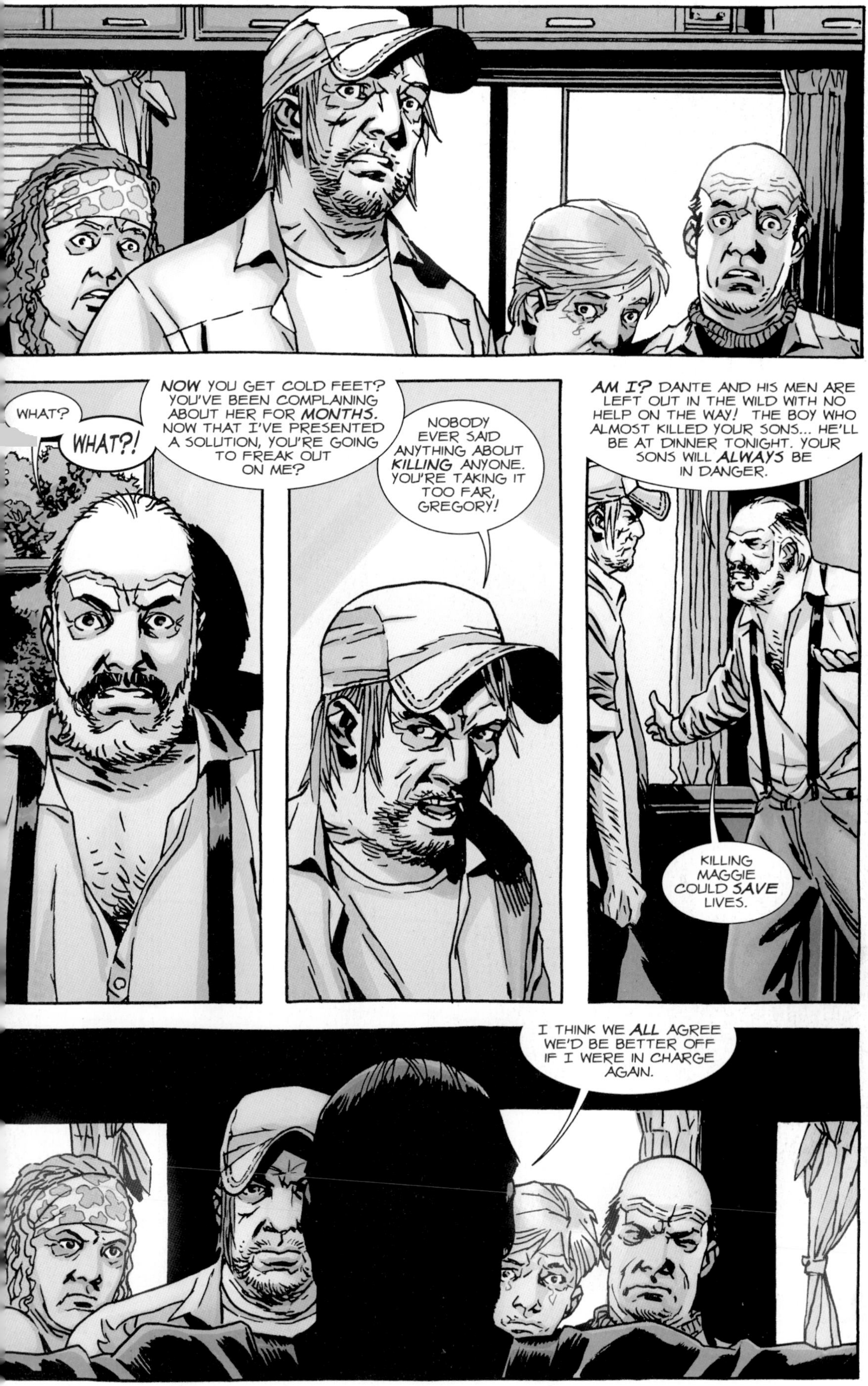

WHAT?
WHAT?!
NOW YOU GET COLD FEET? YOU'VE BEEN COMPLAINING ABOUT HER FOR MONTHS. NOW THAT I'VE PRESENTED A SOLUTION, YOU'RE GOING TO FREAK OUT ON ME?
NOBODY EVER SAID ANYTHING ABOUT KILLING ANYONE. YOU'RE TAKING IT TOO FAR, GREGORY!
AM I? DANTE AND HIS MEN ARE LEFT OUT IN THE WILD WITH NO HELP ON THE WAY! THE BOY WHO ALMOST KILLED YOUR SONS... HE'LL BE AT DINNER TONIGHT. YOUR SONS WILL ALWAYS BE IN DANGER.
KILLING MAGGIE COULD SAVE LIVES.
I THINK WE ALL AGREE WE'D BE BETTER OFF IF I WERE IN CHARGE AGAIN.

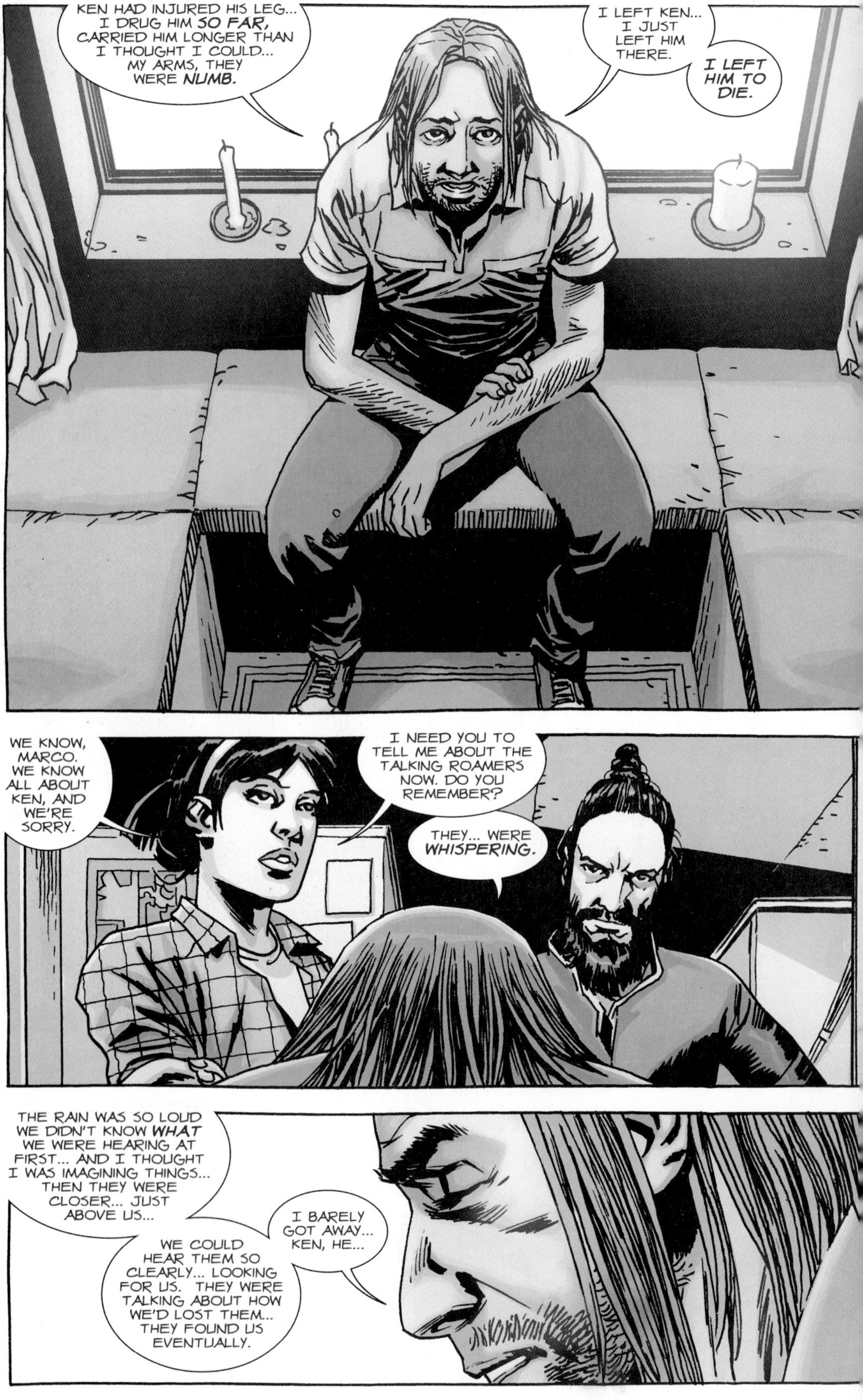
KEN HAD INJURED HIS LEG... I DRUG HIM SO FAR, CARRIED HIM LONGER THAN I THOUGHT I COULD... MY ARMS, THEY WERE NUMB.
I LEFT KEN... I JUST LEFT HIM THERE.
I LEFT HIM TO DIE.
WE KNOW, MARCO. WE KNOW ALL ABOUT KEN, AND WE'RE SORRY.
I NEED YOU TO TELL ME ABOUT THE TALKING ROAMERS NOW. DO YOU REMEMBER?
THEY... WERE WHISPERING.
THE RAIN WAS SO LOUD WE DIDN'T KNOW WHAT WE WERE HEARING AT FIRST... AND I THOUGHT I WAS IMAGINING THINGS... THEN THEY WERE CLOSER... JUST ABOVE US...
WE COULD HEAR THEM SO CLEARLY... LOOKING FOR US. THEY WERE TALKING ABOUT HOW WE'D LOST THEM... THEY FOUND US EVENTUALLY.
I BARELY GOT AWAY... KEN, HE...

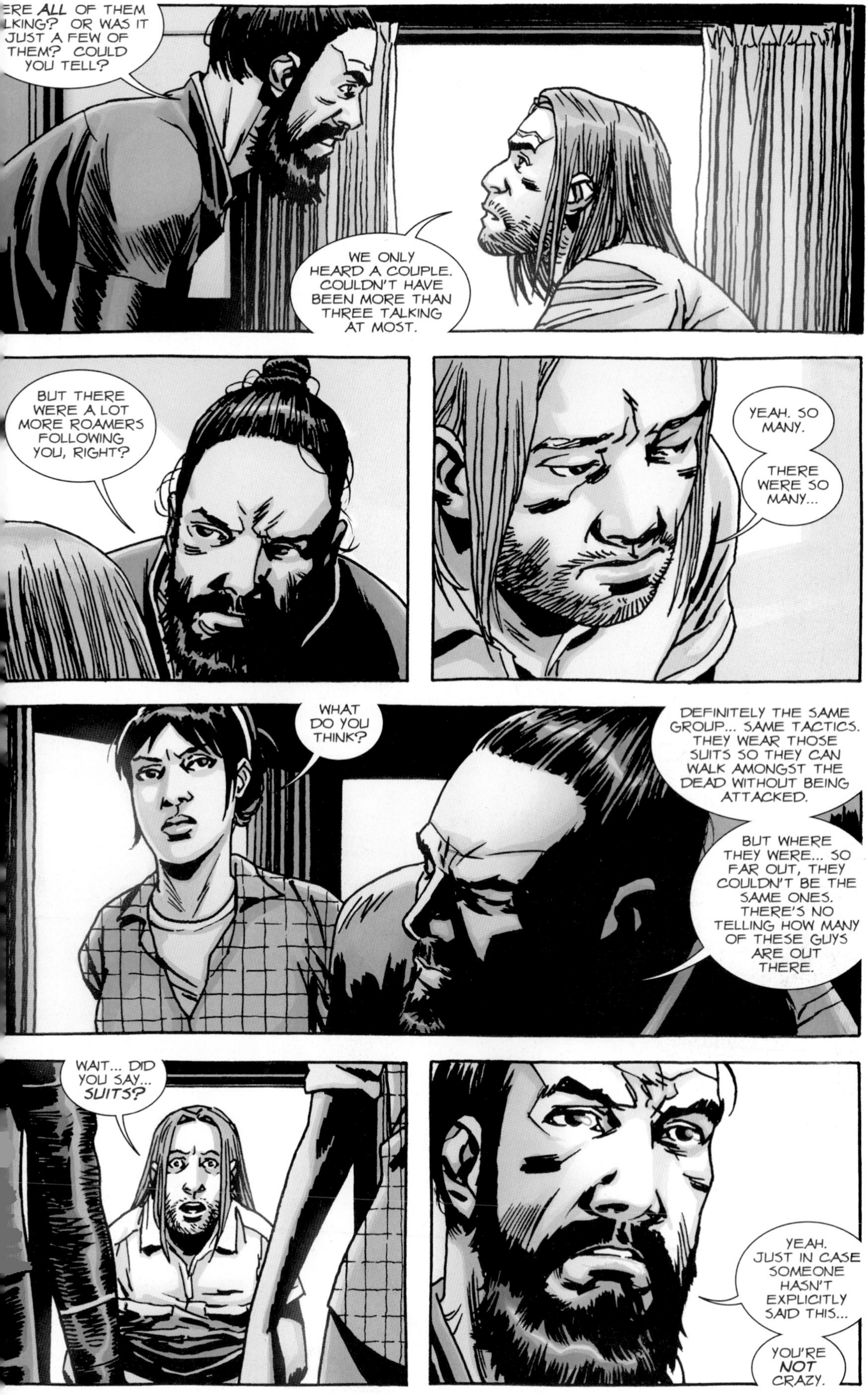
ERE ALL OF THEM LKING? OR WAS IT JUST A FEW OF THEM? COULD YOU TELL?
WE ONLY HEARD A COUPLE. COULDN'T HAVE BEEN MORE THAN THREE TALKING AT MOST.
BUT THERE WERE A LOT MORE ROAMERS FOLLOWING YOU, RIGHT?
YEAH. SO MANY.
THERE WERE SO MANY...
WHAT DO YOU THINK?
DEFINITELY THE SAME GROUP... SAME TACTICS. THEY WEAR THOSE SUITS SO THEY CAN WALK AMONGST THE DEAD WITHOUT BEING ATTACKED.
BUT WHERE THEY WERE... SO FAR OUT, THEY COULDN'T BE THE SAME ONES. THERE'S NO TELLING HOW MANY OF THESE GUYS ARE OUT THERE.
WAIT... DID YOU SAY... SUITS?
YEAH. JUST IN CASE SOMEONE HASN'T EXPLICITLY SAID THIS...
YOU'RE NOT CRAZY.

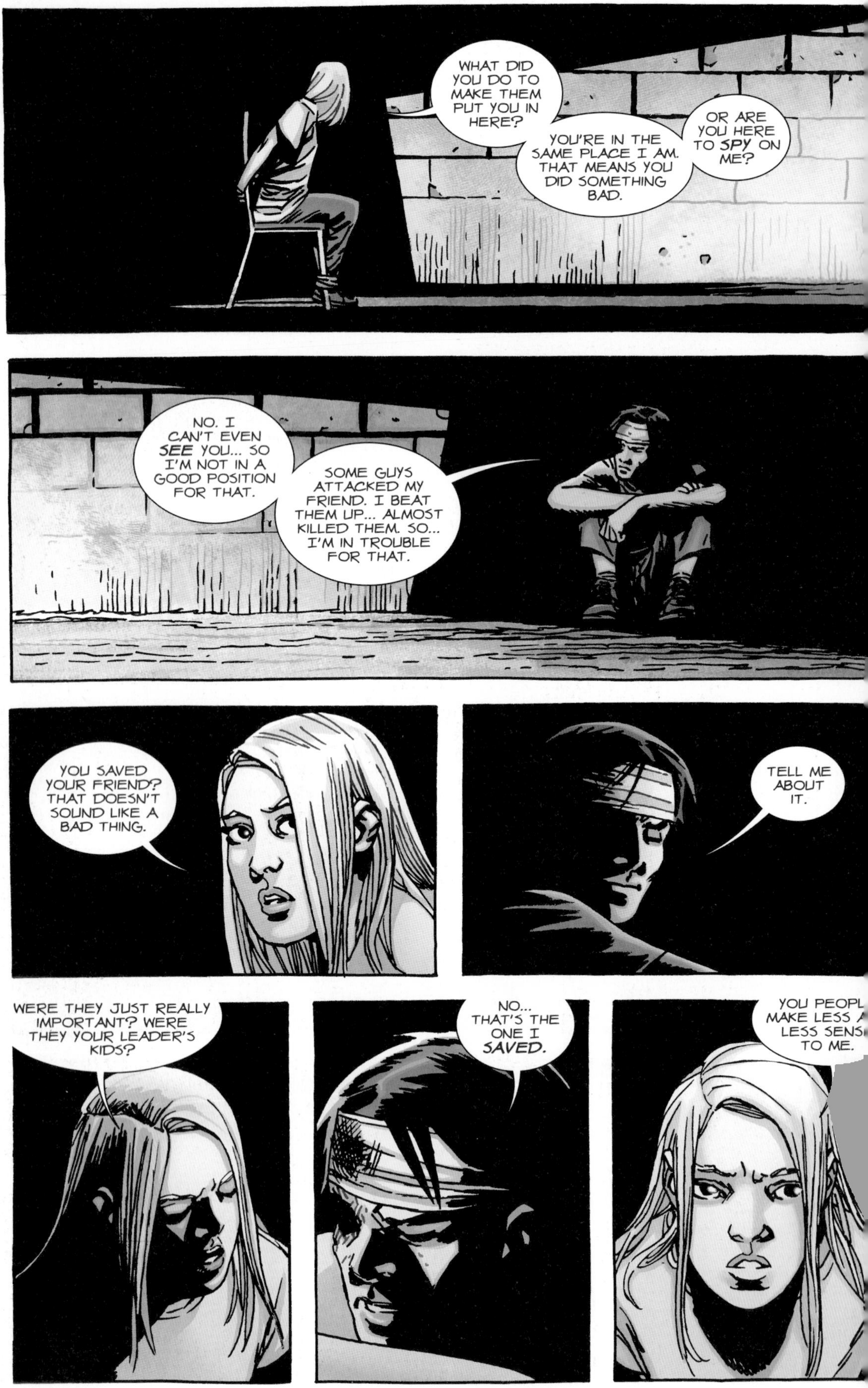
WHAT DID YOU DO TO MAKE THEM PUT YOU IN HERE?
YOU'RE IN THE SAME PLACE I AM. THAT MEANS YOU DID SOMETHING BAD.
OR ARE YOU HERE TO SPY ON ME?
NO. I CAN'T EVEN SEE YOU... SO I'M NOT IN A GOOD POSITION FOR THAT.
SOME GUYS ATTACKED MY FRIEND. I BEAT THEM UP... ALMOST KILLED THEM. SO... I'M IN TROUBLE FOR THAT.
YOU SAVED YOUR FRIEND? THAT DOESN'T SOUND LIKE A BAD THING.
TELL ME ABOUT IT.
WERE THEY JUST REALLY IMPORTANT? WERE THEY YOUR LEADER'S KIDS?
NO... THAT'S THE ONE I SAVED.
YOU PEOPL MAKE LESS A LESS SENS TO ME.

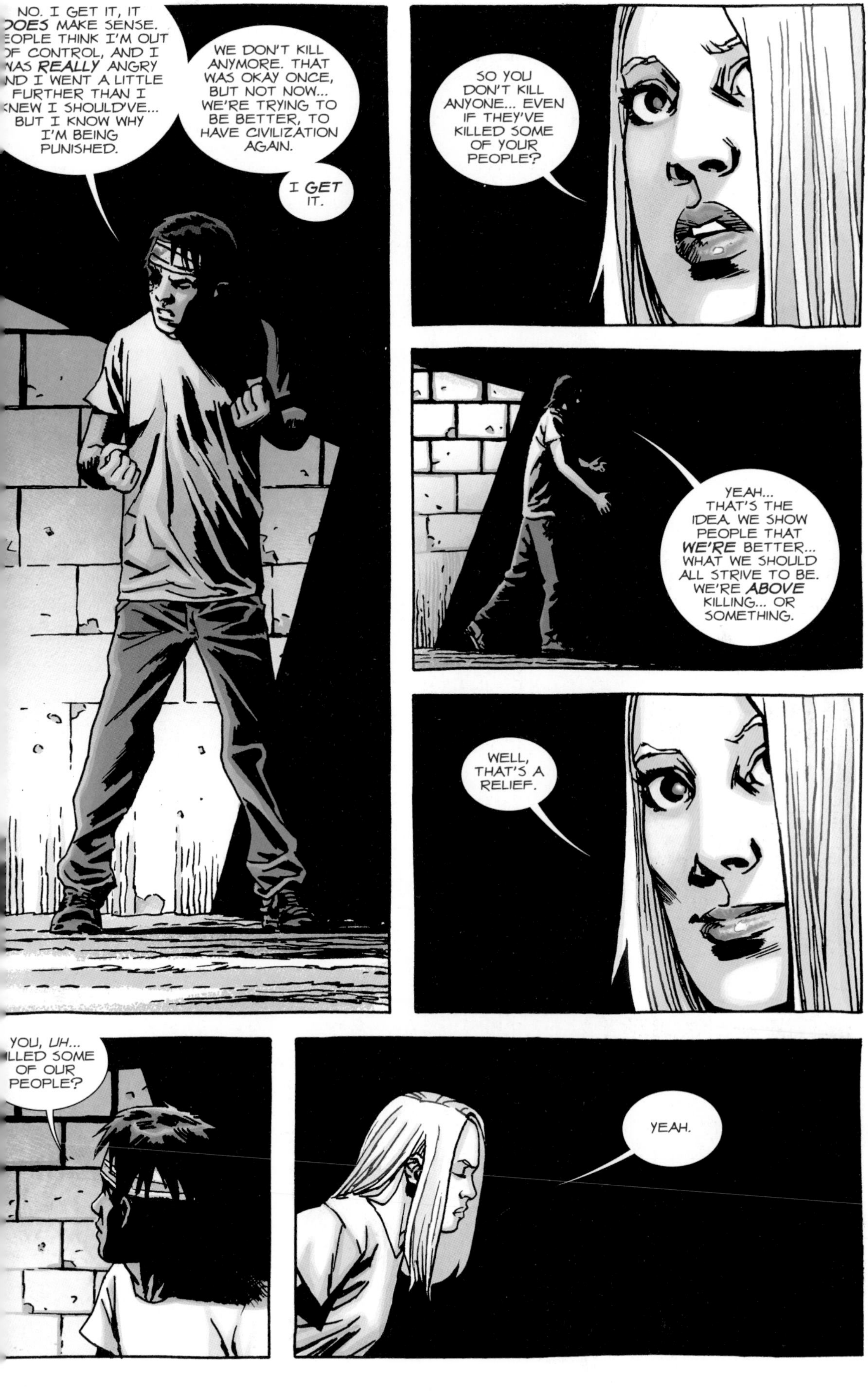
NO. I GET IT, IT DOES MAKE SENSE. EOPLE THINK I'M OUT OF CONTROL, AND I WAS REALLY ANGRY ND I WENT A LITTLE FURTHER THAN I KNEW I SHOULD'VE... BUT I KNOW WHY I'M BEING PUNISHED.
WE DON'T KILL ANYMORE. THAT WAS OKAY ONCE, BUT NOT NOW... WE'RE TRYING TO BE BETTER, TO HAVE CIVILIZATION AGAIN.
I GET IT.
SO YOU DON'T KILL ANYONE... EVEN IF THEY'VE KILLED SOME OF YOUR PEOPLE?
YEAH... THAT'S THE IDEA. WE SHOW PEOPLE THAT WE'RE BETTER... WHAT WE SHOULD ALL STRIVE TO BE. WE'RE ABOVE KILLING... OR SOMETHING.
WELL, THAT'S A RELIEF.
YOU, UH... LLED SOME OF OUR PEOPLE?
YEAH.

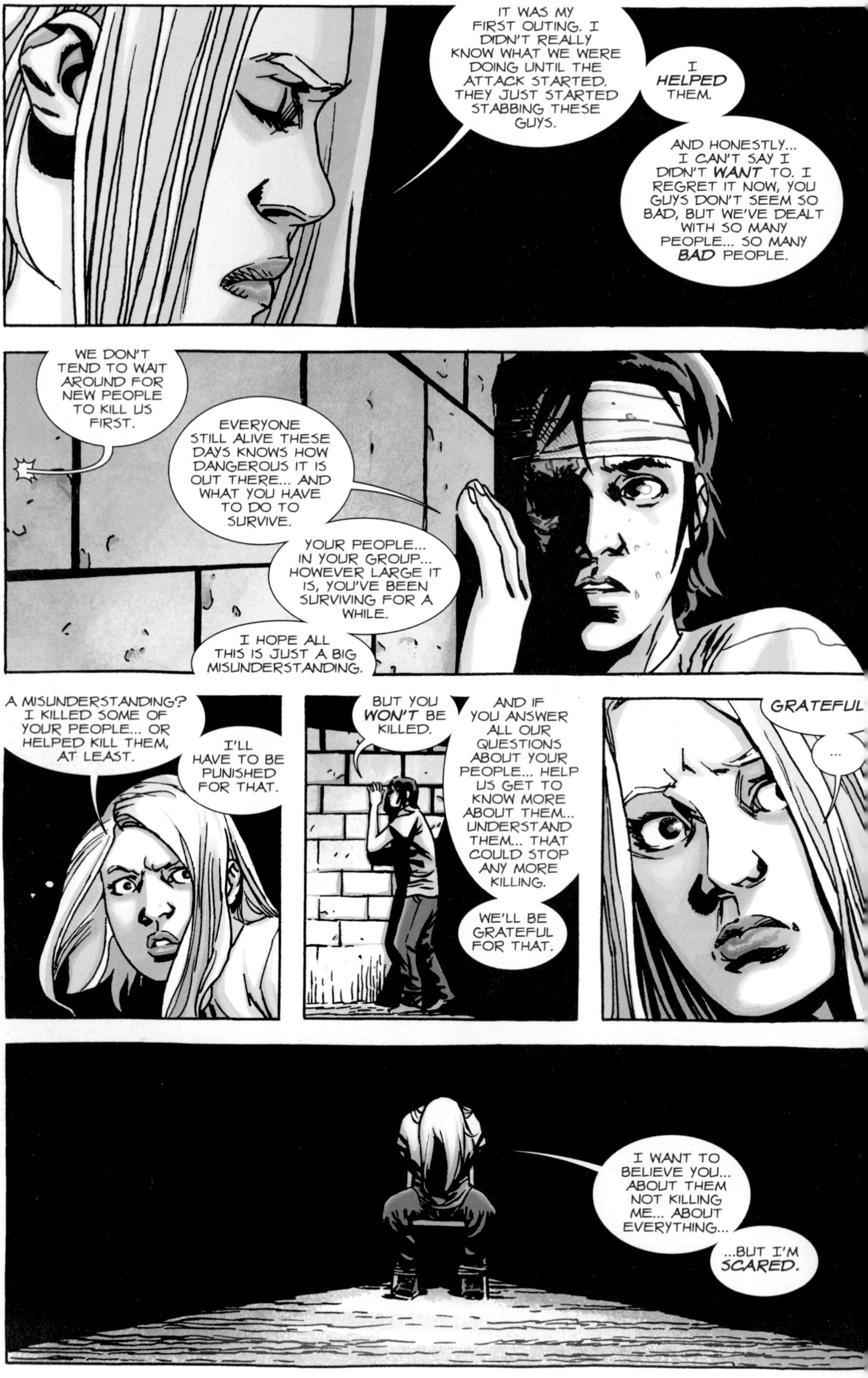
IT WAS MY FIRST OUTING. I DIDN'T REALLY KNOW WHAT WE WERE DOING UNTIL THE ATTACK STARTED. THEY JUST STARTED STABBING THESE GUYS.
I *HELPED* THEM.
AND HONESTLY... I CAN'T SAY I DIDN'T *WANT* TO. I REGRET IT NOW, YOU GUYS DON'T SEEM SO BAD, BUT WE'VE DEALT WITH SO MANY PEOPLE... SO MANY *BAD* PEOPLE.
WE DON'T TEND TO WAIT AROUND FOR NEW PEOPLE TO KILL US FIRST.
EVERYONE STILL ALIVE THESE DAYS KNOWS HOW DANGEROUS IT IS OUT THERE... AND WHAT YOU HAVE TO DO TO SURVIVE.
YOUR PEOPLE... IN YOUR GROUP... HOWEVER LARGE IT IS, YOU'VE BEEN SURVIVING FOR A WHILE.
I HOPE ALL THIS IS JUST A BIG MISUNDERSTANDING.
A MISUNDERSTANDING? I KILLED SOME OF YOUR PEOPLE... OR HELPED KILL THEM, AT LEAST.
I'LL HAVE TO BE PUNISHED FOR THAT.
BUT YOU *WON'T* BE KILLED.
AND IF YOU ANSWER ALL OUR QUESTIONS ABOUT YOUR PEOPLE... HELP US GET TO KNOW MORE ABOUT THEM... UNDERSTAND THEM... THAT COULD STOP ANY MORE KILLING.
WE'LL BE GRATEFUL FOR THAT.
GRATEFUL
...
I WANT TO BELIEVE YOU... ABOUT THEM NOT KILLING ME... ABOUT EVERYTHING...
...BUT I'M *SCARED.*

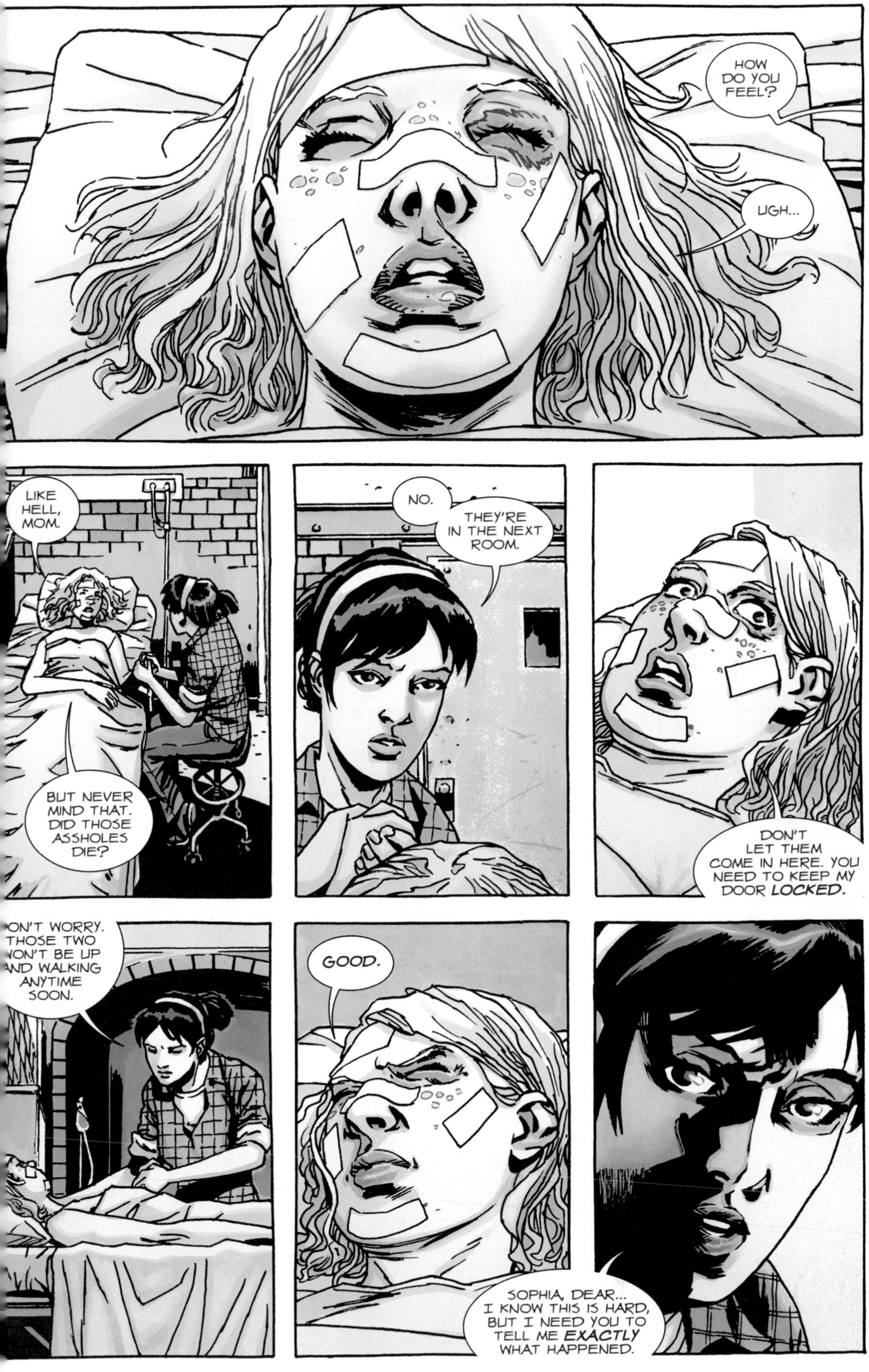
HOW DO YOU FEEL?
UGH...
LIKE HELL, MOM.
BUT NEVER MIND THAT. DID THOSE ASSHOLES DIE?
NO.
THEY'RE IN THE NEXT ROOM.
DON'T LET THEM COME IN HERE. YOU NEED TO KEEP MY DOOR *LOCKED.*
ON'T WORRY. THOSE TWO VON'T BE UP AND WALKING ANYTIME SOON.
GOOD.
SOPHIA, DEAR... I KNOW THIS IS HARD, BUT I NEED YOU TO TELL ME *EXACTLY* WHAT HAPPENED.

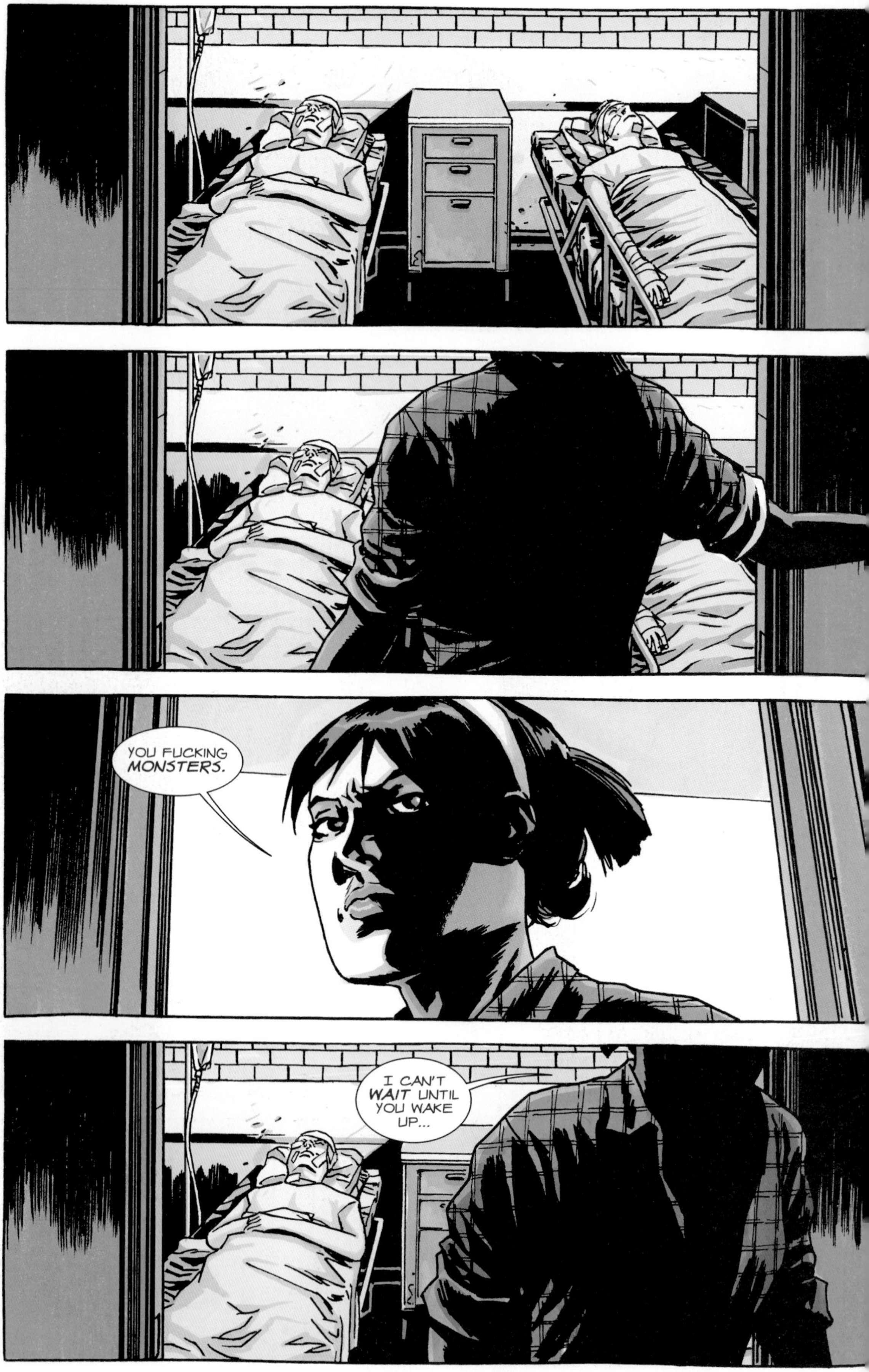
YOU FUCKING MONSTERS.
I CAN'T WAIT UNTIL YOU WAKE UP...

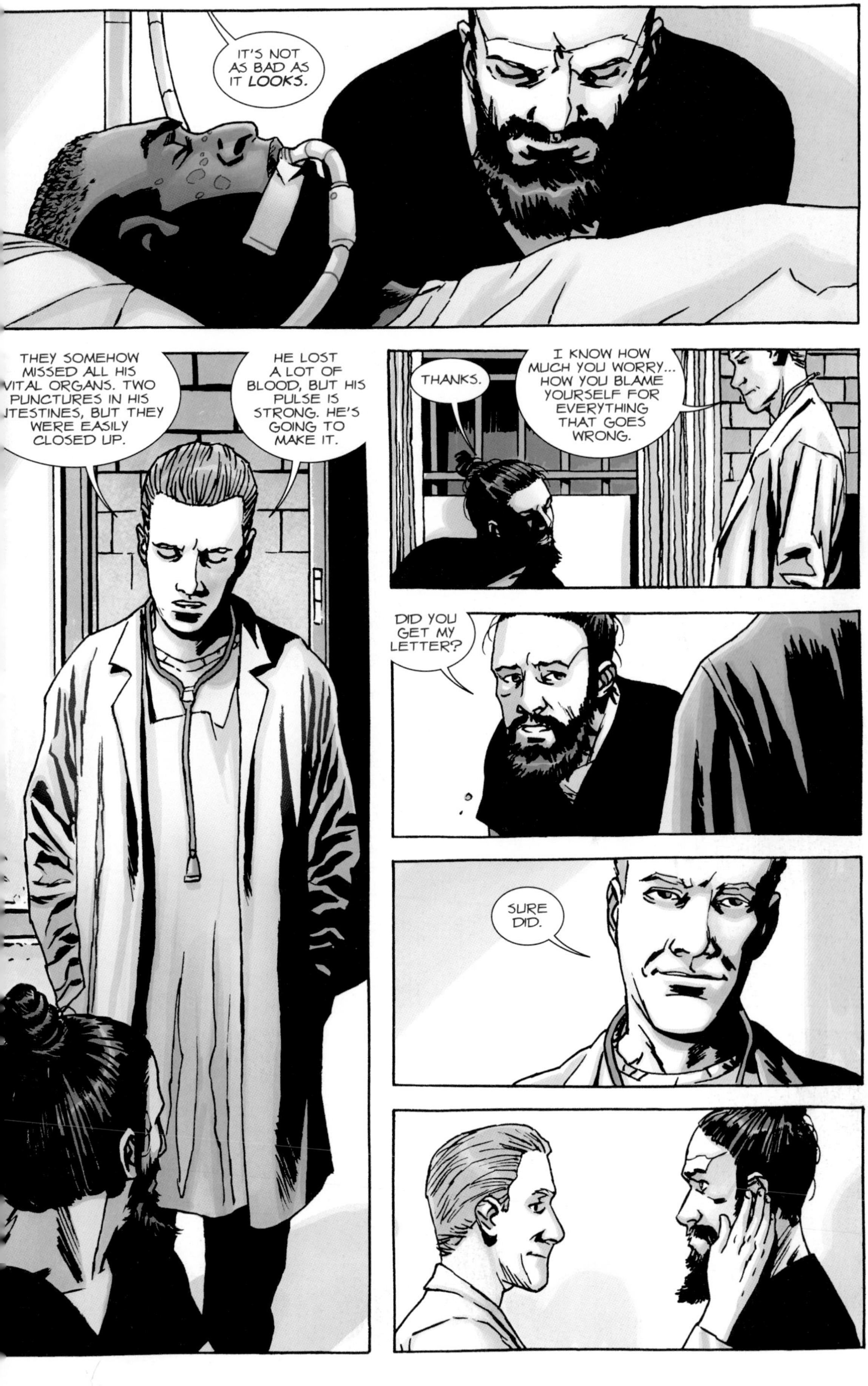
IT'S NOT AS BAD AS IT LOOKS.
THEY SOMEHOW MISSED ALL HIS VITAL ORGANS. TWO PUNCTURES IN HIS INTESTINES, BUT THEY WERE EASILY CLOSED UP.
HE LOST A LOT OF BLOOD, BUT HIS PULSE IS STRONG. HE'S GOING TO MAKE IT.
THANKS.
I KNOW HOW MUCH YOU WORRY... HOW YOU BLAME YOURSELF FOR EVERYTHING THAT GOES WRONG.
DID YOU GET MY LETTER?
SURE DID.

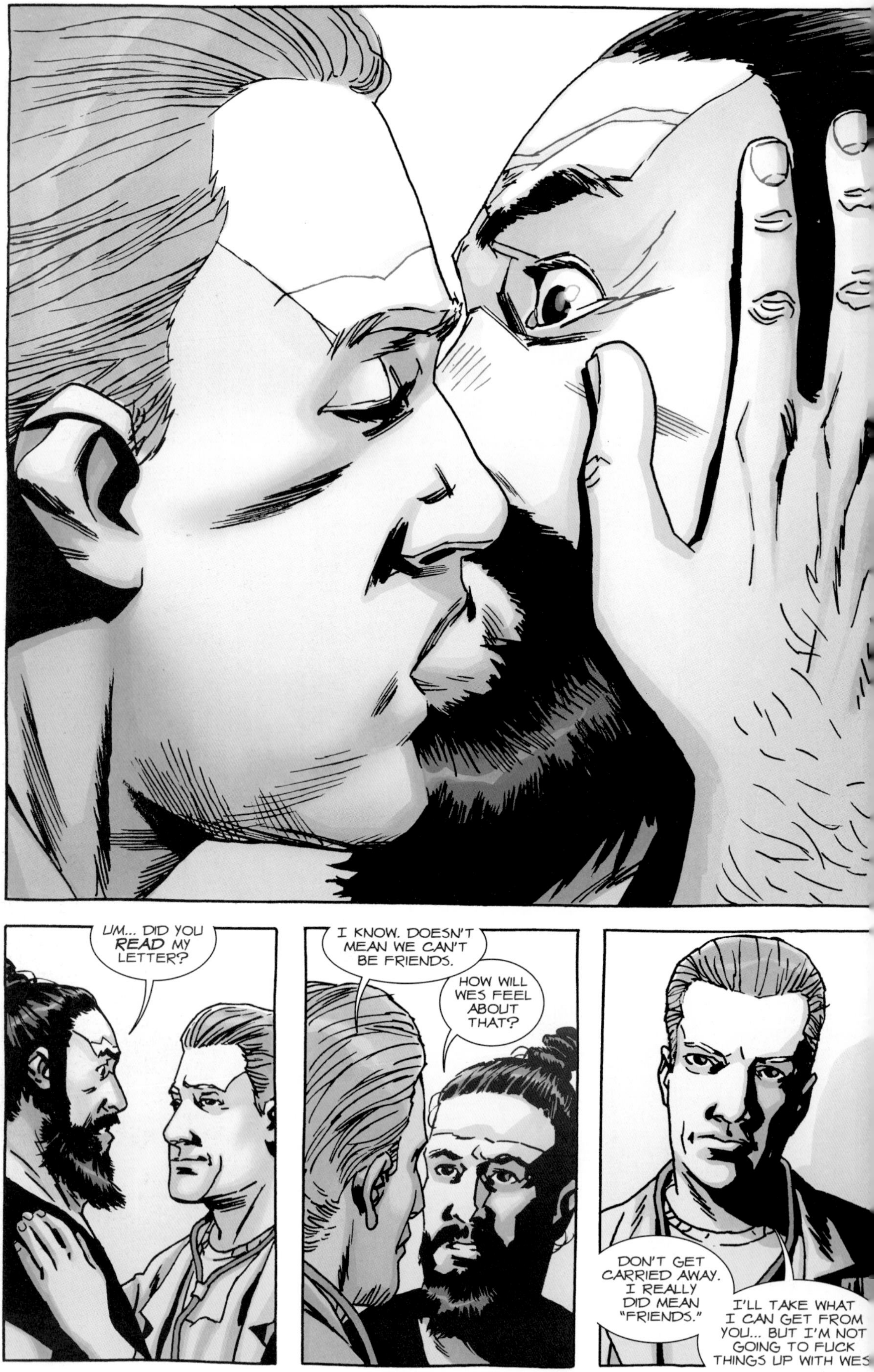
UM... DID YOU READ MY LETTER?
I KNOW. DOESN'T MEAN WE CAN'T BE FRIENDS.
HOW WILL WES FEEL ABOUT THAT?
DON'T GET CARRIED AWAY. I REALLY DID MEAN "FRIENDS."
I'LL TAKE WHAT I CAN GET FROM YOU... BUT I'M NOT GOING TO FUCK THINGS UP WITH WES.

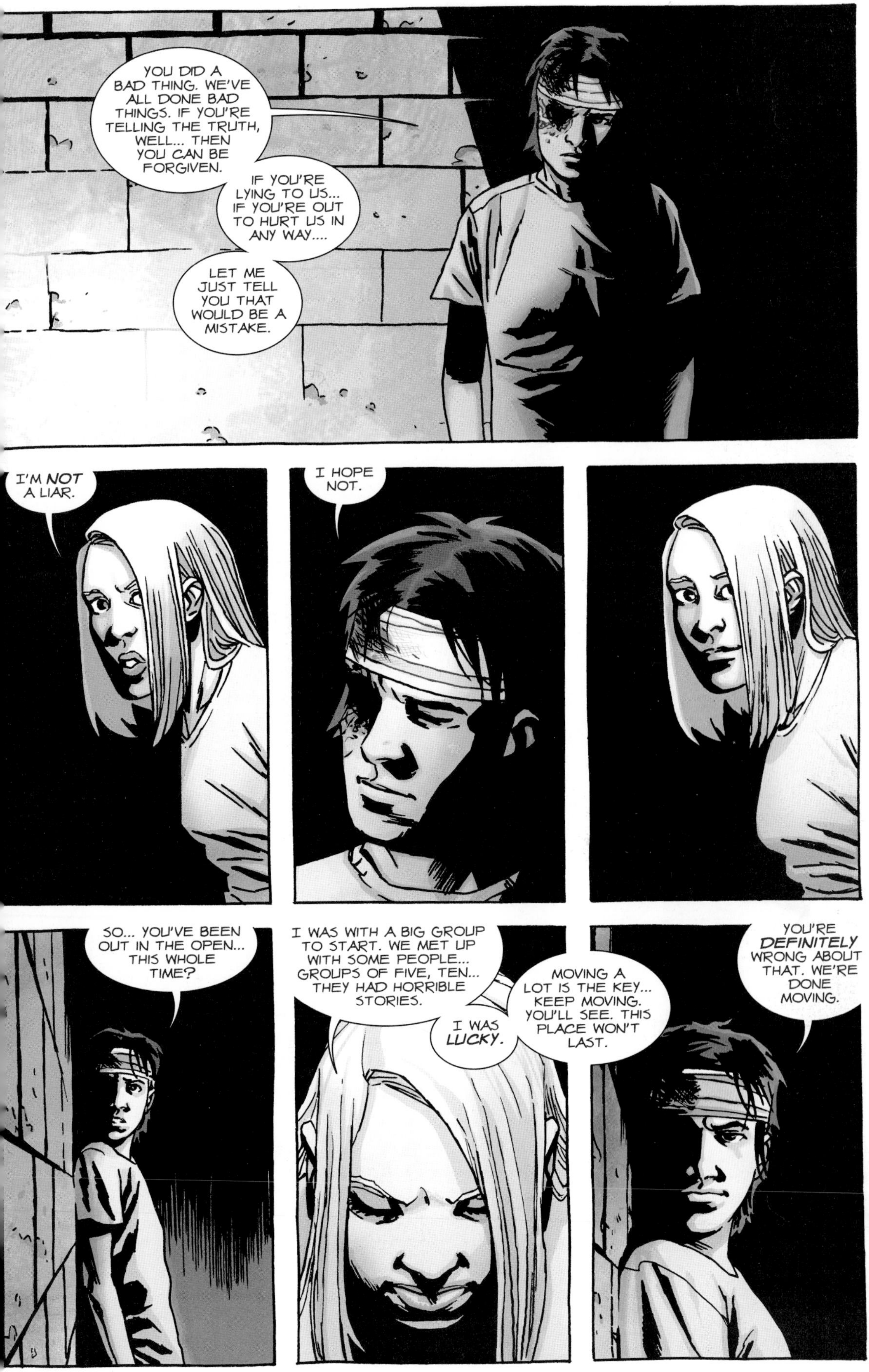
YOU DID A BAD THING. WE'VE ALL DONE BAD THINGS. IF YOU'RE TELLING THE TRUTH, WELL... THEN YOU CAN BE FORGIVEN.
IF YOU'RE LYING TO US... IF YOU'RE OUT TO HURT US IN ANY WAY....
LET ME JUST TELL YOU THAT WOULD BE A MISTAKE.
I'M *NOT* A LIAR.
I HOPE NOT.
SO... YOU'VE BEEN OUT IN THE OPEN... THIS WHOLE TIME?
I WAS WITH A BIG GROUP TO START. WE MET UP WITH SOME PEOPLE... GROUPS OF FIVE, TEN... THEY HAD HORRIBLE STORIES.
I WAS *LUCKY*.
MOVING A LOT IS THE KEY... KEEP MOVING. YOU'LL SEE. THIS PLACE WON'T LAST.
YOU'RE *DEFINITELY* WRONG ABOUT THAT. WE'RE DONE MOVING.

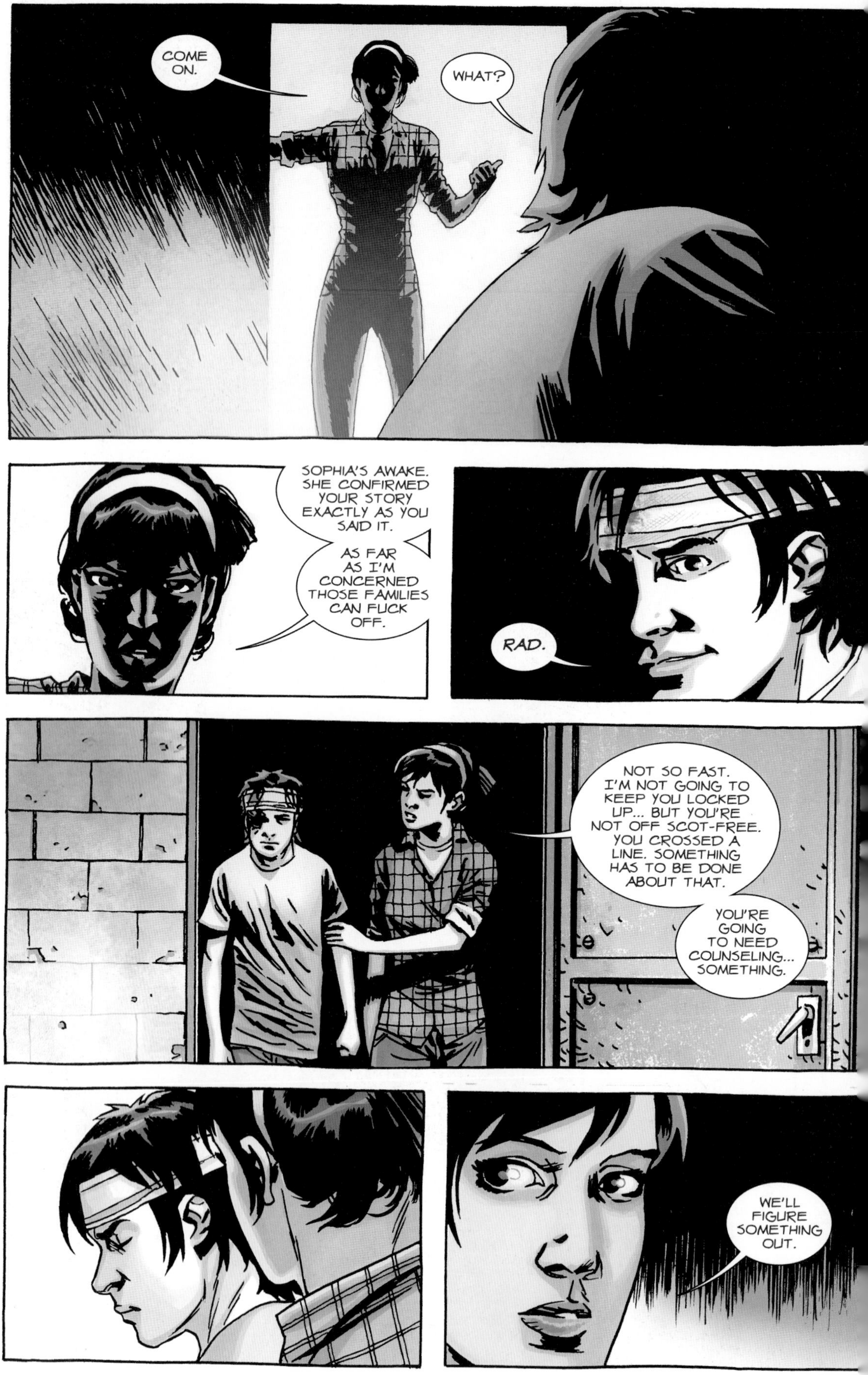
COME ON.
WHAT?
SOPHIA'S AWAKE. SHE CONFIRMED YOUR STORY EXACTLY AS YOU SAID IT.
AS FAR AS I'M CONCERNED THOSE FAMILIES CAN FUCK OFF.
RAD.
NOT SO FAST. I'M NOT GOING TO KEEP YOU LOCKED UP... BUT YOU'RE NOT OFF SCOT-FREE. YOU CROSSED A LINE. SOMETHING HAS TO BE DONE ABOUT THAT.
YOU'RE GOING TO NEED COUNSELING... SOMETHING.
WE'LL FIGURE SOMETHING OUT.

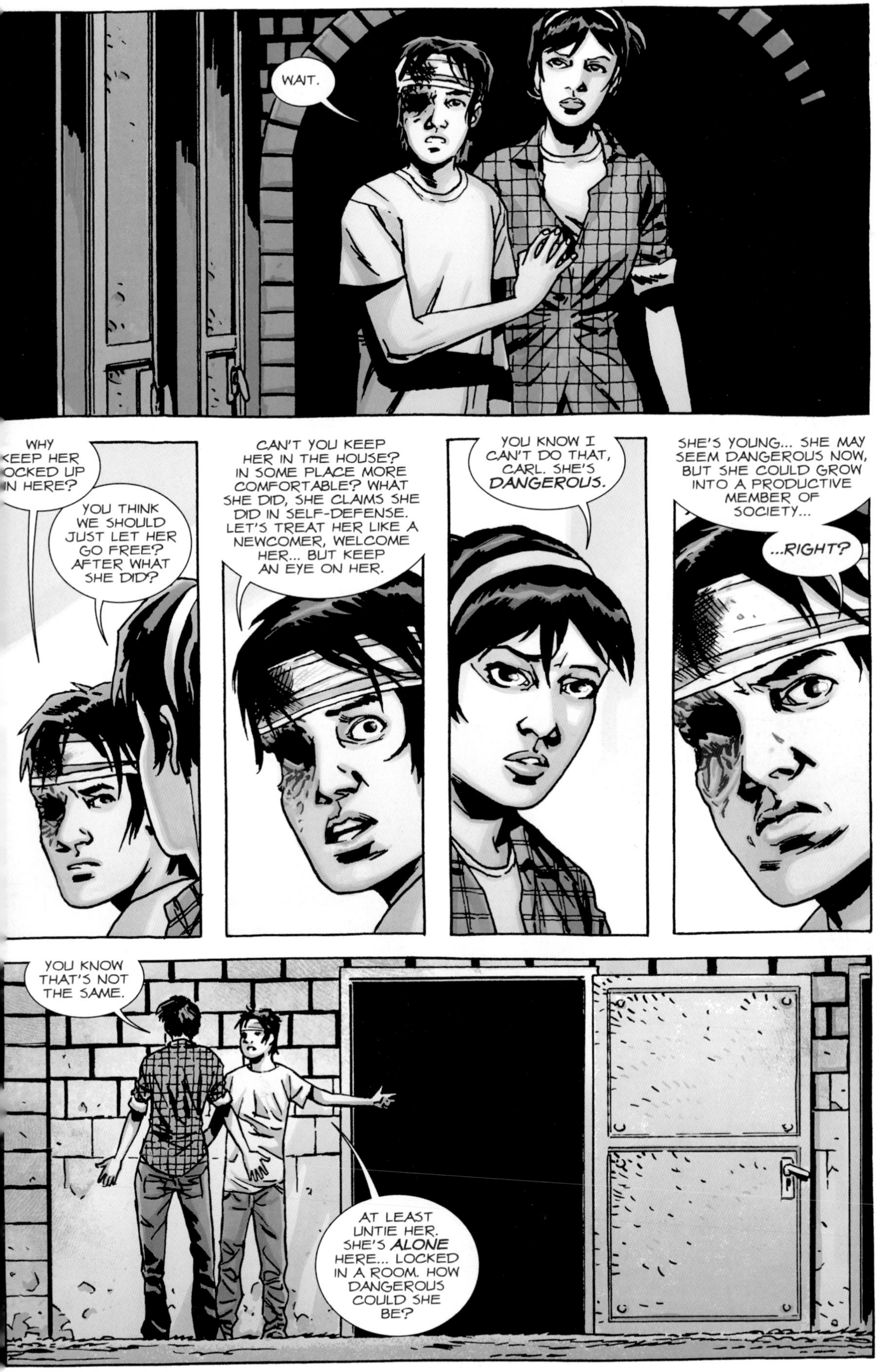
WAIT.
WHY KEEP HER LOCKED UP IN HERE?
YOU THINK WE SHOULD JUST LET HER GO FREE? AFTER WHAT SHE DID?
CAN'T YOU KEEP HER IN THE HOUSE? IN SOME PLACE MORE COMFORTABLE? WHAT SHE DID, SHE CLAIMS SHE DID IN SELF-DEFENSE. LET'S TREAT HER LIKE A NEWCOMER, WELCOME HER... BUT KEEP AN EYE ON HER.
YOU KNOW I CAN'T DO THAT, CARL. SHE'S *DANGEROUS.*
SHE'S YOUNG... SHE MAY SEEM DANGEROUS NOW, BUT SHE COULD GROW INTO A PRODUCTIVE MEMBER OF SOCIETY...
...*RIGHT?*
YOU KNOW THAT'S NOT THE SAME.
AT LEAST UNTIE HER. SHE'S *ALONE* HERE... LOCKED IN A ROOM. HOW DANGEROUS COULD SHE BE?

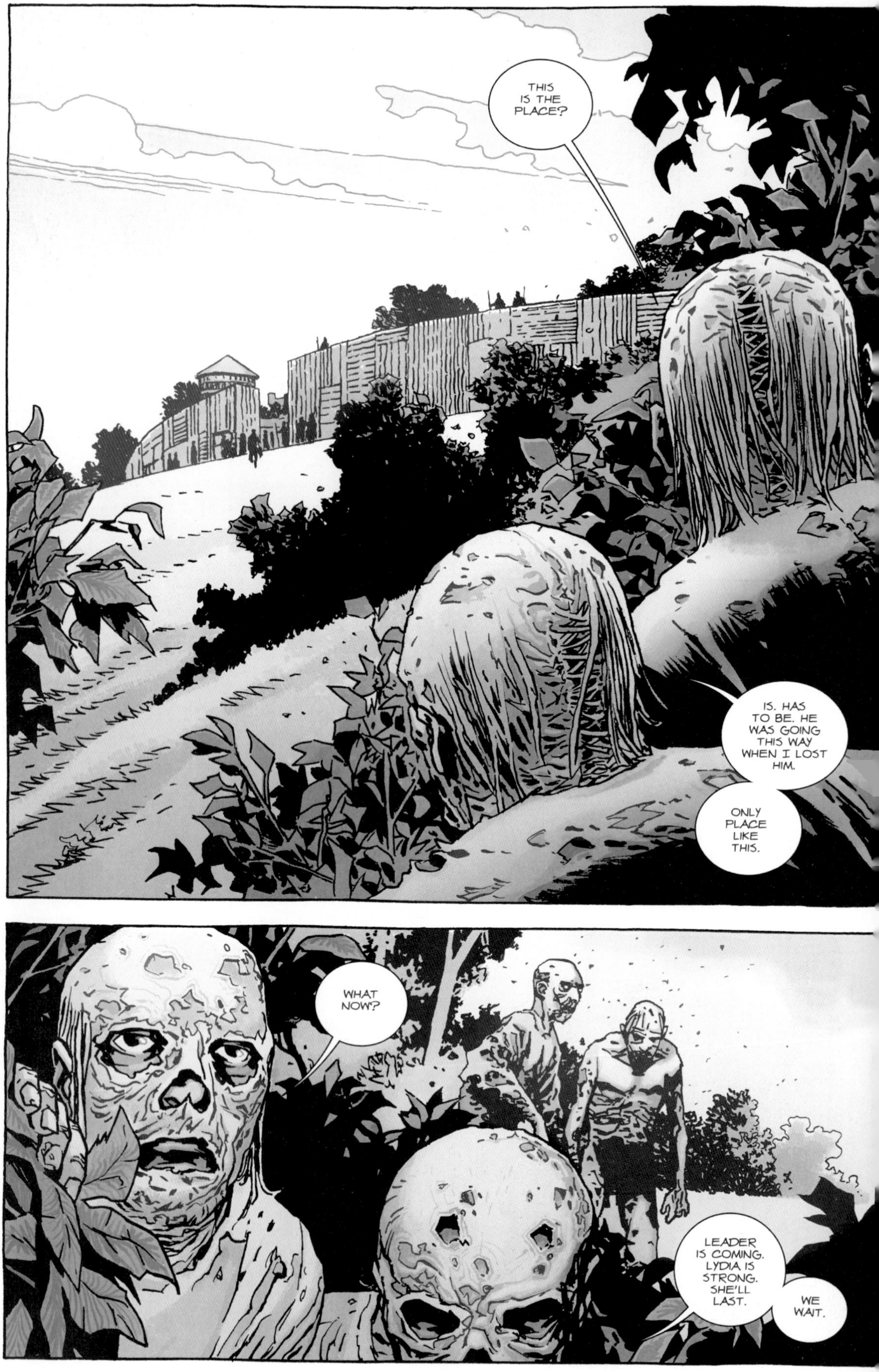
THIS IS THE PLACE?
IS. HAS TO BE. HE WAS GOING THIS WAY WHEN I LOST HIM.
ONLY PLACE LIKE THIS.
WHAT NOW?
LEADER IS COMING. LYDIA IS STRONG. SHE'LL LAST.
WE WAIT.

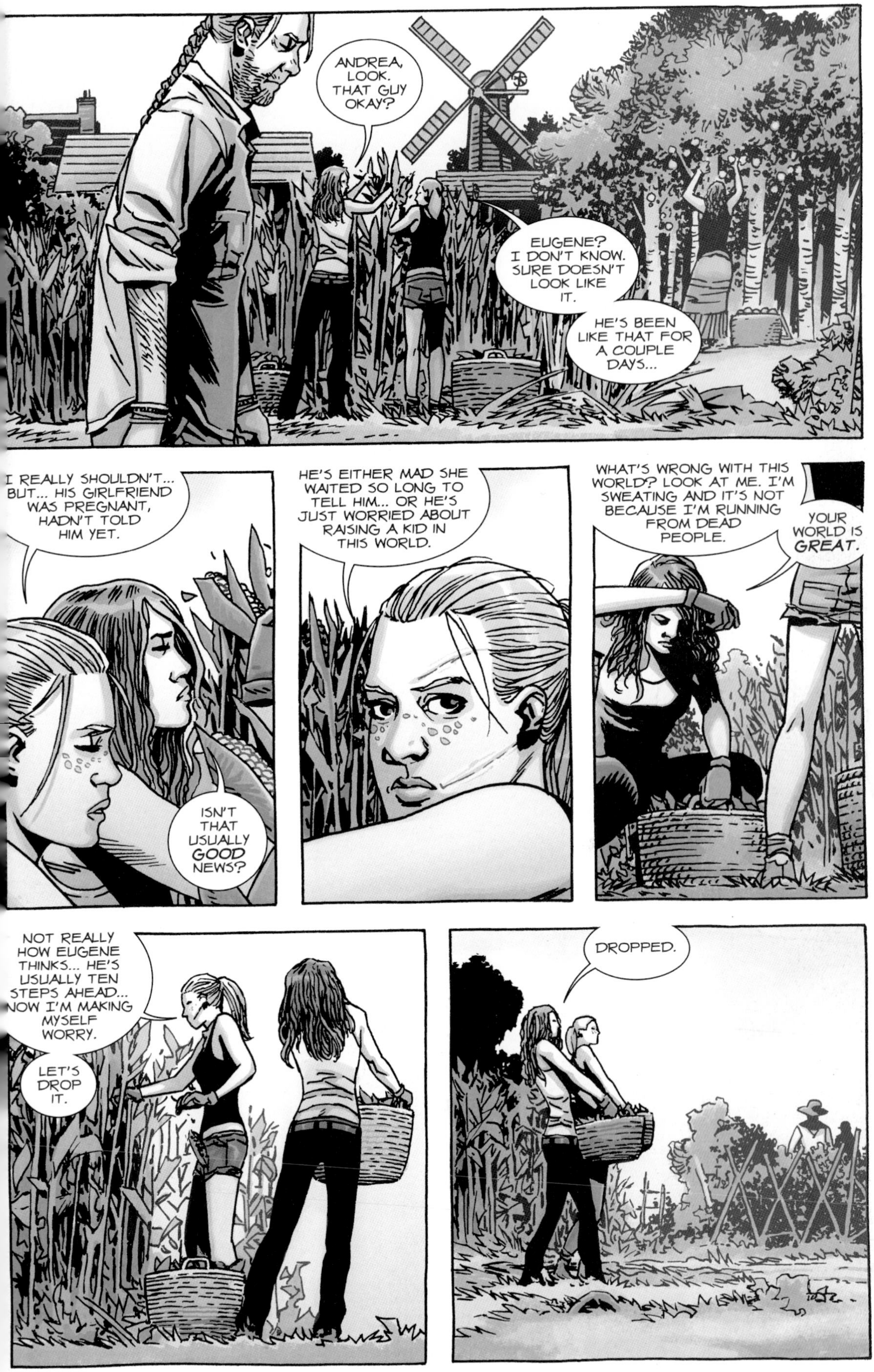
ANDREA, LOOK. THAT GUY OKAY?
EUGENE? I DON'T KNOW. SURE DOESN'T LOOK LIKE IT.
HE'S BEEN LIKE THAT FOR A COUPLE DAYS...
I REALLY SHOULDN'T... BUT... HIS GIRLFRIEND WAS PREGNANT, HADN'T TOLD HIM YET.
ISN'T THAT USUALLY GOOD NEWS?
HE'S EITHER MAD SHE WAITED SO LONG TO TELL HIM... OR HE'S JUST WORRIED ABOUT RAISING A KID IN THIS WORLD.
WHAT'S WRONG WITH THIS WORLD? LOOK AT ME. I'M SWEATING AND IT'S NOT BECAUSE I'M RUNNING FROM DEAD PEOPLE.
YOUR WORLD IS GREAT.
NOT REALLY HOW EUGENE THINKS... HE'S USUALLY TEN STEPS AHEAD... NOW I'M MAKING MYSELF WORRY.
LET'S DROP IT.
DROPPED.

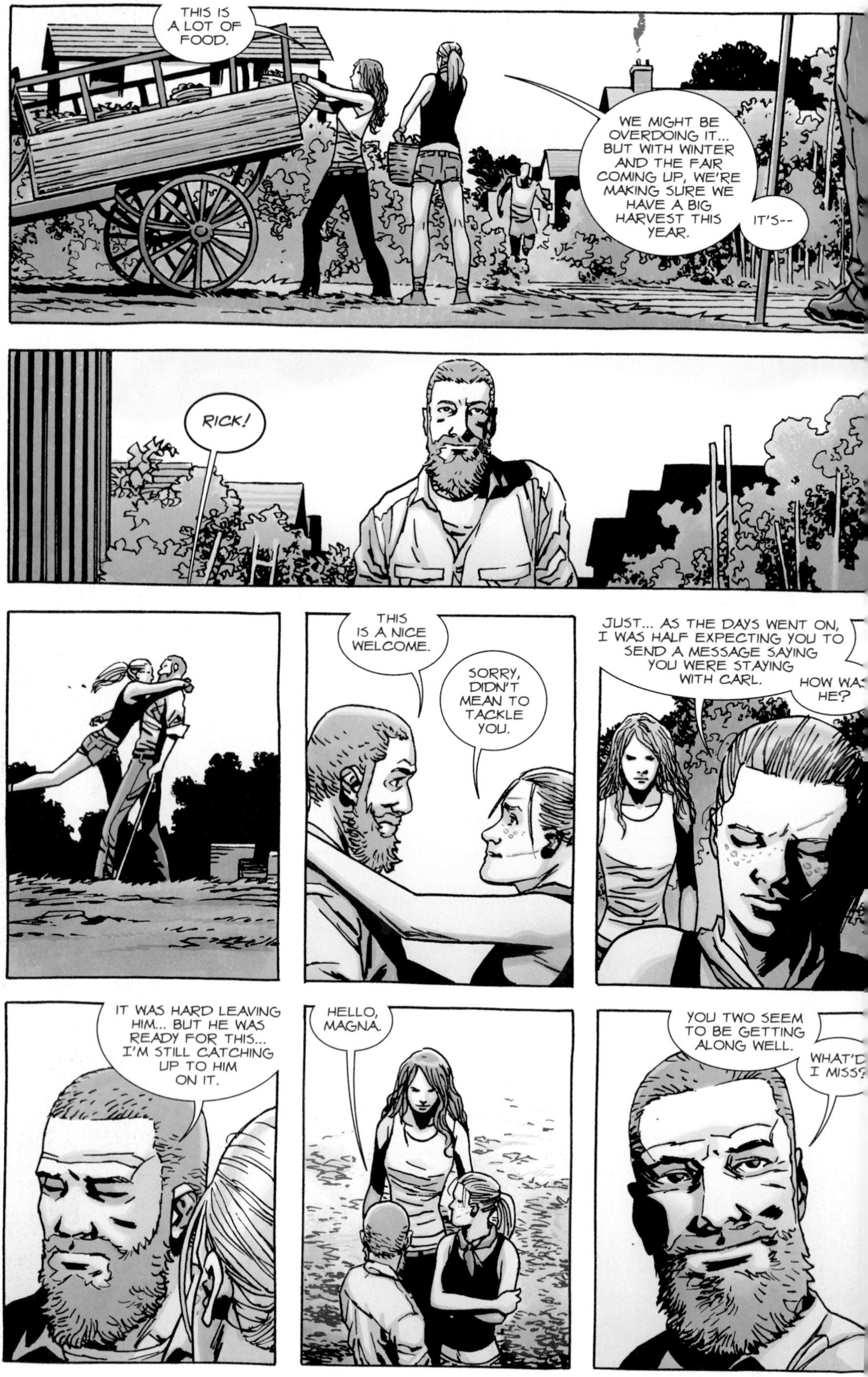
THIS IS A LOT OF FOOD.
WE MIGHT BE OVERDOING IT... BUT WITH WINTER AND THE FAIR COMING UP, WE'RE MAKING SURE WE HAVE A BIG HARVEST THIS YEAR.
IT'S--
RICK!
THIS IS A NICE WELCOME.
SORRY, DIDN'T MEAN TO TACKLE YOU.
JUST... AS THE DAYS WENT ON, I WAS HALF EXPECTING YOU TO SEND A MESSAGE SAYING YOU WERE STAYING WITH CARL.
HOW WAS HE?
IT WAS HARD LEAVING HIM... BUT HE WAS READY FOR THIS... I'M STILL CATCHING UP TO HIM ON IT.
HELLO, MAGNA.
YOU TWO SEEM TO BE GETTING ALONG WELL.
WHAT'D I MISS?

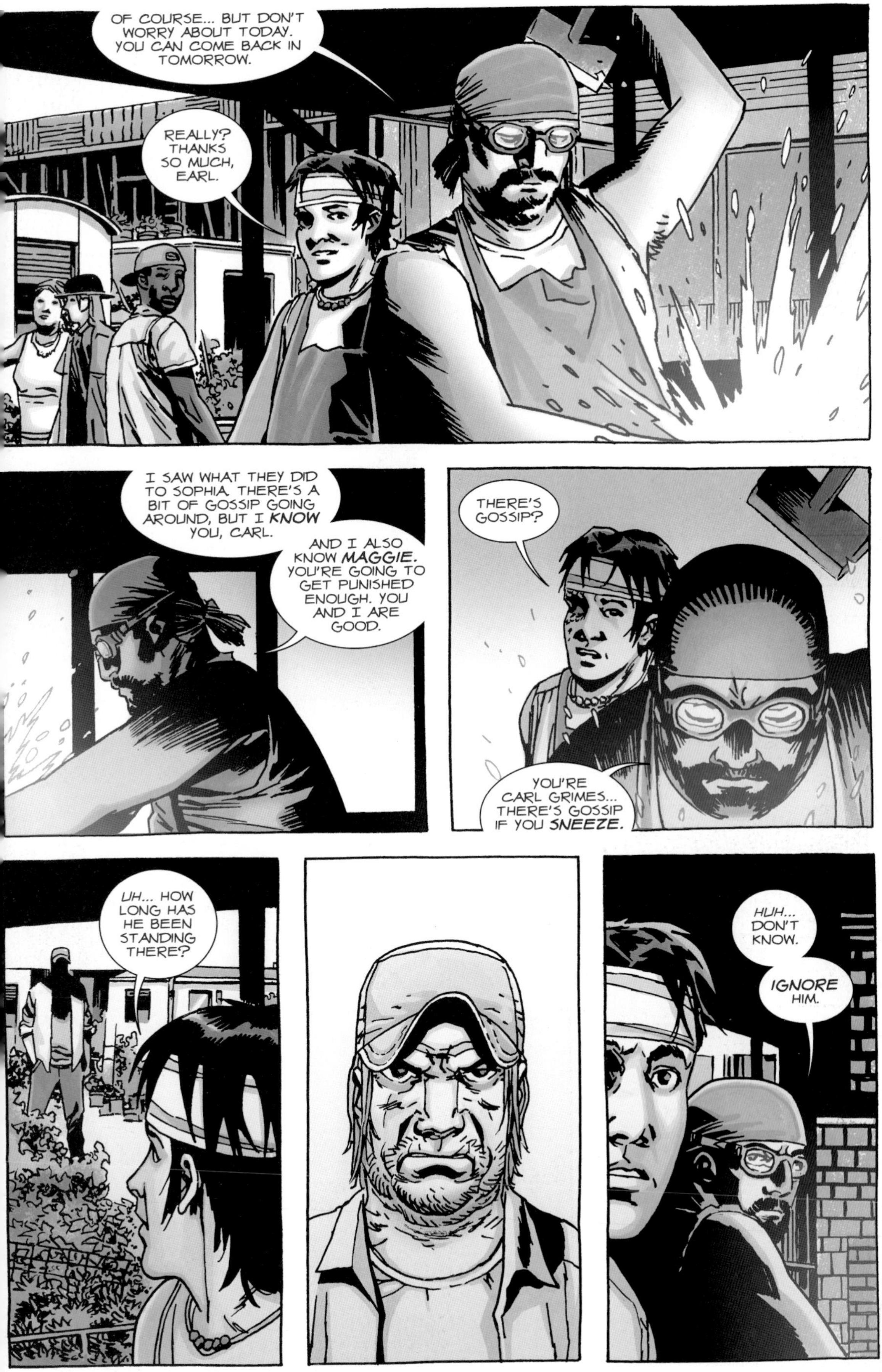
OF COURSE... BUT DON'T WORRY ABOUT TODAY. YOU CAN COME BACK IN TOMORROW.
REALLY? THANKS SO MUCH, EARL.
I SAW WHAT THEY DID TO SOPHIA. THERE'S A BIT OF GOSSIP GOING AROUND, BUT I KNOW YOU, CARL.
AND I ALSO KNOW MAGGIE. YOU'RE GOING TO GET PUNISHED ENOUGH. YOU AND I ARE GOOD.
THERE'S GOSSIP?
YOU'RE CARL GRIMES... THERE'S GOSSIP IF YOU SNEEZE.
UH... HOW LONG HAS HE BEEN STANDING THERE?
HUH... DON'T KNOW.
IGNORE HIM.

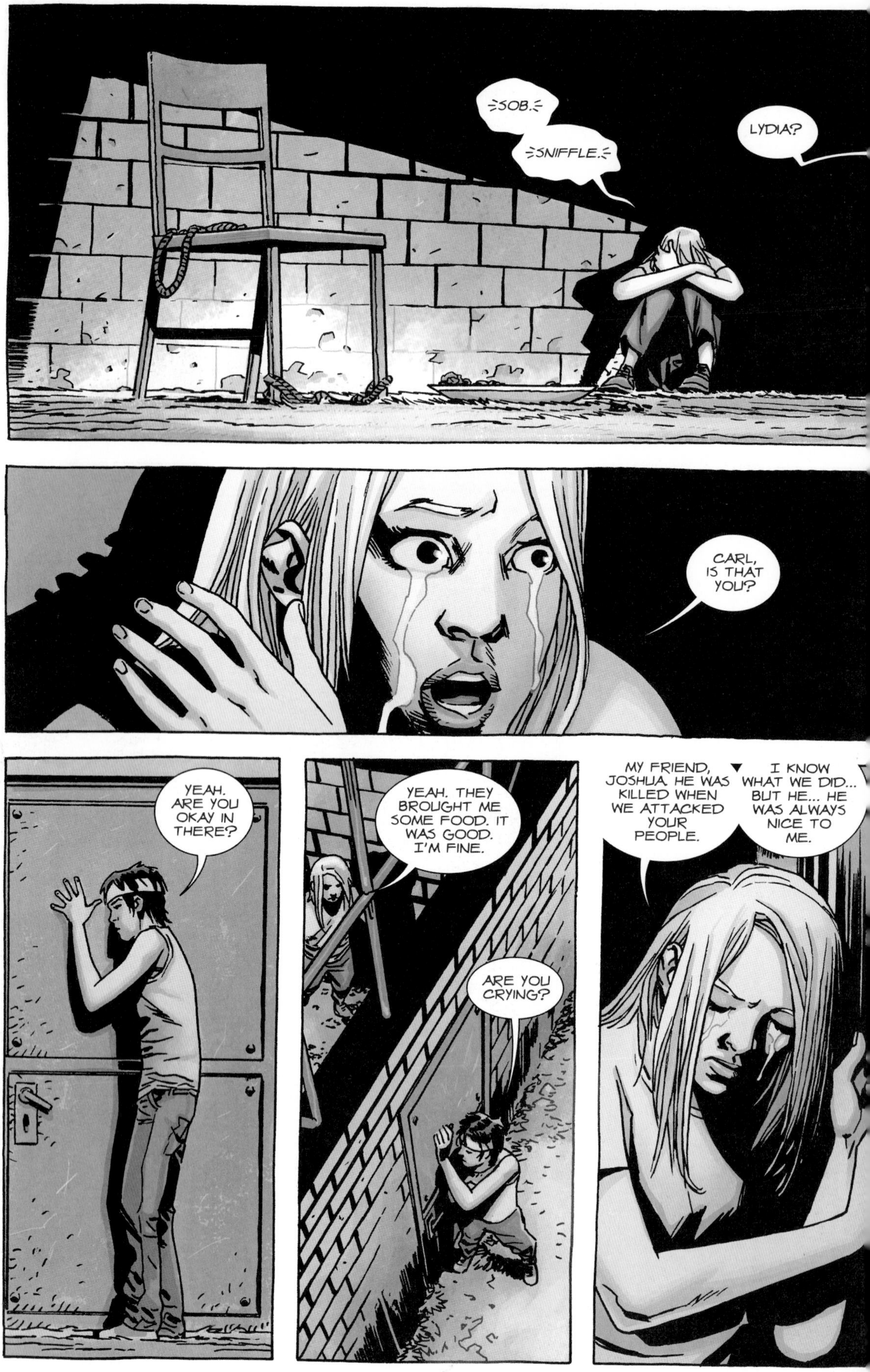
SOB.
SNIFFLE.
LYDIA?
CARL, IS THAT YOU?
YEAH. ARE YOU OKAY IN THERE?
YEAH. THEY BROUGHT ME SOME FOOD. IT WAS GOOD. I'M FINE.
ARE YOU CRYING?
MY FRIEND, JOSHUA. HE WAS KILLED WHEN WE ATTACKED YOUR PEOPLE.
I KNOW WHAT WE DID... BUT HE... HE WAS ALWAYS NICE TO ME.

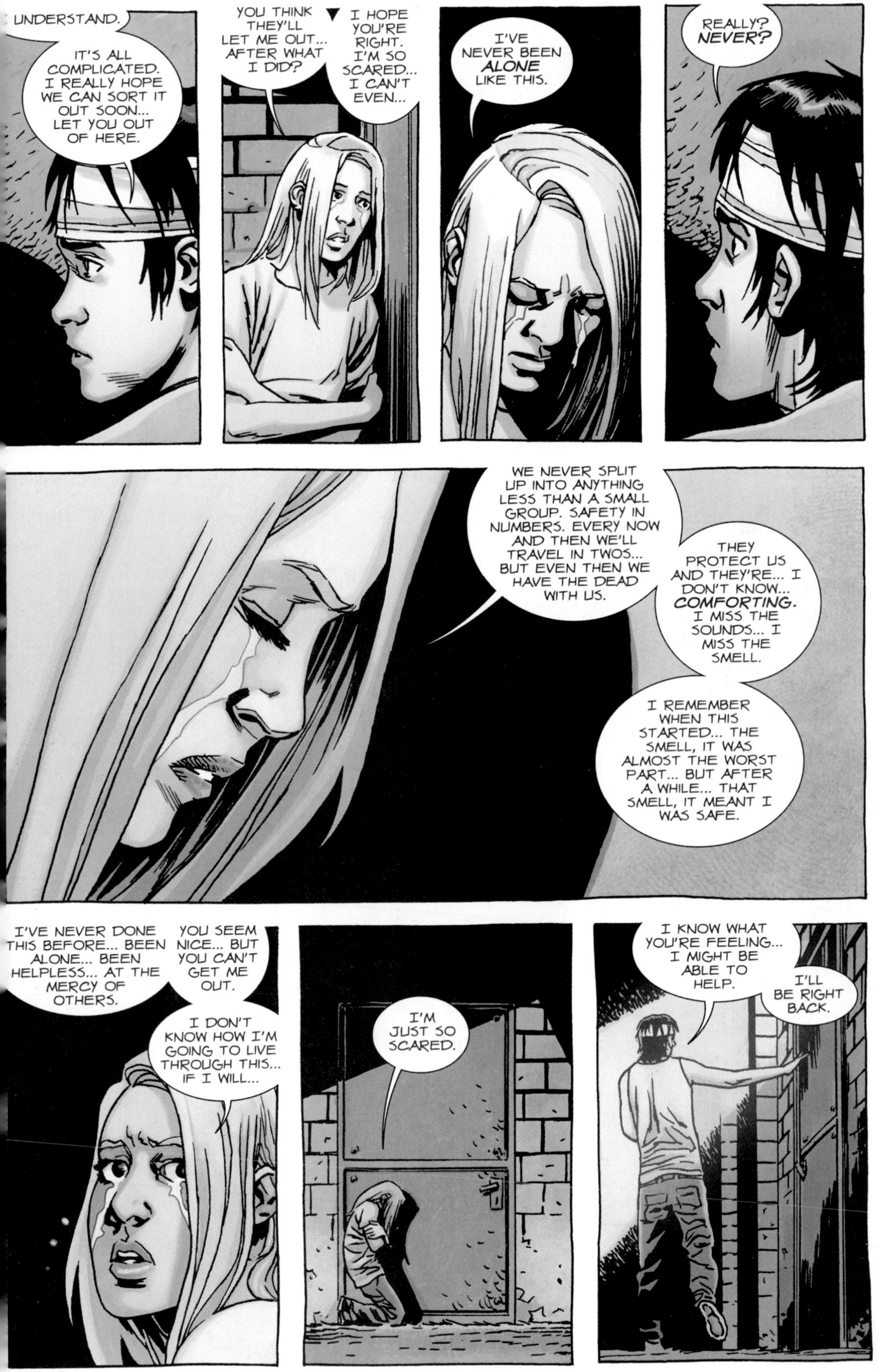

UNDERSTAND.
IT'S ALL COMPLICATED. I REALLY HOPE WE CAN SORT IT OUT SOON... LET YOU OUT OF HERE.
YOU THINK THEY'LL LET ME OUT... AFTER WHAT I DID?
I HOPE YOU'RE RIGHT. I'M SO SCARED... I CAN'T EVEN...
I'VE NEVER BEEN ALONE LIKE THIS.
REALLY? NEVER?
WE NEVER SPLIT UP INTO ANYTHING LESS THAN A SMALL GROUP. SAFETY IN NUMBERS. EVERY NOW AND THEN WE'LL TRAVEL IN TWOS... BUT EVEN THEN WE HAVE THE DEAD WITH US.
THEY PROTECT US AND THEY'RE... I DON'T KNOW... COMFORTING. I MISS THE SOUNDS... I MISS THE SMELL.
I REMEMBER WHEN THIS STARTED... THE SMELL, IT WAS ALMOST THE WORST PART... BUT AFTER A WHILE... THAT SMELL, IT MEANT I WAS SAFE.
I'VE NEVER DONE THIS BEFORE... BEEN ALONE... BEEN HELPLESS... AT THE MERCY OF OTHERS.
YOU SEEM NICE... BUT YOU CAN'T GET ME OUT.
I DON'T KNOW HOW I'M GOING TO LIVE THROUGH THIS... IF I WILL...
I'M JUST SO SCARED.
I KNOW WHAT YOU'RE FEELING... I MIGHT BE ABLE TO HELP.
I'LL BE RIGHT BACK.

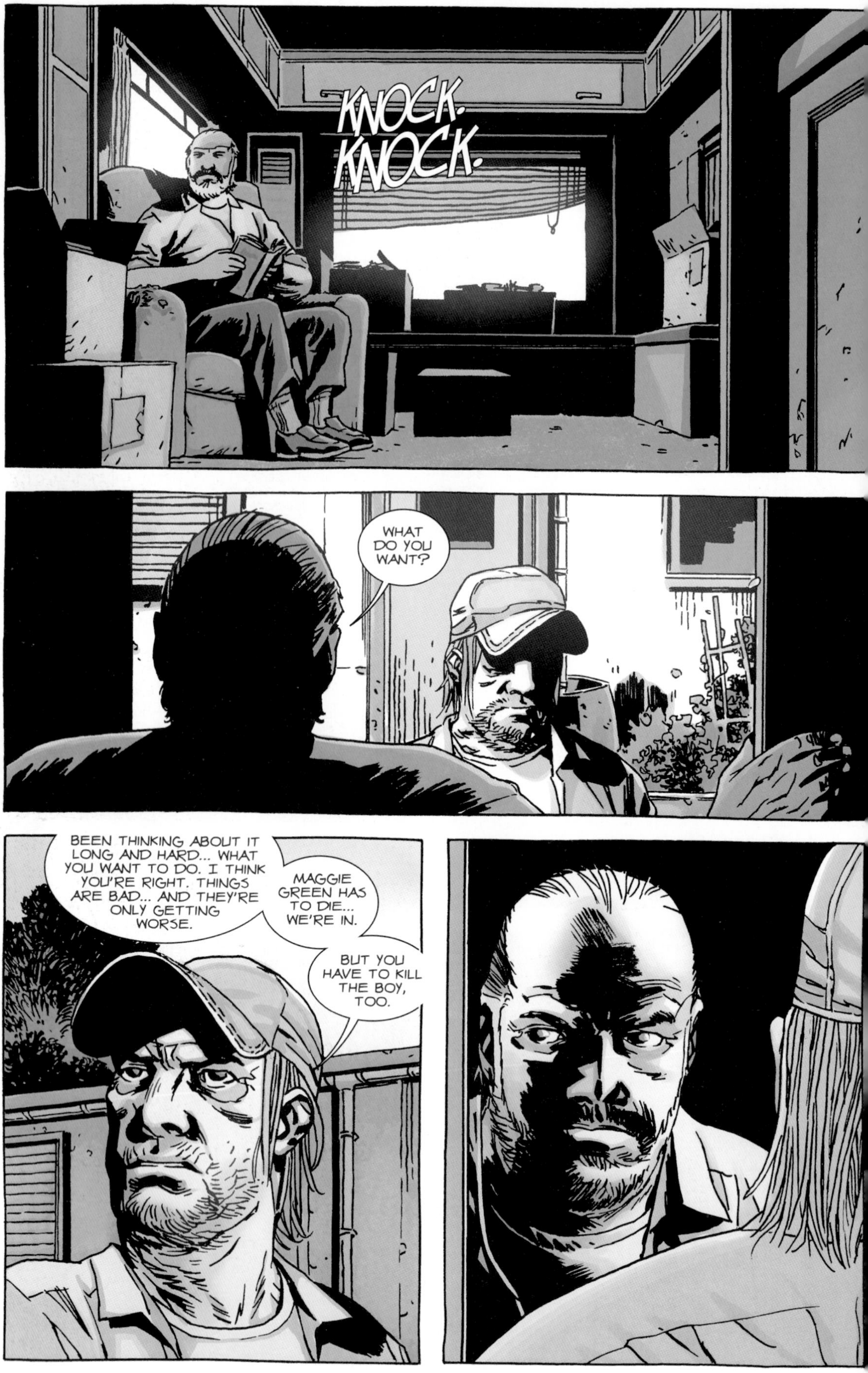
KNOCK. KNOCK.
WHAT DO YOU WANT?
BEEN THINKING ABOUT IT LONG AND HARD... WHAT YOU WANT TO DO. I THINK YOU'RE RIGHT. THINGS ARE BAD... AND THEY'RE ONLY GETTING WORSE.
MAGGIE GREEN HAS TO DIE... WE'RE IN.
BUT YOU HAVE TO KILL THE BOY, TOO.

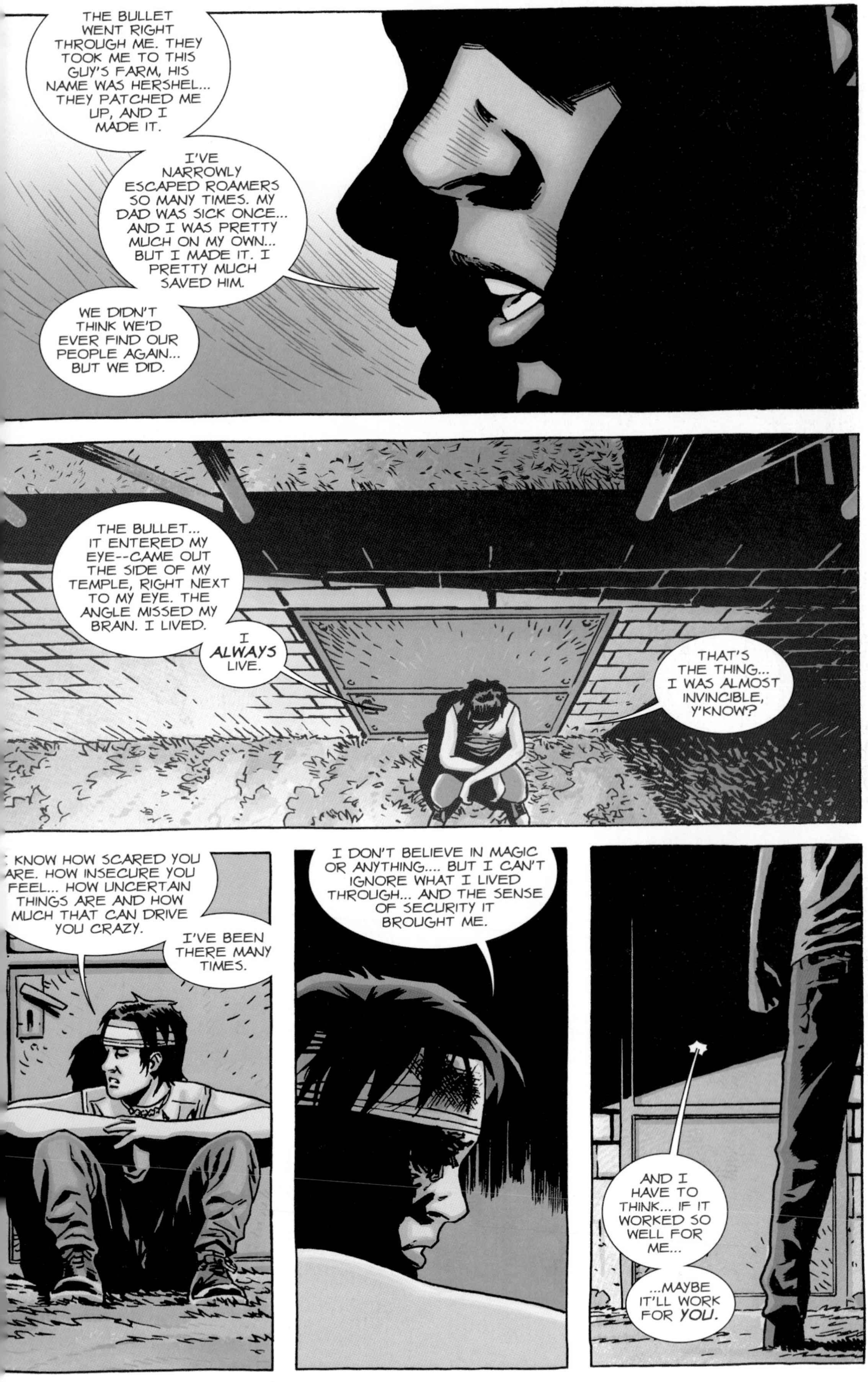
THE BULLET WENT RIGHT THROUGH ME. THEY TOOK ME TO THIS GUY'S FARM, HIS NAME WAS HERSHEL... THEY PATCHED ME UP, AND I MADE IT.
I'VE NARROWLY ESCAPED ROAMERS SO MANY TIMES. MY DAD WAS SICK ONCE... AND I WAS PRETTY MUCH ON MY OWN... BUT I MADE IT. I PRETTY MUCH SAVED HIM.
WE DIDN'T THINK WE'D EVER FIND OUR PEOPLE AGAIN... BUT WE DID.
THE BULLET... IT ENTERED MY EYE--CAME OUT THE SIDE OF MY TEMPLE, RIGHT NEXT TO MY EYE. THE ANGLE MISSED MY BRAIN. I LIVED.
I *ALWAYS* LIVE.
THAT'S THE THING... I WAS ALMOST INVINCIBLE, Y'KNOW?
KNOW HOW SCARED YOU ARE. HOW INSECURE YOU FEEL... HOW UNCERTAIN THINGS ARE AND HOW MUCH THAT CAN DRIVE YOU CRAZY.
I'VE BEEN THERE MANY TIMES.
I DON'T BELIEVE IN MAGIC OR ANYTHING.... BUT I CAN'T IGNORE WHAT I LIVED THROUGH... AND THE SENSE OF SECURITY IT BROUGHT ME.
AND I HAVE TO THINK... IF IT WORKED SO WELL FOR ME...
...MAYBE IT'LL WORK FOR *YOU*.

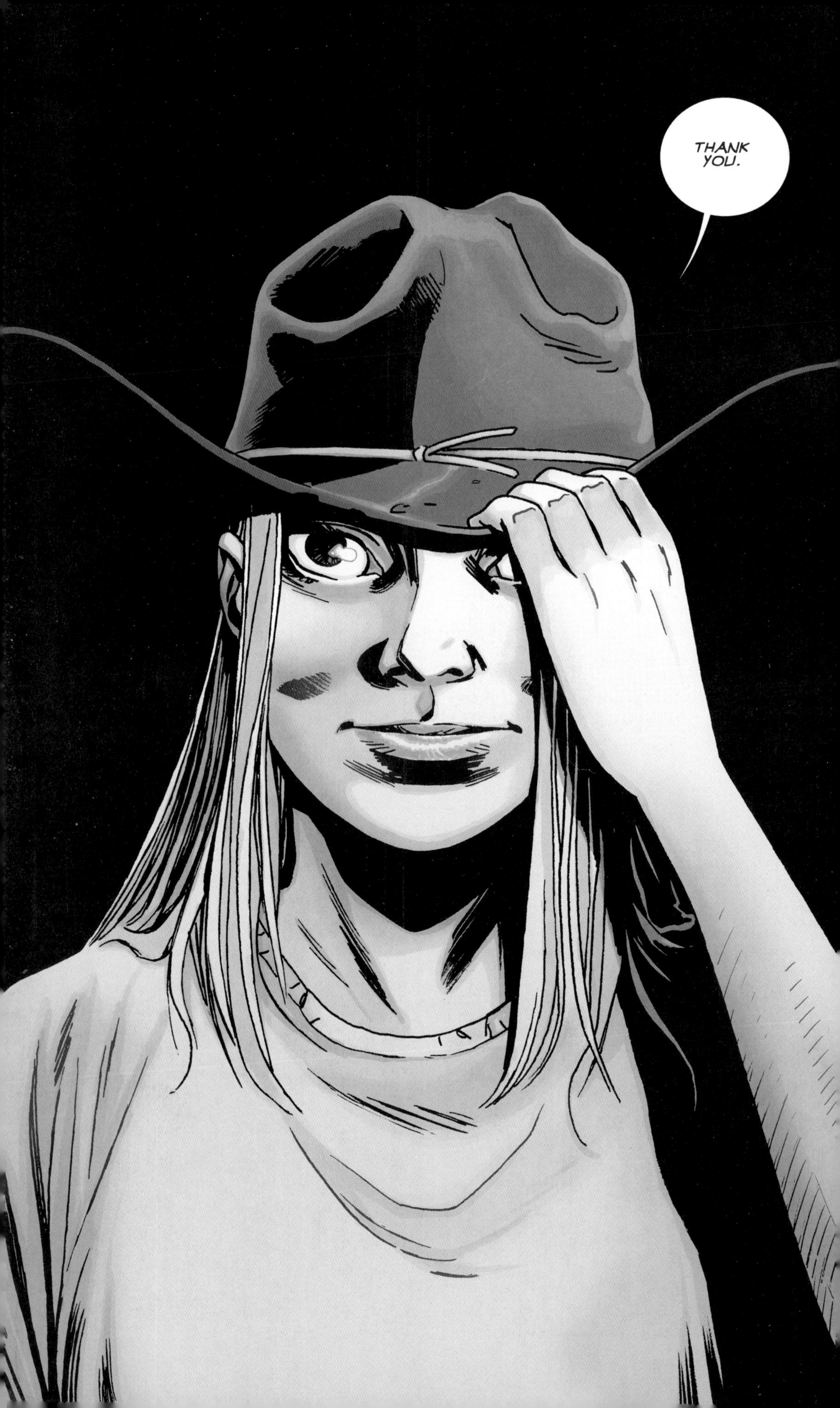
THANK YOU.

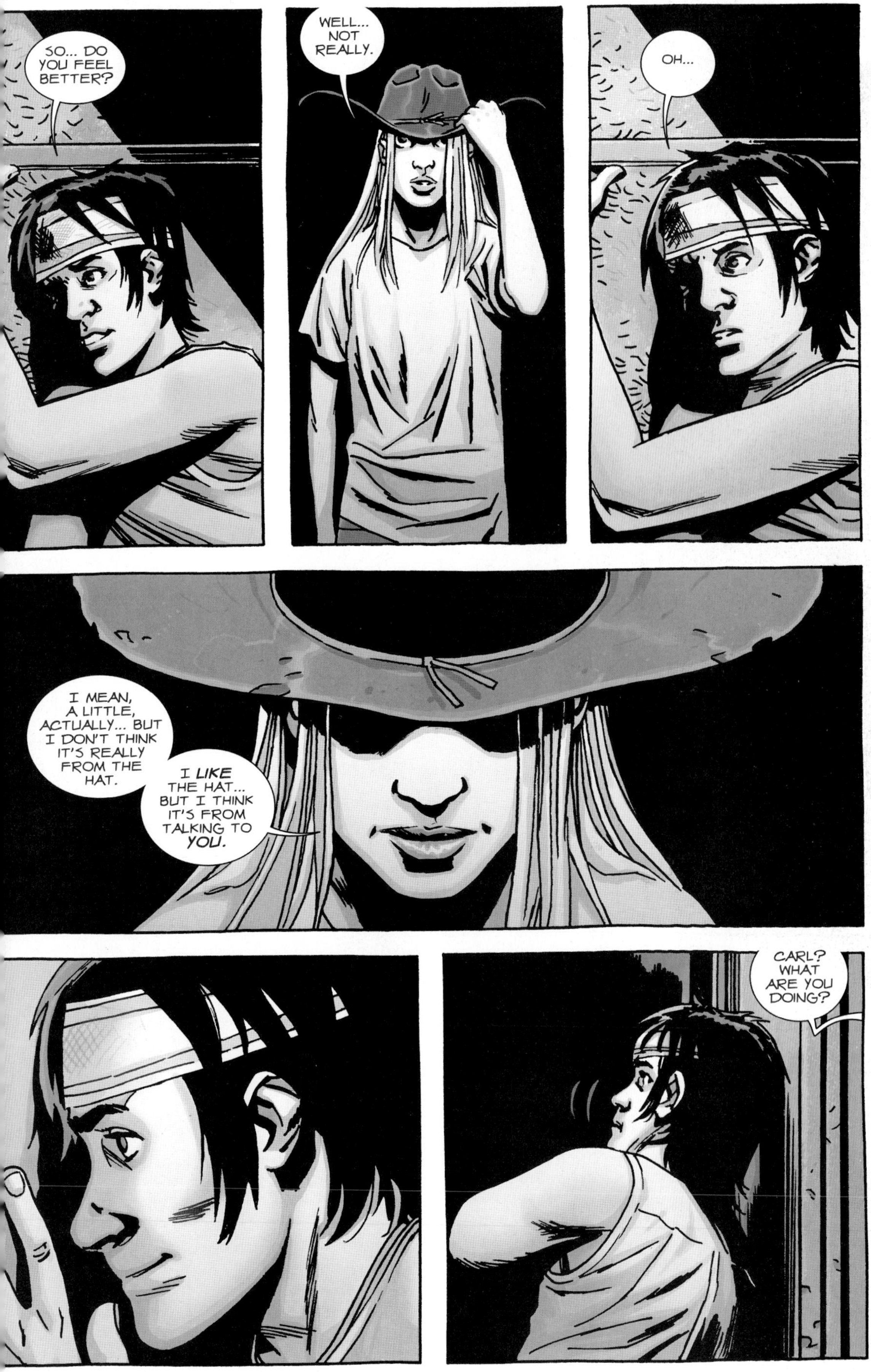
SO... DO YOU FEEL BETTER?
WELL... NOT REALLY.
OH...
I MEAN, A LITTLE, ACTUALLY... BUT I DON'T THINK IT'S REALLY FROM THE HAT.
I *LIKE* THE HAT... BUT I THINK IT'S FROM TALKING TO *YOU*.
CARL? WHAT ARE YOU DOING?

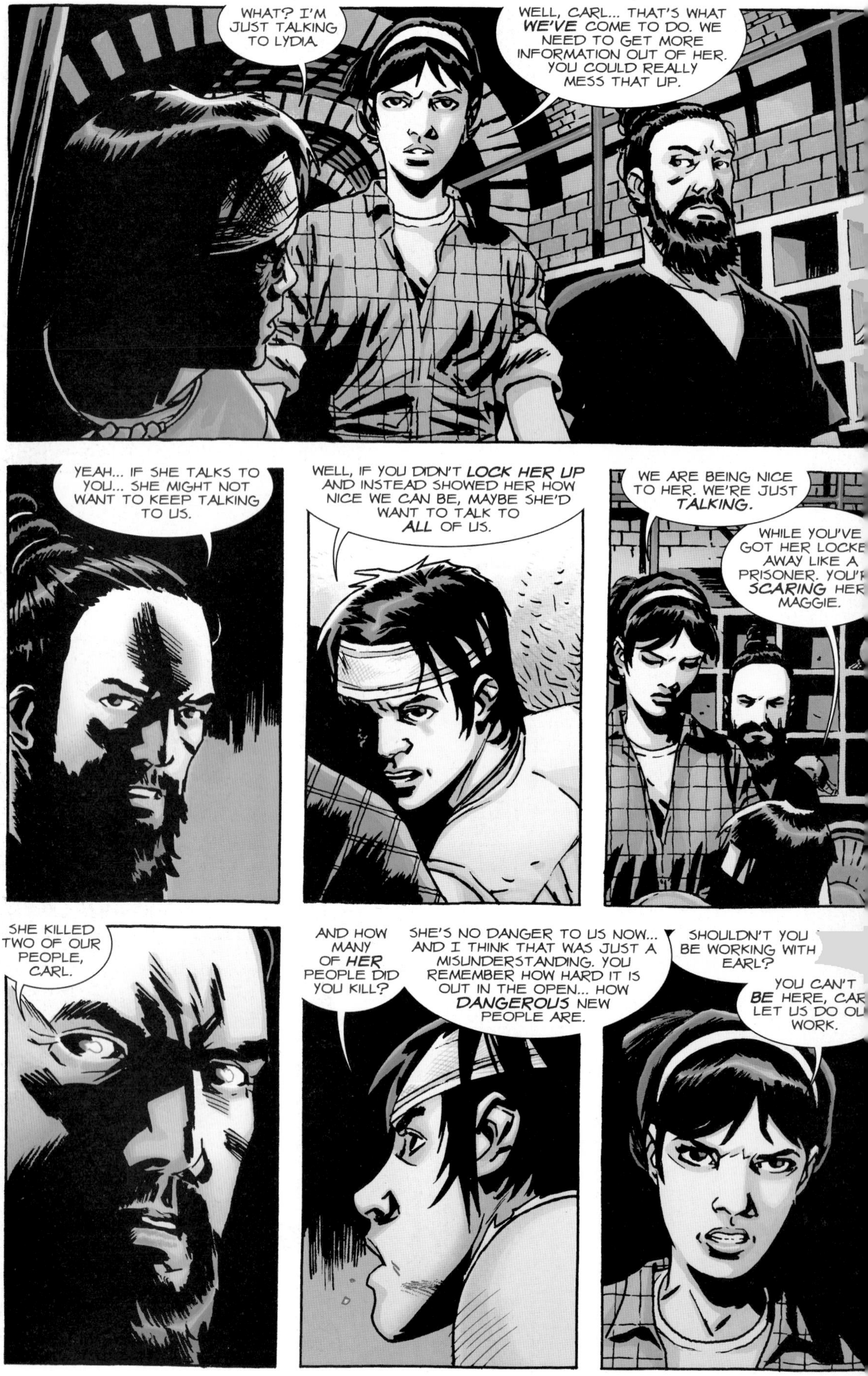
WHAT? I'M JUST TALKING TO LYDIA.
WELL, CARL... THAT'S WHAT *WE'VE* COME TO DO. WE NEED TO GET MORE INFORMATION OUT OF HER. YOU COULD REALLY MESS THAT UP.
YEAH... IF SHE TALKS TO YOU... SHE MIGHT NOT WANT TO KEEP TALKING TO US.
WELL, IF YOU DIDN'T *LOCK HER UP* AND INSTEAD SHOWED HER HOW NICE WE CAN BE, MAYBE SHE'D WANT TO TALK TO *ALL* OF US.
WE ARE BEING NICE TO HER. WE'RE JUST *TALKING.*
WHILE YOU'VE GOT HER LOCKE AWAY LIKE A PRISONER. YOU' *SCARING* HER MAGGIE.
SHE KILLED TWO OF OUR PEOPLE, CARL.
AND HOW MANY OF *HER* PEOPLE DID YOU KILL?
SHE'S NO DANGER TO US NOW... AND I THINK THAT WAS JUST A MISUNDERSTANDING. YOU REMEMBER HOW HARD IT IS OUT IN THE OPEN... HOW *DANGEROUS* NEW PEOPLE ARE.
SHOULDN'T YOU BE WORKING WITH EARL?
YOU CAN'T *BE* HERE, CAR LET US DO OU WORK.

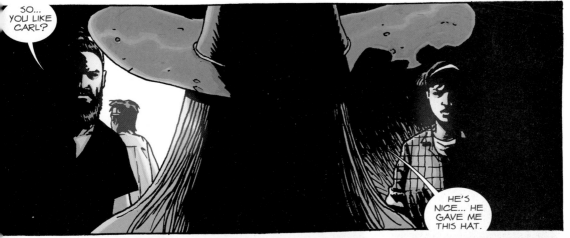

SO... YOU LIKE CARL?

HE'S NICE... HE GAVE ME THIS HAT.

HE DID, DID HE? THAT WAS REALLY NICE OF HIM.

WHAT ARE YOU GOING TO ASK ME?

WHO IS THE LEADER OF YOUR GROUP?

I DON'T WANT TO TALK TO YOU ANYMORE.

WELL, THAT'S JUST--

MAGGIE?

WHAT IS IT, ALEX?

IT'S THE BOYS... YOU WANTED ME TO MAKE SURE YOU KNEW FIRST WHEN THEY WOKE UP.

WHERE IS SHE?!

WHERE IS THAT FUCKING BITCH?!

SHE'S RIGHT HERE.

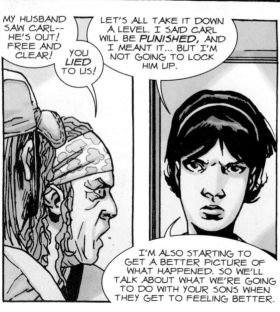

MY HUSBAND SAW CARL-- HE'S OUT! FREE AND CLEAR!

YOU LIED TO US!

LET'S ALL TAKE IT DOWN A LEVEL. I SAID CARL WILL BE PUNISHED, AND I MEANT IT... BUT I'M NOT GOING TO LOCK HIM UP.

I'M ALSO STARTING TO GET A BETTER PICTURE OF WHAT HAPPENED. SO WE'LL TALK ABOUT WHAT WE'RE GOING TO DO WITH YOUR SONS WHEN THEY GET TO FEELING BETTER.

WHAT THE HELL DOES THAT MEAN?

ARE YOU FUCKING JOKING? IS THAT A JOKE?! YOU CAN'T FUCKING BE SERIOUS!

I HONESTLY THIN IT'S TIME TO STAR DISCUSSING RELOCATION.

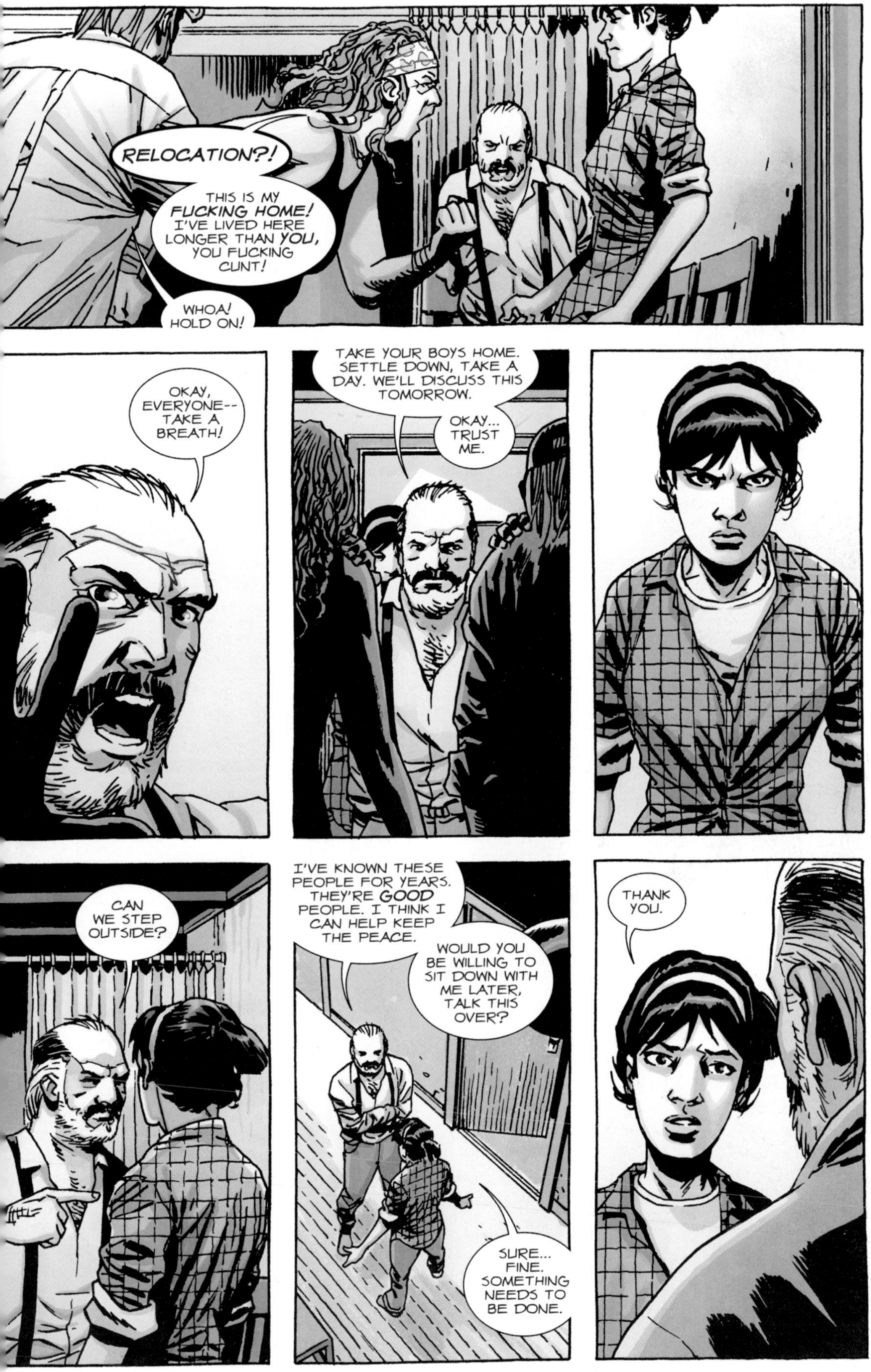
RELOCATION?!
THIS IS MY FUCKING HOME! I'VE LIVED HERE LONGER THAN YOU, YOU FUCKING CUNT!
WHOA! HOLD ON!
OKAY, EVERYONE-- TAKE A BREATH!
TAKE YOUR BOYS HOME. SETTLE DOWN, TAKE A DAY. WE'LL DISCUSS THIS TOMORROW.
OKAY... TRUST ME.
CAN WE STEP OUTSIDE?
I'VE KNOWN THESE PEOPLE FOR YEARS. THEY'RE GOOD PEOPLE. I THINK I CAN HELP KEEP THE PEACE.
WOULD YOU BE WILLING TO SIT DOWN WITH ME LATER, TALK THIS OVER?
SURE... FINE. SOMETHING NEEDS TO BE DONE.
THANK YOU.

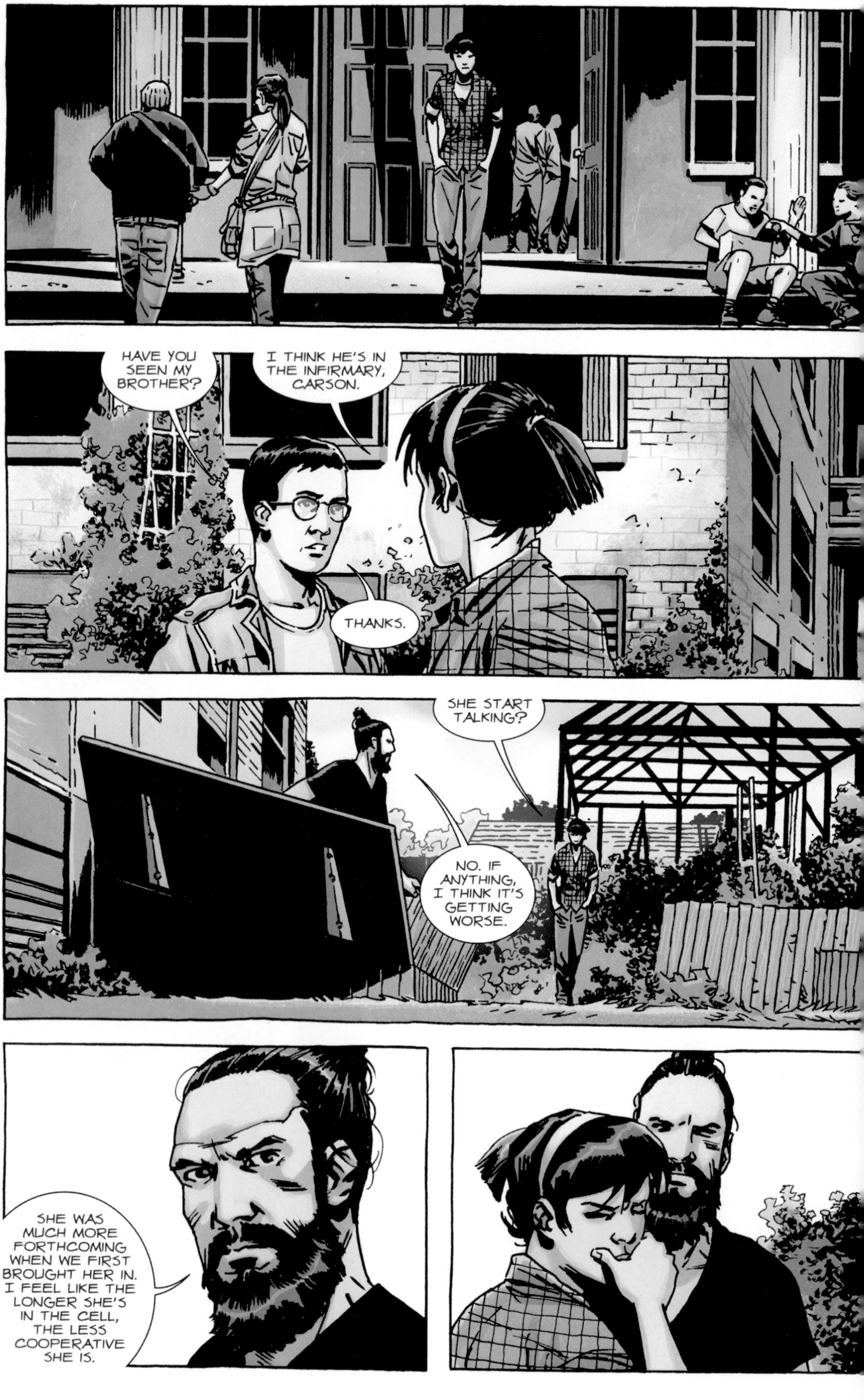
HAVE YOU SEEN MY BROTHER?
I THINK HE'S IN THE INFIRMARY, CARSON.
THANKS.
SHE START TALKING?
NO. IF ANYTHING, I THINK IT'S GETTING WORSE.
SHE WAS MUCH MORE FORTHCOMING WHEN WE FIRST BROUGHT HER IN. I FEEL LIKE THE LONGER SHE'S IN THE CELL, THE LESS COOPERATIVE SHE IS.

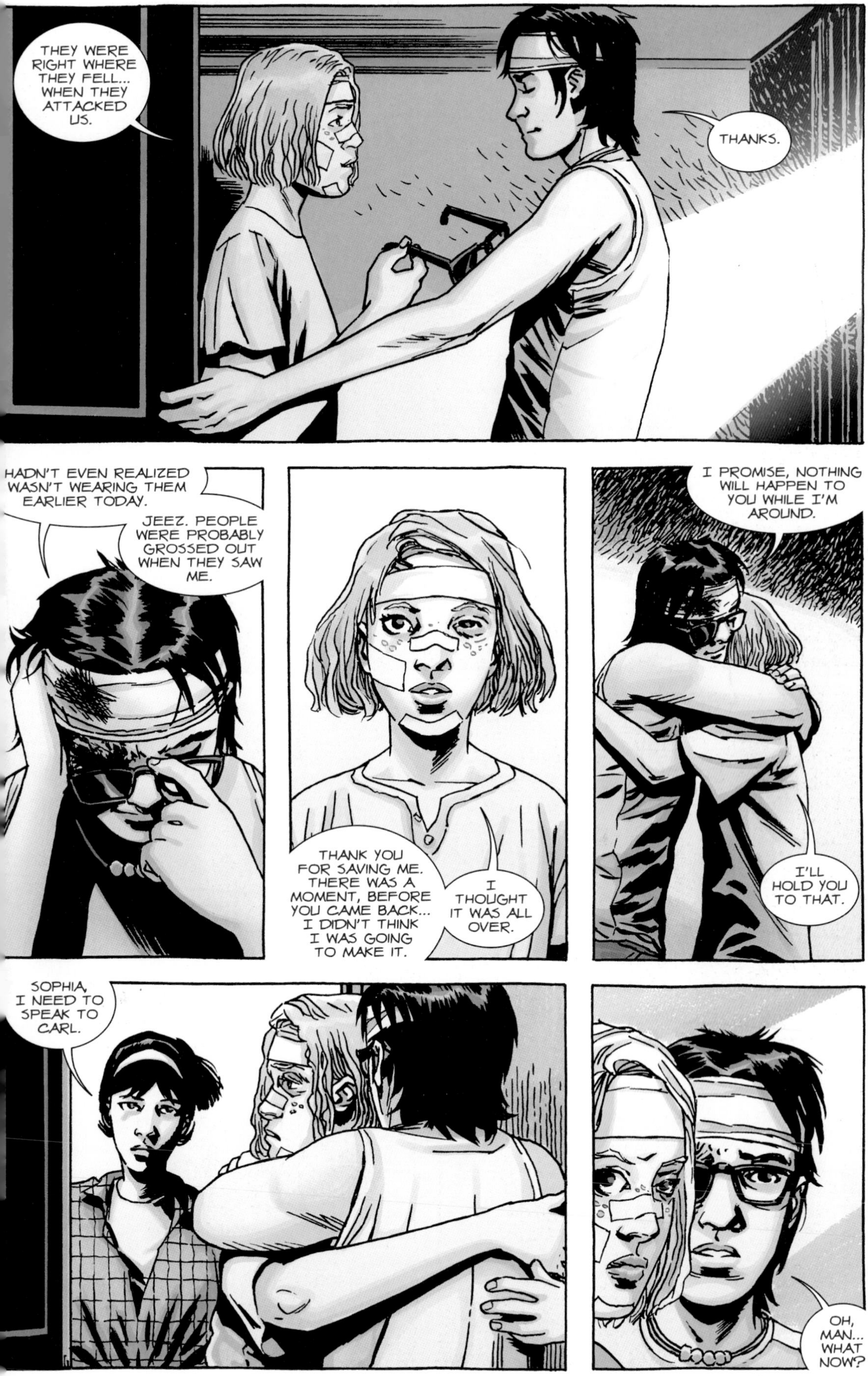
THEY WERE RIGHT WHERE THEY FELL... WHEN THEY ATTACKED US.
THANKS.
HADN'T EVEN REALIZED WASN'T WEARING THEM EARLIER TODAY.
JEEZ. PEOPLE WERE PROBABLY GROSSED OUT WHEN THEY SAW ME.
THANK YOU FOR SAVING ME. THERE WAS A MOMENT, BEFORE YOU CAME BACK... I DIDN'T THINK I WAS GOING TO MAKE IT.
I THOUGHT IT WAS ALL OVER.
I PROMISE, NOTHING WILL HAPPEN TO YOU WHILE I'M AROUND.
I'LL HOLD YOU TO THAT.
SOPHIA, I NEED TO SPEAK TO CARL.
OH, MAN... WHAT NOW?

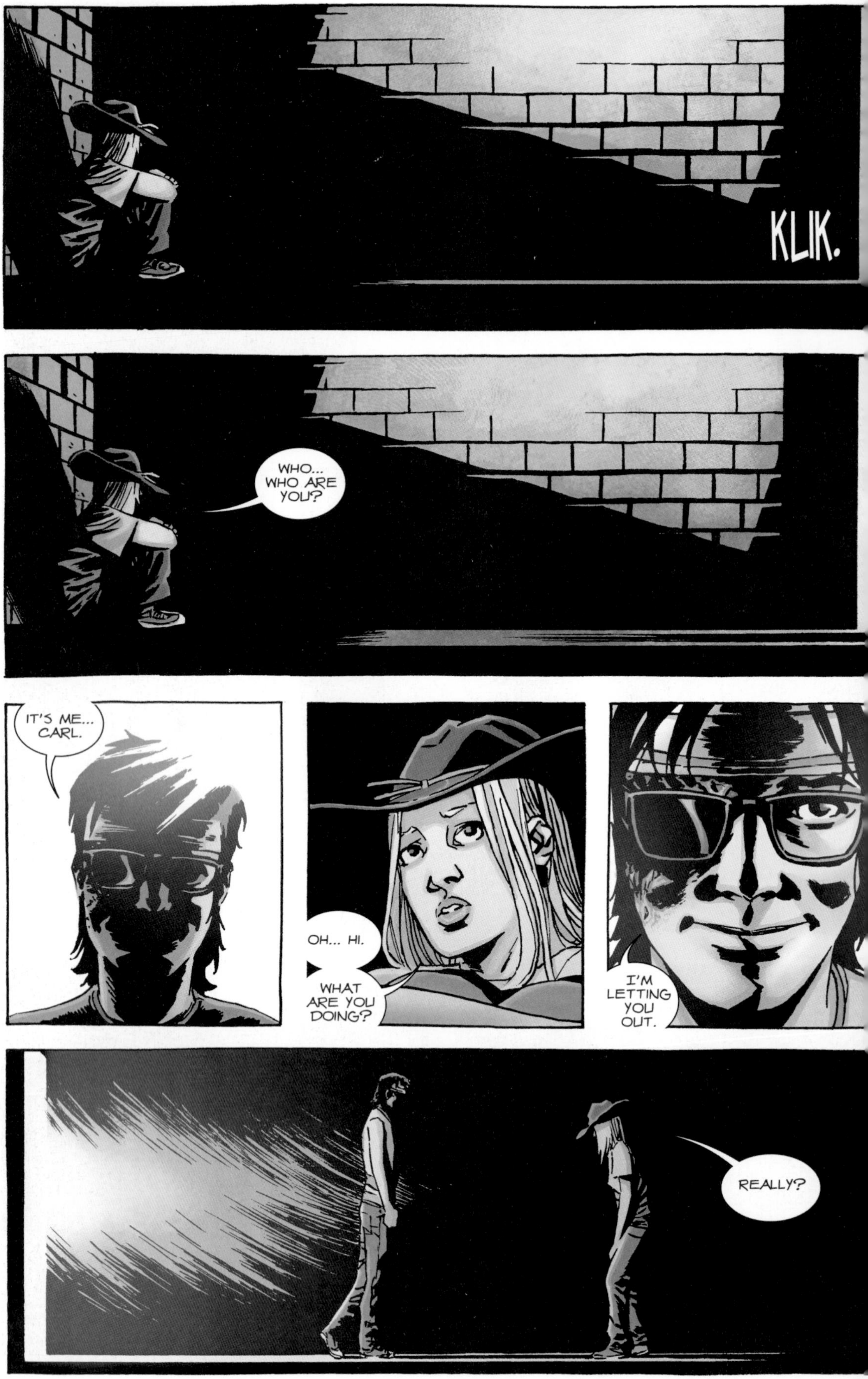
KLIK.
WHO... WHO ARE YOU?
IT'S ME... CARL.
OH... HI.
WHAT ARE YOU DOING?
I'M LETTING YOU OUT.
REALLY?

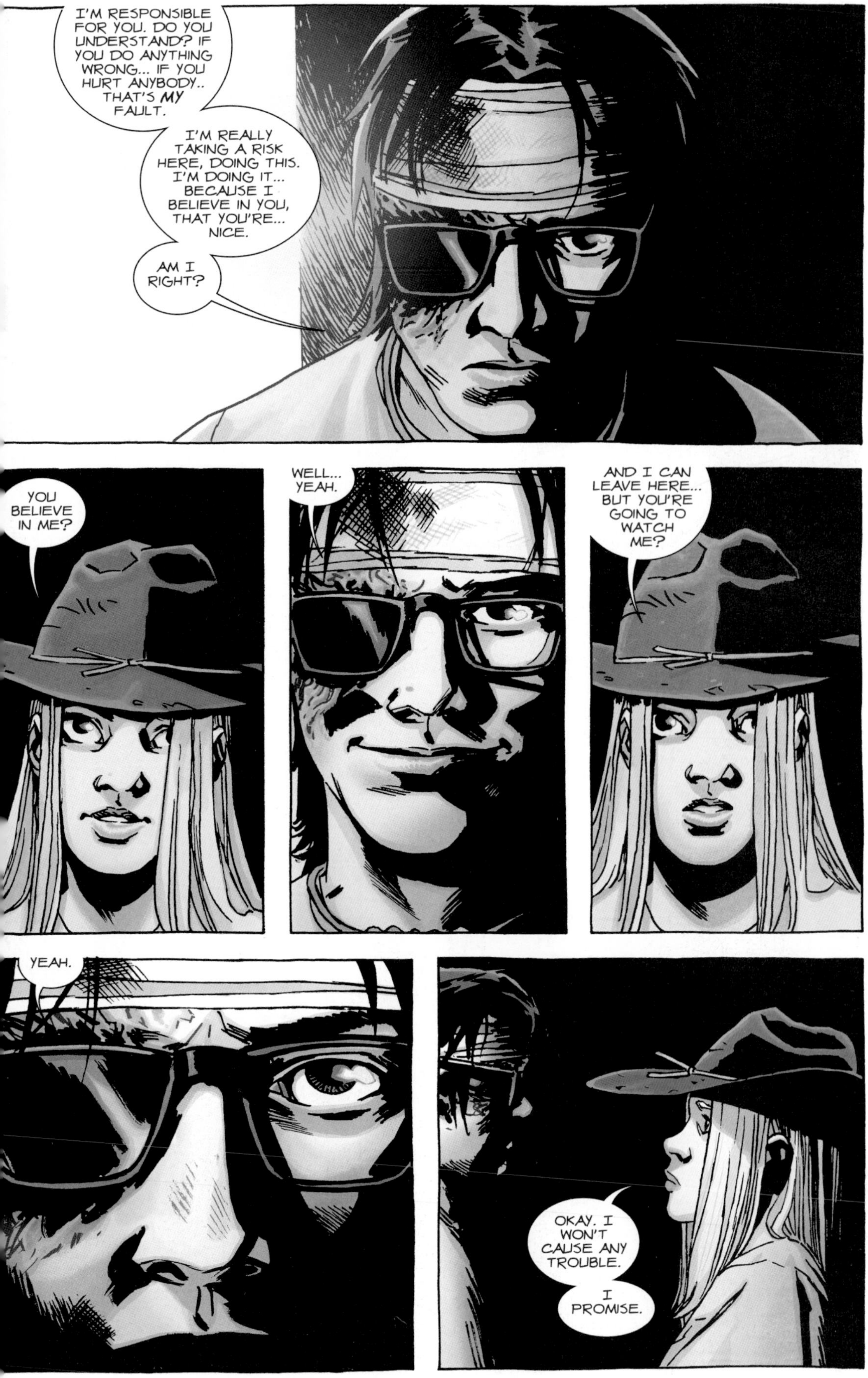
I'M RESPONSIBLE FOR YOU. DO YOU UNDERSTAND? IF YOU DO ANYTHING WRONG... IF YOU HURT ANYBODY.. THAT'S *MY* FAULT.
I'M REALLY TAKING A RISK HERE, DOING THIS. I'M DOING IT... BECAUSE I BELIEVE IN YOU, THAT YOU'RE... NICE.
AM I RIGHT?
YOU BELIEVE IN ME?
WELL... YEAH.
AND I CAN LEAVE HERE... BUT YOU'RE GOING TO WATCH ME?
YEAH.
OKAY. I WON'T CAUSE ANY TROUBLE.
I PROMISE.

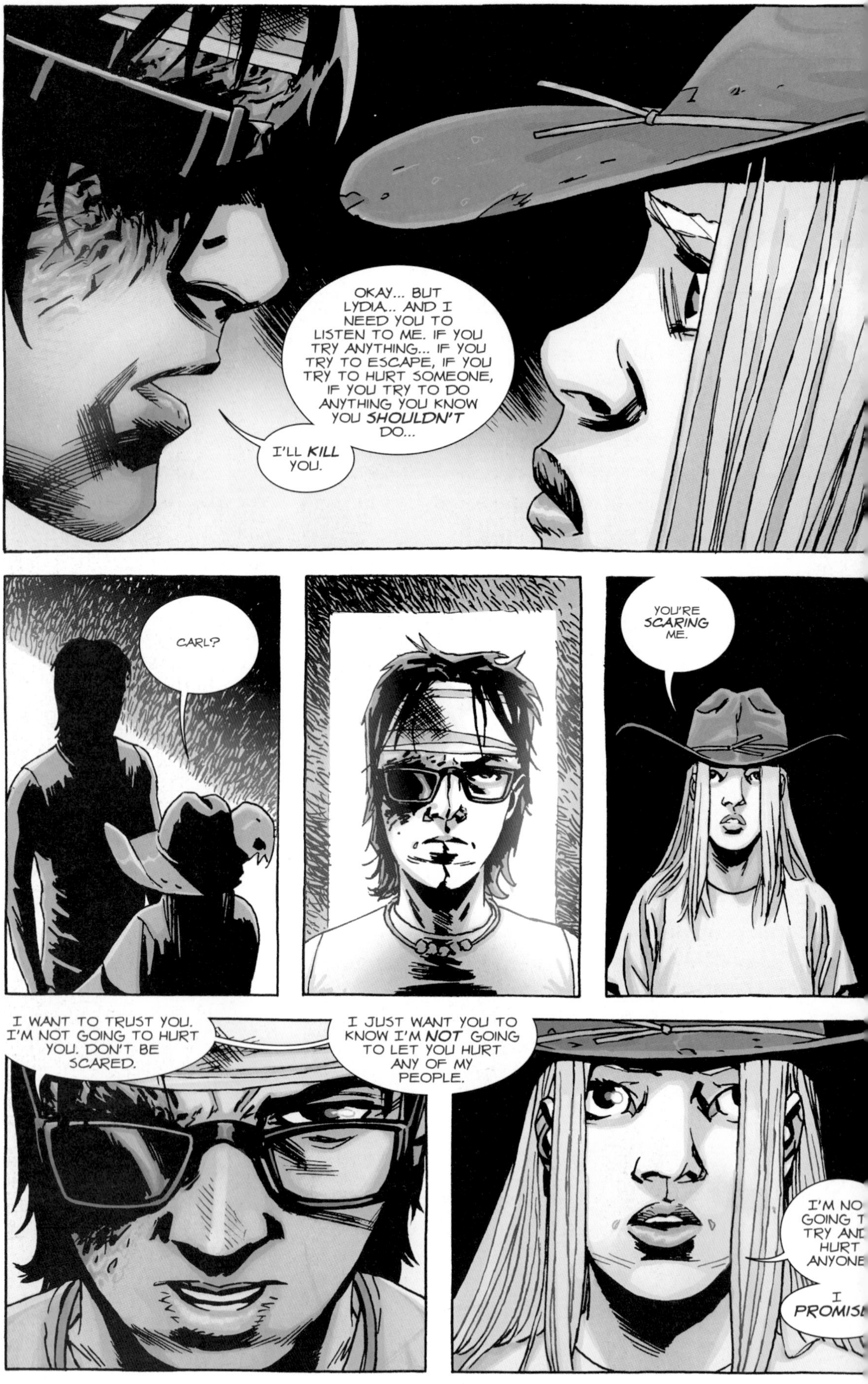
OKAY... BUT LYDIA... AND I NEED YOU TO LISTEN TO ME. IF YOU TRY ANYTHING... IF YOU TRY TO ESCAPE, IF YOU TRY TO HURT SOMEONE, IF YOU TRY TO DO ANYTHING YOU KNOW YOU SHOULDN'T DO...
I'LL KILL YOU.
CARL?
YOU'RE SCARING ME.
I WANT TO TRUST YOU. I'M NOT GOING TO HURT YOU. DON'T BE SCARED.
I JUST WANT YOU TO KNOW I'M NOT GOING TO LET YOU HURT ANY OF MY PEOPLE.
I'M NO GOING T TRY AN HURT ANYONE
I PROMIS

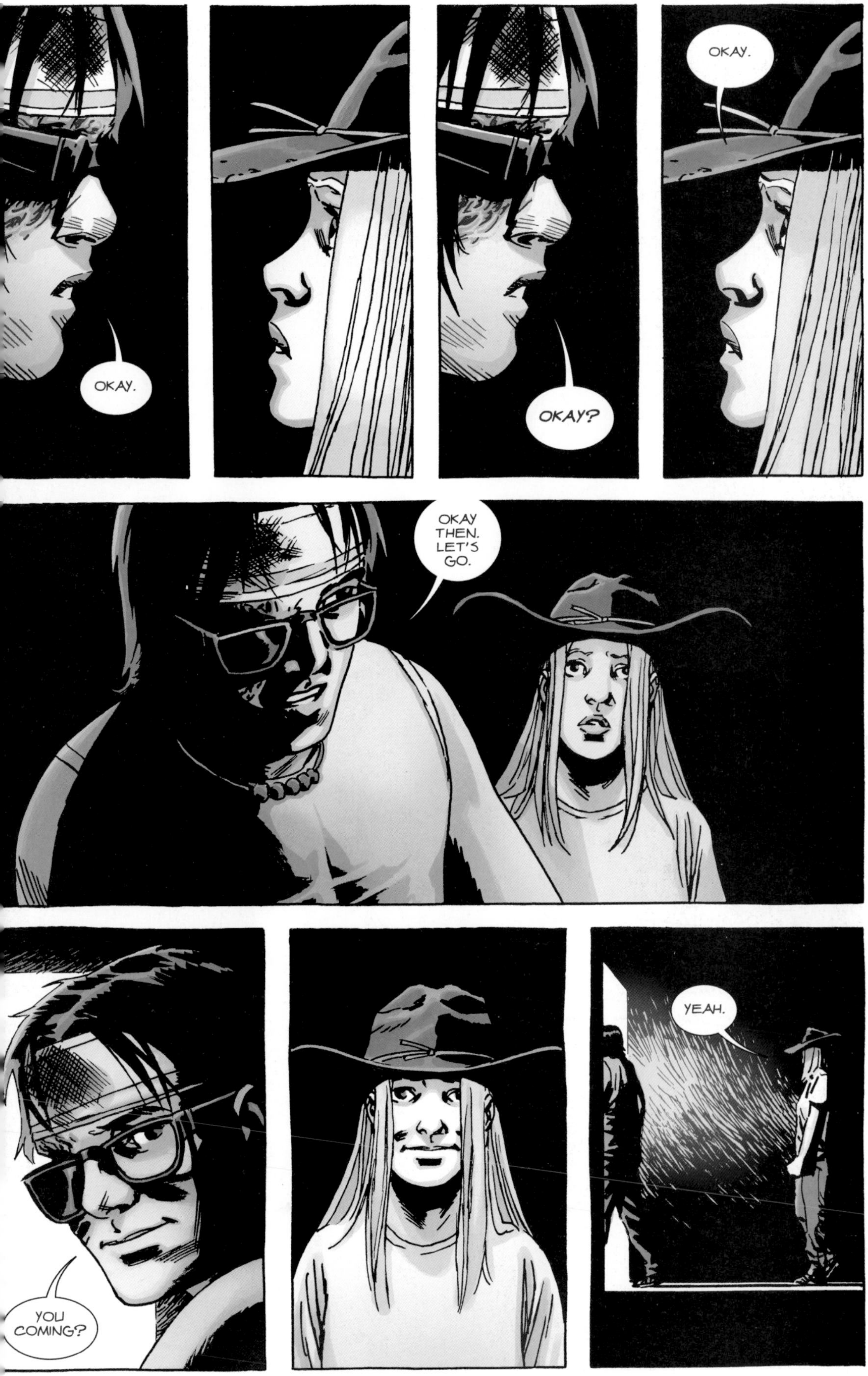
OKAY.
OKAY?
OKAY.
OKAY THEN. LET'S GO.
YOU COMING?
YEAH.

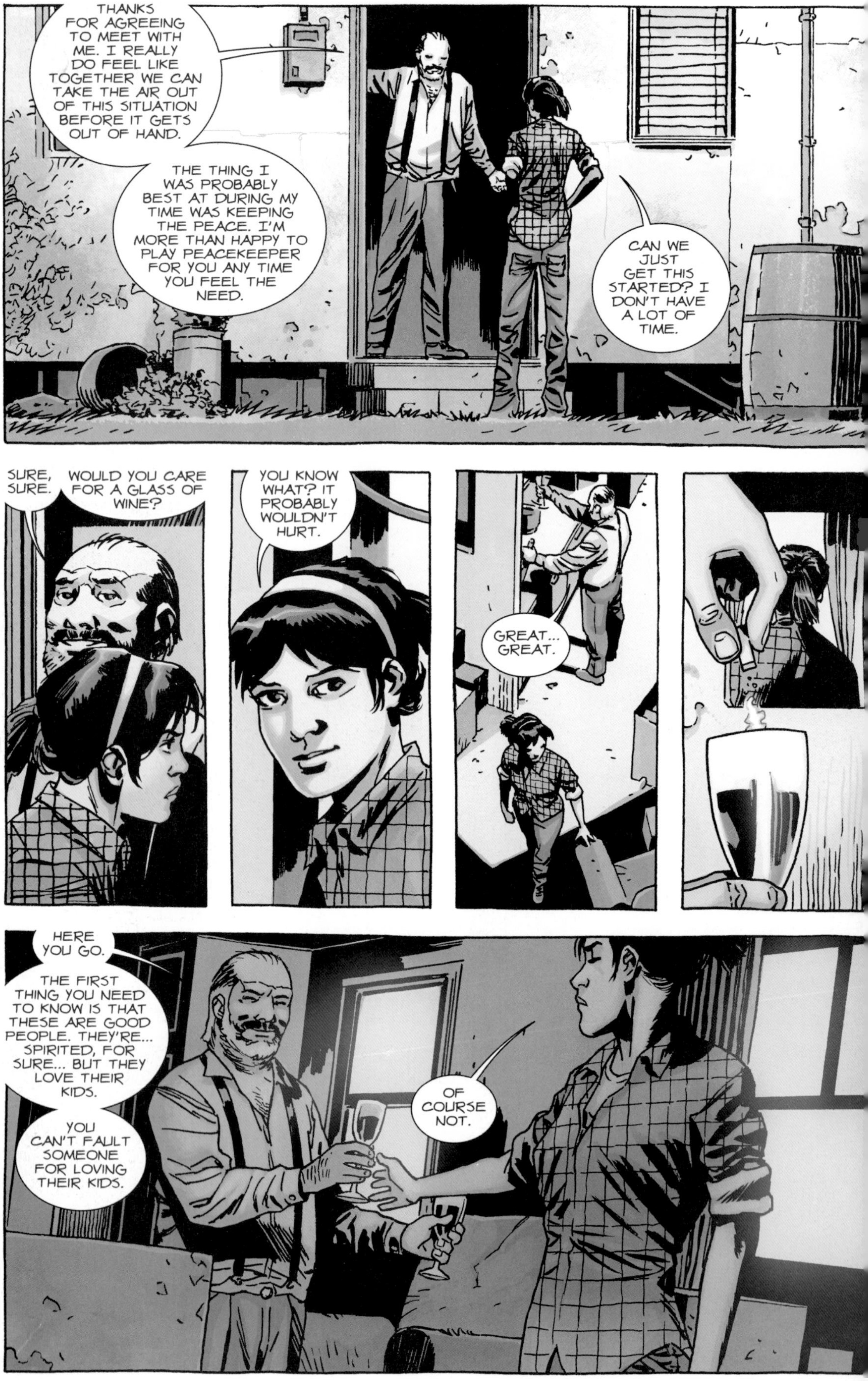
THANKS FOR AGREEING TO MEET WITH ME. I REALLY DO FEEL LIKE TOGETHER WE CAN TAKE THE AIR OUT OF THIS SITUATION BEFORE IT GETS OUT OF HAND.
THE THING I WAS PROBABLY BEST AT DURING MY TIME WAS KEEPING THE PEACE. I'M MORE THAN HAPPY TO PLAY PEACEKEEPER FOR YOU ANY TIME YOU FEEL THE NEED.
CAN WE JUST GET THIS STARTED? I DON'T HAVE A LOT OF TIME.
SURE, SURE.
WOULD YOU CARE FOR A GLASS OF WINE?
YOU KNOW WHAT? IT PROBABLY WOULDN'T HURT.
GREAT... GREAT.
HERE YOU GO.
THE FIRST THING YOU NEED TO KNOW IS THAT THESE ARE GOOD PEOPLE. THEY'RE... SPIRITED, FOR SURE... BUT THEY LOVE THEIR KIDS.
YOU CAN'T FAULT SOMEONE FOR LOVING THEIR KIDS.
OF COURSE NOT.

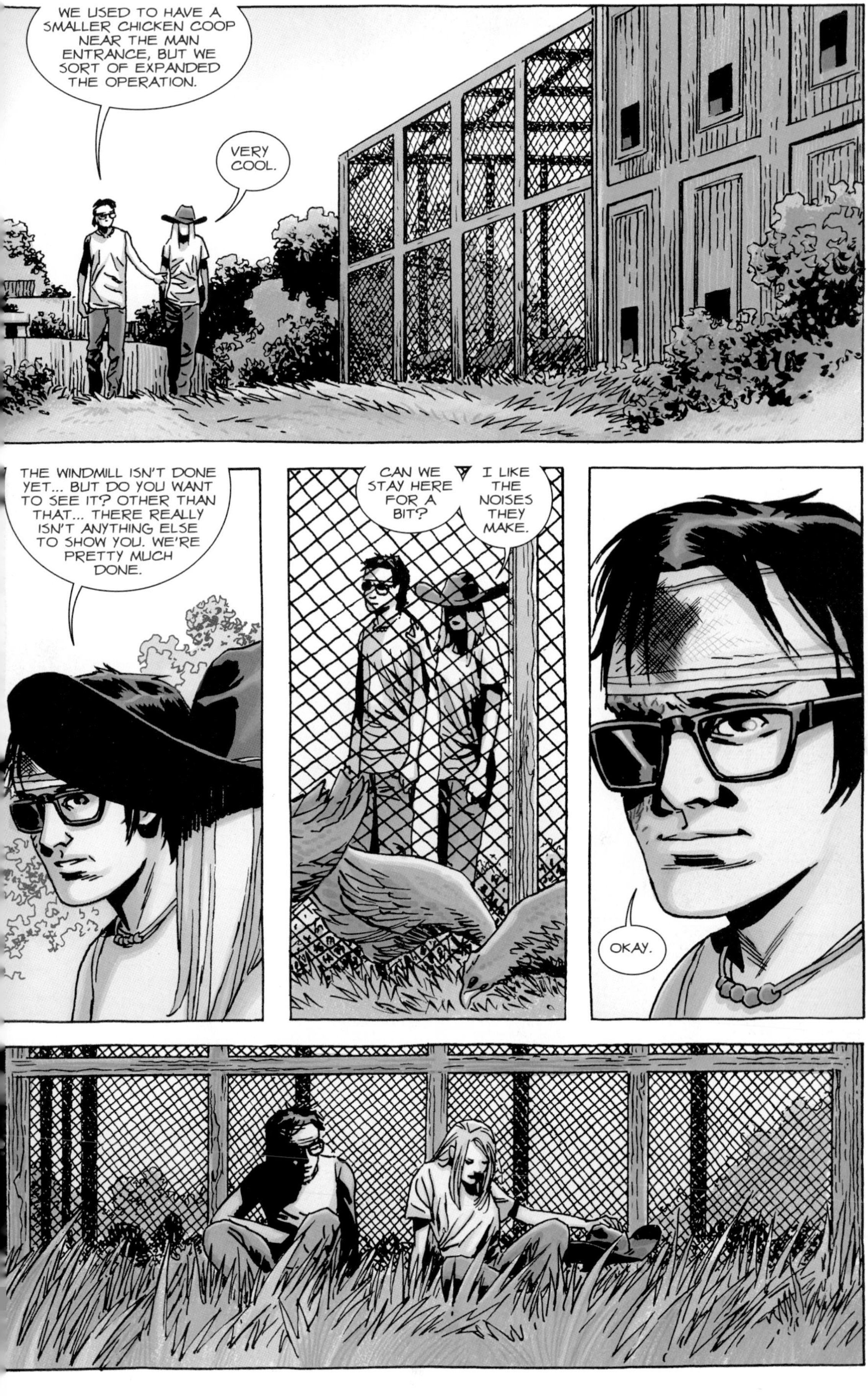
WE USED TO HAVE A SMALLER CHICKEN COOP NEAR THE MAIN ENTRANCE, BUT WE SORT OF EXPANDED THE OPERATION.
VERY COOL.
THE WINDMILL ISN'T DONE YET... BUT DO YOU WANT TO SEE IT? OTHER THAN THAT... THERE REALLY ISN'T ANYTHING ELSE TO SHOW YOU. WE'RE PRETTY MUCH DONE.
CAN WE STAY HERE FOR A BIT?
I LIKE THE NOISES THEY MAKE.
OKAY.

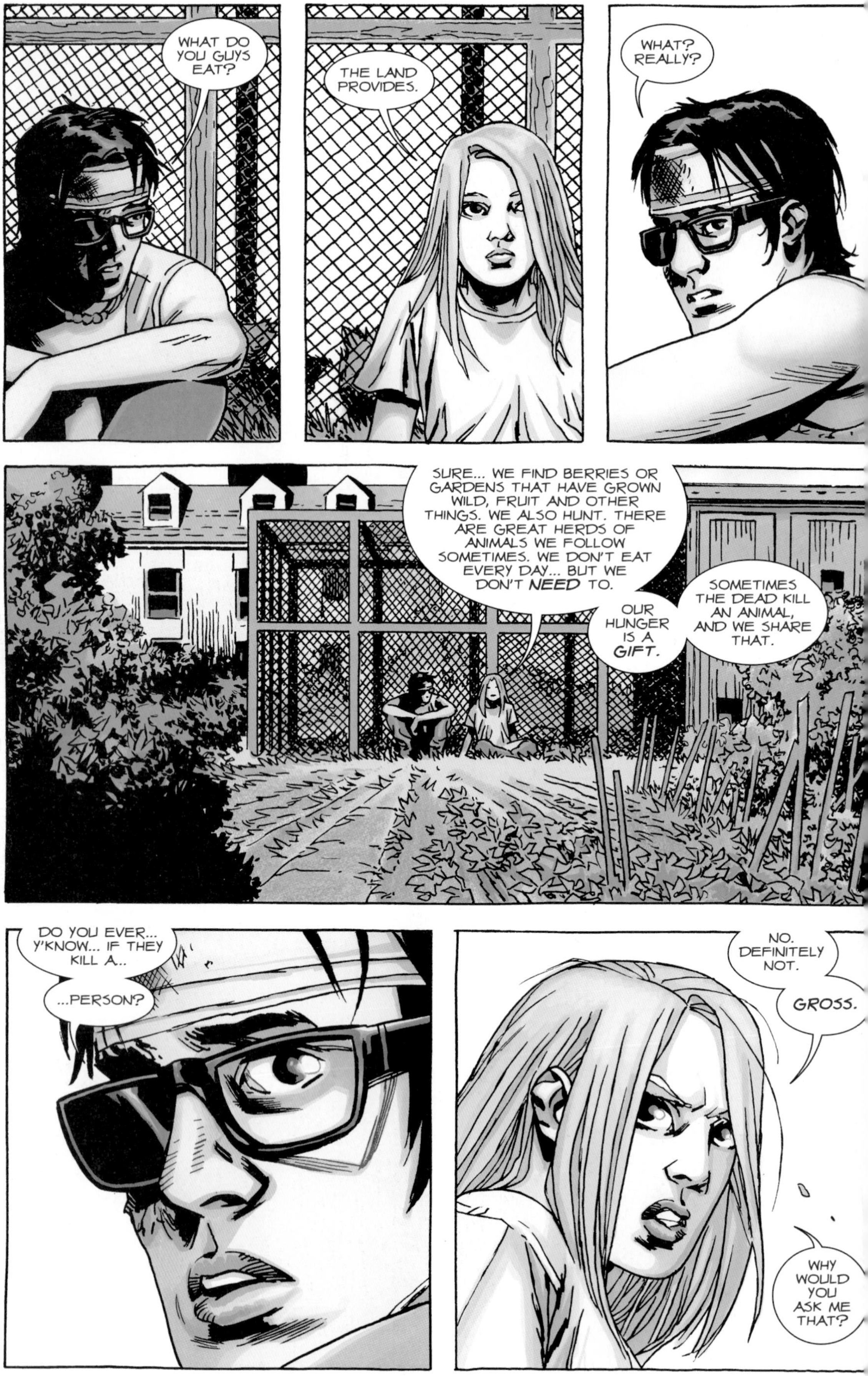
WHAT DO YOU GUYS EAT?
THE LAND PROVIDES.
WHAT? REALLY?
SURE... WE FIND BERRIES OR GARDENS THAT HAVE GROWN WILD, FRUIT AND OTHER THINGS. WE ALSO HUNT. THERE ARE GREAT HERDS OF ANIMALS WE FOLLOW SOMETIMES. WE DON'T EAT EVERY DAY... BUT WE DON'T NEED TO.
OUR HUNGER IS A GIFT.
SOMETIMES THE DEAD KILL AN ANIMAL, AND WE SHARE THAT.
DO YOU EVER... Y'KNOW... IF THEY KILL A..
...PERSON?
NO. DEFINITELY NOT.
GROSS.
WHY WOULD YOU ASK ME THAT?

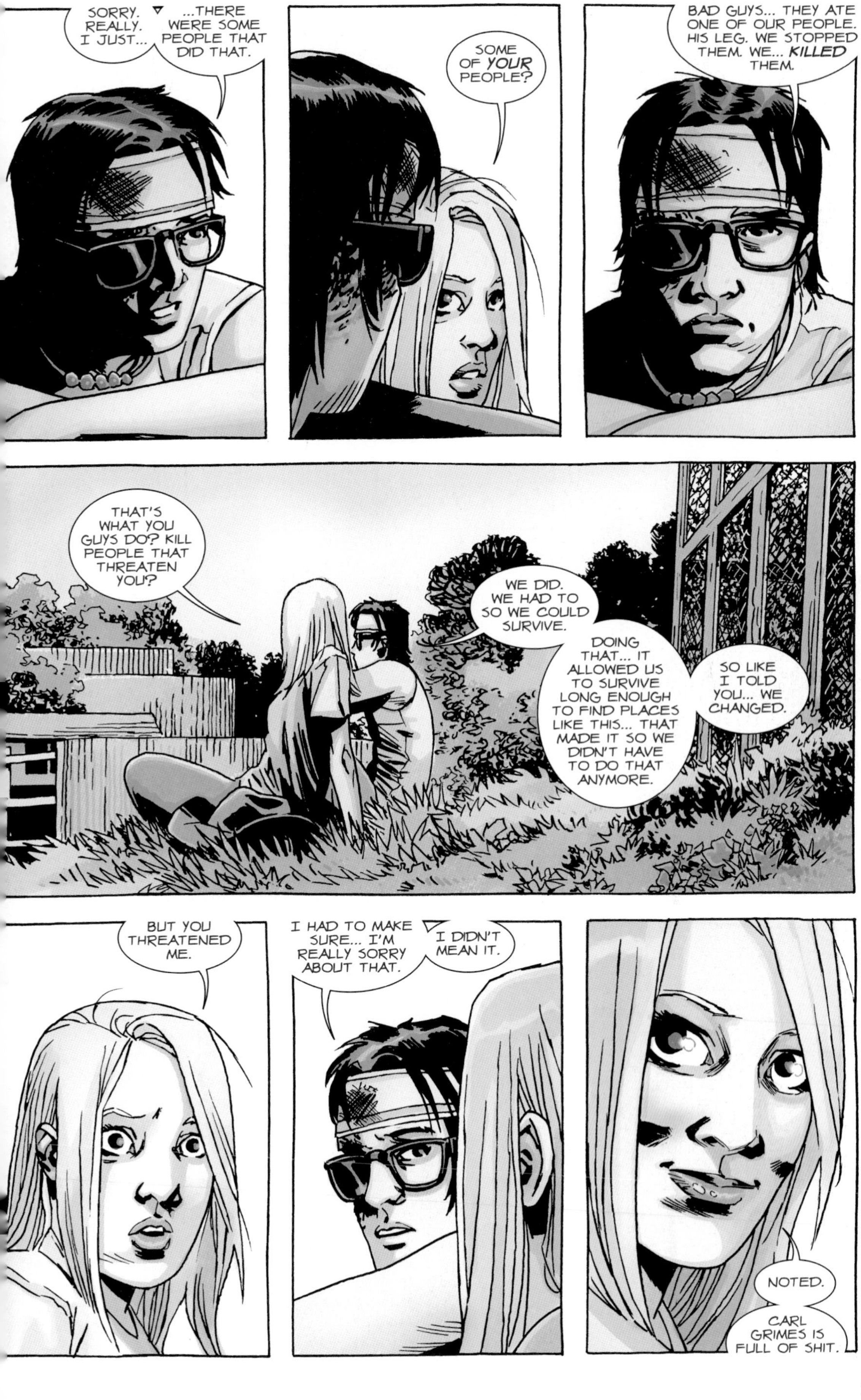
SORRY. REALLY. I JUST...
...THERE WERE SOME PEOPLE THAT DID THAT.
SOME OF *YOUR* PEOPLE?
BAD GUYS... THEY ATE ONE OF OUR PEOPLE. HIS LEG. WE STOPPED THEM. WE... ***KILLED*** THEM.
THAT'S WHAT YOU GUYS DO? KILL PEOPLE THAT THREATEN YOU?
WE DID. WE HAD TO SO WE COULD SURVIVE.
DOING THAT... IT ALLOWED US TO SURVIVE LONG ENOUGH TO FIND PLACES LIKE THIS... THAT MADE IT SO WE DIDN'T HAVE TO DO THAT ANYMORE.
SO LIKE I TOLD YOU... WE CHANGED.
BUT YOU THREATENED ME.
I HAD TO MAKE SURE... I'M REALLY SORRY ABOUT THAT.
I DIDN'T MEAN IT.
NOTED.
CARL GRIMES IS FULL OF SHIT.

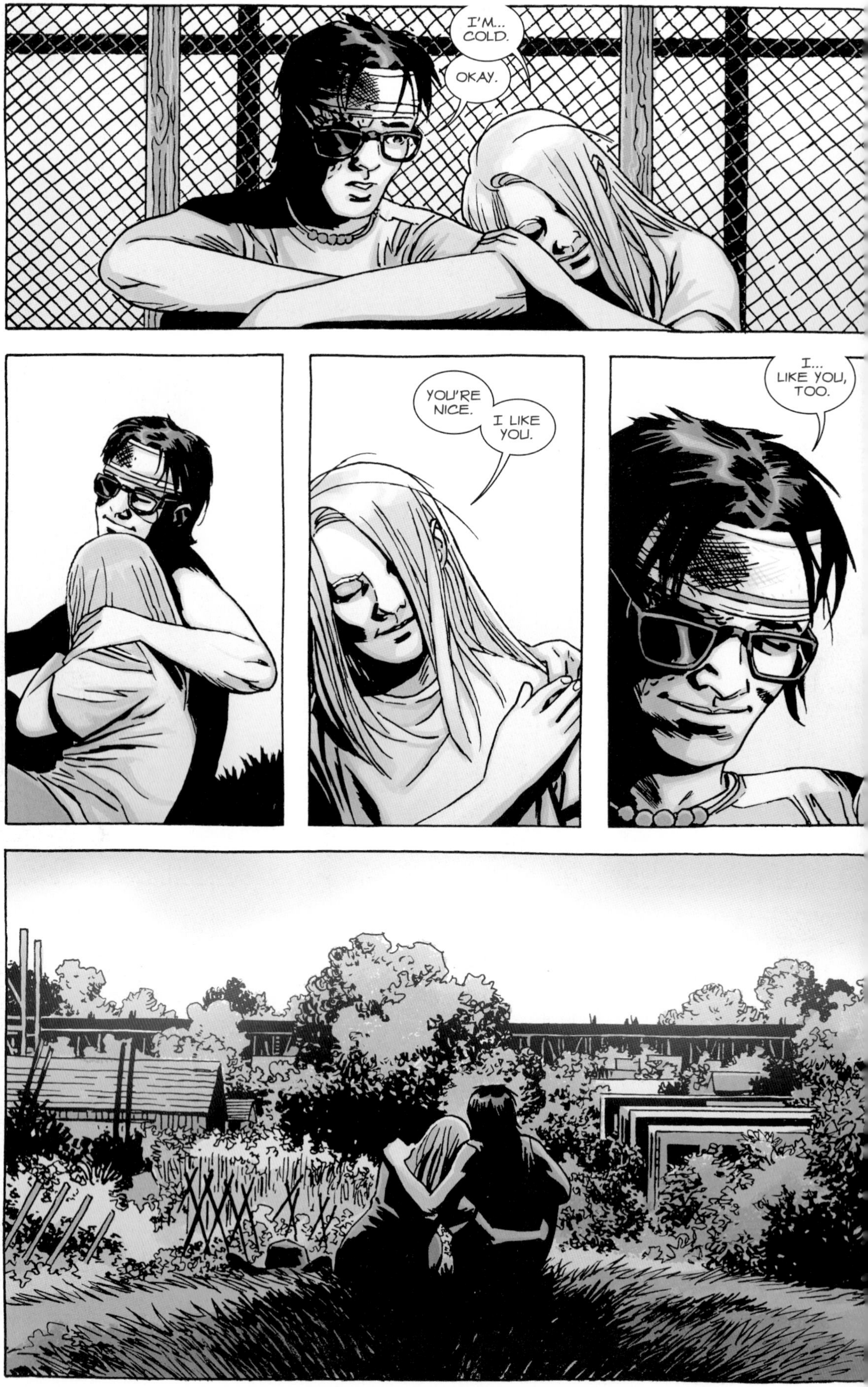
I'M... COLD.
OKAY.
YOU'RE NICE.
I LIKE YOU.
I... LIKE YOU, TOO.

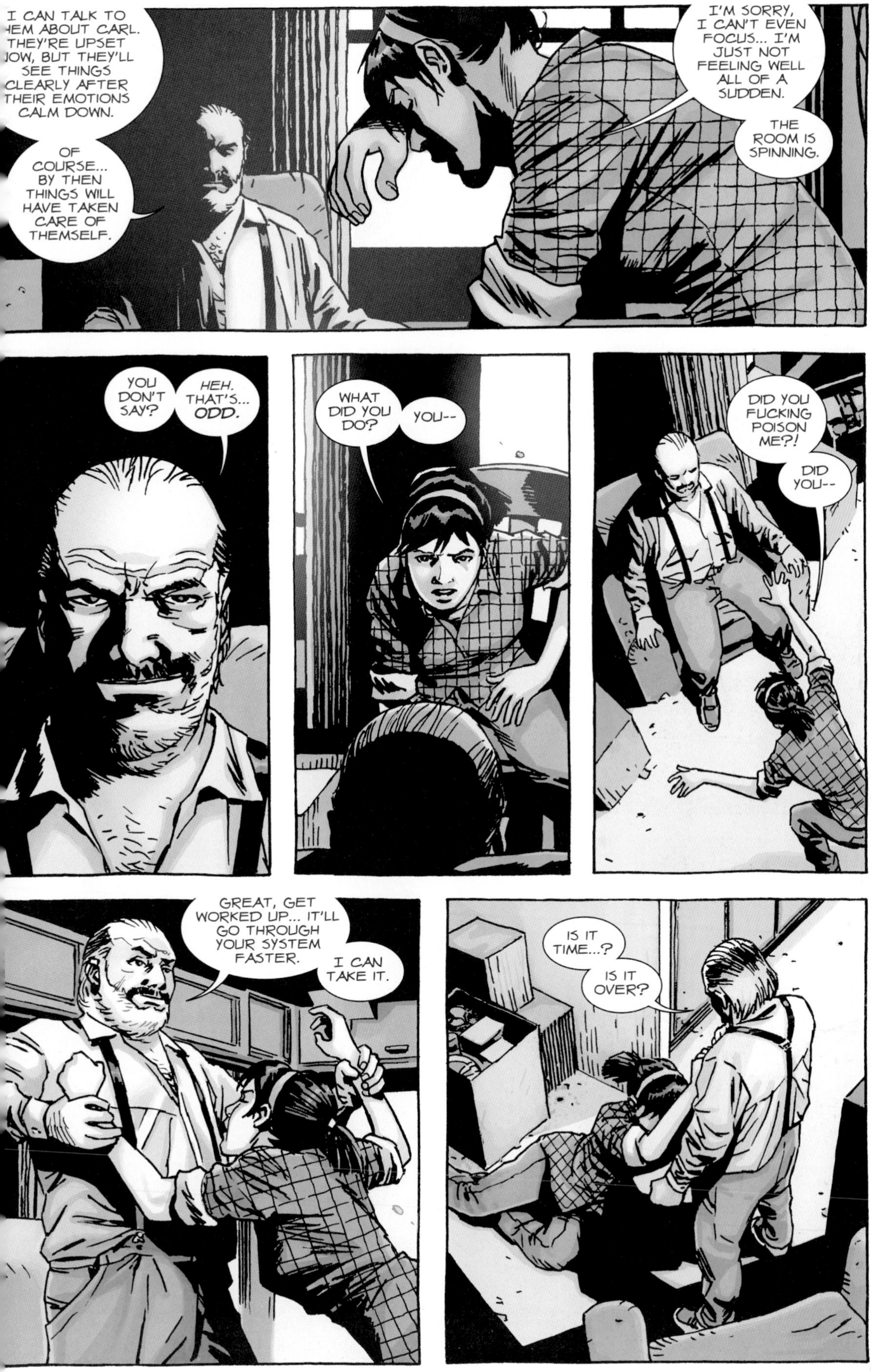
I CAN TALK TO HEM ABOUT CARL. THEY'RE UPSET OW, BUT THEY'LL SEE THINGS CLEARLY AFTER THEIR EMOTIONS CALM DOWN.
I'M SORRY, I CAN'T EVEN FOCUS... I'M JUST NOT FEELING WELL ALL OF A SUDDEN.
THE ROOM IS SPINNING.
OF COURSE... BY THEN THINGS WILL HAVE TAKEN CARE OF THEMSELF.
YOU DON'T SAY?
HEH. THAT'S... ODD.
WHAT DID YOU DO?
YOU--
DID YOU FUCKING POISON ME?!
DID YOU--
GREAT, GET WORKED UP... IT'LL GO THROUGH YOUR SYSTEM FASTER.
I CAN TAKE IT.
IS IT TIME...?
IS IT OVER?

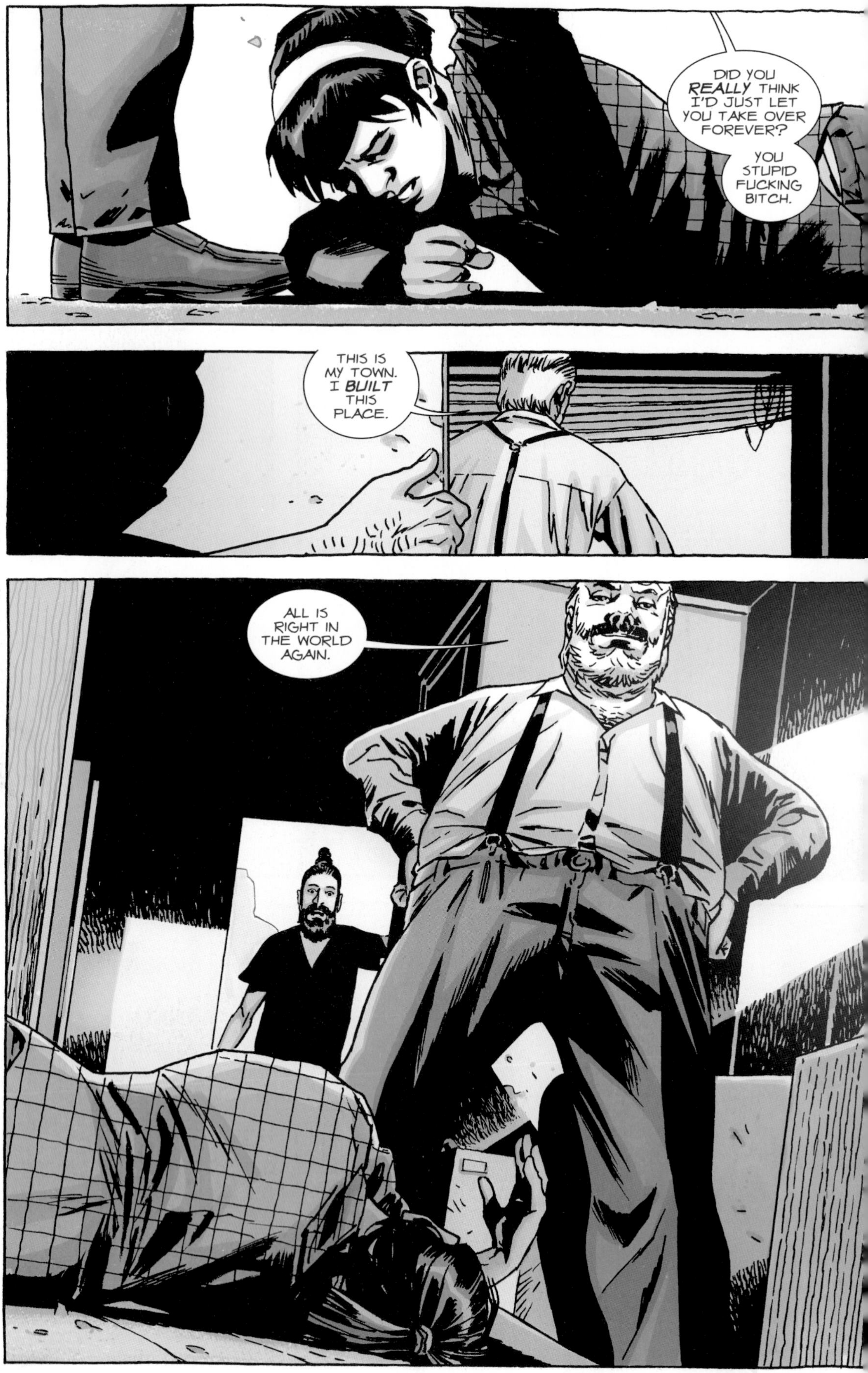
DID YOU REALLY THINK I'D JUST LET YOU TAKE OVER FOREVER?
YOU STUPID FUCKING BITCH.
THIS IS MY TOWN. I BUILT THIS PLACE.
ALL IS RIGHT IN THE WORLD AGAIN.

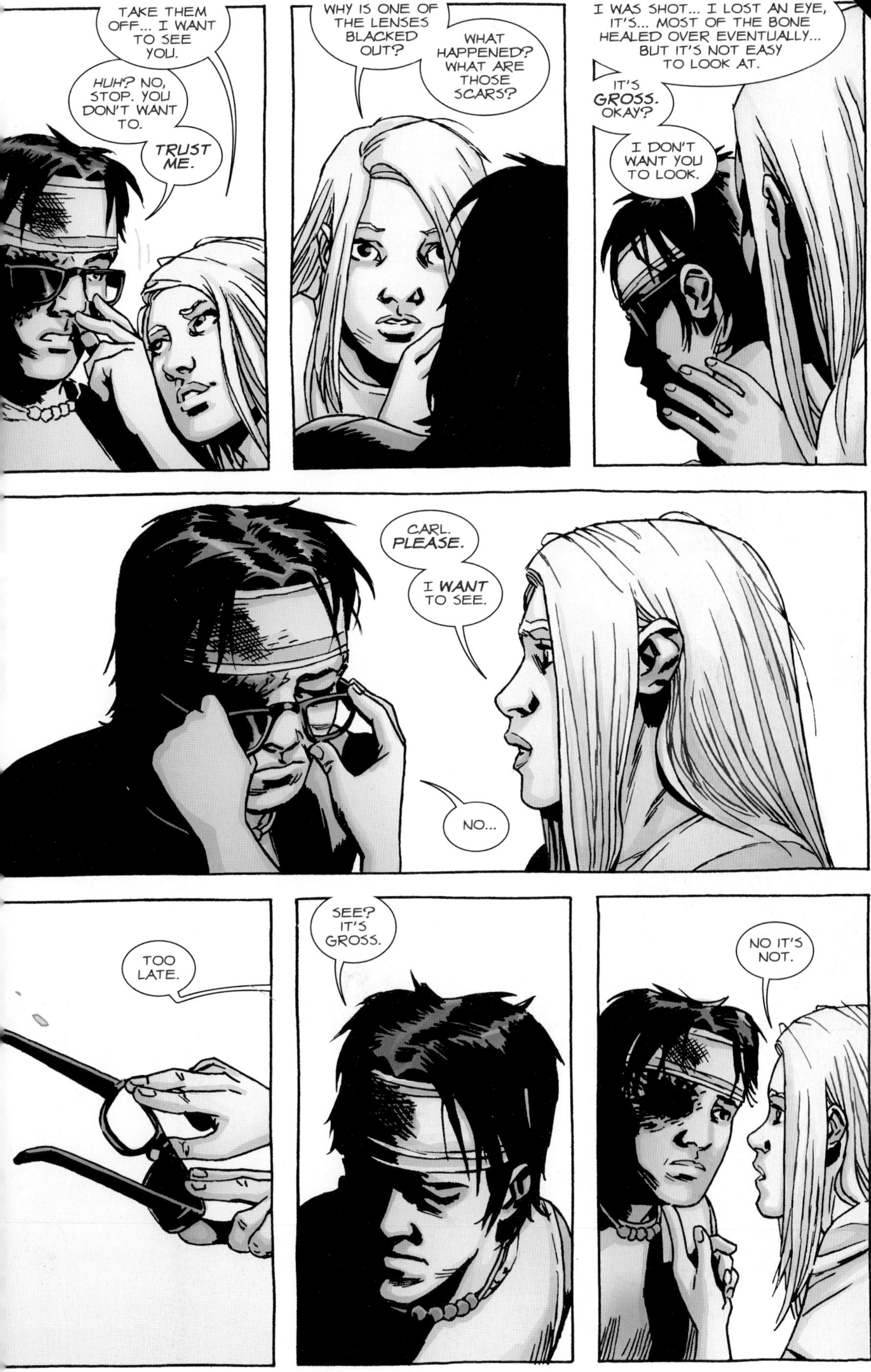
TAKE THEM OFF... I WANT TO SEE YOU.
HUH? NO, STOP. YOU DON'T WANT TO.
TRUST ME.
WHY IS ONE OF THE LENSES BLACKED OUT?
WHAT HAPPENED? WHAT ARE THOSE SCARS?
I WAS SHOT... I LOST AN EYE, IT'S... MOST OF THE BONE HEALED OVER EVENTUALLY... BUT IT'S NOT EASY TO LOOK AT.
IT'S GROSS. OKAY?
I DON'T WANT YOU TO LOOK.
CARL. PLEASE.
I WANT TO SEE.
NO...
TOO LATE.
SEE? IT'S GROSS.
NO IT'S NOT.

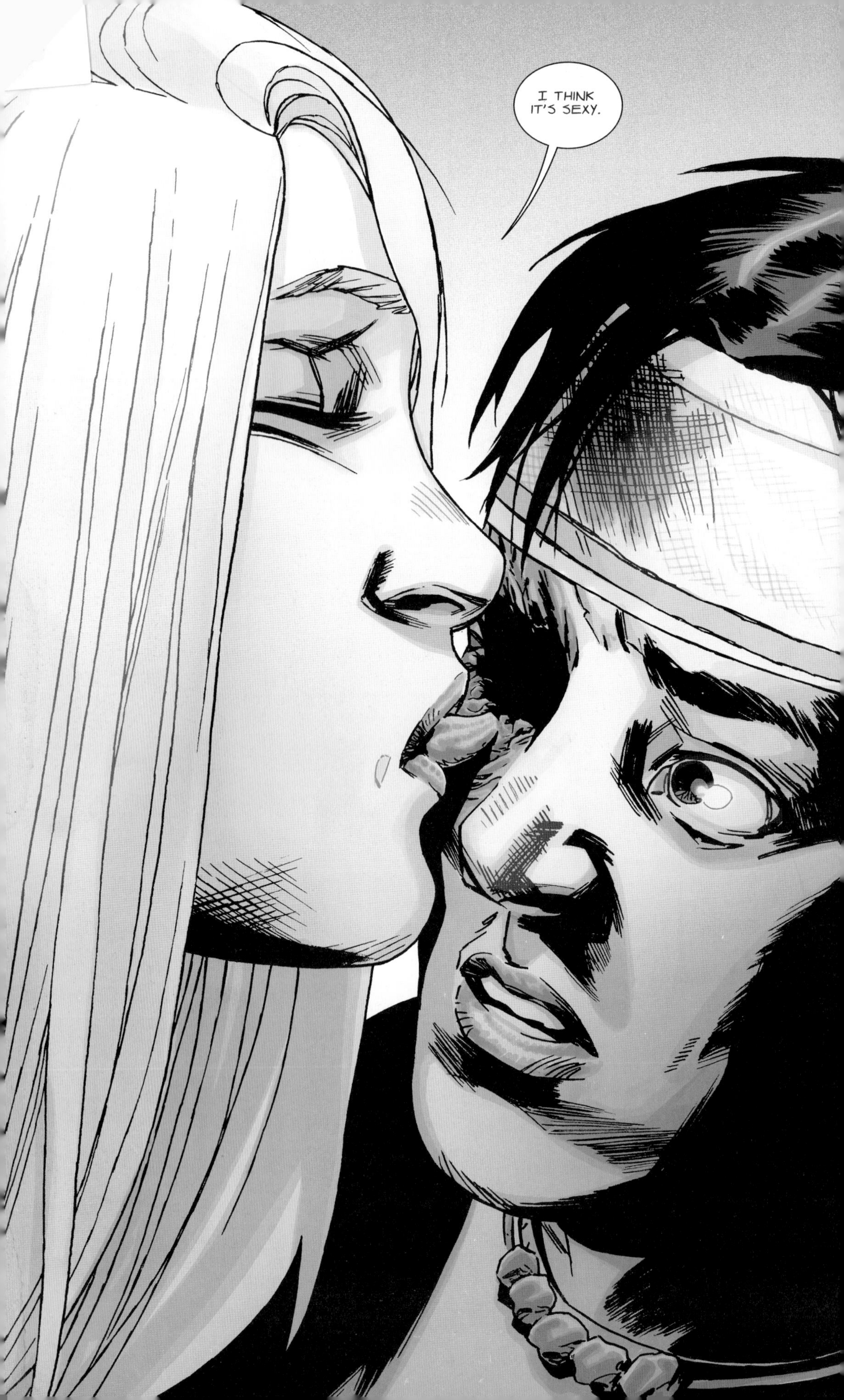
I THINK IT'S SEXY.

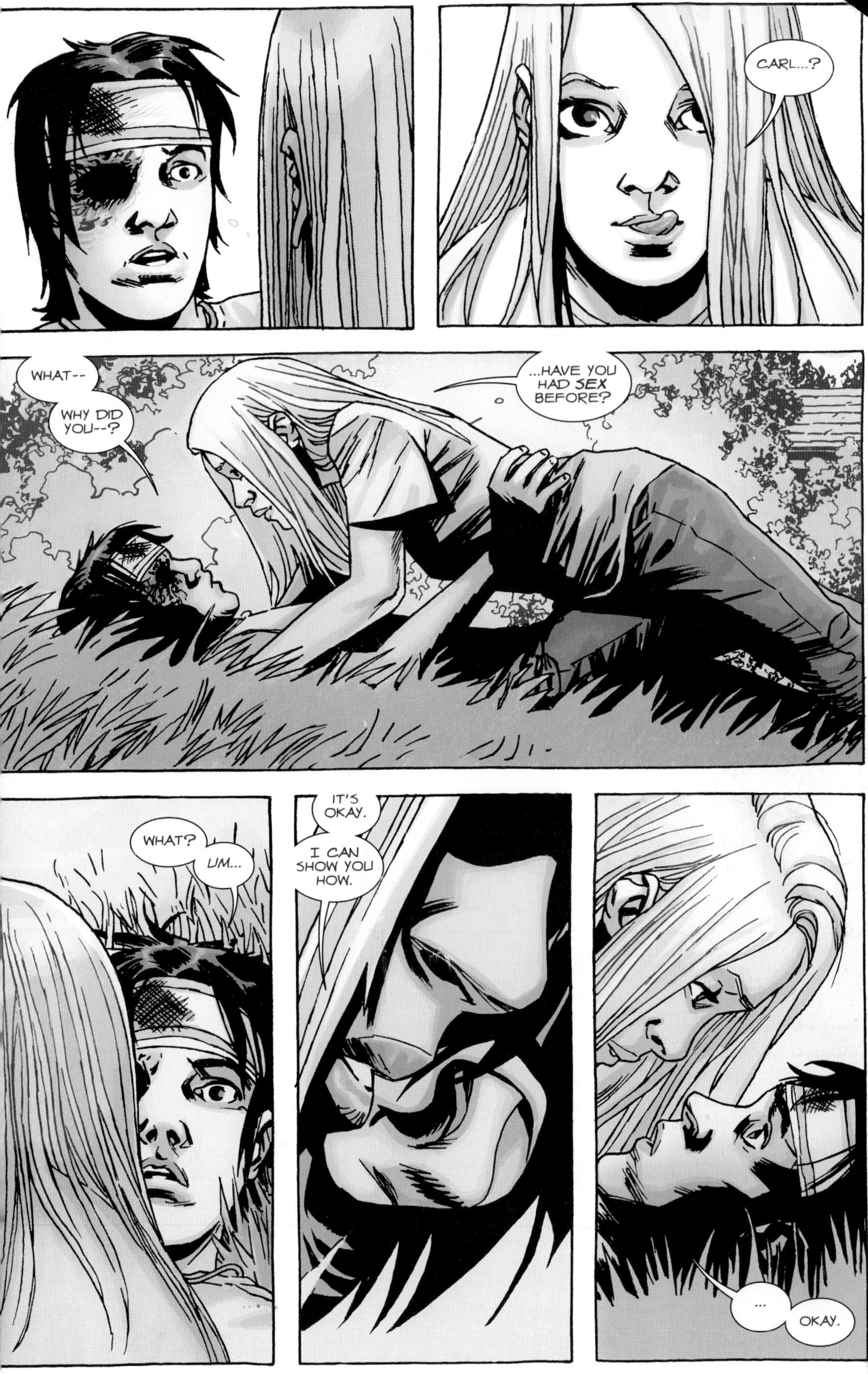
CARL...?
WHAT--
WHY DID YOU--?
...HAVE YOU HAD SEX BEFORE?
WHAT?
UM...
IT'S OKAY.
I CAN SHOW YOU HOW.
...
OKAY.

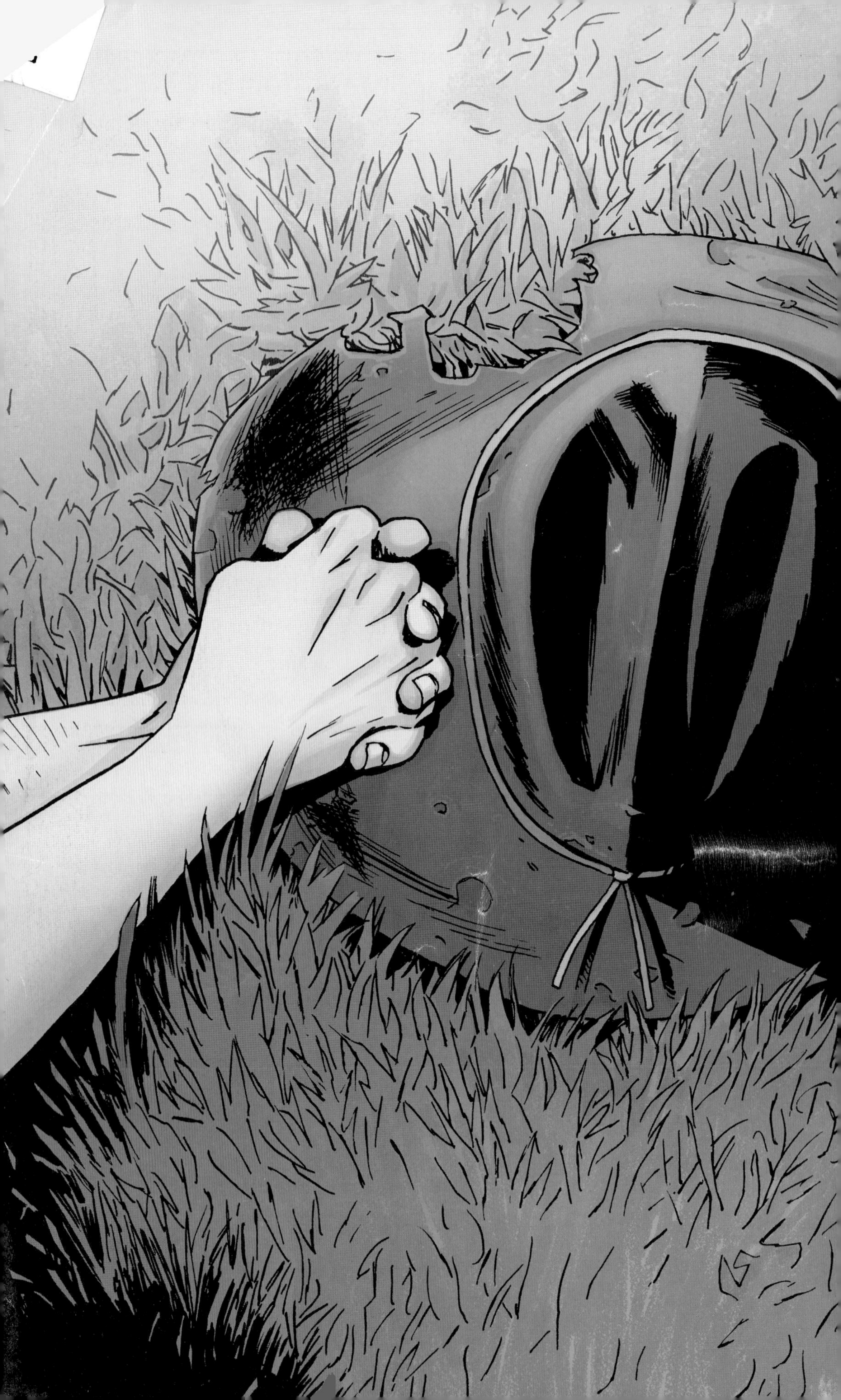

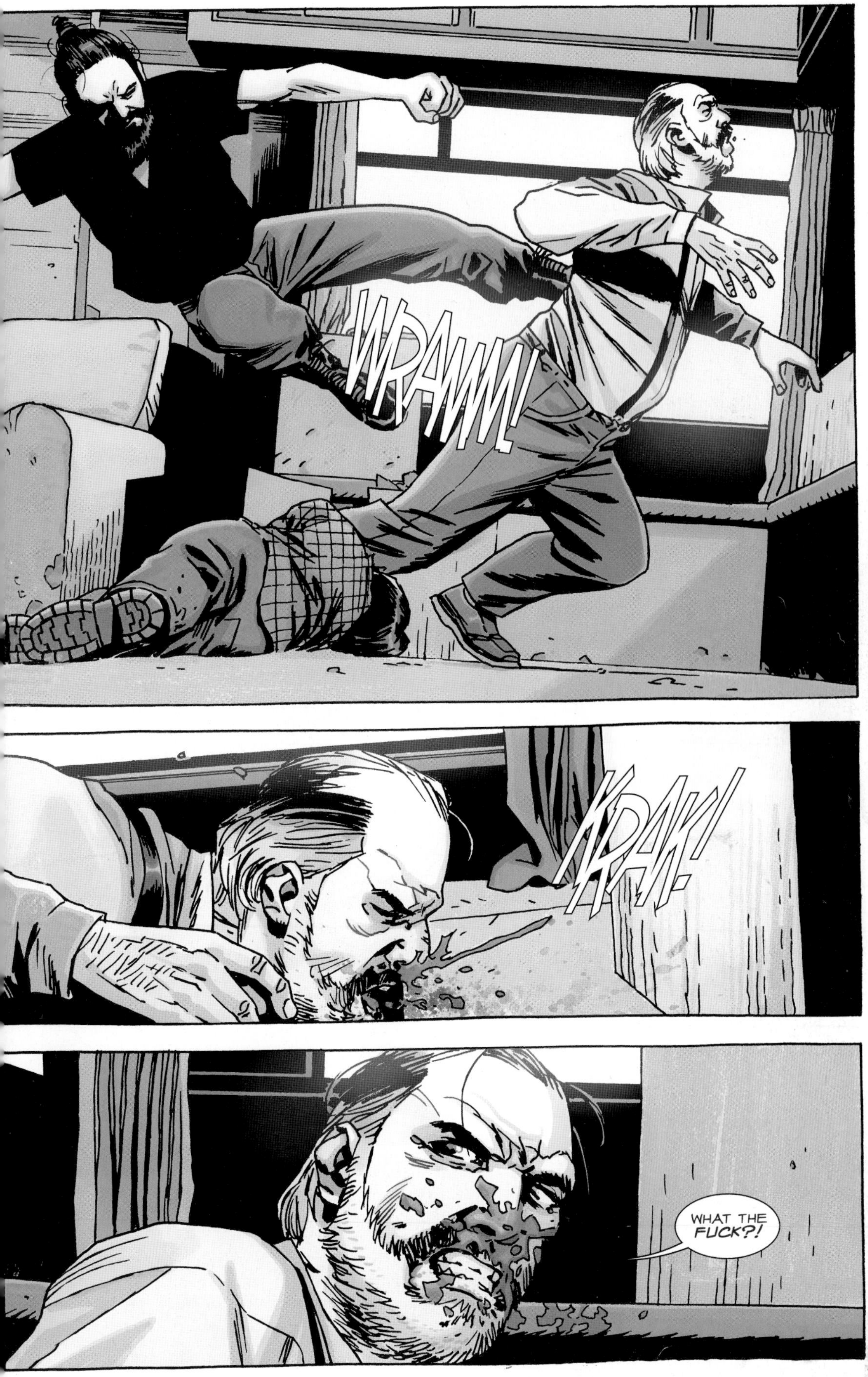
WRAMM!
KRAK!
WHAT THE FUCK?!

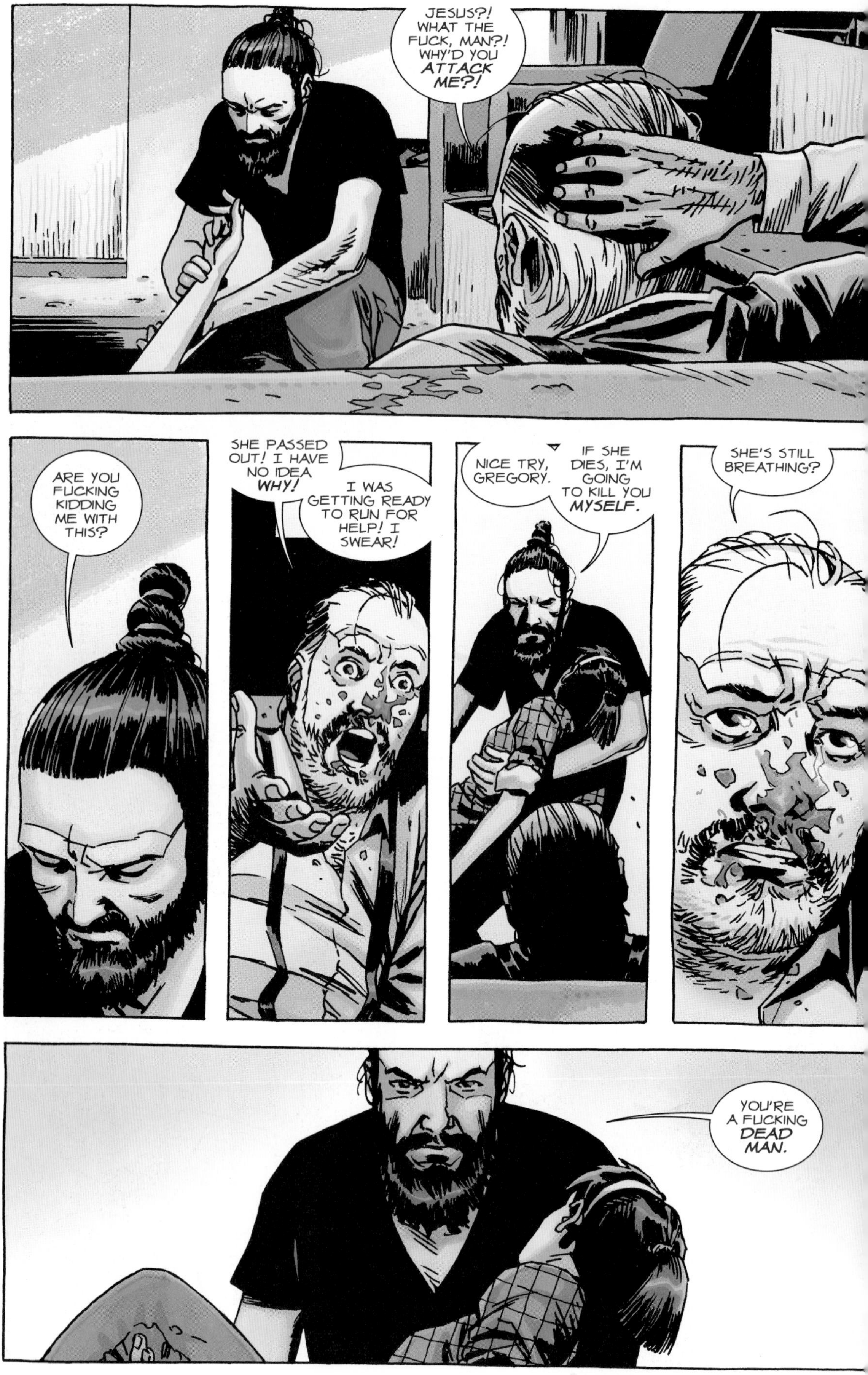
JESUS?! WHAT THE FUCK, MAN?! WHY'D YOU ATTACK ME?!
ARE YOU FUCKING KIDDING ME WITH THIS?
SHE PASSED OUT! I HAVE NO IDEA WHY!
I WAS GETTING READY TO RUN FOR HELP! I SWEAR!
NICE TRY, GREGORY.
IF SHE DIES, I'M GOING TO KILL YOU MYSELF.
SHE'S STILL BREATHING?
YOU'RE A FUCKING DEAD MAN.

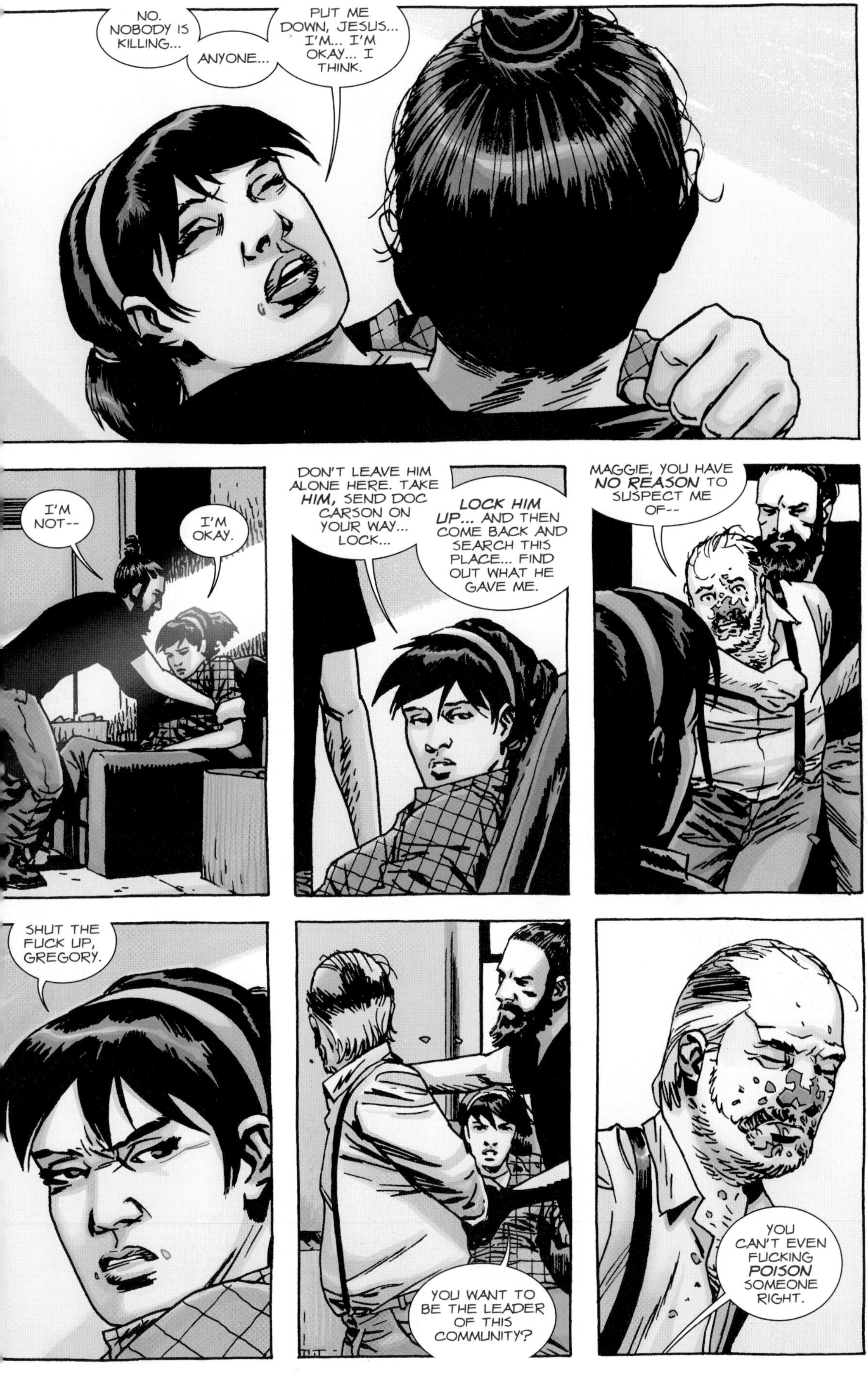
NO. NOBODY IS KILLING...
ANYONE...
PUT ME DOWN, JESUS... I'M... I'M OKAY... I THINK.
I'M NOT--
I'M OKAY.
DON'T LEAVE HIM ALONE HERE. TAKE HIM, SEND DOC CARSON ON YOUR WAY... LOCK...
LOCK HIM UP... AND THEN COME BACK AND SEARCH THIS PLACE... FIND OUT WHAT HE GAVE ME.
MAGGIE, YOU HAVE NO REASON TO SUSPECT ME OF--
SHUT THE FUCK UP, GREGORY.
YOU WANT TO BE THE LEADER OF THIS COMMUNITY?
YOU CAN'T EVEN FUCKING POISON SOMEONE RIGHT.

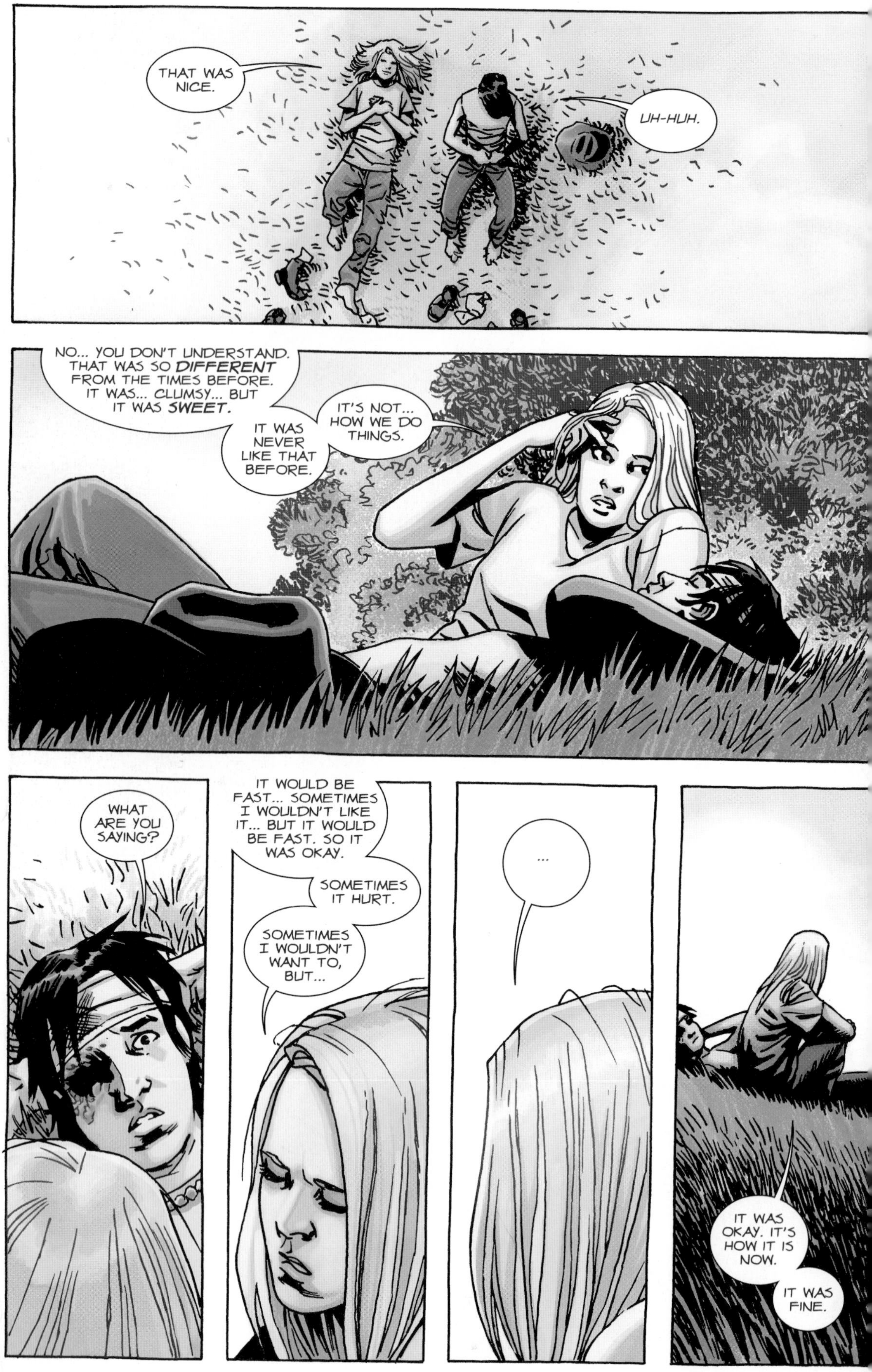
THAT WAS NICE.
UH-HUH.
NO... YOU DON'T UNDERSTAND. THAT WAS SO *DIFFERENT* FROM THE TIMES BEFORE. IT WAS... CLUMSY... BUT IT WAS *SWEET.*
IT WAS NEVER LIKE THAT BEFORE.
IT'S NOT... HOW WE DO THINGS.
WHAT ARE YOU SAYING?
IT WOULD BE FAST... SOMETIMES I WOULDN'T LIKE IT... BUT IT WOULD BE FAST. SO IT WAS OKAY.
SOMETIMES IT HURT.
SOMETIMES I WOULDN'T WANT TO, BUT...
...
IT WAS OKAY. IT'S HOW IT IS NOW.
IT WAS FINE.

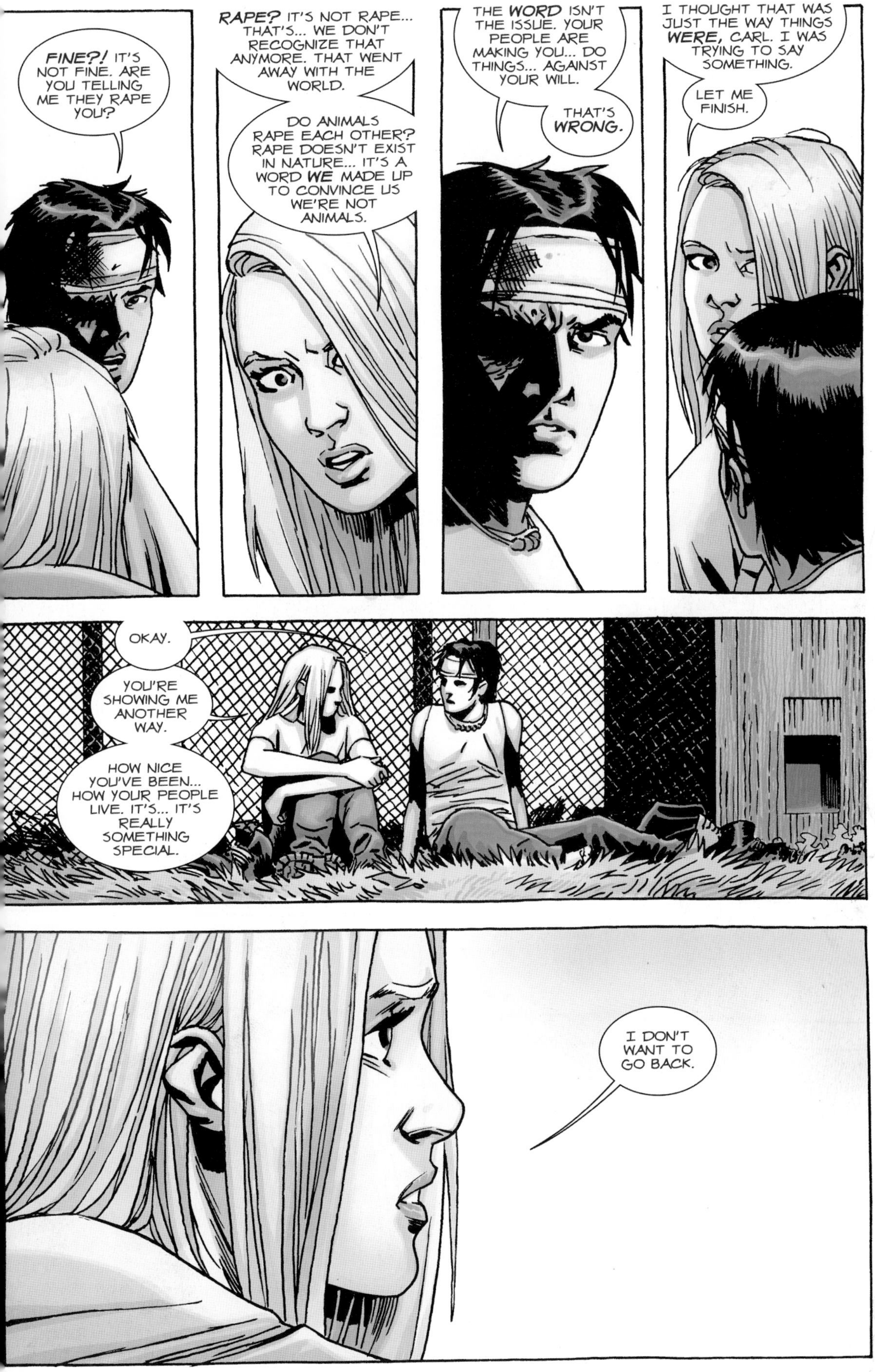

FINE?! IT'S NOT FINE. ARE YOU TELLING ME THEY RAPE YOU?
RAPE? IT'S NOT RAPE... THAT'S... WE DON'T RECOGNIZE THAT ANYMORE. THAT WENT AWAY WITH THE WORLD.
DO ANIMALS RAPE EACH OTHER? RAPE DOESN'T EXIST IN NATURE... IT'S A WORD WE MADE UP TO CONVINCE US WE'RE NOT ANIMALS.
THE WORD ISN'T THE ISSUE. YOUR PEOPLE ARE MAKING YOU... DO THINGS... AGAINST YOUR WILL.
THAT'S WRONG.
I THOUGHT THAT WAS JUST THE WAY THINGS WERE, CARL. I WAS TRYING TO SAY SOMETHING.
LET ME FINISH.
OKAY.
YOU'RE SHOWING ME ANOTHER WAY.
HOW NICE YOU'VE BEEN... HOW YOUR PEOPLE LIVE. IT'S... IT'S REALLY SOMETHING SPECIAL.
I DON'T WANT TO GO BACK.

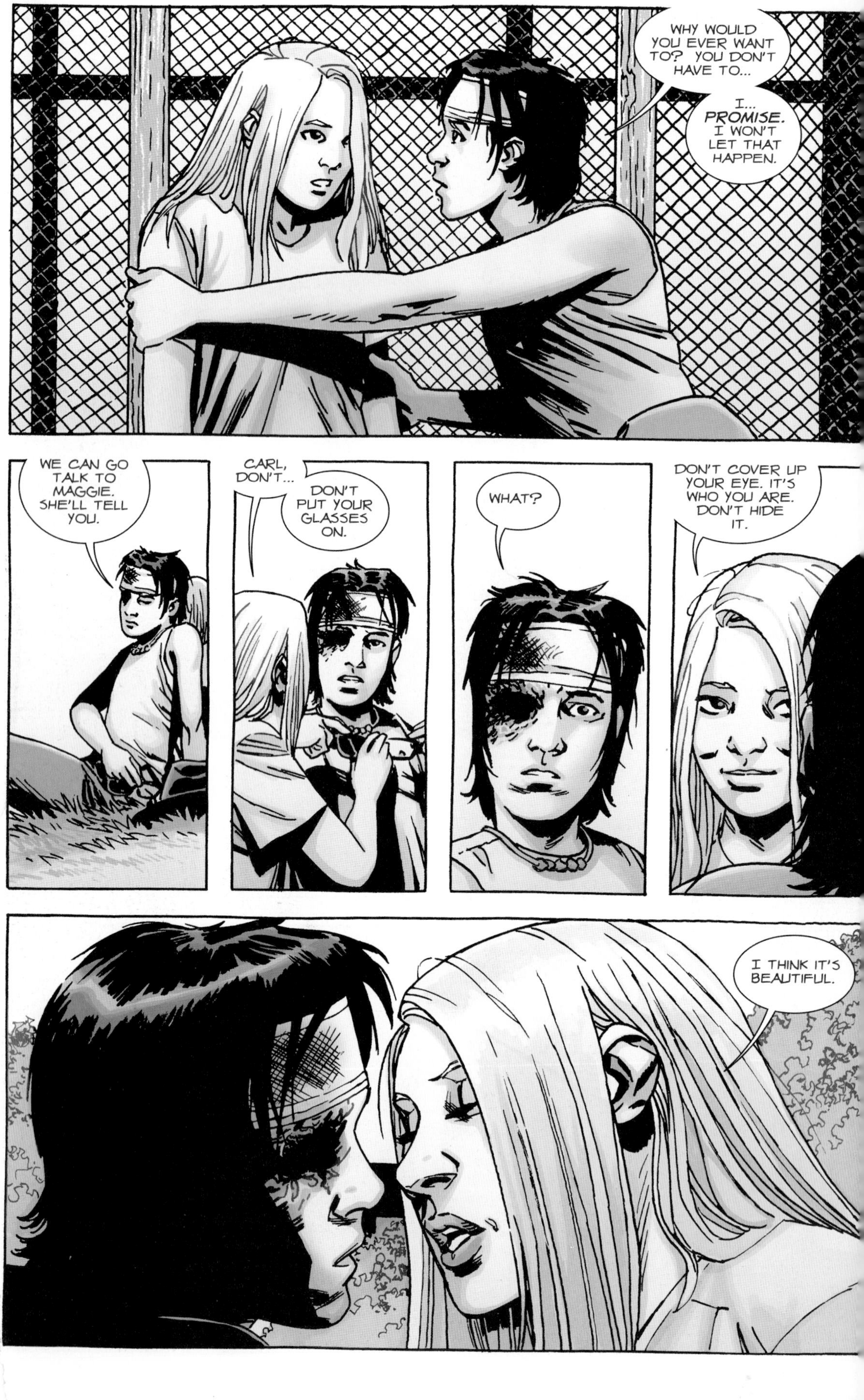
WHY WOULD YOU EVER WANT TO? YOU DON'T HAVE TO...
I... **PROMISE.** I WON'T LET THAT HAPPEN.
WE CAN GO TALK TO MAGGIE. SHE'LL TELL YOU.
CARL, DON'T...
DON'T PUT YOUR GLASSES ON.
WHAT?
DON'T COVER UP YOUR EYE. IT'S WHO YOU ARE. DON'T HIDE IT.
I THINK IT'S BEAUTIFUL.

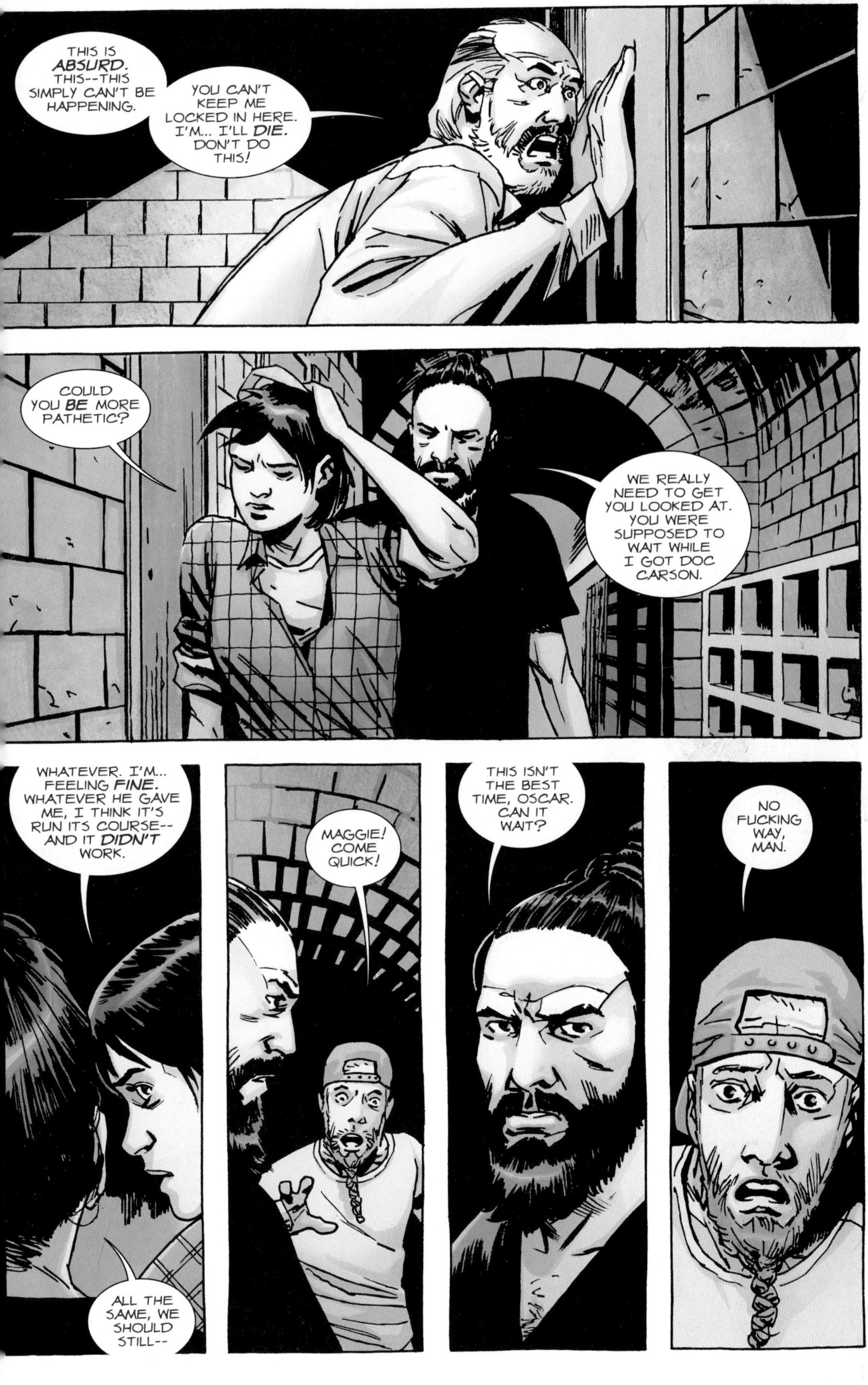
THIS IS ABSURD. THIS--THIS SIMPLY CAN'T BE HAPPENING.
YOU CAN'T KEEP ME LOCKED IN HERE. I'M... I'LL DIE. DON'T DO THIS!
COULD YOU BE MORE PATHETIC?
WE REALLY NEED TO GET YOU LOOKED AT. YOU WERE SUPPOSED TO WAIT WHILE I GOT DOC CARSON.
WHATEVER. I'M... FEELING FINE. WHATEVER HE GAVE ME, I THINK IT'S RUN ITS COURSE-- AND IT DIDN'T WORK.
ALL THE SAME, WE SHOULD STILL--
MAGGIE! COME QUICK!
THIS ISN'T THE BEST TIME, OSCAR. CAN IT WAIT?
NO FUCKING WAY, MAN.

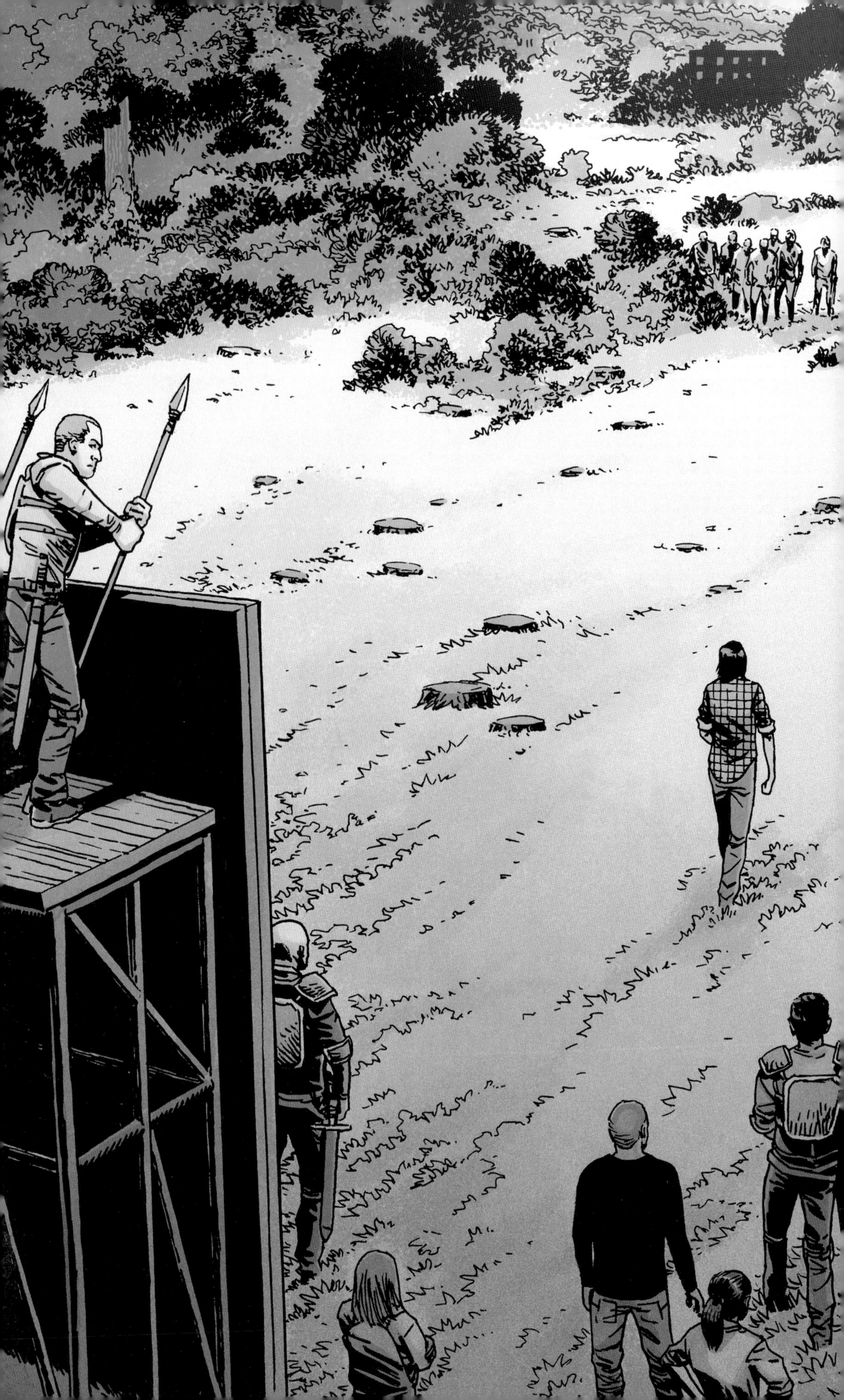

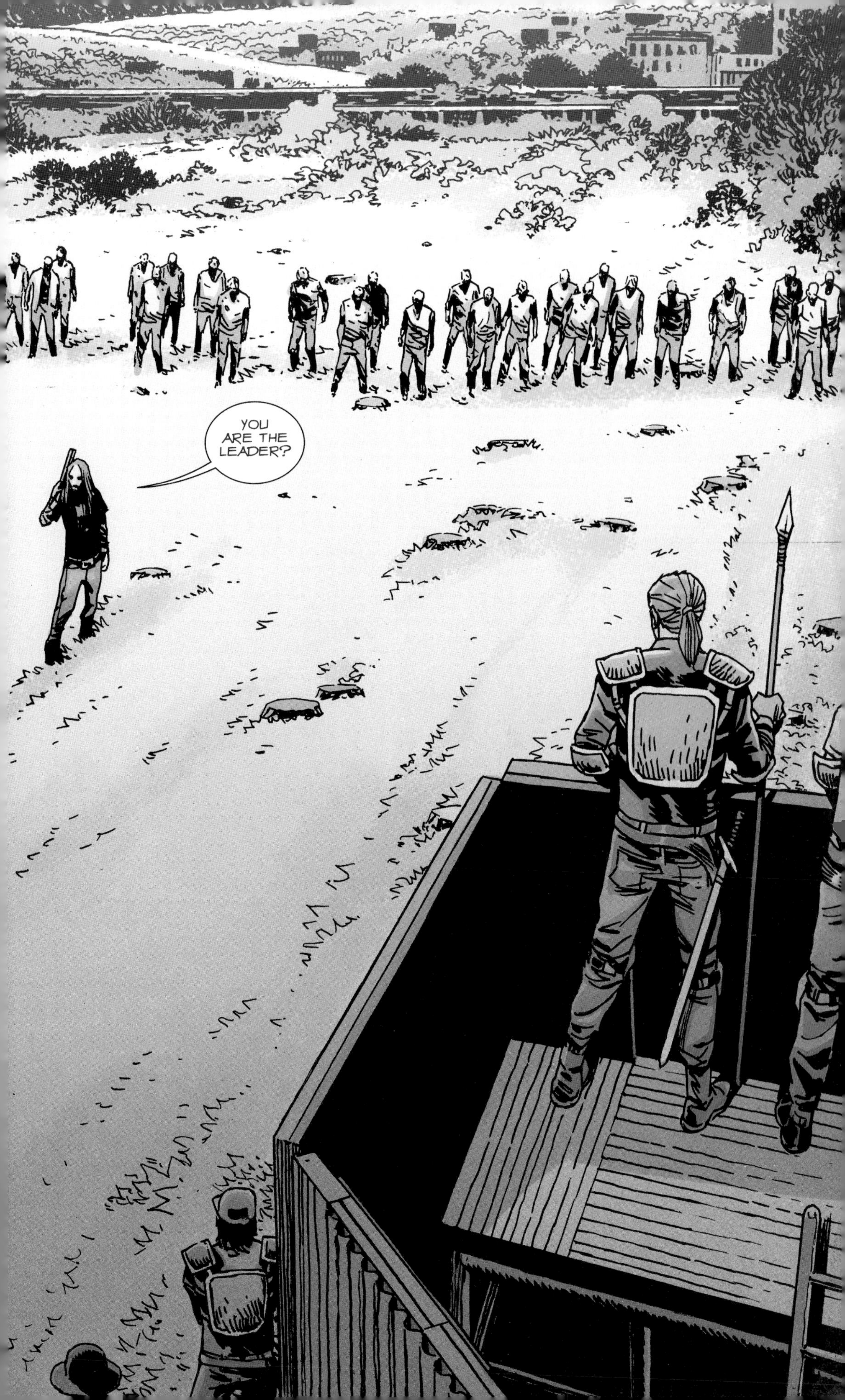
YOU ARE THE LEADER?

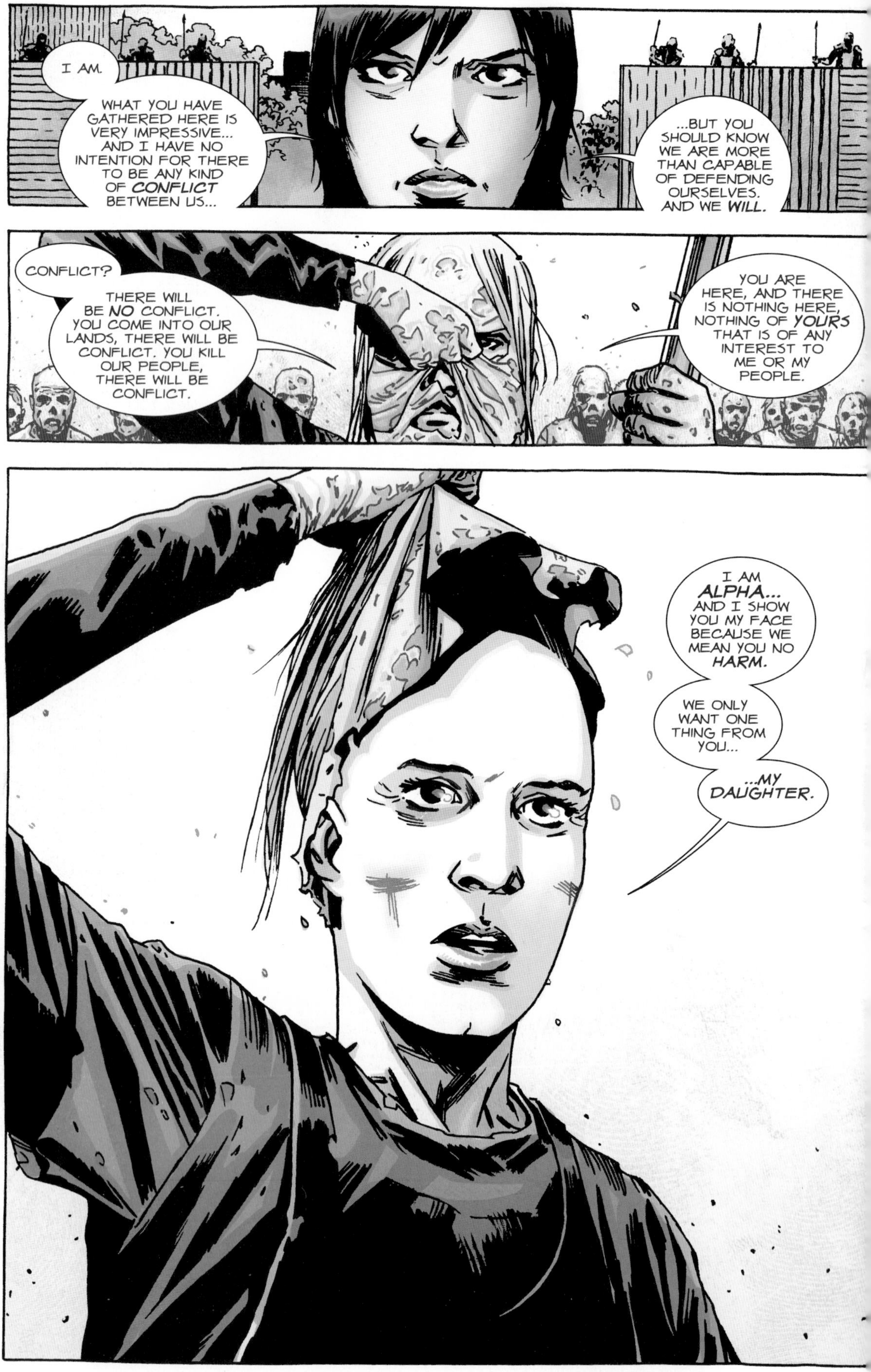

I AM.
WHAT YOU HAVE GATHERED HERE IS VERY IMPRESSIVE... AND I HAVE NO INTENTION FOR THERE TO BE ANY KIND OF CONFLICT BETWEEN US...
...BUT YOU SHOULD KNOW WE ARE MORE THAN CAPABLE OF DEFENDING OURSELVES. AND WE WILL.
CONFLICT?
THERE WILL BE NO CONFLICT. YOU COME INTO OUR LANDS, THERE WILL BE CONFLICT. YOU KILL OUR PEOPLE, THERE WILL BE CONFLICT.
YOU ARE HERE, AND THERE IS NOTHING HERE, NOTHING OF YOURS THAT IS OF ANY INTEREST TO ME OR MY PEOPLE.
I AM ALPHA... AND I SHOW YOU MY FACE BECAUSE WE MEAN YOU NO HARM.
WE ONLY WANT ONE THING FROM YOU...
...MY DAUGHTER.

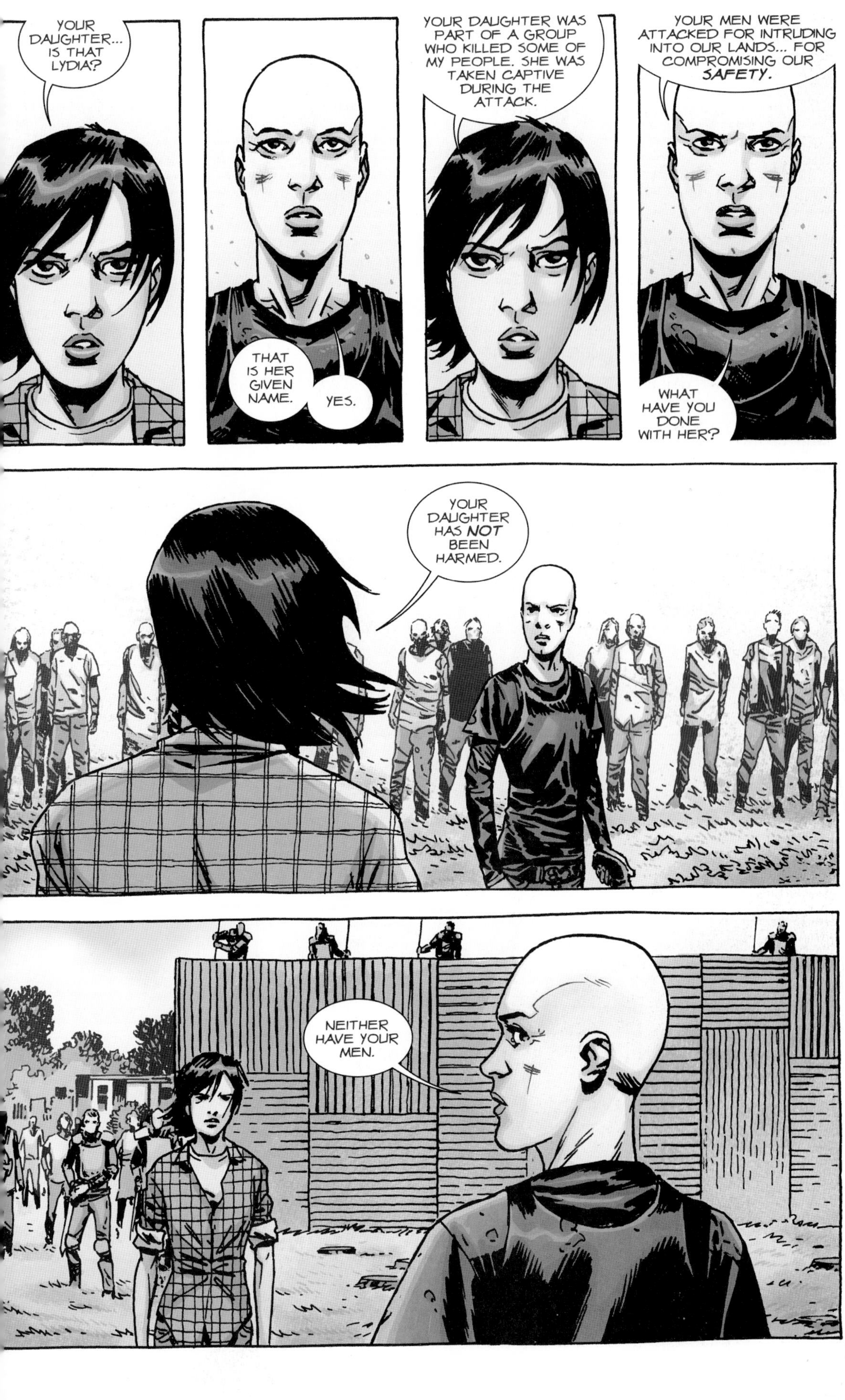
YOUR DAUGHTER... IS THAT LYDIA?
THAT IS HER GIVEN NAME.
YES.
YOUR DAUGHTER WAS PART OF A GROUP WHO KILLED SOME OF MY PEOPLE. SHE WAS TAKEN CAPTIVE DURING THE ATTACK.
YOUR MEN WERE ATTACKED FOR INTRUDING INTO OUR LANDS... FOR COMPROMISING OUR SAFETY.
WHAT HAVE YOU DONE WITH HER?
YOUR DAUGHTER HAS NOT BEEN HARMED.
NEITHER HAVE YOUR MEN.

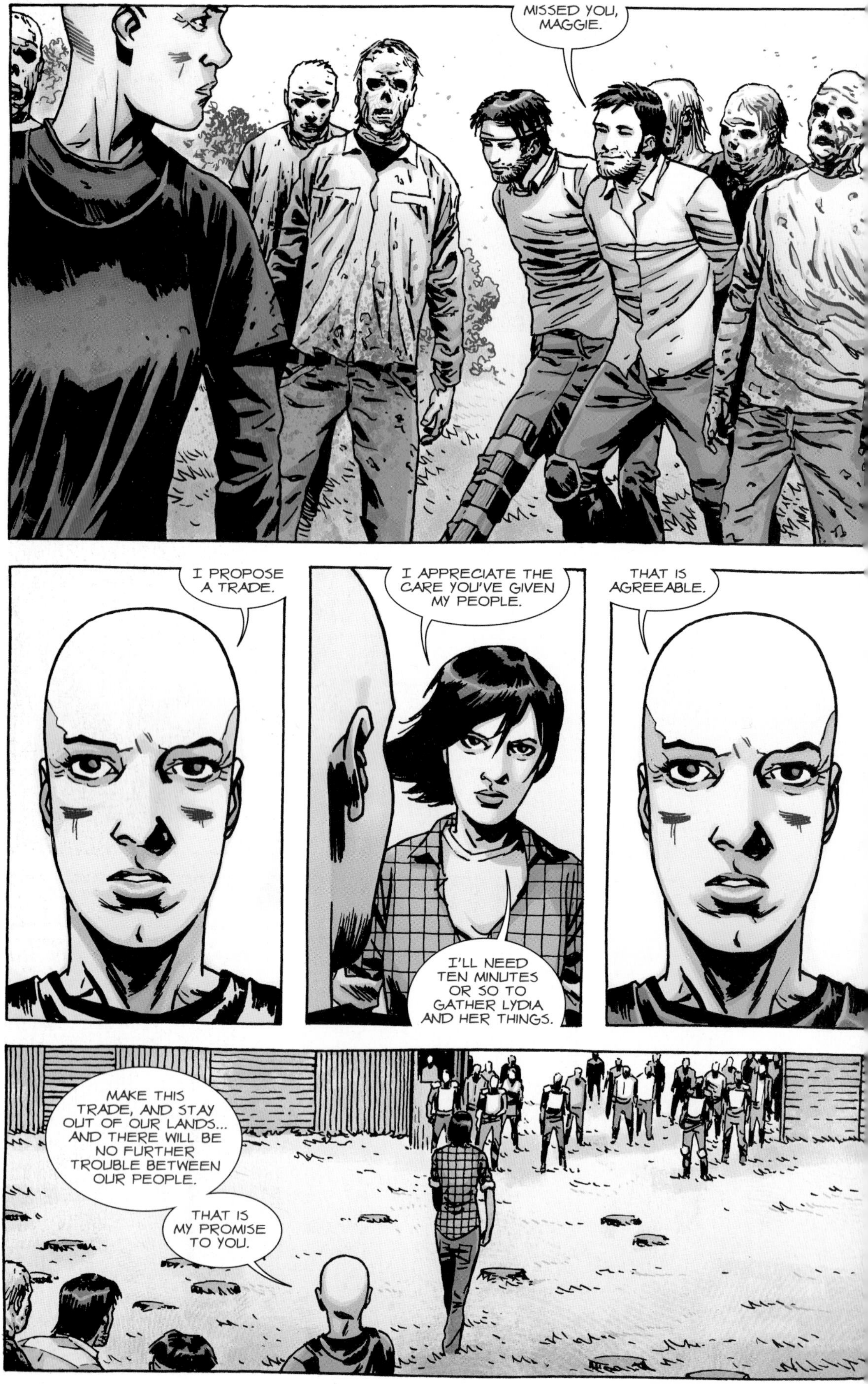
MISSED YOU, MAGGIE.
I PROPOSE A TRADE.
I APPRECIATE THE CARE YOU'VE GIVEN MY PEOPLE.
I'LL NEED TEN MINUTES OR SO TO GATHER LYDIA AND HER THINGS.
THAT IS AGREEABLE.
MAKE THIS TRADE, AND STAY OUT OF OUR LANDS... AND THERE WILL BE NO FURTHER TROUBLE BETWEEN OUR PEOPLE.
THAT IS MY PROMISE TO YOU.

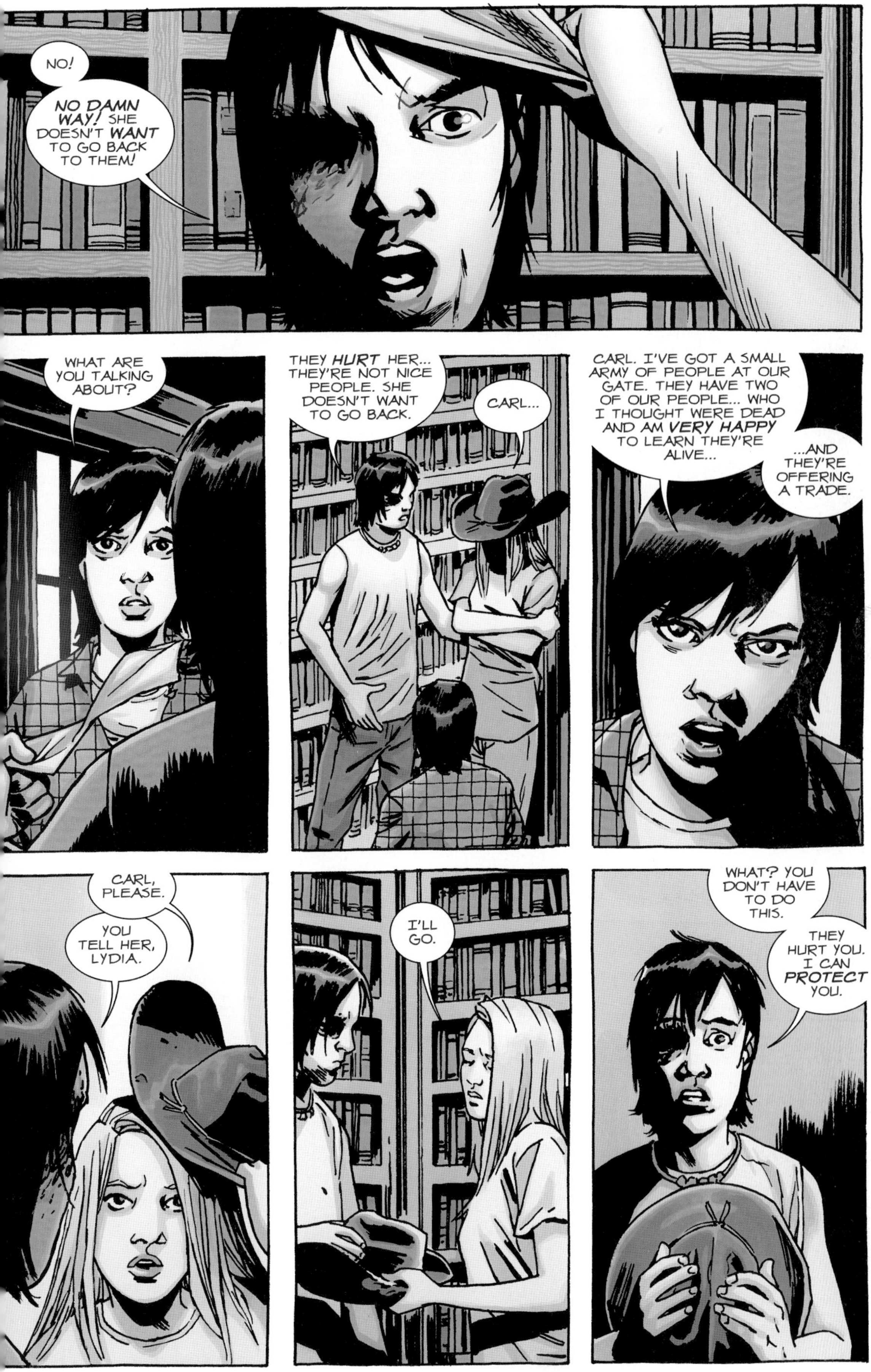
NO!
NO DAMN WAY! SHE DOESN'T WANT TO GO BACK TO THEM!
WHAT ARE YOU TALKING ABOUT?
THEY HURT HER... THEY'RE NOT NICE PEOPLE. SHE DOESN'T WANT TO GO BACK.
CARL...
CARL. I'VE GOT A SMALL ARMY OF PEOPLE AT OUR GATE. THEY HAVE TWO OF OUR PEOPLE... WHO I THOUGHT WERE DEAD AND AM VERY HAPPY TO LEARN THEY'RE ALIVE...
...AND THEY'RE OFFERING A TRADE.
CARL, PLEASE.
YOU TELL HER, LYDIA.
I'LL GO.
WHAT? YOU DON'T HAVE TO DO THIS.
THEY HURT YOU. I CAN PROTECT YOU.

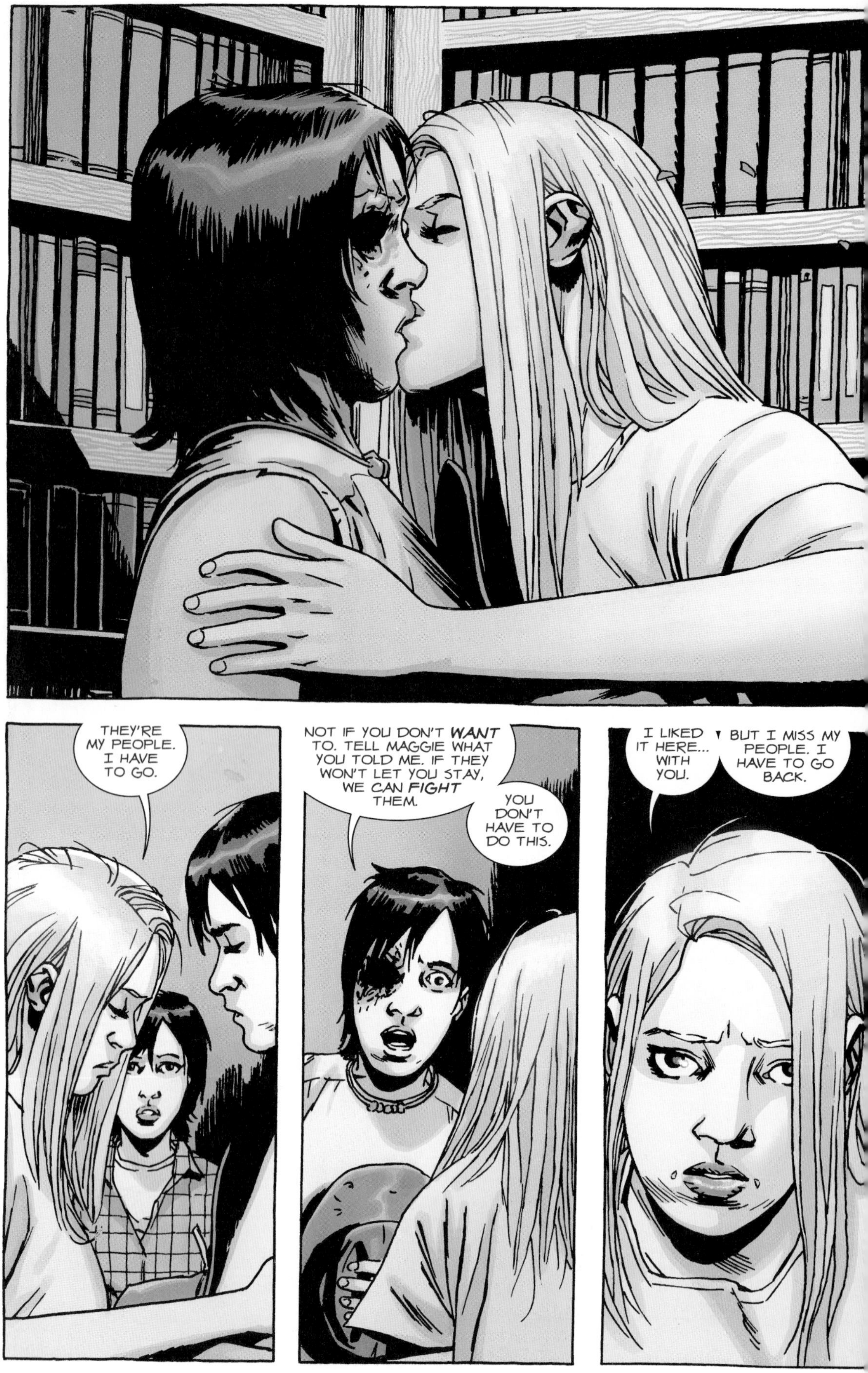
THEY'RE MY PEOPLE. I HAVE TO GO.
NOT IF YOU DON'T **WANT** TO. TELL MAGGIE WHAT YOU TOLD ME. IF THEY WON'T LET YOU STAY, WE CAN **FIGHT** THEM.
YOU DON'T HAVE TO DO THIS.
I LIKED IT HERE... WITH YOU.
BUT I MISS MY PEOPLE. I HAVE TO GO BACK.

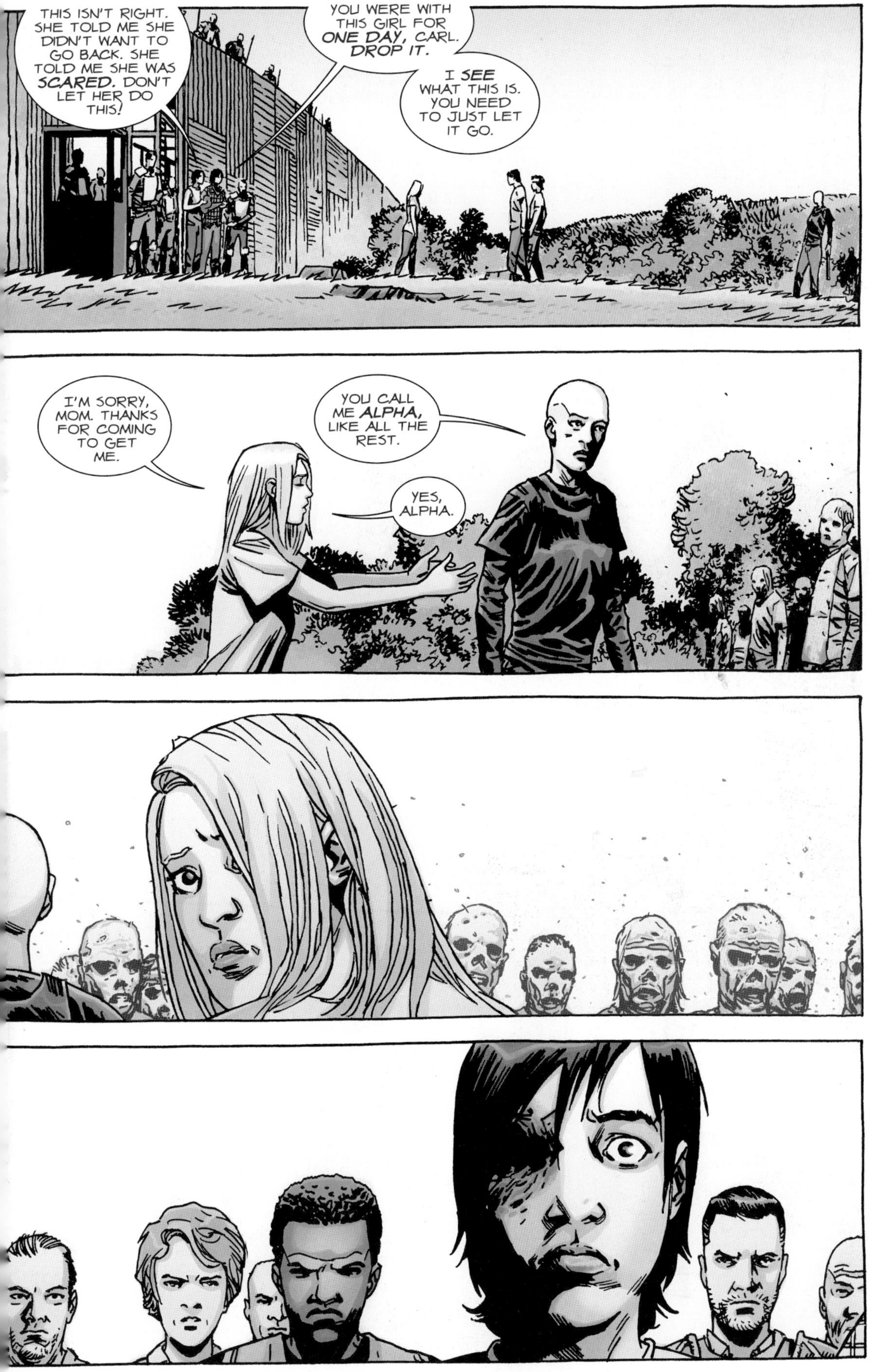
THIS ISN'T RIGHT. SHE TOLD ME SHE DIDN'T WANT TO GO BACK. SHE TOLD ME SHE WAS SCARED. DON'T LET HER DO THIS!
YOU WERE WITH THIS GIRL FOR ONE DAY, CARL. DROP IT.
I SEE WHAT THIS IS. YOU NEED TO JUST LET IT GO.
I'M SORRY, MOM. THANKS FOR COMING TO GET ME.
YOU CALL ME ALPHA, LIKE ALL THE REST.
YES, ALPHA.

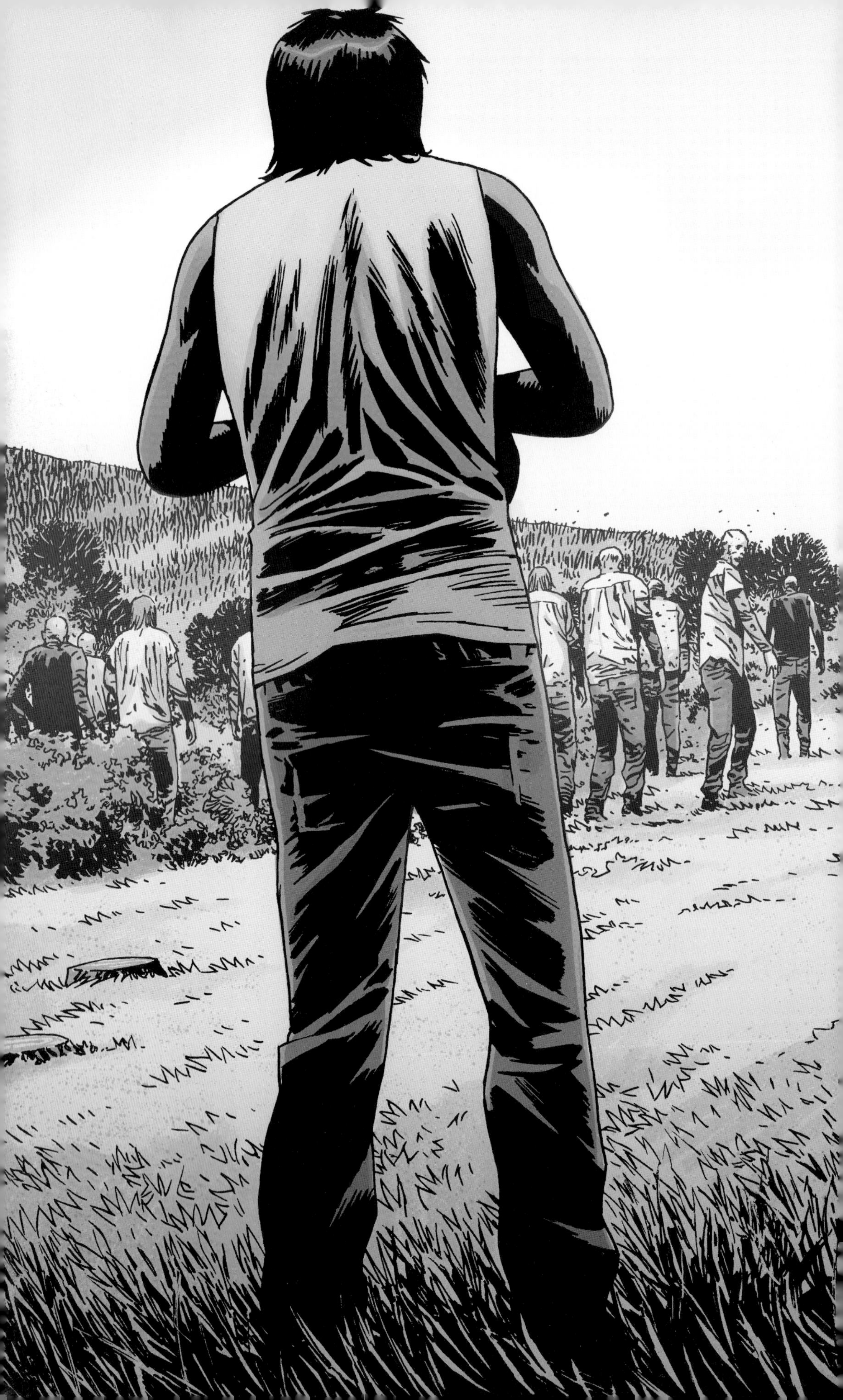

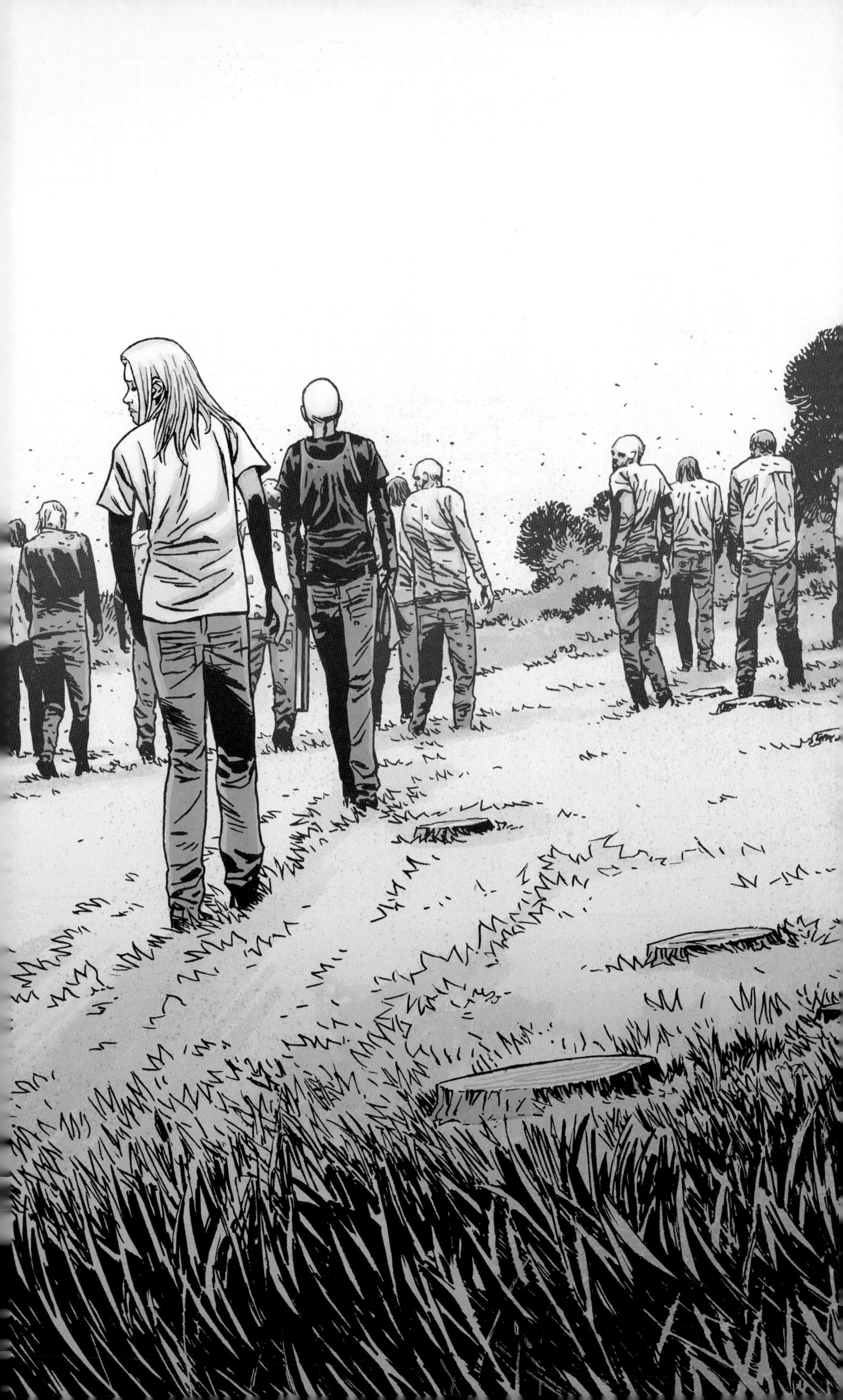

CARL, PLEASE. I'M JUST ASKING YOU TO BE REASONABLE.

REASONABLE?!

I TOLD YOU SHE WAS IN DANGER. I TOLD YOU SHE DIDN'T WANT TO GO BACK. THEY *MADE* HER DO THINGS AGAINST HER WILL.

I KNOW YOU WANTED DANTE AND KEN BACK. I WANTED THEM BACK, TOO. I *UNDERSTAND* WHAT YOU DID. I'M NOT SOME STUPID CHILD.

BUT YOU *SACRIFICED* LYDIA. YOU DIDN'T SPEND TIME WITH HER LIKE I DID... YOU DIDN'T *KNOW* HER.

KNOW HER? YOU SPENT *ONE DAY* WITH THE GIRL. SHE *KILLED* SOME OF OUR PEOPLE. YOU DON'T *KNOW* HER OR IF ANYTHING SHE SAID WAS TRUE!

SHE COUL HAVE BEEN MURDERIN SAVAGE FO ALL WE KNOW.

BUT WHAT IF YOU'RE *WRONG?* WHAT IF SHE WAS A VICTIM AND YOU SENT HER BACK TO THOSE PEOPLE?

CARL, I HAVE OTHER THINGS TO ATTEND TO. I NEED TO DROP THIS FOR NOW.

...

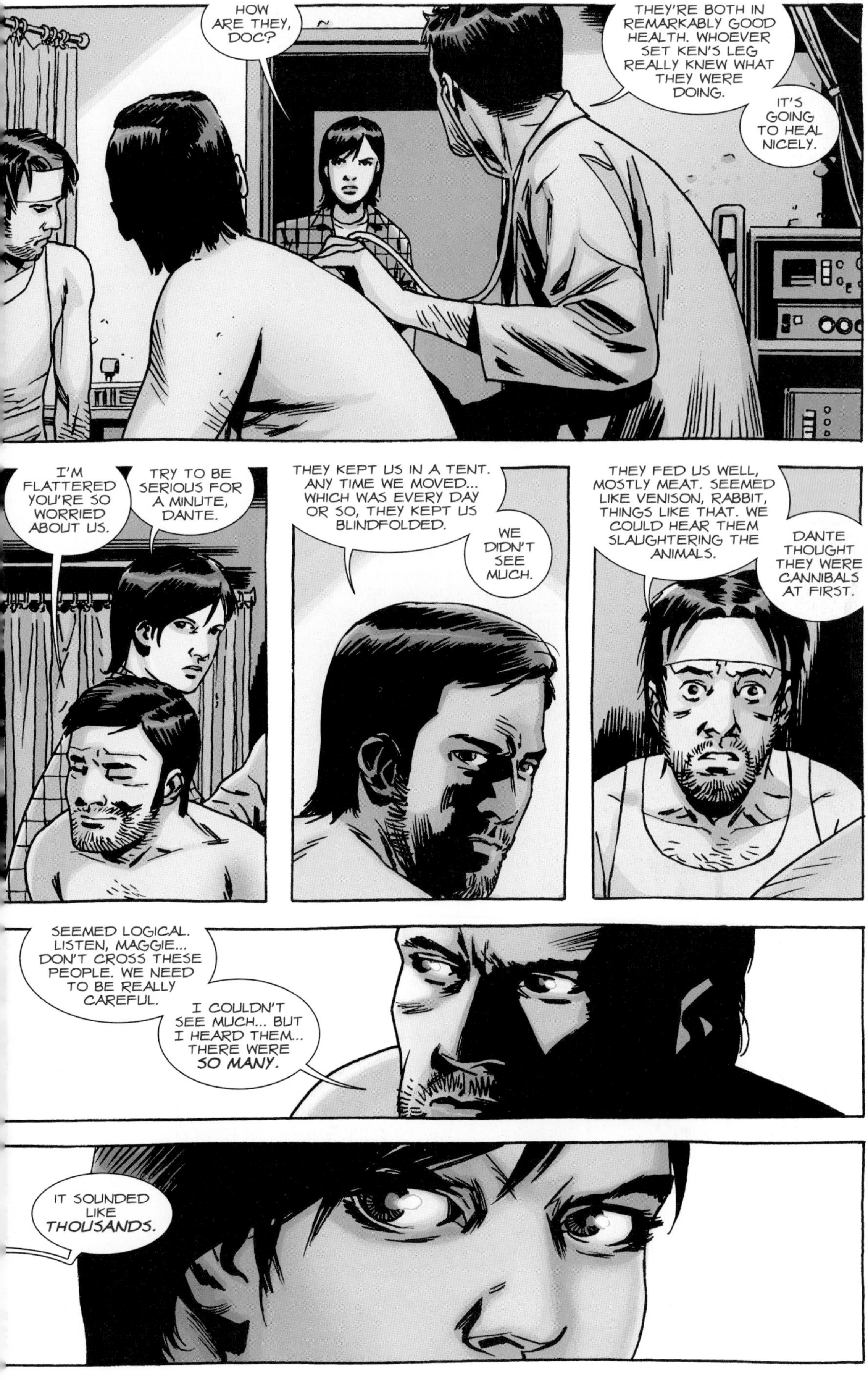
HOW ARE THEY, DOC?
THEY'RE BOTH IN REMARKABLY GOOD HEALTH. WHOEVER SET KEN'S LEG REALLY KNEW WHAT THEY WERE DOING.
IT'S GOING TO HEAL NICELY.
I'M FLATTERED YOU'RE SO WORRIED ABOUT US.
TRY TO BE SERIOUS FOR A MINUTE, DANTE.
THEY KEPT US IN A TENT. ANY TIME WE MOVED... WHICH WAS EVERY DAY OR SO, THEY KEPT US BLINDFOLDED.
WE DIDN'T SEE MUCH.
THEY FED US WELL, MOSTLY MEAT. SEEMED LIKE VENISON, RABBIT, THINGS LIKE THAT. WE COULD HEAR THEM SLAUGHTERING THE ANIMALS.
DANTE THOUGHT THEY WERE CANNIBALS AT FIRST.
SEEMED LOGICAL. LISTEN, MAGGIE... DON'T CROSS THESE PEOPLE. WE NEED TO BE REALLY CAREFUL.
I COULDN'T SEE MUCH... BUT I HEARD THEM... THERE WERE *SO MANY.*
IT SOUNDED LIKE *THOUSANDS.*

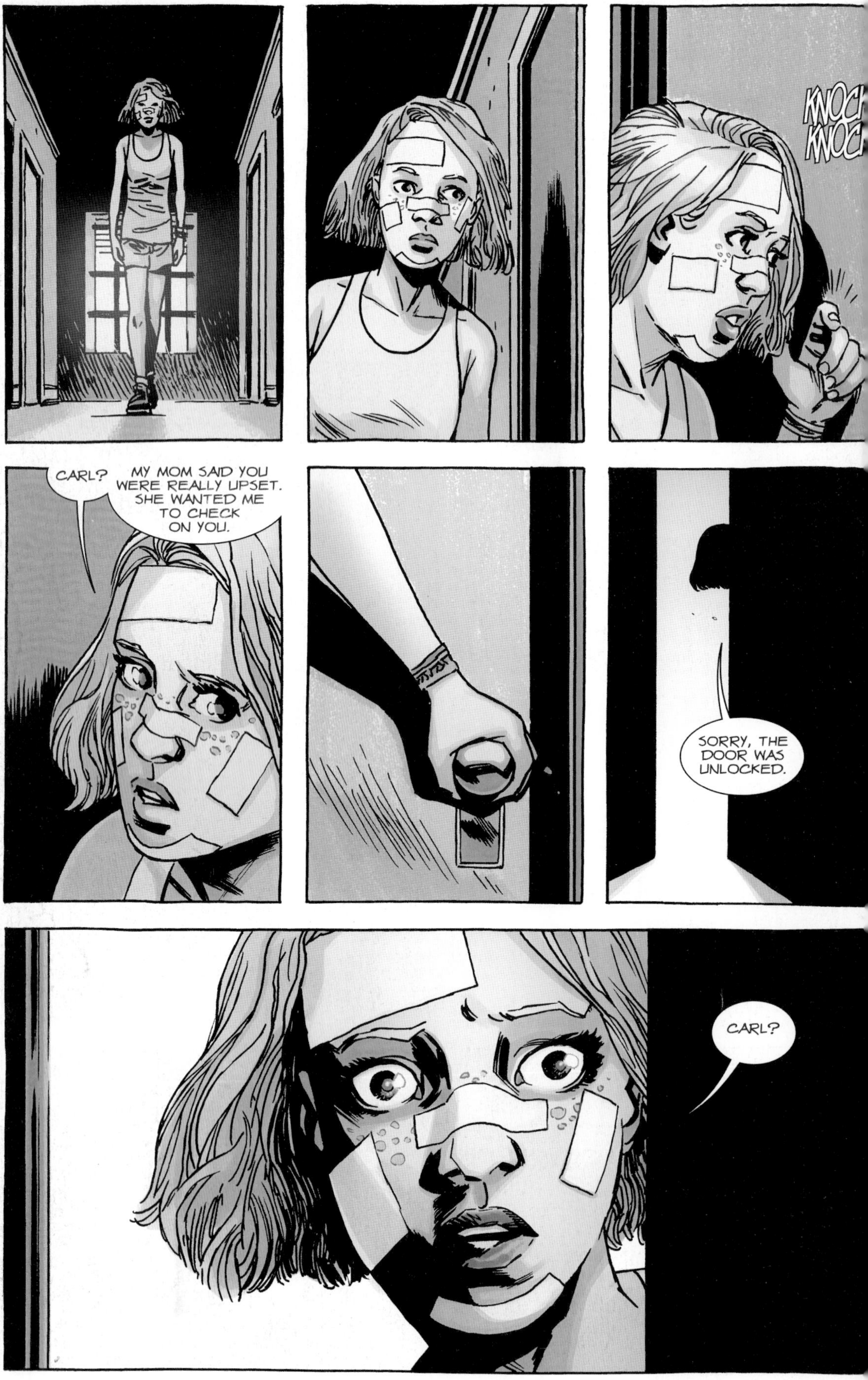
KNOCK KNOCK
CARL?
MY MOM SAID YOU WERE REALLY UPSET. SHE WANTED ME TO CHECK ON YOU.
SORRY, THE DOOR WAS UNLOCKED.
CARL?

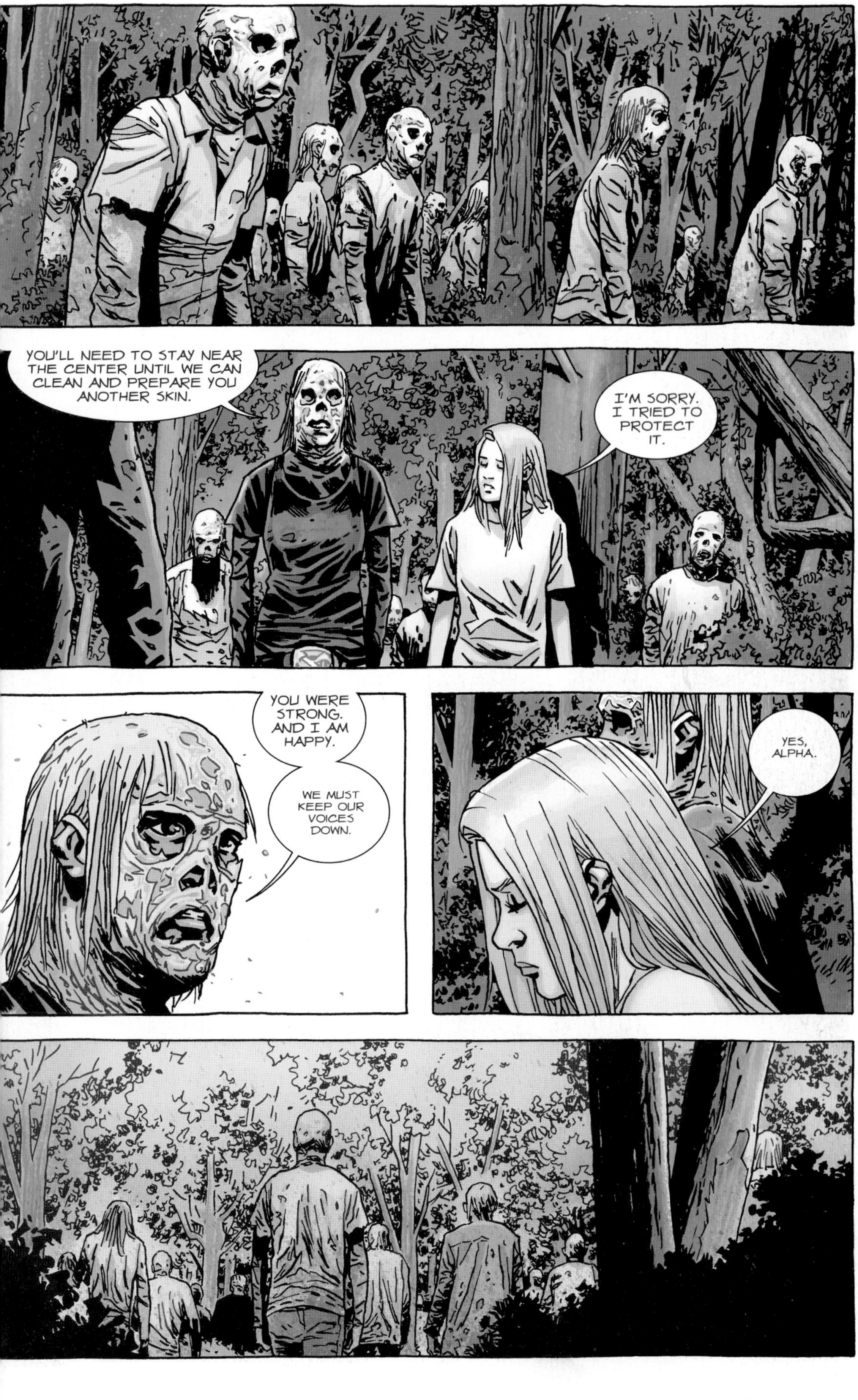
YOU'LL NEED TO STAY NEAR THE CENTER UNTIL WE CAN CLEAN AND PREPARE YOU ANOTHER SKIN.
I'M SORRY. I TRIED TO PROTECT IT.
YOU WERE STRONG. AND I AM HAPPY.
WE MUST KEEP OUR VOICES DOWN.
YES, ALPHA.

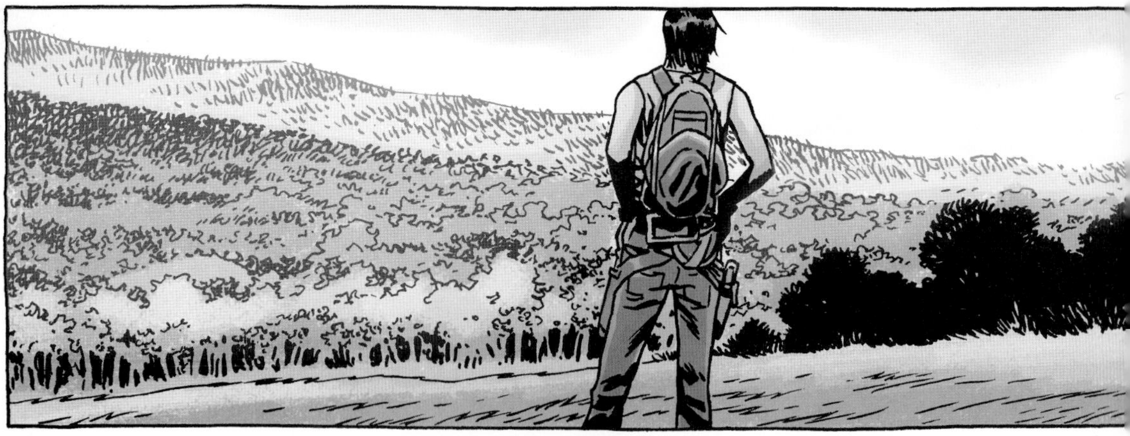
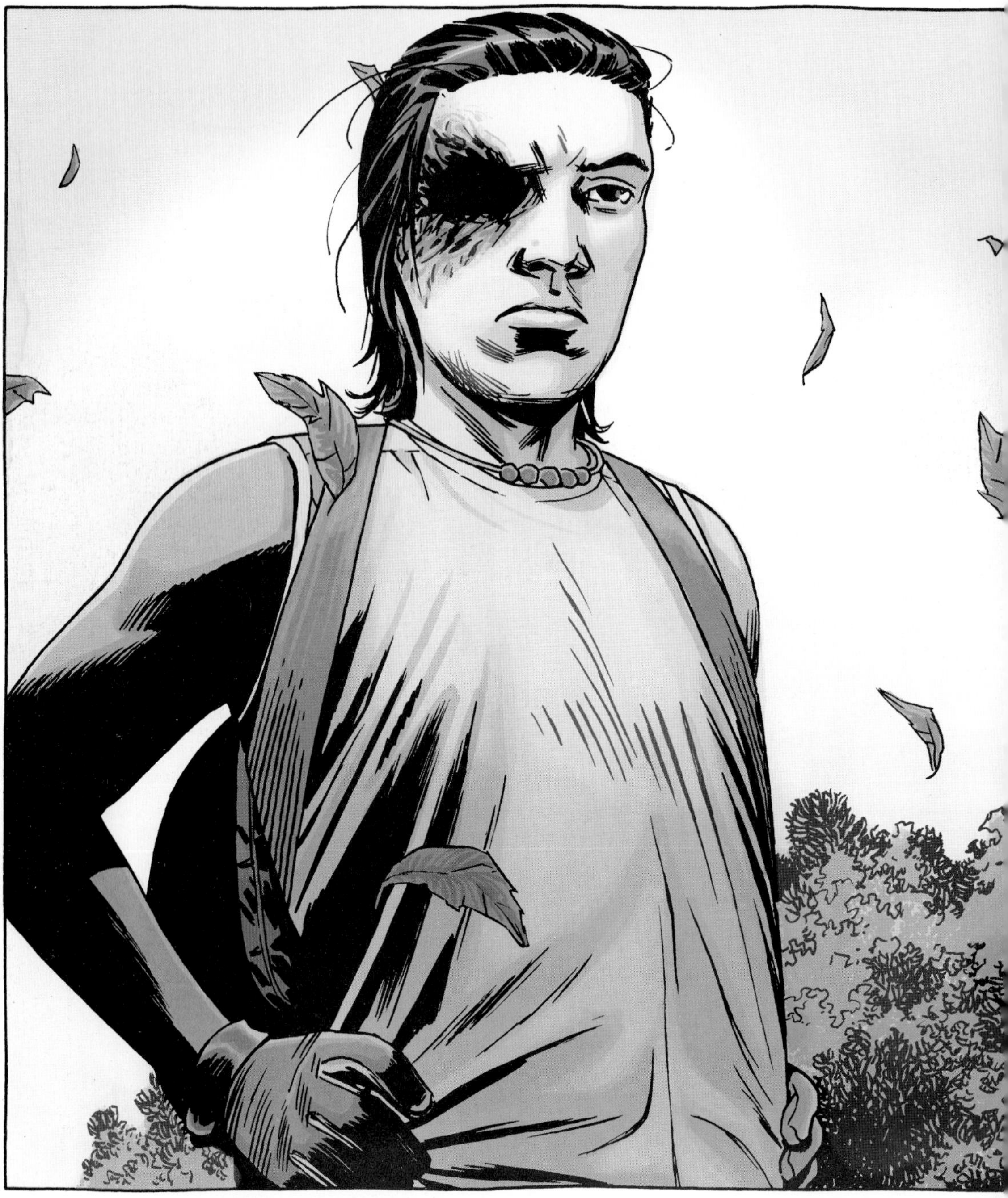

TO BE CONTINUED...

FOR MORE OF THE WALKING DEA

TRADEPAPERBACKS

ROBERT KIRKMAN TONY MOORE
THE WALKING DEAD
VOLUME 1
DAYS GONE BYE

VOL. 1: DAYS GONE BYE TP
ISBN: 978-1-58240-672-5
$14.99
VOL. 2: MILES BEHIND US TP
ISBN: 978-1-58240-775-3
$14.99
VOL. 3: SAFETY BEHIND BARS TP
ISBN: 978-1-58240-805-7
$14.99
VOL. 4: THE HEART'S DESIRE TP
ISBN: 978-1-58240-530-8
$14.99
VOL. 5: THE BEST DEFENSE TP
ISBN: 978-1-58240-612-1
$14.99
VOL. 6: THIS SORROWFUL LIFE TP
ISBN: 978-1-58240-684-8
$14.99
VOL. 7: THE CALM BEFORE TP
ISBN: 978-1-58240-828-6
$14.99

VOL. 8: MADE TO SUFFER TP
ISBN: 978-1-58240-883-5
$14.99
VOL. 9: HERE WE REMAIN TP
ISBN: 978-1-60706-022-2
$14.99
VOL. 10: WHAT WE BECOME TP
ISBN: 978-1-60706-075-8
$14.99
VOL. 11: FEAR THE HUNTERS TP
ISBN: 978-1-60706-181-6
$14.99
VOL. 12: LIFE AMONG THEM TP
ISBN: 978-1-60706-254-7
$14.99
VOL. 13: TOO FAR GONE TP
ISBN: 978-1-60706-329-2
$14.99
VOL. 14: NO WAY OUT TP
ISBN: 978-1-60706-392-6
$14.99

VOL. 15: WE FIND OURSELVES TP
ISBN: 978-1-60706-440-4
$14.99
VOL. 16: A LARGER WORLD TP
ISBN: 978-1-60706-559-3
$14.99
VOL. 17: SOMETHING TO FEAR TP
ISBN: 978-1-60706-615-6
$14.99
VOL. 18: WHAT COMES AFTER TP
ISBN: 978-1-60706-687-3
$14.99
VOL. 19: MARCH TO WAR TP
ISBN: 978-1-60706-818-1
$14.99
VOL. 20: ALL OUT WAR PART ONE TP
ISBN: 978-1-60706-882-2
$14.99
VOL. 21: ALL OUT WAR PART TWO TP
ISBN: 978-1-63215-030-1
$14.99

VOL. 22: A NEW BEGINI
ISBN: 978-1-6321
$14.99
VOL. 23: WHISPERS INTO
ISBN: 978-1-63215
$14.99
VOL. 1: SPANISH EDITI
ISBN: 978-1-6070
$14.99
VOL. 2: SPANISH EDITI
ISBN: 978-1-6070
$14.99
VOL. 3: SPANISH EDITI
ISBN: 978-1-6070
$14.99
VOL. 4: SPANISH EDITI
ISBN: 978-1-63215
$14.99

HARDCOVERS

THE WALKING DEAD
BOOK ONE
a continuing story of survival horror.

BOOK ONE HC
ISBN: 978-1-58240-619-0
$34.99
BOOK TWO HC
ISBN: 978-1-58240-698-5
$34.99
BOOK THREE HC
ISBN: 978-1-58240-825-5
$34.99
BOOK FOUR HC
ISBN: 978-1-60706-000-0
$34.99
BOOK FIVE HC
ISBN: 978-1-60706-171-7
$34.99
BOOK SIX HC
ISBN: 978-1-60706-327-8
$34.99
BOOK SEVEN HC
ISBN: 978-1-60706-439-8
$34.99
BOOK EIGHT HC
ISBN: 978-1-60706-593-7
$34.99
BOOK NINE HC
ISBN: 978-1-60706-798-6
$34.99
BOOK TEN HC
ISBN: 978-1-63215-034-9
$34.99
BOOK ELEVEN HC
ISBN: 978-1-63215-271-8
$34.99

COMPENDIUMS

The ultimate edition of The New York Times bestseller!
THE WALKING DEAD
COMPENDIUM ONE
Robert Kirkman • Charlie Adlard • Tony Moore • Cliff Rathburn

COMPENDIUM TP, VOL. 1
ISBN: 978-1-60706-076-5
$59.99
COMPENDIUM TP, VOL. 2
ISBN: 978-1-60706-596-8
$59.99

SPECIALTY BOOKS

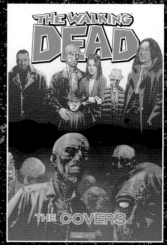

THE WALKING DEAD
THE COVERS

THE WALKING DEAD: THE COVERS, VOL. 1 HC
ISBN: 978-1-60706-002-4
$24.99
THE WALKING DEAD SURVIVORS' GUIDE
ISBN: 978-1-60706-458-9
$12.99
THE WALKING DEAD: ALL OUT WAR HC
ISBN: 978-1-63215-038-7
$34.99

OMNIBUS

THE WALKING DEAD

OMNIBUS, VOL. 1
ISBN: 978-1-60706-503-6
$100.00
OMNIBUS, VOL. 2
ISBN: 978-1-60706-515-9
$100.00
OMNIBUS, VOL. 3
ISBN: 978-1-60706-330-8
$100.00
OMNIBUS, VOL. 4
ISBN: 978-1-60706-616-3
$100.00
OMNIBUS, VOL. 5
ISBN: 978-1-63215-042-4
$100.00